To David – for his unending kindness and patience

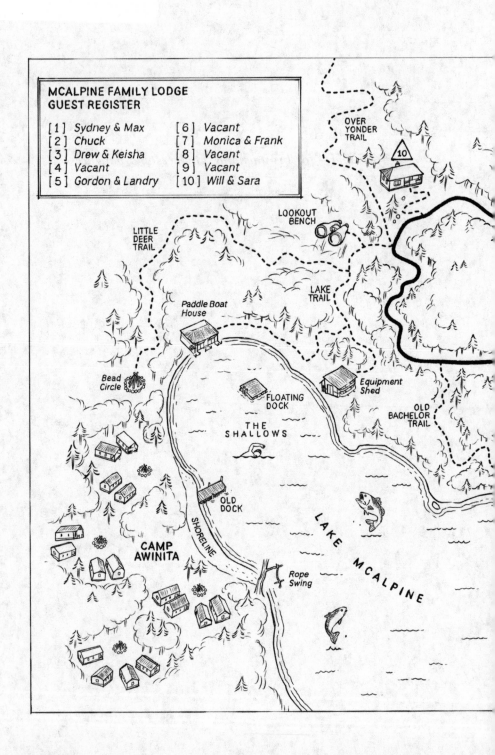

PROLOGUE

Will Trent sat down at the edge of the lake to take off his hiking boots. The numbers on his watch glowed in the darkness. An hour away from midnight. He could hear an owl in the distance. A gentle breeze whispered through the trees. The moon was a perfect circle in the night sky, light bouncing off the figure in the water. Sara Linton was swimming toward the floating dock. A cool blue light bathed her body as she cut through the gently rolling waves. Then she turned, doing a lazy backstroke as she smiled at Will.

"Are you coming in?"

Will couldn't answer. He knew that Sara was accustomed to his awkward silences, but this wasn't one of those times. He felt speechless just looking at her. All he could think was the same thing everybody thought when they saw them together: what the hell was she doing with him? She was so damn clever and funny and beautiful and he couldn't even get the knot out of his shoe-lace in the dark.

He forced off the boot as she swam back toward him. Her long auburn hair was sleek to her head. Her bare shoulders were peeking out from the blackness of the water. She had stripped off her clothes before diving in, laughing at his observation that it seemed like a bad idea to jump into something you couldn't see in the middle of the night when no one knew where you were.

But it seemed like a worse idea not to follow the wishes of a naked woman asking you to join her.

Will took off his socks, then stood so that he could unbutton his pants. Sara let out a low, appreciative whistle as he started to undress.

1

"Whoa," she said. "A little more slowly, please."

He laughed, but he didn't know what to do with the feeling of lightness inside his chest. Will had never experienced this type of prolonged happiness. Sure, there were times that he'd known bursts of joy—his first kiss, his first sexual encounter, his first sexual encounter that had lasted more than three seconds, graduating from college, cashing an actual paycheck, the day he had finally managed to divorce his hateful ex-wife.

This was different.

Will and Sara were two days out from their wedding, and the euphoria he had experienced during the ceremony hadn't subsided. If anything, the feeling was heightened with every passing hour. She would smile at him, or laugh at one of his stupid jokes, and it was like his heart turned into a butterfly. Which he understood wasn't a manly thing to think, but there were things you thought and things you shared, and this was one of the many reasons he preferred an awkward silence.

Sara gave a *whoop* when Will made a show of peeling off his shirt before he stepped into the lake. He wasn't used to walking around naked, especially outdoors, so he ducked under a lot more quickly than he should've. The water was cold, even for mid-summer. Chills prickled his skin. He could feel mud unpleasantly sucking around his feet. Then Sara wrapped her body around his and Will had no complaints.

He said, "Hey."

"Hey." She stroked back his hair. "Have you ever been in a lake before?"

"Not by choice," he admitted. "Are you sure the water's safe?"

She thought about it. "Copperheads are usually more active at dusk. We're probably too far north for cottonmouths."

Will hadn't considered snakes. He had grown up in downtown Atlanta, surrounded by dirty concrete and used syringes. Sara had grown up in a college town in rural South Georgia, surrounded by nature.

And snakes, apparently.

"I have a confession," she said. "I told Mercy we lied to her."

"I figured," Will said. The incident between Mercy and her family tonight had been intense. "Is she gonna be okay?"

"Probably. Jon seems like a good kid." Sara shook her head over the futility of it all. "It's hard being a teenager."

Will tried to lighten things up. "There's something to be said for growing up in an orphanage."

She pressed her finger to his lips, which he guessed was her way of saying *not funny*. "Look up."

Will looked up. Then he let his head drop back as a sense of awe washed over him. He had never seen actual stars in the sky. Not stars like these, at least. Bright, individual pinpricks in the velvety black expanse of night. Not flattened out by light pollution. Not dulled by smog or haze. He took in a deep breath. Felt his heartbeat start to slow. The only sound was literal crickets. The only man-made light was a distant twinkle coming from the wrap-around porch on the main house.

He kind of loved it here.

They'd hiked five miles through rocky terrain to get to the McAlpine Family Lodge. The place had been around so long that Will had heard about it when he was a kid. He had dreamed about going one day. Canoeing, paddle boarding, mountain bike riding, hiking, eating s'mores by a campfire. That he had made the trip with Sara, that he was a happily married man on his honeymoon, was a fact that brought him more wonder than every star in the sky.

Sara said, "Places like this, you scratch a little bit under the surface and all sorts of bad things come out."

Will knew that she was still thinking about Mercy. The brutal argument with her son. The cold response from her parents. Her pitiful brother. Her total dick of an ex-husband. Her eccentric aunt. Then there were the other guests with their problems, which had been amplified by the liberal amount of alcohol poured at the communal dinner. Which reminded Will again that when he'd dreamed about this place as a kid, he hadn't anticipated that other people would be here. Especially one asshole in particular.

"I know what you're going to say," Sara told him. "This is why we lied."

That wasn't exactly what he was going to say, but it was close.

Will was a special agent with the Georgia Bureau of Investigation. Sara had trained as a pediatrician and was currently serving as a medical examiner with the GBI. Both occupations tended to elicit long conversations from strangers, not all of them good and some of them very bad. Concealing their jobs had felt like a better way to enjoy their honeymoon.

Then again, saying you were one thing didn't stop you from being the other. They were both the kind of people who worried about other people. Particularly Mercy. She seemed to have the entire world against her right now. Will knew how much strength it took to keep your head up, to keep moving forward, when everyone else in your life was trying to pull you down.

"Hey." Sara hugged him closer, wrapping her legs around his waist. "I have another confession."

Will smiled because she was smiling. The butterfly in his chest started to stir. Then other things stirred because he could feel the heat of her pressing against his body.

He asked, "What's your confession?"

"I can't get enough of you." Sara kissed her way up the side of his neck, using her teeth to tease out a response. The chills came back. The feel of her breath in his ear flooded his brain with need. He let his hand slowly travel down. Her breath caught when he touched her. He could feel the rise and fall of her breasts against his bare chest.

Then a sharp, loud scream pierced the night air.

"Will." Sara's body had tensed. "What was that?"

He had no idea. He couldn't tell if it was human or animal. The scream had been high-pitched, blood-curdling. Not a word or a cry for help, but a sound of unrestrained terror. The kind of noise that made the primal part of your brain kick into fight or flight.

Will wasn't built for flight.

He held onto Sara's hand as they quickly made their way toward shore. He picked up his clothes, gave Sara her things. Will looked out over the water as he put on his shirt. He knew from the map that the lake spread out like a slumbering snowman. The swimming area was at the head. The shoreline disappeared into the darkness around the curve of the abdomen. Sound was hard to pin down. The obvious source of the scream was where the people were. Four other couples and a single man were staying at the lodge. The McAlpine family was in the main house. Leaving out Will and Sara, the guests were in five of the ten cottages that fanned away from the dining hall. That brought the total number to eighteen people on the compound.

Any one of them could've screamed.

"The fighting couple at dinner." Sara worked the buttons on her dress. "The dentist was wasted. The IT guy was—"

"What about the single guy?" Will's cargo pants skidded up his wet legs. "The one who kept needling Mercy?"

"Chuck," Sara provided. "The lawyer was obnoxious. How did he get on the Wi-Fi?"

"His horse-obsessed wife annoyed everybody." Will shoved his bare feet into his boots. His socks went into his pocket. "The lying app guys are up to something."

"What about the Jackal?"

Will looked up from tying his bootlace.

"Babe?" Sara kicked over her sandals so she could slide them on. "Are you—"

He left the lace untied. He didn't want to talk about the Jackal. "Ready?"

They started up the path. Will felt the urge to move, picking up the pace until Sara started to lag. She was incredibly athletic, but her shoes were made for strolling, not running.

He stopped, turning to her. "Is it okay if—"

"Go," she said. "I'll catch up."

Will left the path, taking a straight line through the woods. He used the porch light as his guide, his hands pushing away limbs and prickly vines that caught at his shirt sleeves. His wet feet were rubbing inside his boots. It had been a mistake to leave the one lace untied. He thought about stopping, but the wind shifted, carrying an odor like copper pennies in the air. Will couldn't tell if he was smelling blood or if his cop brain was throwing out sense memories of past crime scenes.

The scream could've come from an animal.

Even Sara hadn't been sure. Will's only certainty was the thing that had made the sound was in fear of its life. Coyote. Bobcat. Bear. There were a lot of creatures in the woods that could make other creatures feel that way.

Was this an overreaction?

He stopped trudging through the overgrowth, turning around to locate the path. He could tell where Sara was, not by sight but by the sound of her shoes on the gravel. She was halfway between the main house and the lake. Their cottage was on the far end of the compound. She was probably trying to form a plan. Were there any lights on in the other cottages? Should she start knocking on doors? Or was she thinking the same as Will, that they were being overly vigilant considering what they both did for a living, and this was going to be a really funny story to tell her sister about how they heard an animal give a death cry and rushed off to investigate rather than having hot lake sex.

Will could not appreciate the humor right now. Sweat had pasted his hair to his head. A blister was rubbing on the back of his heel. Blood trickled from his forehead where a vine had ripped open the skin. He listened to the silence in the woods. Not even the crickets were chirping now. He slapped at an insect that bit him on the side of his neck. Something scurried in the trees overhead.

Maybe he didn't love this place after all.

Worse, at a very deep level, he blamed the Jackal for this misery. Nothing had ever gone right in Will's life when that asshole was around, dating back to when they were kids. The sadistic prick had always been a walking bad luck charm.

Will rubbed his face with his hands like he could erase any thoughts of the Jackal from his brain. They weren't kids anymore. Will was a grown man on his honeymoon.

He headed back toward Sara. Or at least in the direction he thought Sara had gone. Will had lost all sense of time and direction in the dark. There was no telling how long he'd run through the forest like he was tackling a Ninja Warrior set. Walking through the overgrowth was a lot harder without the adrenaline pushing him to run face-first into hanging vines. Will silently formed his own plan. Once he reached the path, he would put on his socks and tie his bootlace so he wasn't limping through the rest of the week. He would locate his beautiful wife. He would take her back to the cottage and they could pick up where they had left off.

"Help!"

Will froze.

There wasn't any uncertainty this time. The scream was so pronounced that he knew it had come from the mouth of a woman.

Then she screamed again—

"Please!"

Will bolted away from the path, running toward the lake. The sound had come from the opposite side of the swimming area, toward the bottom of the snowman. He kept his head down. Legs pumping. He could hear the blood rushing through his ears alongside the echo of the screams. The woods quickly turned into a dense forest. Low-hanging limbs slashed at his arms. Gnats swarmed around his face. The terrain suddenly dropped. He landed sideways on his foot. His ankle rolled.

He ignored the sharp pain, forcing himself to keep going. Will tried to get his adrenaline in check. He had to slow his pace. The compound was at a higher elevation than the lake. There was a steep drop-off near the dining hall. He found the back end of the Loop Trail, then followed another zig-zagging path down. His heart was still pumping. His brain was still reeling with recriminations. He should've paid attention to his instincts the first time. He should've figured this out. He felt sick about what he was going to find, because the woman had screamed for her life, and there was no predator more vicious than a human being.

He coughed as the air turned thick with smoke. The moonlight broke through the trees just in time for him to see the ground was terraced. Will stumbled into a clearing. Empty beer cans and cigarette butts littered the ground. Tools were everywhere. Will kept his head on a swivel as he jogged past sawhorses and extension cords and a generator that had been turned on its side. There were three more cottages, all of them in various stages of repair. A tarp covered one roof. Windows were boarded up in the next. The last cabin was on fire. Flames licked out between the log siding. The door was half-open. Smoke ribboned from a busted side window. The roof wasn't going to hold for much longer.

The screams for help. The fire.

Someone had to be inside.

Will took a deep breath before he ran up the porch stairs. Kicked the door wide open. A blast of heat snatched the moisture from his eyes. All but one of the windows was boarded up. The only light was from the fire. He crouched down, keeping himself below the smoke as he made his way through the living room. Into the tiny kitchen. The bathroom with space for a soaking tub. The small closet. His lungs started to ache. He was running out of breath. He inhaled a mouthful of black smoke as he headed toward the bedroom. No door. No fixtures. No closet. The back wall of the cottage had been stripped to the studs.

They were too narrow for him to fit through.

Will heard a loud creak over the roar of the fire. He jogged back into the living room. The ceiling was fully engulfed. Flames were chewing away the support beams. The roof was collapsing. Chunks of burning wood rained down. Will could barely see for the smoke.

The front door was too far away. He ran toward the busted window, jumping at the last minute, hurtling past falling debris. He rolled to the ground. Coughs racked his body. His skin was tight, as though it wanted to boil from the heat. He tried to stand up, but could only make it to his hands and knees before he coughed out a wad of black soot. His nose was running. Sweat poured from his face. He coughed again. His lungs felt like shattered glass. He pressed his forehead to the ground. Mud smacked at his singed eyebrows. He pulled in a sharp breath through his nose.

Copper.

Will sat up.

There was a belief among police officers that you could smell the iron in blood when it hit oxygen. This wasn't true. The iron needed a chemical reaction to activate the scent. At crime scenes, that something was usually the fatty compounds in skin. The odor was amplified in the presence of water.

Will looked out at the lake. His eyes blurred. He wiped away the mud and sweat. Silenced the cough that wanted to come.

In the distance, he could make out the soles of a pair of Nikes.

Blood-stained jeans pulled down to the knees.

Arms floating out to the sides.

The body was face up, half in the water, half out.

Will felt momentarily transfixed by the sight. It was the way the moon turned the skin a waxy, pale blue. Maybe joking about growing up in an orphanage had put it in his mind, or maybe he was still feeling the absence of any family members on his side of the aisle at the wedding, but Will found himself thinking of his own mother.

As far as he knew, there were only two photographs that documented the seventeen years of his mother's short life. One was a mugshot from an arrest that had taken place a year before Will was born. The other was taken by the medical examiner who had performed her autopsy. Polaroid. Faded. The waxy blue of his mother's skin was the same color as the dead woman lying twenty feet away.

Will stood. He limped toward the body.

He wasn't under any illusion that he would see his mother's face. His gut had already told him who he would find. Still, standing over the body, knowing he was right, etched another scar in the darkest place of his heart.

Another woman lost. Another son who would grow up without his mother.

Mercy McAlpine lay in the shallow water, rippling waves sending her shoulders into tiny shrugs. Her head rested on a cluster of rocks that kept her nose and mouth above water. Floating tendrils of blonde hair gave her an ethereal effect—a fallen angel, a fading star.

Cause of death wasn't a mystery. Will could tell that she'd been repeatedly stabbed. The white button-down shirt Mercy had worn at dinner had disappeared into the bloody pulp of her chest. Water had washed clean some of the wounds. He could see the angry gouges in her shoulder where the knife had been twisted. Dark red squares showed the only thing that had kept the blade from going deeper was the handle.

In his career, Will had seen more horrific crime scenes, but this woman had been alive, walking around, joking, flirting, arguing with her sullen son, warring with her toxic family, less than an hour ago, and now she was dead. She would never be able to make things right with her child. She would never see him fall in love. Never sit in the front row as she watched him marry the love of his life. No more holidays or birthdays or graduations or quiet moments together.

And all Jon would be left with was the aching loss of her absence.

Will allowed himself a few seconds of sorrow before he summoned his training. He scanned the woods in case the killer was still around. He checked for weapons on the ground. The assailant had taken the knife with him. Will studied the woods again. Listened for strange sounds. He swallowed down the soot and bile in his throat. Knelt beside Mercy. Pressed his fingers against the side of her neck to check for a pulse.

He felt the quick jolt of her heartbeat.

She was alive.

"Mercy?" Will gently turned her head in his direction. Her eyes were open, the whites gleaming like shiny marbles. He made his voice firm. "Who did this to you?"

Will heard a whistling sound, but not from her nose or mouth. Her lungs were trying to draw in air through the open wounds in her chest.

"Mercy." He grabbed her face in his hands. "Mercy McAlpine. My name is Will Trent. I'm an agent with the Georgia Bureau of Investigation. I need you to look at me right now."

Her eyelids started to flutter.

"Look at me, Mercy," Will ordered. "Look at me."

The white flickered for a moment. Her pupils rolled. Seconds passed, maybe a minute, before she finally focused on Will's face. There was a brief spark of recognition, then a rush of fear. She was back in her body now, filled with terror, filled with pain.

"You're gonna be okay." Will started to stand. "I'm going to get help."

Mercy grabbed Will's collar, pulling him back down. She looked at him—really looked at him. They both knew that she would not be okay. Instead of panicking, instead of letting him go, she was keeping him here. Her life was coming into focus. The last words she had said to her family, the fight with her son.

"J-Jon . . . tell him . . . tell him he h-has to . . . he has to g-get away from h-huh . . ."

Will watched her eyelids start to flutter again. He wasn't going to tell Jon anything. Mercy was going to say her last words to her son's face. He raised his voice, yelling, "Sara! Get Jon! Hurry!"

"N-no . . ." Mercy started to tremble. She was going into shock. "J-Jon can't . . . he c-can't . . . stay . . . Get away from . . . from . . ."

"Listen to me," Will said. "Give your son the chance to say goodbye."

"L-love . . ." she said. "Love him . . . s-so much."

Will could hear his own heartbreak in her voice. "Mercy, please stay with me for just a while longer. Sara's gonna bring Jon here. He needs to see you before—"

"I'm s-sorry . . ."

"Don't be sorry," Will said. "Just stay with me. Please. Think about the last thing Jon said to you. That can't be the end of it. You know he doesn't hate you. He doesn't want you dead. Don't leave him with that. Please."

"F-forgive . . . him . . ." She coughed, spraying out blood. "Forgive him . . ."

"Tell him yourself. Jon needs to hear it from you."

Her fist twisted into his shirt. She pulled him even closer. "F-forgive him . . ."

"Mercy, please don't—" Will's voice broke. She was slipping away too fast. It suddenly hit him what Jon would see if Sara brought him here. This was not a tender moment to say goodbye. No son should have to live with the evidence of his mother's violent death.

He tried to swallow down his own grief. "Okay. I'll tell Jon. I promise."

Mercy took his vow as permission.

Her body went slack. She let go of his collar. Will watched her hand fall away, the ripples as it splashed into the water. The trembling had stopped. Her mouth gaped open. A slow, pained sigh left her body. Will waited for her to take another raspy breath, but her chest went still.

He panicked in the silence. He couldn't let her go. Sara was a doctor. She could save Mercy. She would bring Jon and he would have his last chance to say goodbye.

"Sara!"

Will's voice echoed around the lake. He ripped off his shirt, covered up her wounds. Jon wouldn't see the damage. He would see his mother's face. He would know that she loved him. He wouldn't have to live the rest of his life wondering what might have been.

"Mercy?" Will shook her so hard that her head lolled to the side. "Mercy?"

He slapped his palm against her face. Her skin was ice cold. There was no more color left to drain. The blood had stopped flowing. She wasn't breathing. He couldn't find a pulse. He had to start compressions. Will laced together his hands, placed his palms on Mercy's chest, locked his elbows, squared his shoulders, and pushed down with his full weight.

Pain sliced through his hand like a lightning strike. He tried to pull back, but he was caught.

"Stop!" Sara had come out of nowhere. She grabbed his hands, trapping them against Mercy's chest. "Don't move. You'll cut the nerves."

It took a moment for him to understand that Sara wasn't worried about Mercy. She was worried about Will.

He looked down. His brain had no explanation for what he was seeing. Slowly, he came back to his senses. He was looking at the murder weapon. The attack had been frenzied, violent, filled with rage. The killer hadn't just stabbed Mercy in the chest. He'd attacked her from behind, driving the knife into her back with such force that the handle had snapped off. The blade was still embedded inside Mercy's chest.

Will had impaled his hand on the broken knife.

1

TWELVE HOURS BEFORE THE MURDER

Mercy McAlpine stared up at the ceiling thinking through her week. All ten couples had checked out of the lodge this morning. Five new ones were hiking in today. Five more would arrive on Thursday, giving them another full house over the weekend. She needed to get the right suitcases put into the right cottages. The shipper had dumped the last of them on the parking pad this morning. She would have to figure out what to do with her brother's idiot friend, who kept showing up like a stray dog on their doorstep. The kitchen staff needed to be notified he was here again because Chuck had a peanut allergy. Or maybe she wouldn't notify them and the level of bullshit in her life would be cut roughly in half.

The other half was grinding away on top of her. Dave was huffing like a steam train that was never going to reach the end of the tunnel. His eyes bulged in his head. His cheeks were bright red. Mercy had quietly orgasmed five minutes ago. She probably should've told him, but she hated giving him the win.

She turned her head, trying to see the clock by the bed. They were on the floor of cottage five because Dave wasn't worth changing out the sheets. It had to be close to noon. Mercy couldn't be late for the family meeting. Guests would start trickling in around two. Phone calls needed to be made. Two of the couples had asked for massages. Another couple had signed up at the last minute for white water rafting. She needed to confirm the horseback riding

13

place had the right time for the morning. She had to check the weather again, see if that storm was still heading their way. The supplier had brought nectarines instead of peaches. Did he really think she didn't know the difference?

"Merce?" Dave was still chugging away, but she could hear the defeat in his voice. "I think I need to call it."

Mercy patted his shoulder twice, tapping him out. Dave's tired cock flopped against her leg as he collapsed onto his back. He stared up at the ceiling. She stared at him. He'd just turned thirty-five years old and he looked closer to eighty. His eyes were rheumy. His nose was crisscrossed with burst capillaries. His breath had a wheeze. He'd started smoking again because the liquor and pills weren't killing him fast enough.

He said, "Sorry."

There was no need for Mercy to respond because they'd done this so many times that her words existed like a perpetual echo. *Maybe if you weren't high . . . maybe if you weren't drunk . . . maybe if you weren't a worthless piece of shit . . . maybe if I wasn't a lonely, stupid moron who kept fucking her loser ex-husband on the floor . . .*

"You want me to—" He gestured downward.

"I'm good."

Dave laughed. "You're the only woman I know who fakes not having an orgasm."

Mercy didn't want to joke with him. She kept harping on Dave for making bad decisions, but then she kept having sex with him like she was any better. She pulled on her jeans. The button was tight because she'd put on a few pounds. She hadn't taken off anything else but her shoes. The lavender Nikes were beside his toolbox, which reminded her, "You need to fix that toilet in three before the guests get here."

"You got it, boss lady." Dave rolled onto his side in preparation to stand. He was never in a hurry. "You think you can cut me some money loose?"

"Take it out of child support."

He winced. He was sixteen years behind.

She asked, "What about the money Papa paid you to fix up the bachelor cottages?"

"That was a deposit." Dave's knee gave a loud pop as he stood. "I had to buy materials."

She assumed most of the materials came from his dealer or his bookie. "A tarp and a used generator doesn't equal a thousand bucks."

"Come on now, Mercy Mac."

Mercy gave an audible sigh as she checked her reflection in the mirror. The scar that sliced down her face was an angry red against her pale skin. Her hair was still tightly pulled back. Her shirt wasn't even wrinkled. She looked like she'd had the least satisfying orgasm given to her by the world's most disappointing man.

Dave asked, "What do you think about this investment thing?"

"I think Papa's gonna do whatever he wants to do."

"It's not him I'm asking."

She looked at Dave in the mirror. Her father had sprung the news about the wealthy investors over breakfast. Mercy hadn't been consulted, so she assumed this was Papa's way of reminding her that he was still in control. The lodge had been handed down through the McAlpine family for seven generations. In the past, there had been small loans, usually from long-time guests who wanted to keep the place going. They helped get roofs repaired or buy new water heaters, or once, replace the power line from the road. This sounded a hell of a lot bigger. Papa had said the money from the investors was enough to build an annex to the main compound.

Mercy said, "I think it's a good idea. That section of old campsite sits on the best part of the property. We can build some bigger cottages, maybe start marketing to weddings and family reunions."

"Still gonna call it Camp A-Wanna-Pedo?"

Mercy didn't want to laugh, but she did. Camp Awinita was a one-hundred-acre campground with access to the lake, a stream full of trout, and a magnificent long-range mountain view. The land had also been a reliable cash cow until fifteen years ago, when every organization that rented it out, from the Boy Scouts to the Southern Baptists, experienced some kind of pedophile scandal. There was no telling how many kids had suffered over there. The only option had been to close it down before the taint spread to the lodge.

"I dunno," Dave said. "Most of that land's in a conservation easement. You can't really build out past where the creek hits the lake. Plus, I don't see Papa giving anybody any input on how that money's spent."

Mercy quoted her father, "'There's only one name on that sign by the road.'"

"Your name's on that sign, too," Dave said. "You're doing a great job running this place. You were right about upgrading the bathrooms. That marble was a pain hauling in, but it's sure impressive. The faucets and bathtubs look like they came out of a magazine. Guests are spending more for extras. Coming back for repeats. Those investors wouldn't be offering any money except for what you've done here."

Mercy resisted the urge to preen. Compliments were not handed out lightly in her family. No one had said a word about the accent walls in the cottages, the addition of coffee bars and window boxes overflowing with flowers so that guests felt like they were walking into a fairy tale.

She said, "If we spend this money right, people will pay twice, maybe even three times, what they're paying now. Especially if we give them road access instead of making them hike in. We could even do some of those UTVs to get to the bottom of the lake. It's beautiful down there."

"It surely is beautiful, I'll give you that." Dave spent most of his days on the site, ostensibly remodeling the three ancient cottages. He asked, "Bitty have anything to say about the money?"

Her mother always sided with her father, but Mercy said, "She'd talk to you before she talked to me."

"Haven't heard a peep." Dave shrugged. Bitty would confide in him eventually. She loved Dave more than her own children. "You ask me, bigger ain't always better."

Bigger was exactly what Mercy was hoping for. After the shock from hearing the news had worn off, she'd come around to the idea. The influx of cash could shake things up. She was tired of running in quicksand.

Dave said, "It's a lot of change."

She leaned her back against the dresser, looking at him. "Would it be so bad if things were different?"

They stared at each other. There was a lot of weight to the question. She looked past the rheumy eyes and the red nose and saw the eighteen-year-old boy who had promised to take her away from here. Then she saw the car accident that had split open her face. The rehab. The rehab again. The custody battle for Jon. The threat of falling off the wagon. And always the constant, unrelenting disappointment.

Her phone pinged from the bedside table. Dave looked down at the notification. "You got somebody at the trailhead."

Mercy unlocked the screen. The camera was at the parking pad, which meant she had around two hours before the first guests completed the five-mile hike to the lodge. Or maybe less. They looked like they could easily handle the trail. The man was tall and lanky with a runner's build. The woman had long, curly red hair and was carrying a backpack that looked like it had been used before.

The couple shared a deep kiss before they headed toward the trailhead. Mercy felt a pang of jealousy to see them holding hands. The man kept looking down at the woman. She kept looking up at him. Then they both laughed, like they realized how ridiculously in love they were acting.

"Dude looks dick drunk," Dave said.

Mercy's jealousy intensified. "She looks pretty tipsy herself."

"BMW," Dave noticed. "Those the investors?"

"Rich people aren't that happy. Has to be the honeymooners. Will and Sara."

Dave took a closer look, though the couple's back was to the camera now. "You know what they do for a living?"

"He's a mechanic. She's a chemistry teacher."

"Where're they from?"

"Atlanta."

"Real Atlanta or metro Atlanta?"

"I don't know, Dave. Atlanta-Atlanta."

He walked toward the window. She watched him stare across the compound at the main house. She knew something had set him off, but she didn't have it in her to ask. Mercy had put in her time with Dave. Trying to help him. Trying to heal him. Trying to love him enough. Trying to be enough. Trying, trying, trying not to drown in the quicksand of his aching need.

People thought he was Mr. Laid Back Easy-Going Life-of-the-Party Dave, but Mercy knew that he walked around with a giant ball of angst inside his chest. Dave wasn't an addict because he was at peace. He had spent the first eleven years of his life in the foster care system. No one had bothered to look for him when he'd run away. He'd hung around the campsite until Mercy's father had found him sleeping in one of the bachelor cottages. Then her mother had cooked him dinner, then Dave had started showing up every night, then he'd moved into the main house and the McAlpines had adopted him, which had led to a lot of nasty rumors when Mercy had gotten pregnant with Jon. It didn't help that Dave was eighteen and Mercy had just turned fifteen when it happened.

They had never thought of each other as siblings. They were more like two idiots passing in the night. He had hated her until he'd loved her. She had loved him until she'd hated him.

"Heads-up." Dave turned away from the window. "Fishtopher's comin' in hot."

Mercy was tucking her phone into her back pocket when her brother opened the door. He was holding one of the cats, a plump ragdoll that flopped over his arms. Christopher was dressed the way he was always dressed: fishing vest, bucket hat hooked with fishing flies, cargo shorts with too many pockets, flip-flops so he could quickly pull on his waders and stand in the middle of a stream all day throwing out lines. Hence the nickname.

Dave asked, "What lured you here, Fishtopher?"

"Dunno." Fish raised his eyebrows. "Something reeled me in."

Mercy knew they could go on like this for hours. "Fish, did you tell Jon to get the canoes cleaned out?"

"Yep, and he told me to go fuck myself."

"Jesus." Mercy shot Dave a look, like he was solely responsible for Jon's behavior. "Where is he now?"

Fish placed the cat on the porch alongside the other one. "I sent him into town to get some peaches."

"Why?" She looked at the clock again. "We've got five minutes until family meeting. I'm not paying him to ass his way around town all summer. He needs to know the schedule."

"He needs to be gone." Fish crossed his arms the way he always did when he thought he had something important to say. "Delilah's here."

He could've said Lucifer was dancing a jig on the front porch and gotten less shock out of her. Without thinking, Mercy grabbed for Dave's arm. Her heart was gonging against her ribcage. Twelve years had passed since she'd faced off against her aunt inside a cramped courtroom. Delilah had been trying to get permanent custody of Jon. Mercy still felt the deep wounds from the fight to get him back.

"What's that crazy bitch doing here?" Dave demanded. "What does she want?"

"Dunno," Fish said. "She passed right by me on the lane, then went into the house with Papa and Bitty. I found Jon and sent him off before he saw her. You're welcome."

Mercy couldn't thank him. She had started to sweat. Delilah lived an hour away inside her own little bubble. Her parents had brought her up here because they were up to something. "Papa and Bitty were on the porch waiting for Delilah?"

"They're always on the porch in the morning. How would I know if they were waiting?"

"Fish!" Mercy stamped her foot. He could tell the difference between a smallmouth and a redeye from twenty yards, but he couldn't read people for shit. "How did they look when Delilah pulled up? Were they surprised? Did they say anything?"

"Don't think so. Delilah got out of her car. She was holding her purse like this."

Mercy watched him grip together his hands in front of his belly.

"Then she walked up the stairs and they all went inside."

Dave asked, "She still dressing like Pippi Longstocking?"

"Who's Pippi Longstocking?"

"Hush," Mercy hissed. "Delilah didn't say anything about Papa being in a wheelchair?"

"Nope. None of them said anything at all, now that I think

about it. Strangely silent." Fish held up his finger to indicate that he remembered another detail. "Bitty started to push Papa's chair inside, but Delilah took over."

Dave mumbled, "Sounds like Delilah all right."

Mercy felt her teeth clench. Delilah hadn't been surprised to find her brother in a wheelchair, which meant she already knew about the accident, which meant that they had talked on the phone. The question was, who had made the phone call? Had she been invited here or just shown up?

As if on cue, her phone started to ring. Mercy slid it out of her pocket. She saw the caller ID. "Bitty."

Dave said, "Put it on speaker."

Mercy tapped the screen. Her mother started every phone call the same way whether she was calling or answering. "This is Bitty."

Mercy answered, "Yes, Mother."

"Are you kids coming for family meeting?"

Mercy looked at the clock. She was two minutes late. "I sent Jon into town. Fish and I are on the way."

"Bring Dave."

Mercy's hand was hovering over the phone. She had been ready to hang up. Now her fingers were trembling. "Why do you want Dave there?"

There was a click as her mother ended the call.

Mercy looked at Dave, then at Fish. She could feel a fat drop of sweat rolling down her back. "Delilah's going to try to get Jon back."

"No she ain't. Jon just had his birthday. He's practically an adult." For once, Dave was the logical one. "Delilah can't snatch him away. Even if she tries, it won't go to court for a couple years, at least. He'll be eighteen by then."

Mercy pressed her palm to her heart. He was right. Jon acted like a baby sometimes, but he was sixteen years old. Mercy wasn't a serial fuck-up with two DUIs trying to ween herself off of heroin with zanies. She was a responsible citizen. She was running the family business. She'd been clean for thirteen years.

"Guys," Fish said, "are we even supposed to know Delilah's here?"

Dave asked, "She didn't see you when she came up the lane?"

"Maybe?" Fish was asking, not telling. "I was stacking logs by the shed. She was going pretty fast. You know how she is. Like she's on a mission."

Mercy thought of an explanation that was almost too awful to speak. "The cancer could be back."

Fish looked stricken. Dave took a few steps away, turning his back to them both. Bitty had been diagnosed with metastatic melanoma four years ago. Aggressive treatment had put the cancer into remission, but remission did not mean cured. The oncologist had told her to keep her affairs in order.

"Dave?" Mercy asked. "Have you noticed anything? Is she acting any different?"

Mercy watched Dave shake his head. He used his fist to wipe his eyes. He'd always been a mama's boy, and Bitty still doted on him like a baby. Mercy couldn't begrudge him the extra affection. His own mother had abandoned him in a cardboard box outside a fire station.

"She—" Dave cleared his throat a few times so he could speak. "She would get me alone and tell me if it was back. She wouldn't spring it on me at a family meeting."

Mercy knew this was true, if only because Dave had been the first person Bitty had told the last time. Dave had always had a special connection with her mother. He was the one who'd nicknamed her Bitty Mama because she was so small. When she was fighting cancer, Dave had taken her to every doctor's appointment, every surgery, every treatment. He was also the one who'd changed her surgical dressings, kept up with her pill regimen, even washed her hair.

Papa had been too busy running the lodge.

Fish said, "We're missing the obvious."

Dave was wiping his nose with the hem of his T-shirt when he turned back around. "What?"

Fish supplied, "Papa wants to talk about the investors."

Mercy felt like an idiot for not thinking of this first. "Do we have to call a board meeting to vote on taking the money?"

"No." Dave knew the rules of the McAlpine Family Trust better than anyone. Delilah had tried to force him out because he was adopted. "Papa's the trustee, so he gets to make those decisions. Besides, you only need a quorum to call a vote. Mercy, you've got Jon's proxy, so all he needs is you, Fish and Bitty. No reason for me to be there. Or Delilah."

Fish anxiously looked at his watch. "We should go, right? Papa's waiting."

"Waiting to ambush us," Dave said.

Mercy figured that was what her father was planning. She was under no illusion that they were about to share a warm family moment.

She told them, "Let's get this over with."

Mercy led the boys across the compound. The two cats trotted alongside them. She struggled against her natural state of anxiety. Jon was safe. Mercy was not helpless. She was too old for a spanking, and it wasn't like Papa could outrun her anymore.

Heat rushed into her face. She was an awful daughter for even thinking such a thing. Eighteen months ago, her father had been guiding a group up the mountain bike trail when he'd flipped head-first over his handlebars and plunged into the gorge. An air ambulance had winched him out on a stretcher while the guests watched in horror. His skull had been cracked open. Two vertebrae in his neck were fractured. His back was broken. There was no question that he would end up in a wheelchair. He had nerve damage in his right arm. If he was lucky, he would have limited control of his left hand. He could still breathe on his own, but in those first few days, the surgeons had talked about him like he was already dead.

Mercy hadn't had time to grieve. Guests were still at the lodge. Even more were coming in the following weeks. Schedules had to be made. Guides had to be assigned. Supplies had to be ordered. Bills had to be paid.

Fish was the oldest, but he'd never been interested in management. His passion was taking guests out on the water. Jon was too young, and what's more, he hated it here. Dave couldn't be trusted to show up. Delilah was not an option. Bitty, understandably, wouldn't leave Papa's side. By default, Mercy had been given the job. That she was actually good at it should've been a source of family pride. That her changes had led to a large profit in the first year, that she was on track to double that now, should've warranted a celebration.

Yet from the moment her father had gotten out of the rehab facility, he'd seethed with anger. Not about the accident. Not about his loss of athletic ease in his body. Not even about his loss of freedom. For some unfathomable reason, all of his rage, all of his animosity, was directed squarely at Mercy.

Every day, Bitty would wheel Papa around the main compound. Every day, he would find fault with everything Mercy did. The beds weren't being made the right way. The towels weren't being folded the right way. The guests weren't being handled the right way. The meals weren't being served the right way. And of course, *the right way* was always *his way*.

In the beginning, Mercy had struggled to please him, to stroke his ego, to pretend like she couldn't do it without him, to beg him for advice and approval. Nothing worked. His anger only festered. She could've shit out gold bars and he would've found a problem with every single one. She had known Papa could be a demanding bully. What she hadn't realized was that he was just as petty as he was cruel.

"Hold up." Fish's voice was low, like they were kids sneaking off to the lake. "How're we gonna play this, my peeps?"

"Like we always do," Dave told him. "You're gonna stare at the floor with your mouth shut. I'm gonna piss everybody off. Mercy's gonna dig in and fight."

That earned him a smile, at least. Mercy squeezed Dave's arm before opening the front door.

As always, she was greeted by darkness. Dark, weather-worn walls. Two tiny, slitted windows. No sunlight. The foyer of the main house had served as the original lodge when it opened after the Civil War. The place was little more than a fishing shack back then. You could see the ax marks in the wood paneling where the planks had been cut from trees felled on the property.

By luck and necessity, the house had expanded over the years. A second entrance was added on the side of the porch so hikers saw something more inviting when they came off the trail. Private rooms were built for more affluent guests, which necessitated a back set of stairs to the upper floor. A parlor and a dining room were added for would-be Teddy Roosevelts who'd flooded in to explore the new national forest. The kitchen had been connected to the house when wood-burning stoves stopped being a thing. The wrap-around porch was a concession to the crushing summer heat. At one point, there were twelve McAlpine brothers stuffed into bunkbeds on the upper floor. One half had hated the other, which had necessitated building the three bachelor cottages around the lake.

They had mostly scattered when the Great Depression hit, leaving a lone, resentful McAlpine hanging on by the skin of his teeth. He had stored their ashes on a shelf in the basement as one-by-one they had returned to the property. This great-grandfather to Mercy and Fish was responsible for creating the tightly controlled family trust, and his bitterness toward his siblings was writ large in every paragraph.

He was also the only reason this place hadn't been sold for parts years ago. Most of the campsite was in a conservation easement that could never be developed. The other part was restricted by covenants that limited how that land could be used. The trust required a consensus before anything major could be done, and over the years, there had only been asshole McAlpines battling against asshole McAlpines who avoided consensus if only out of spite. That her father was the biggest asshole in a long line should've come as no surprise.

Yet here they were.

Mercy squared her shoulders as she walked down the long hallway toward the back. Her eyes watered at the rush of sunlight pouring through the crank casement windows, then the Palladian windows, then the sleek accordion doors that led to the back of the porch. Each room was like the rings in a tree. You could mark the passage of time by the horsehair plaster and popcorn ceilings and avocado green appliances that complemented the brand-new Wolf six-burner cooktop in the kitchen.

That's where she found her parents waiting. Papa's wheelchair was pulled up under the round pedestal table Dave had built after the accident. Bitty sat beside him, back straight, lips pursed, hand resting on a stack of schedules. There was something timeless about her appearance. Barely a line etched her face. She had always looked more like Mercy's older sister than her mother. Except for the air of disapproval. As usual, Bitty didn't smile until she saw Dave, then her face lit up like Elvis had carried Jesus Christ through the door.

Mercy barely clocked the exchange. Delilah was nowhere to be seen, which sent Mercy's brain spinning all over again. Where was she hiding? Why was she here? What did she want? Had she run into Jon on the narrow road?

"Is it so hard to be on time?" Papa made a show of looking at the kitchen clock. He wore a watch, but turning his left wrist took effort. "Sit down."

Dave ignored the order and leaned down to kiss Bitty's cheek. "Doing okay, Bitty Mama?"

"I'm good, dear." Bitty reached up and patted his face. "Go on and sit."

Her light touch temporarily smoothed the worry from Dave's brow. He winked at Mercy as he pulled out his chair. *Mama's boy*. Fish took his usual seat on her left; eyes on the floor, hands in his lap, no surprise.

Mercy let her gaze rest on her father. His face had more scars than hers now, with deep wrinkles that fanned from the corners of his eyes and dueling parentheses that sliced into the hollows of his cheeks. He'd turned sixty-eight this year, but he looked ninety. He'd always been an active outdoorsman. Before the bike accident, Mercy had never seen her father sit still for more time than it took to shovel a meal into his mouth. The mountains were his home. He knew every inch of the trails. The name of every bird. Every flower. Guests adored him. The men wanted his life. The women wanted his sense of purpose. They called him their favorite guide, their kindred spirit, their confidant.

He wasn't their father.

"All right, children." Bitty always started the family meeting with the same phrase like they were all still toddlers. She leaned up in her chair so she could pass out the schedules. She was a petite woman, barely five feet tall, with a soft voice and cherubic face. "We'll get five couples today. Five more on Thursday."

"Another packed house," Dave said. "Good job, Mercy Mac."

25

The fingers of Papa's left hand wrapped around the arm of his chair. "We'll need to bring in extra guides for the weekend."

Mercy took a moment to find her voice. Were they really doing the meeting like Delilah wasn't lurking in the shadows? Papa was clearly up to something. There was nothing to do but play along.

She told him, "I've already lined up Xavier and Gil. Jedediah's on standby."

"Standby?" Papa demanded. "What the hell is *standby*?"

Mercy choked back the offer to google the word for him. They had strict policies about the guest-to-guide ratios—not only for safety reasons, but because their curated experiences brought in hefty fees. "In case a guest signs up for the hike at the last minute."

"You tell them it's too late. We don't leave guides hanging. They work for money, not promises."

"Jed's fine with it, Papa. He said he'd come if he could."

"And what if he's not available?"

Mercy felt her teeth grit. He always moved the goalpost. "Then I'll take the guests up the trail myself."

"And who's going to look after the place while you're galivanting up the mountains?"

"The same people who looked after it when you did."

Papa's nostrils flared in anger. Bitty looked profoundly disappointed. Less than a minute into the meeting and they were already at a stand-off. Mercy was never going to win. She could go fast or she could go slow, but she was still running in quicksand.

"Fine," Papa said. "You're just going to do whatever you want to do."

He wasn't giving in. He was getting in the last word while telling her she was wrong. Mercy was about to respond when Dave's leg pressed against hers under the table, urging her to drop it.

Papa had already moved on anyway. He trained his sights on Fish. "Christopher, you need to put your best foot forward with the investors. Names are Sydney and Max, a woman and a man, but she wears the pants. Take them to the Falls where they'll be sure to catch something good. Don't bore them with all your ecology talk."

"Absolutely. Understood." Fish had earned his Master of Natural Resource Management with an emphasis on fisheries and aquatic sciences at UGA. Most of the guests were enthralled by his passions. "I was thinking they'd enjoy the—"

"Dave," Papa said. "What's going on with the bachelor cottages? Am I paying you by the nail?"

In a scattershot of passive aggressiveness that hit everyone at the table, Dave took his time answering. His hand slowly reached up to his face. He absently scratched his chin. Finally, he said, "Found some dry rot in the third cottage. Had to gut out the back and start over. Might be in the foundation. Who knows?"

Papa's nostrils flared again. There was no way for him to fact-check Dave's claim. He couldn't make it down to that part of the property, even if they strapped him on an ATV.

"I want photos," Papa said. "Document the damage. And make sure you put all your shit away. There's a storm coming. I'm not paying for another table saw because you didn't have the sense to get it out of the rain."

Dave was picking grime out from under his fingernail. "Sure thing, Papa."

Mercy watched her father's left hand gripping the arm of his chair. Two years ago, he would've come across the table. Now, he had to save up every ounce of energy just to scratch his ass.

Mercy asked her father, "When do you want me to meet with the investors?"

Papa snorted at the question. "Why would you meet with them?"

"Because I'm the manager. Because I have all the spreadsheets and P&Ls. Because I'm a McAlpine. Because each of us has an equal share in the trust. Because I have a right to."

"You have a right to shut your mouth before I shut it for you." Papa turned to Fish. "Why is Chuck back on the property? We're not a homeless shelter."

Mercy exchanged a look with Dave. He took it as his cue to throw a bomb in the middle of the room. "Are you gonna tell us why Delilah's here?"

Bitty shifted uncomfortably in her chair.

Papa started smiling, which brought its own special sense of fear. His cruelty always left a mark. "Why do you think she's here?"

"I think—" Dave started drumming his fingers on the table. "I think the investors aren't here to invest. They're here to buy."

Fish's jaw dropped. "What?"

Mercy felt like her lungs were out of air. "Y-you can't. The trust says—"

"It's done," Papa said. "We've got to get ourselves out of this place before you run it into the ground."

"Run it into the ground?" Mercy couldn't believe what she was hearing. "Are you fucking kidding me?"

"Mercy!" her mother hissed. "Mind your language."

"We're booked out through the season!" She couldn't stop yelling. "Profits are up thirty percent off last year!"

"Which you squandered on marble bathrooms and fancy sheets."

"Which we've made back in repeat bookings."

"How long is that going to last?"

"For as long as you stay the fuck out of it!"

Mercy heard the angry screech in her voice as it bounced around the room. Guilt flooded through her body. She had never spoken to her father this way. None of them had.

They'd been too afraid.

"Mercy," Bitty said. "Sit down, child. Show some respect."

Mercy slowly sank into her chair. Tears streamed from her eyes. This was such a betrayal. She was a McAlpine. She was supposed to be the seventh generation. She had given up everything—everything—to stay here.

"Mercy," Bitty repeated. "Apologize to your father."

Mercy felt her head shaking. She tried to swallow down the splinters in her throat.

"You listen to me, Miss Thirty Percent." Papa's tone was like a razor flaying apart her skin. "Any asshole can have a good year. It's the lean years you won't be able to handle. The pressure will grind you into the ground."

She wiped her eyes. "You don't know that."

Papa huffed a laugh. "How many times have I had to bail your ass out of jail? Pay for your rehabs? Your lawyers? Your parole?

Slip the sheriff some cash to look the other way? Take care of your boy because you were so blind drunk you were pissing yourself?"

Mercy stared at the stove over his shoulder. This was the deepest part of the quicksand, the past that she would never, ever escape.

Dave said, "Delilah drove down for a vote, right?"

Papa said nothing.

Dave said, "The family trust says you've gotta have sixty percent of the vote in order to sell the commercial part of the property. You've got me working on those cottages so we can include that land in the commercial part, right?"

Mercy could barely hear what he was saying. The family trust was byzantine. She had never really studied the language because there had never been a chance it would matter. Every generation going back decades had either despised the place enough to leave or begrudgingly worked for the common good.

Dave said, "There's seven of us. That means you've gotta have four votes to sell."

Mercy barked out a surprised laugh. "You don't have it. I've got Jon's proxy until he turns eighteen. We're both a no. Dave's a no. Fish is a no. You don't have the votes. Even with Delilah."

"Christopher?" Papa lasered in on Fish. "Is that true?"

"I—" Fish kept his gaze on the floor. He loved this land, knew every rise and fall of the earth, every good fishing hole and quiet spot. But that didn't stop him from being who he was. "I can't get in the middle of this. I recuse. Or abstain. Whatever you wanna call it. I'm out."

Mercy wished that she was surprised by his retreat. She told her father, "That puts us each at fifty percent. Fifty percent is not sixty."

"I've got a number for you," Papa said. "Twelve million bucks."

Mercy heard Dave's throat work as he swallowed. Money always changed him. It was the Dr. Jekyll's potion that turned him into a monster.

"Take off half for taxes," Mercy said. "Six million divided by seven, right? Papa and Bitty get equal shares. Fish gets his part whether he votes or not."

Dave said, "So does Jon."

"Dave, please." She waited for him to look at her. He was too busy seeing the dollar signs, running through all the shit he would buy, the people he would impress. Mercy was in a room full of people, surrounded by her family, but as always, she was completely alone.

Bitty said, "Think about what you kids could do with that kind of money. Travel. Start your own business. Go back to school, maybe?"

Mercy knew exactly what they would do. Jon wouldn't be able to hold on to it. Dave would snort it and drink it and still want more. Fish would donate it to whatever the hell river conservation society he could find. Mercy would have to watch every penny because she was a convicted felon with two DUIs who'd dropped out of high school to have a baby. God only knew if the money would last into her old age. If she made it that long.

Her parents, on the other hand, were fine. They had an annuity, a 401(k). The accident policies had covered Papa's hospital bills and rehab. They were both on Medicare, both receiving social security and dividends from the lodge. They didn't need the money. They had everything they needed.

Except for time.

She asked her father, "How long do you think you have left?"

Papa blinked. For just a moment, his guard slipped down. "What are you talking about?"

"You're not doing your physical therapy. You refuse to do your breathing exercises. You only leave the house to check after me." Mercy shrugged. "Covid or RSV or a bad case of the flu could take you out next week."

"Merce," Dave mumbled. "Don't make this mean."

Mercy dried the tears from her eyes. She was past mean. She wanted to hurt them the way they kept hurting her. "What about you, Mother? How long before the cancer comes back?"

"Jesus," Dave said. "That's too far."

"And stealing away my birthright isn't?"

"Your birthright," Papa said. "You stupid bitch. You wanna know what happened to your birthright? Take a look in the mirror at your ugly fucking face."

Mercy felt a vibration go through her body. A sense of tension. A sickening dread.

Papa hadn't moved, but she felt like she was a teenager again with his hands wrapped around her neck. Grabbing Mercy by the hair when she tried to run away. Jerking her arm so hard that the tendon popped. She was late to school again, late for work again, hadn't done her homework, had done her homework too soon. He was always after her, punching her arm, bruising her leg, beating her with his belt, whipping her with the rope in the barn. He had kicked her in the stomach when she was pregnant. Shoved her face into her plate when she was too sick to eat. Put a lock outside her bedroom door so she couldn't see Dave. Testified in front of a judge that she deserved prison time. Told another judge she was mentally ill. Told a third judge she was unfit to be a mother.

She saw him now with a sudden, startling clarity.

Papa wasn't angry about what he had lost in the bike accident.

He was angry about what Mercy had gained.

"You stupid old man." The voice that came out of her mouth sounded possessed. "I've wasted nearly all my life on this godforsaken land. You think I haven't heard your talks and your whispers and your phone calls and your late-night confessions?"

Papa's head reared back. "Don't you dare—"

"Shut up," Mercy snapped. "All of you. Each and every one of you. Fish. Dave. Bitty. Even Delilah, wherever the fuck she's hiding. I could ruin your lives right now. One phone call. One letter. At least two of you motherfuckers could land your asses in jail. The rest of you would never be able to show your faces again. There's not enough money in the world that would buy your lives back. You'll be ruined."

Their fear gave Mercy a sense of power she had never felt in her life. She could see them considering the threats, weighing the odds. They knew she wasn't bluffing. Mercy could burn them all down without even striking a match.

Dave said, "Mercy."

"What, Dave? Are you saying my name, or are you giving up like you always do?"

He tucked his chin to his chest. "I'm just saying be careful."

"Careful of what?" she asked. "You know for a fact I can take a punch. And all of my shit is already out there. It's written on my ugly fucking face. It's carved into that gravestone down at the Atlanta cemetery. I've got nothing to lose but this place, and if it comes to that, I swear to almighty God I'm taking all of you down with me."

The threat was enough to shut them all up for one blissful moment. In the silence, Mercy heard tires crunching on the gravel lane. The old truck needed a new muffler, but she was grateful for the warning. Jon was on his way back from town.

She told them, "We'll talk about this after supper. We've got guests coming. Dave, fix the toilet in three. Fish, get those canoes cleaned out. Bitty, remind the kitchen Chuck's allergic to peanuts. And you, Papa. I know you can't do much, but you damn well better keep your fucking sister away from my son."

Mercy left the kitchen. She walked past the accordion doors, the Palladian windows, the crank casements. In the dark foyer, she wrapped her hand around the doorknob, but paused before opening it. Jon was trying to back the truck into its space. She could hear the gears grinding as he slipped the clutch.

She took a deep breath, then slowly shushed it out.

There was history in this dark room. Sweat and toil and land that had been passed down for over one hundred and sixty years. Photographs covered the walls, all of them marking the important milestones: a daguerreotype of the fishing shack. Sepia-toned prints of various McAlpines working around the property. Digging the first well. The WPA bringing in the power line. The annexation of Camp Awinita. Boy Scouts singing around a campfire. Guests roasting marshmallows by the lake. The first color photo showed off the new indoor plumbing. The bachelor cottages. The floating dock. The paddle boathouse. The family portraits. The generations of McAlpines; the marriages and funerals and babies and life.

Mercy didn't need photographs. She had recorded her own history. Diaries from her childhood. Ledgers she'd found hidden in the office and tucked into the back of an old cupboard in the kitchen. The notebooks she had started keeping on her own. There were secrets that would destroy Dave. Revelations that would tear Fish apart. Crimes that could send Bitty to prison. And the sheer evil that Papa had committed to keep this place in his violent, greedy hands.

None of them were going to take the lodge away from Mercy. They would have to kill her first.

2

TEN HOURS BEFORE THE MURDER

Will was quickly starting to understand that there was a big difference between running five miles a day on the streets of Atlanta and hiking up a mountain. Maybe it had been a bad idea to spend almost his entire life training the muscles in his legs for exactly one thing. It didn't help that Sara was springing up the pass like a gazelle. He always derived a great deal of pleasure watching her go through her morning yoga routine. He hadn't realized she was secretly conditioning herself for an Iron Man competition.

He took his water bottle out of his backpack as an excuse to stop. "We should stay hydrated."

The sly smile on her face told him she knew exactly what he was up to. She turned around, taking in the view. "It's so beautiful up here. I forget how nice it is to be surrounded by trees."

"We've got trees in Atlanta."

"Not like this."

Will had to give her that. The long-range mountain view was jaw-dropping if you didn't feel like murder hornets were attacking your calves.

"Thank you for bringing me here." She rested her hands on his shoulders. "This is a perfect way to start our honeymoon."

"Last night was pretty fantastic."

"This, morning, too." She gave him a lingering kiss. "What time do we have to be at the airport?"

He grinned. Sara had been in charge of the wedding. Will was in charge of the honeymoon, and he'd done everything he could to keep it a secret, down to asking her sister to do the packing. Their suitcases had already been shipped to the lodge. He'd told Sara they were going to go for a day hike, enjoy a leisurely picnic, then head back to Atlanta and fly out to their destination.

Will asked, "What time do you want to be at the airport?"

"Is it an overnight flight?"

"Is it?"

"Are we going to be sitting for a long while? Is that why you wanted to get some exercise first?"

"Are we?"

"You can drop the act." She playfully tugged at his ear. "Tessa told me everything."

Will almost fell for it. Sara was incredibly close to her sister, but there was no way Tessa had ratted him out. "Good try."

"I'm going to need to know what to pack," she said, which was valid but also sneaky. "Do I need a swimsuit or do I need a heavy coat?"

"You mean, are we going to the beach or are we going to the Arctic?"

"Are you seriously going to make me wait until tonight?"

Will had been silently weighing the right time to spring their destination on her. Should he wait until they reached the lodge? Should he tell her before they got there? Would she be happy with his choice? She'd mentioned an overnight flight. Did she think they were going somewhere romantic, like Paris? Maybe he should've taken her to Paris. If he donated enough blood, he could probably swing a youth hostel.

"My love." She smoothed her thumb along his brow. "Wherever we end up, I'm going to be happy because I'm with you."

She kissed him again, and he decided now was as good a time as any. At least if she was disappointed, it wouldn't be in front of an audience.

Will said, "Let's sit down."

He helped her with her backpack. The plastic plates clinked

against the tin silverware as it hit the ground. They'd already stopped for lunch overlooking a meadow full of grazing horses. Will had gotten fancy sandwiches from the French pastry shop in Atlanta, which had cemented his belief that he was not a fancy sandwich man.

But Sara had been delighted, which was all that mattered.

He gently took her hand as they sat on the ground across from each other. Will's thumb automatically went to her ring finger. He played with the thin wedding band that had joined the ring that had belonged to his mother. Will thought about the ceremony, the feeling of euphoria he still hadn't been able to shake. Faith, his partner at the GBI, had stood with him. He'd danced with his boss, Amanda, because she was more like a mother to Will, if your mother was the type of person who would shoot you in the leg so the bad guys would get to you first while she sprinted away.

Sara asked, "Will?"

He felt an awkward smile on his mouth. Out of nowhere, he was nervous. He didn't want to disappoint her. He didn't want to put too much pressure on her, either. The lodge could've been a terrible idea. She could end up hating it.

She said, "Tell me your favorite part about the wedding."

Will felt some of the awkwardness leave his smile. "Your dress was beautiful."

"That's sweet," she said. "My favorite part was when everybody left and you fucked me against the wall."

His laugh was more like a guffaw. "Can I change my answer?"

She gently touched her fingers to the side of his face. "Tell me."

Will took a deep breath and forced himself to get out of his head. "When I was a kid, there was a church group that did summer activities with the children's home. They'd take us to Six Flags or we'd go to the Varsity for hot dogs or to see a movie or whatever."

Sara's smile softened. She knew that his life at the children's home had not been easy.

"They also sponsored kids for summer camp. Two weeks in the mountains. I never got to go, but the kids who did—it's all they talked about for the whole rest of the year. Canoeing and fishing and hiking. All that stuff."

Sara pressed together her lips. She was doing the math. Will had spent eighteen years in the system. Not being able to go to the camp at least once was statistically improbable.

Will explained, "They gave you passages from the Bible to memorize. You had to recite it in front of the whole church. If you got the lines right, then you got to go."

He saw her throat work.

"Shit, I'm sorry." Leave it to Will to make Sara cry on their honeymoon. "It was my choice, not because of my dyslexia. I could memorize the verses, but I didn't want to speak in front of people. They were trying to help us come out of our shells, I think? Like, learn how to speak to strangers or give a presentation or—"

She gripped his hand.

"Anyway." He had to move this along. "I heard about the camp at the end of every summer—kids wouldn't shut up about it—and I thought it would be nice to go there. Not camping, because I know you hate camping."

"I do."

"But there's an eco lodge that you can hike into. You can't reach it by car. It's been in the same family for years. They have guides who take you mountain biking and fishing and paddle boarding and—"

She interrupted him with a kiss. "I love everything about it."

"Are you sure?" Will asked. "Because it's not just for me. I booked you a massage, and there's sunrise yoga by the lake. Plus, there's no Wi-Fi or television or cell reception."

"Holy shit." She looked genuinely astonished. "What are you going to do?"

"I'm going to fuck you against every wall in the cottage."

"We get our own cottage?"

"Hello!"

They both turned at the sound. A man and a woman were twenty yards down the trail. They were dressed in hiking attire and carrying backpacks that were so new Will wondered if they had taken off the tags in their car.

The man called, "Are you guys going to the lodge? We're lost."

"We're not lost," the woman muttered. They were both wearing wedding rings, but Will got the feeling from the sharp look she gave her husband that that was up for debate. "There's only one trail in and out, right?"

Sara looked at Will. He'd been leading the hike, and there actually was just one trail, but he wasn't going to get in the middle of things.

"I'm Sara," she told the couple. "This is my husband, Will."

Will cleared his throat as he stood up. She'd never called him her husband before.

The man looked up at Will. "Wow, what're you, six-three? Six-four?"

Will didn't answer, but the man didn't seem to mind.

"I'm Frank. This is Monica. Mind if we go together?"

"Sure." Sara picked up her backpack. The look she gave Will was an unsubtle reminder that there was a difference between an awkward silence and being rude.

"So," he said. "Nice day, right? Good weather."

Frank said, "I heard there might be a storm."

Monica muttered under her breath.

"This way, right?" Frank took the lead, walking in front of Sara. The trail was narrow, so Will had no choice but to bring up the rear behind Monica. Judging by the huffing noises, the woman was not enjoying the hike. Nor was she prepared. Her Skecher slip-ons kept slipping on the rocks.

". . . got the idea to come here," Frank was saying. "I mean, I love the outdoors, but work keeps me very busy."

Monica huffed again. Will looked over her head at Frank. The man had used some kind of spray on his bald spot to cover the bright pink of his scalp. Sweat had washed the dye down his collar, leaving a dark ring.

". . . and then Monica said, 'If you promise to stop talking about it, I'll go.'" Frank's voice had taken on the cadence of a hammer drill. "And so, I had to schedule time off work, which isn't easy. I've got a team of eight guys answering to me."

Will guessed from the way Frank was talking that he made less money than his wife. And that it bothered him. He looked at his watch. The lodge's website said that guests usually took two hours to hike in. Will and Sara had stopped for lunch, so maybe they had another ten or fifteen minutes to go. Or twenty, since Frank's pace was slow.

Sara shot Will a look over her shoulder. She wasn't going to take this bullet for the team. Will was going to have to make more small talk.

He asked Frank, "How'd you guys hear about this place?"

"Google," Frank said.

Monica muttered, "Thanks, Google."

Frank asked, "What do you guys do?"

Will watched Sara straighten her shoulders. A few weeks ago, they had agreed that no matter where they went, it would be easier to lie about their jobs. Will didn't want to be valorized or denigrated for wearing a badge. Sara didn't want to listen to weird medical complaints or wildly dangerous vaccine theories.

Before she could lose her nerve, he said, "I'm a mechanic. My wife teaches high school chemistry."

He saw Sara smile. This was the first time Will had called her his wife.

"Oh, I sucked at science stuff," Frank said. "Monica's a dentist. Did you take chemistry, Monica?"

Monica grunted rather than answer. She was Will's kind of people.

Frank said, "I do IT for the Afmeten Insurance Group. No one's ever heard of them, don't worry. We deal with mostly high net-worth individuals and institutional investors."

Sara said, "Oh look, more hikers."

Will felt his stomach tying itself into a knot at the thought of more people. The second man and woman must've slipped ahead on the trail while Sara and Will were having lunch. The couple was older, probably in their mid-fifties, but more determined and better equipped to make the hike.

They both smiled as they waited for the group to catch up.

The man said, "Y'all must be heading toward the McAlpine Lodge. I'm Drew, this is my partner, Keisha."

Will waited for his turn to shake hands, trying not to think back to the blissful moments he'd had alone with Sara. His brain was throwing up images from the McAlpine Lodge website. Chef-prepared meals. Curated hikes. Fly-fishing excursions. There were always two or three couples enjoying themselves in each photo. It was only now that Will realized the couples had probably not known each other before arriving at the lodge.

He was going to end up paddle boarding with Frank.

Keisha said, "You just missed Landry and Gordon. They sprinted on ahead of us to the lodge. It's their first time. They're app developers."

"Really?" Frank asked. "Did they mention which app?"

"We were all too caught up in the view to talk about anything else." Drew rested his hand on Keisha's hip. "We made a pledge that we're not gonna talk about work the whole week. Y'all wanna join in?"

"Absolutely," Sara said. "Should we go?"

Will had never loved her more.

They all fell silent as they followed the winding trail up the mountain. The trees thickened overhead. The path narrowed again so they went back to single file. There was a well-maintained wooden footbridge over a rushing stream. Will looked down at the churning water. He wondered how often it flooded the bank, but he let the question go when Frank started verbally debating himself on the differences between creeks and rivers. Sara gave a pained smile at Will as Frank yapped on like a toy poodle at her heels. Will had somehow ended up second from last. Drew was in front of him. Monica took up the rear, head down, feet still slipping on the rocks. Will hoped she'd shipped some hiking boots to the lodge. He was wearing his HAIX tactical boots. He could probably scale the side of a building. If his calves didn't explode.

Frank finally stopped talking when they had to navigate a rocky section. Thankfully, the silence continued as the path widened and the going got smoother. Sara managed to drop back behind Frank so that she could talk to Keisha. Soon, both women were laughing. Will loved the easy way Sara had about her. She could find common ground with almost anybody. Will, not so much, but he was mindful that they were going to be surrounded by these people for the next six days. And also of the look that Sara had given him earlier. She needed him to carry his side of the conversation. The only time Will was good at small talk was when he was sitting across the table from a suspect.

He thought about his four fellow guests, wondering what kind of criminals they would hypothetically be. Considering the hefty cost of the lodge, he assumed at least three of them would lean more toward white-collar crimes. Frank would definitely be embroiled in something to do with crypto. Keisha had the sly, competent look of an embezzler. Drew reminded Will of a guy he'd busted for running a Ponzi scheme involving nutritional supplements. That left Monica, who legitimately looked like she was going to murder Frank. Of the group, Will figured she'd be the one most likely to get away with it. She'd have an alibi. She'd have a lawyer. She sure as hell wouldn't sit for an interview.

And he would have a hard time blaming her for the crime.

"Will," Drew said. Which was how you started a conversation when you weren't gaming out criminals in your head. "First time at the lodge?"

"Yeah." Will kept his voice low because Drew had. "You?"

"Third time. We love it up there." His looped his thumbs through the straps on his backpack. "Keisha and I own a catering business on the West Side. Hard to clock out. She dragged me kicking and screaming the first time. Couldn't believe there was no phone or internet. Thought I was gonna go into shock by the end of the day. But then—"

Will watched him stretch out his arms and take a deep, cleansing breath.

Drew said, "Being in nature resets you. Know what I mean?"

Will nodded, but he had some concerns. "So, everything at the lodge is done in groups?"

"Meals are communal. The activities are limited to four guests per guide."

Will did not like those odds. "How is that assigned?"

"You can ask for a specific couple," Drew said. "Why do you think I dropped back to talk to you?"

Will guessed it was pretty obvious. "There's really no internet? No reception?"

"Not for us." Drew was grinning. "They've got a landline for emergencies. The staff has access to Wi-Fi, but they aren't allowed to give out the password. Believe me, that first time, I tried to wear them down, but Papa runs a tight ship."

"Papa?"

"Wowza!" Frank yelled.

Will saw a deer darting across the path. A large clearing was a hundred yards on. Sunlight poured through the gap. Will saw a rainbow arcing across the blue sky. It was like something out of a movie. All that was missing was a singing nun. He felt his heart slow in his chest. A calmness took over. Sara was looking at him again, a huge smile on her face. Will let go of a breath he hadn't realized he'd been holding.

She was happy.

"Here." Drew handed a map to Will. "It's old, but it'll help you get your bearings."

Old was an accurate description. The map looked like something from the seventies, with press-on letters and line drawings to indicate various points of interest. An irregular loop lassoed around the top quadrant, with dashed lines indicating smaller trails. Will spotted the footbridge where they'd crossed over the creek. The scale had to be off. They'd walked for at least twenty minutes to get here. He guessed by the McAlpine stamp at the bottom that the owners hadn't been going for accuracy.

He studied the images as he walked. The sprawling house at the bottom of the lasso looked central to the property. He assumed the smaller houses were the cottages. Each was numbered one through ten. An octagonal building served as the dining hall, judging by the plate and silverware drawn beside it. Another trail led to a waterfall with clusters of fish jumping through the air. Another had an equipment shed with canoes. Yet another trail meandered toward a boathouse. The lake was shaped like a snowman leaning against a wall. The head was apparently the area for swimming. There was a floating dock. What looked like a scenic viewpoint had a bench overlooking the vista.

Will noted with interest that there was only one access road, which ended near the main house. He assumed the road crossed the creek somewhere near the footbridge and wound its way down into town. The family wasn't carrying in supplies on their backs. A place this size would need bulk deliveries and a way to get staff in and out. Plus water and electricity. He assumed the land-line was buried. No one wanted to get trapped inside an Agatha Christie novel.

"Damn," Drew said. "Never gets old."

Will looked up. They had entered the clearing. The main house was a hodge-podge of bad architecture. The second story looked slapped on. The ground floor had brick on one side and clapboard on the other. There seemed to be two main entrances, one at the front and one at the side. A third, smaller set of stairs went up the back, along with a wheelchair ramp. A spacious, wrap-around porch was doing its best to lend some architectural cohesion, but there was no explanation for the mismatched windows. Some of the more narrow slits reminded Will of the cells inside the Fulton County Jail.

An outdoorsy-looking woman with blonde hair tightly tied behind her head stood at the bottom of the side porch stairs. She was dressed in cargo shorts and a white button-down shirt with lavender-colored Nikes. The table beside her held an array of snacks, cups of water, and glasses of champagne. Will checked behind him to make sure Monica was still there. She'd come alive at the sight of the table. She passed Will at the home stretch, grabbed a glass of champagne and downed it in one gulp.

"I'm Mercy McAlpine, the manager of the McAlpine Family Lodge," the outdoorsy woman told the group. "Three generations of McAlpines live here on the property. We all wanna welcome you to our home. If I could have your attention for a moment, I'll quickly run through a few of the rules and some safety in-formation, then I'll get to the fun parts."

Predictably, Sara stood at the front, listening intently like the beautiful nerd she was. Frank stayed glued to her side. Keisha and Drew hung back with Will like the bad kids in class. Monica took another glass of champagne and sat on the bottom stair. A muscular-looking cat rubbed against her leg. Will saw a second cat fall over onto the ground and roll on its back. He guessed the app developers, Landry and Gordon, had already gone through the orientation and were blissfully alone.

"In the unlikely event of an emergency—a fire, or dangerous weather—you'll hear us clanging on this bell." Mercy pointed to a large bell hanging on a post. "If you hear the bell, we ask you to stage at the parking pad on the other side of the house."

Will alternated between brownie bites and potato chips as Mercy detailed the evacuation plan. Then it started to feel too much like a briefing at work, so he tuned out her voice and looked around the compound. It reminded him of college campuses he'd seen on television. Ceramic pots overflowed with flowers. There were park benches and grassy areas and pavers where he imagined the cats enjoyed the sun.

Eight cottages were nestled inside their own little garden areas around the main house. Will guessed the other two were on the back end of the lasso. Which meant that the family probably lived together in the main house. Will assumed from the size that there were at least six bedrooms on the top floor. He couldn't imagine choosing to live on top of people like that. Then again, Sara's sister lived one floor below her condo, so maybe Will was thinking too much of the Atlanta Children's Home and not enough of the Waltons.

"Now," Mercy said. "The fun part."

She started passing around folders. Three couples, three sets. Sara eagerly flipped hers open. She loved an informational packet. Will felt his attention being pulled back toward Mercy as she ran through how the activities worked, where they were supposed to meet, what equipment would be provided. Her face was unremarkable but for the long scar that ran from her forehead, over her eyelid, down the side of her nose, then took a sharp turn toward her jaw line.

Will was well versed in the scars that came from violence. A fist or shoe couldn't be that precise. The blade of a knife couldn't be that straight. A baseball bat could cause a linear wound, but the scar tended to be rippled at the deepest point of impact. If Will had to guess, a piece of sharp metal or glass had caused the damage. That meant either an industrial accident or something involving a car.

"Cottage assignments." Mercy looked down at her clipboard. "Sara and Will are at the end of the lane in number ten. My son, Jon, will show you the way."

Mercy turned toward the house, a warm smile softening her

face. The affection was lost on the kid, who slowly walked down the porch stairs. He looked to be around sixteen and had the kind of hard muscle that teenage boys packed on simply by existing. Will noted the slow once-over Jon gave Sara. Then the kid brushed back his curly hair and showed her a set of straight white teeth.

"Hi there." Jon walked straight past Frank and focused all of his charm on Sara. "Did you enjoy the hike in?"

"I did, thank you." Sara had always been good with kids, but she was missing the fact that this kid was not looking at her like a kid. "You're a McAlpine, too?"

"Guilty. Third generation living on the mountain." He ran his fingers through his hair again. Maybe he needed a comb. "You can call me Jon. I hope you enjoy your stay on the property."

"Jon." Will stepped in front of Frank. "I'm Will. Sara's husband."

The kid had to crane his neck to look up at Will, but the important part was that he got the message. "This way, sir."

Will gave the hand-drawn map back to Drew, who offered a nod of approval. Not a bad way to start the week. Will had married a beautiful woman. He'd climbed a mountain. He'd made Sara happy. He had intimidated a thirsty teenager.

Jon took them across the compound. He had a goofy way of walking, like he was still learning how to use his body. Will could remember what that felt like, not knowing one day to the next whether you were going to wake up with a mustache or your voice cracking like a tween girl's. He would not go back to that time for all of the money in the world.

They picked up the lasso trail between cottages five and six. The ground was lined with crushed stone. One of the cats darted into the underbrush, probably going after a chipmunk. Will was glad to see that low voltage lighting would help them navigate at night. Darkness in the woods was not the same as darkness in the city. The tree canopy was tight over their heads. He could feel the temperature drop as Jon pulled ahead of them. The terrain started to slope down gradually. Someone had trimmed back the vines and branches around the path, but Will had the feeling of going deep into the forest.

"This is called the Loop Trail." Sara had opened the folder to the map. She had slowed her pace, putting more distance between them and Jon. "Two circles around is roughly one mile. We're on the top half. We can explore the bottom half when we go for supper. We'll probably need ten or fifteen minutes to get to the dining hall."

Will's stomach rumbled.

She flipped the page to the calendar. She looked up at Will in surprise. "You signed both of us up for morning yoga."

"I figured I'd give it a try." Will figured he would look like an ass. "Your sister said you love fishing."

"My sister is right. I haven't been since I moved to Atlanta." She traced her finger across the days. "White water rafting. Mountain biking. I don't see where you signed up for a pissing contest with a teenager."

Will fought a grin. "I think they comp the first one."

"Good. I'd hate for you to pay for a second one."

Will got the message, which Sara softened by looping her arm through his. She leaned her head against his shoulder as they walked. They fell into a companionable silence. Will didn't feel the incline in the trail so much as his calves reminded him that they weren't used to this. The walk was not a short one. He guessed five minutes passed before the terrain got steeper. The trees pulled back. The sky opened up above their heads. He could see the mountains rolling in the distance like a never-ending magic carpet. Will didn't know if it was the changes in elevation or the way the sun was moving, but every time he took in the view, it looked different. The colors were an explosion of greens. The air was so fresh that his lungs felt shaky.

Jon had stopped. He pointed twenty yards ahead to a fork in the trail. "Lake's down that way. You're not supposed to swim after dark. Cottage ten is the farthest away from the main house, but if you go left at the fork, it loops back around to the dining hall."

Will asked, "There used to be a campsite around here, right?"

"Camp Awinita," Jon said.

Sara asked, "Is *awinita* a native American word?"

"It's Cherokee for fawn, but a guest told me a while back it's supposed to be two words, and spelled with a *d*, like *ahwi anida*."

Will asked, "Do you know where the camp is?"

"They closed it down when I was little." Jon shrugged as he continued up the trail. "If you're interested in all that stuff, you can ask my grandma Bitty. You'll see her at supper. She knows more about this place than just about anybody."

Will watched Jon disappear around a curve. He let Sara go ahead of him. The view was even better from behind. He studied the shape of her legs. The curve of her ass. The toned muscles along her bare shoulders. Her hair was up in a ponytail. The back of her neck had a sheen of sweat from the hike. Will was sweaty, too. They should probably take a long shower together before dinner.

"Oh, wow." Sara was looking up an offshoot from the trail.

Will followed her gaze. Jon was climbing a set of stone stairs that looked like they had been etched into the hill for Glorfindel. Ferns crowded at the edges. Moss covered the adjacent stones. At the top was a small cottage with rustic board and batten siding. Colorful flowers spilled from the window boxes. There was a hammock swaying on the front porch. Will could've spent the next ten years trying to make something this perfect and never come close.

"It's like a fairy tale." Sara's voice had a winsome quality. She was never more beautiful than when she smiled. "I love it."

Jon said, "You can see three states from this ridge."

Sara unclipped the compass from her backpack. She opened the folder, found the map. She pointed into the distance. "I think that must be Tennessee, right?"

"Yes, ma'am." Jon walked back down the stairs to do his own pointing. "That's the eastern slope of Lookout Mountain. There's a bench on the lake trail called the lookout bench where you can see it better. We're in the Cumberland Plateau."

"Which means that Alabama is that way." Sara pointed behind Will. "And North Carolina is way over there."

Will turned around. All he could see was millions and millions of trees undulating across the mountain range. He pivoted, catching the glare as the afternoon sun turned part of the lake into a mirror. From above, the expanse looked less like a snowman and more like a giant amoeba that disappeared into the curve of the earth.

Jon said, "That's the Shallows. The water comes off the mountaintops, so it's still a little cold this time of year."

Sara held the folder open like a book. She read, "Lake McAlpine spreads out over four hundred acres, with depths up to sixty-eight feet. The Shallows, located at the end of the Lake Trail, is less than fifteen feet, which makes this area ideal for swimming. There are smallmouth bass, walleye, bluegill and yellow perch. Eighty percent of the lake sits in a conservation easement that can never be developed. The lodge compound is abutted by the 750,000-acre Muscogee State Forest to the west and the 800,000-acre Cherokee National Forest to the east."

Jon said, "Cherokee and Muscogee are two of the tribes that were in this area. The lodge was founded after the Civil War, seven generations of McAlpines ago."

Will assumed the land had come at a literal steal. The original inhabitants were removed from their home and forced to march west. Most of them had died on the journey.

Sara referred to the map. "What about this part along the creek, Lost Widow Trail?"

"That's way down a steep hill to the very backside of the lake," Jon said. "The story is, the first Cecil McAlpine who started this place had his throat slit by some bad guys. His wife thought he was dead. She disappeared down that trail. Only, he didn't die, but she didn't know that. He searched for days, but she was lost to him for ever."

"You know a lot about this place," Sara said.

"My grandma drilled it into me every single day when I was a kid. She loves it here." Jon shrugged, but Will caught the blush of pride on his face. "Ready?"

Jon didn't wait for a response. He walked up the stairs and swung open the front door to the cottage. There was no key. All of the windows were already open to take advantage of the breeze.

Sara was smiling again. "It's beautiful, Will. Thank you."

"Suitcases are already in your room." Jon started a clearly practiced routine. "Coffeemaker's there. Pods are in the box there. Mugs are hanging from the hooks. There's a small fridge under the counter with all the stuff you asked for."

Will looked around the space as Jon pointed out the obvious.

He'd booked the two-bedroom cottage because the view was supposed to be better. The additional cost meant he'd probably have to pack his own lunch for the next year, but judging by Sara's reaction, it was worth it.

He was pretty pleased with the choice himself. The main area of the cottage was big enough for a couch and two club chairs. The leather looked worn and comfortable. The corded rug underfoot was springy soft. The lamps were mid-century modern. Everything seemed thoughtfully placed and had an air of quality to it. Will assumed if you took the time to haul something up a mountain, you wanted to make sure it would last.

He followed Jon and Sara into the larger bedroom. Their suitcases were on the bed, which was high off the ground and covered in a dark blue velvet blanket. Another soft rug. Matching lamps. Another comfortable leather chair in the corner with a side table.

Will stuck his head into the bathroom, surprised by the contemporary feel. White marble, modern, industrial-looking fixtures. There was a large soaking tub in front of a huge window that overlooked the valley. Will couldn't think of any additional ways to describe the breathtaking view, so he thought about sitting in the tub with Sara and decided it was worth a year of PB&Js for lunch.

Jon said, "One of us makes a loop on the trail at eight in the morning and then again at ten in the evening. If you need something, leave a note on the steps under the rock, or wait on your porch and you'll see us walk by. Otherwise you gotta hoof it back to the lodge. Can I get you anything else?"

"We're good, thanks." Will reached for his wallet.

Jon said, "We're not allowed to take tips."

Sara asked, "How about I buy that vape pen in your back pocket?"

Will felt as surprised as Jon looked. Sara had a pediatrician's disgust for vaping. She'd seen too many kids destroy their lungs.

"Please don't tell my mom." Jon lost about five years with the desperate request. His voice squeaked. He turned jittery. "I got it in town today."

She said, "I'll give you twenty for it."

"Really?" Jon was already pulling out the metal pen. It was bright blue with a silver tip, maybe ten bucks at a 7-Eleven. "There's some Red Zeppelin in there. Do you need more cartridges?"

"No, thank you." Sara nodded for Will to pay.

He would've been more comfortable confiscating a tobacco product from an underage minor, but that didn't seem like something a car mechanic would do. Will reluctantly handed over the cash.

"Thanks." Jon carefully folded the twenty. Will could practically see the kid's brain trying to work out how to get more. "We're not supposed to, but if you uh, I mean if you need it, I've got the Wi-Fi password. It won't reach out here, but it goes in the dining hall and—"

Sara said, "No, thank you."

Will opened the door to move the kid along. Jon gave them a salute on his way out. It was hard not to follow him. The Wi-Fi password wouldn't be bad information to have.

Sara asked, "You're not thinking about getting the password, right?"

Will closed the door, pretending to be a man who did not want to know how Atlanta United was doing against FC Cincinnati. He watched Sara take a Ziploc bag out of her backpack. She sealed the vape pen inside, then zipped it back in the front pocket.

She explained, "I don't want Jon getting it out of the trash."

"You know he'll just buy another one."

"Probably," she said. "But not tonight."

Will didn't care what Jon did. "You like it here?"

"It's lovely. Thank you for bringing me to such a special place." She nodded for him to follow her back into the bedroom. Before he could get his hopes up, she started dialing in the combination on her suitcase. "What am I going to find in here?"

"I got Tessa to pack for you."

"That was very sneaky." Sara unzipped the top of her bag. She opened it, then closed it. "What should we do first? Go down to the lake? Walk around the property? Meet the other guests?"

"We'll both need to shower before dinner."

Sara looked at her watch. "We could take a long soak in the bath, then try out the bed."

"That's a good plan."

"Are these pillows going to work for you?"

Will checked the pillows. The foam was as tight as a seal's ass. He preferred a pancake.

"That part you weren't listening to before—Jon told us there are other types of pillows at the main house." She smiled again. "I could unpack and start running the bath while you get your pillows."

Will kissed her before he left.

The sunlight was dancing off the Shallows when he walked down the stone stairs. He held up his hand to block the light until he made it down to the path. Instead of following the Loop Trail back to the main compound, Will headed in the direction of the lake to familiarize himself with the way. The scenery changed as he got closer to the water. He could feel moisture in the air. Hear the soft lapping of waves. The sun was lower in the sky. He passed the lookout bench, which, as advertised, looked out. Will felt that same peacefulness envelope him. Drew was right about getting a reset from being in nature. And Sara was right about the trees. Everything felt different here. Slower. Less stressful. It was going to be hard to leave at the end of the week.

Will stared out into the distance, allowing himself a few minutes to blank out his mind and enjoy the moment. He hadn't realized how much tension he'd been holding in his body until it was no longer there. He looked down at the ring on his finger. Except for the Timex on his wrist, he wasn't a jewelry guy, but he liked the dark finish on the titanium ring Sara had picked out for him. They had basically proposed to each other at the same time. Will had read that you were supposed to spend three months of your salary on an engagement ring. Sara's doctor's salary had given him the better part of the bargain.

He should probably be finding ways to thank her for it rather than staring slack-jawed into the distance. Will turned back the way he'd come. He could watch the sun's progress from the bathtub with Sara. She had obviously wanted him out of the cottage for a few minutes. Will worked to turn off his detective brain as he passed by the stone stairs. Sara knew it would've been easier to pick up some new pillows after dinner. She probably wanted to surprise him with something nice. The thought made Will grin as he turned a sharp bend in the trail.

"Hey, Trashcan."

Will looked up. There was a man standing twenty feet away. Smoking a cigarette, spoiling the clean air. Will hadn't been called by that nickname in a long while. It had been given to him at the children's home. There wasn't a clever reason behind it. As an infant, the police had found him inside a trash can.

"Come on, Trash," the man said. "Don't you recognize me?"

Will studied the stranger. He was dressed in painter's pants and a stained white T-shirt. Shorter than Will. Rounder. The yellow in his eyes and the spiderweb of broken blood vessels indicated a long-standing issue with substances. Still, that didn't narrow down his identity. Most of the kids Will had grown up with had struggled with addiction. It was hard not to.

"Are you fucking with me?" The man blew out a stream of smoke as he slowly walked toward Will. "You really don't recognize me?"

Will felt a sense of dread. It was the deliberate slowness that triggered a memory. One minute, Will was standing on a mountain path with a stranger, the next minute, he was sitting in the common room at the children's home watching the boy they all called *the Jackal* slowly make his way down the stairs. One step. Then the next. His finger dragging along the railing like a sickle.

There was an unwritten rule in adoption circles that you didn't want a child who was older than six. They were too lost after that. Too damaged. Will had seen this play out dozens of times at the children's home. Older kids would go out to foster families or, rarely, adoptions. The ones that came back always had a certain look in their eyes. Sometimes they would tell you their stories. Other times, you could read what had happened by the scars on their bodies. Cigarette burns. The distinctive hook of a wire hanger. The rippled scar of a baseball bat. The bandaged wrists where they had tried to end the misery on their own terms.

They all tried to heal their damage in different ways. Binging and purging. Night terrors. Lashing out. Some couldn't stop cutting themselves. Some disappeared into a pipe or a bottle. Some couldn't control their rage. Others became masters of the awkward silence.

A few learned to weaponize their damage against others. They were given nicknames like *the Jackal* because they were cunning, aggressive predators. They didn't make friendships. They made strategic alliances that were easily dropped when a better opportunity came along. They lied to your face. Stole your things. Spread shitty rumors about you. Broke into the main office and read your file. Found out what had happened to you, things you didn't even know about yourself. Then they came up with a nickname for you. Like Trashcan. And it followed you around for the rest of your life.

"There it is," the Jackal said. "You remember me now."

Will felt all the tension flood back into his body. "What do you want, Dave?"

3

Mercy pointed in the direction of the small kitchen inside cottage three. "Coffeemaker's there. Pods are in the box there. Mugs are—"

"We got this." Keisha had a knowing smile on her face. She ran a catering business in Atlanta. She knew what it was like to go through the same routine day after day. "Thank you, Mercy. We're overjoyed to be back."

"Extra overjoyed." Drew was standing at the open French doors off the living room. All the one-bedroom cottages overlooked the Cherokee Ridge. "I can already feel my blood pressure dropping."

"You're still taking your pills, mister." Keisha turned to Mercy. "How's your daddy doing?"

"He's doing," Mercy said, trying not to clench her teeth. She hadn't seen any of her family since she'd threatened to ruin their lives. "It's y'all's third time here. We're all real happy you came back again."

Keisha said, "Make sure Bitty knows we'd still like to talk with her."

Mercy noted her voice had an edge to it, but she had enough shit on her plate right now without turning everything into a shit sandwich. "Will do."

"Seems like you've got a good group this time," Drew said. "With a few exceptions."

Mercy kept her smile plastered on. She'd met the dentist and her yippy husband. It hadn't been surprising when Monica had handed over her Amex and told Mercy to keep the liquor flowing.

54

Keisha said, "I really liked the teacher, Sara. We got to know each other on the trail."

"Husband seemed like a nice guy," Drew said. "Mind if we team up?"

"No problem." Mercy kept her tone light, even though she'd have to redo the entire schedule after supper. "Fishtopher has some great spots picked out for you guys. I think you're going to be really pleased."

"I'm already pleased." Drew looked down at Keisha. "Are you pleased?"

"Oh, honey, I'm always pleased."

Mercy took that as her cue to exit. They were embracing when she closed the door. She should've been impressed that they were twenty years older than her and still going at it, but she was envious. And also irritated. She'd heard their toilet running in the bathroom, which meant that Dave hadn't bothered to fix it.

She made a note on her pad as she walked toward cottage five. Mercy could feel Papa's disapproving gaze tracking her from the porch. Bitty was beside him knitting something no one would ever wear. The cats were laid out at her feet. Both her parents were acting like the family meeting had gone as usual. Still no sign of Delilah. Dave had disappeared. Fish had scampered off to the equipment shed. Of all of them, he was probably the only person actually doing what Mercy had told him to do. He was probably the most worried, too.

She should find her brother and apologize. She should tell him he was going to be okay. There had to be a way Mercy could convince Dave to vote against the sell. She would have to scrape up some money to bribe him. Dave would always take $100 today versus $500 in a week. Then he'd whine about the lost $400 for the rest of his damn life.

"Mercy Mac!" Chuck bellowed across the compound. He was carrying his usual gigantic water jug like he was some kind of elite athlete desperately in need of hydration. He walked like he was throwing one foot after the other, which was why Dave had started calling him Chuck—*dude chucks his feet like he's tossing sledgehammers.* Mercy couldn't even remember the man's real name anymore. What she knew was that he had a giant crush on her, and that he had always made her skin crawl.

She lied, "Fish is waiting for you down at the equipment shed."

"Oh." He blinked behind his thick glasses. "Thanks. I was looking for you, though. Wanted to make sure you knew about my—"

"Peanut allergy," Mercy finished. She had known about the allergy for seven years, but he always reminded her. "I told Bitty to let the kitchen know. You should check with her."

"All right." He glanced back at Bitty, but didn't leave. "You need any help with anything? I'm stronger than I look."

Mercy watched him flex a fat-wrapped muscle. She bit her lip so she didn't tell him to please, for the love of God, fuck off. He was her brother's best friend. His only friend, if she was being honest. The least she could do was tolerate the creepy fucker. "You'd better go talk to Bitty. It'd take at least an hour for an ambulance to get here. Don't wanna lose you from peanut poisoning."

She turned away so she didn't have to see the disappointment register on his moon-pie face. Mercy's entire life had been filled with Chucks. Well-meaning, goofy guys who had good jobs and practiced basic hygiene. Mercy had dated some of them. Met their mamas. Even went to their churches. And then she always found herself screwing it up by going back to Dave.

Maybe Papa wasn't that far off when he said that Mercy's biggest tragedy was that she was smart enough to know how stupid she was. There was nothing in her past that would indicate otherwise. The only good thing she'd ever done was get her son back. Most days, Jon would probably agree with her. She wondered how he would feel when he found out that Mercy was blocking the sale. She would have to jump off that bridge when she got to it.

Mercy walked up the stairs to cottage five. She knocked harder than she'd meant to.

"Yes?" The door was opened by Landry Peterson. They had met during the intake, but now he was only wearing a towel around his waist. He was a good-looking man. His right nipple was pierced. There was a tattoo over his heart, lots of colorful flowers and a butterfly surrounding a looping cursive that read *Gabbie*.

Mercy's eyes started to burn as she focused on the name. She felt all of the spit leave her mouth. She forced her gaze away from the tattoo. Looked up at Landry.

His smile was pleasant enough. Then he said, "Quite a scar you've got there."

"I—" Mercy's hand went to the scar on her face, but there was no covering the entire thing.

"Sorry for prying, I was a maxillofacial surgeon in a former life." Landry tilted his head, studying her like she was a specimen under glass. "They did a good job. Must've taken quite a few sutures. How long were you in the OR?"

Mercy finally managed to swallow. She flipped on that McAlpine switch in her head that let her pretend like everything was fine. "I'm not sure. It was a long time ago. Anyway, I wanted to check with you guys that everything's okay. Do you need anything?"

"I think we're fine for now." He looked behind her, first left, then right. "Nice situation you've got here. Must bring in a pretty penny. Supports the whole family, right?"

Mercy was taken aback. She wondered if this man was somehow tied up with the investors. She tried to put the topic back on familiar ground. "You'll see the schedule in your folder. Dinner is at—"

"Hon?" Gordon Wylie called from inside the cottage. Mercy recognized his rich baritone. "Are you coming?"

Mercy started to back away. "I hope you enjoy your stay."

"Just a minute," Landry told Mercy. "What were you saying about dinner?"

"Cocktails at six. Meal is served at six-thirty."

Mercy took out her notepad and pretended to write as she walked down the stairs. She didn't hear the door close. Landry was watching her, adding a second set of eyes to Papa's white-hot glare of disapproval. She felt like her back was on fire as she headed toward the Loop.

Was Landry acting strange? Was Mercy making it strange? Gabbie could be anything. A song, a place, a woman. Lots of gay men experimented before they came out. Or maybe Landry was bi. Maybe he was flirting with Mercy. She'd had that happen before. Or she could be freaking out because seeing that damn tattoo had made her heart feel like it was about to slide down the mountain like an avalanche.

Gabbie.

Mercy touched her fingers to the scar on her face. There was never a better representation of before and after. Before, when Mercy had only been a disappointing fuck-up. After, when Mercy had destroyed the only good thing that had ever happened in her life. Not just the good thing, but her chance at happiness. At peace. At a future that didn't leave her desperate to go back and change the past.

She willed the McAlpine switch to flip back on and take her to everything-is-fine land. Mercy had enough stress without looking for more things to stress about. She looked down at her to-do list. She needed to check on the honeymooners. She should go by the kitchen because there was no way Bitty had told them about Chuck's allergy. She should find Fish and make things right. She should fix the broken toilet herself. The investors would show up at some point. Apparently, they were too good for the hike and would drive in on the access road. Mercy hadn't spent much time considering how she would act around them. She was torn between being coldly polite and scratching their eyes out.

Gabbie.

The switch failed her. She stepped off the trail and found a tree to lean against. Sweat was rolling down her back. Her stomach had turned sour. She leaned over and coughed up bile. The splatter bowed the fronds of a maidenhair fern down to the ground. Mercy felt the same way; like a heavy sickness was constantly weighing her down.

"Mercy Mac?"

Fucking Dave.

"What're you doing hiding in the trees?" Dave pushed his way through the overgrowth. He smelled like cheap beer and cigarettes.

She said, "I found vape cartridges in Jon's room. That's down to you."

"What?" He put on his insulted look. "Jesus, girl, you gonna lay into me every time you see me today?"

"What do you want, Dave? I've got work to do."

"Come on, now," he said. "I was gonna tell you something funny, but I don't know if you're in the mood."

Mercy leaned against the tree. She knew he wasn't going to let her leave. "What is it?"

"Not with that attitude."

She wanted to smack him. Three hours ago, he was flopping on top of her like a gasping whale. Two hours ago, she was threatening to ruin his life. And now he wanted to tell her a funny story.

She relented, "I'm sorry. What is it?"

"You sure?" He didn't wait for more coaxing. "Remember that kid I told you about from the home?"

He had a lot of stories about kids from the children's home. "Which one?"

"Trashcan," he said. "He's the tall guy that showed up today. Will Trent. The dude with the redhead."

Mercy couldn't help herself. "That's the girl who gave you your first blowjob?"

"Nah, that was another girl, Angie. Guess she finally dropped his sorry ass. Or she's dead in a ditch somewhere. Never thought that dumbass would end up with somebody normal."

Normal was Dave's word for people who weren't screwed up by their shitty childhoods. Mercy had rarely met someone who fell into the category, but Sara Linton seemed to be one of those lucky few. She gave off that vibe that only other women could pick up on. She had her shit together.

Mercy wiped her mouth with the back of her hand. Her shit was scattered around like broken Legos on the floor.

Dave said, "It's weird seeing him up here. I told you he don't read too good. Couldn't memorize the Bible verses. Kind of pathetic him showing up near the campground all these years later. Like, dude, you had your chance. Time to move on."

Mercy leaned back against the tree. She was still sweating. The puked-on fern was less than twelve inches from his foot. As usual, Dave was too caught up in himself to notice. As usual, she had to pretend to be interested. Or maybe *pretend* wasn't the right word because Mercy was actually interested. Trashcan had always featured prominently in Dave's stories of his tragic youth. The bumbling kid was the punchline to almost every joke.

This would not be the first time Dave had read somebody wrong. Mercy hadn't spoken a word to Will Trent, but his wife was not the type of woman who'd be with a walking punchline. That was more Mercy's speed.

She asked, "What's the real story? You were acting kind of strange when you saw him on the trailhead camera."

Dave shrugged. "Bad blood. If it was up to me, I'd tell him he could hike right back where he came from."

Mercy had to hold back a laugh at his idiotic bluster. "What'd he do to you?"

"Nothing. It's what he *thinks* I did to him." Dave let out an exaggerated, phlegmy sigh. "Dude got pissed at me cause he thought I was the one that gave him the nickname."

She watched Dave hold out his arms in an open shrug, completely innocent of giving people stupid nicknames like Bitty Mama, Mercy Mac, Chuck, or Fishtopher.

He said, "I mean, whatever happened way back then at the children's home, I tried to be the bigger man today. Dude was a straight-up asshole."

"You talked to him?"

"I was heading up the path to fix that toilet. Ran into him."

Mercy wondered how dumb Dave really thought she was. Cottage ten was on the back end of the Loop. The leaking toilet was in cottage three, directly behind her.

Still, she prompted, "And?"

Dave shrugged again. "I tried to do the right thing. It wasn't my fault what happened to him, but I thought maybe an apology would help him work through some of the trauma. Wish somebody would be that nice to me."

Mercy had been on the receiving end of Dave's half-assed apologies. They were not nice. "What'd you say exactly?"

"I don't know. Something like, let's leave the past in the past." Dave shrugged again. "Tried to be magnanimous."

Mercy bit her lip. That was a big word for Dave. "What'd he say?"

"He started counting down from ten." Dave hooked his thumbs into his pockets. "Like, was I supposed to feel threatened? I told you he ain't smart."

Mercy looked down so he wouldn't see her reaction. Will Trent was a foot taller than Dave and had more muscle on him than Jon. She would've bet her stake in the lodge that Dave had scampered before Will could reach the count of five. Otherwise, Dave would've been carried off the mountain in a body bag.

She asked him, "What'd you do?"

"Walked away. What else could I do?" Dave scratched his stomach, one of his many tells when he was lying. "Like I said, he's kind of pathetic. Dude was always quiet, didn't know how to talk to people. And he's up here at the campground after how many years? Some kids, they never shake what they went through. Not my fault he's still screwed up."

Mercy could say a lot about people who wouldn't let things go.

"Anyway," Dave groaned out the word. "What you said in the family meeting. That was just you talking bullshit, right?"

Mercy felt her spine stiffen. "No, it wasn't just bullshit, Dave. I'm not gonna let Papa sell this place out from under me. From under Jon."

"So you're gonna take almost a million bucks away from your own kid?"

"I'm not taking away anything," Mercy said. "Look around you, Dave. Look at this place. The lodge can take care of Jon for the rest of his life. He can pass it on to his kids and grandkids. That's his name on the sign by the road, too. All he's gotta do is work. I owe him that much."

"You owe him a choice," Dave said. "Ask Jon what he wants to do. He's practically a man. This should be his decision, too."

Mercy felt her head shaking before he finished. "Hell. No."

"That's what I thought." Dave snorted in disappointment. "You're not asking Jon because you're too much of a coward to hear his answer."

"I'm not asking Jon because he's still a kid," Mercy said. "I won't put that kind of pressure on him. Jon will know you want to sell. He'll know I don't. It'd be like asking him to choose between us. Do you really want to do that to him?"

"He could go to college."

Mercy was shocked by the suggestion. Not because she didn't want Jon to have an education, but because Dave had bullied Jon for years into thinking college was a waste of time. He'd done the same thing to Mercy when she'd started taking night classes to get her GED. He never wanted anybody to do more than he had.

"Merce," Dave said. "Think about what you're trying to pass up. You been wanting to get off this mountain as long as I've known you."

"I wanted to get off the mountain with *you*, Dave. And I was fifteen years old when I told you that. I'm not a baby anymore. I like running this place. You said I was good at it."

"That was just—" he waved his hand, dismissing the compliment that had made her feel so damn proud. "You gotta see sense. We're talking about life-changing money."

"Not the good kind," she said. "I'm not gonna say what I'm thinking, but we both know how hateful you get around money."

"Watch it."

"There's nothing to watch. It doesn't matter. We might as well be talking about the price of hot-air balloons. I'm not letting you take this place from me. Not after I poured my heart into it. Not after all I've been through."

"What the hell have you been through?" Dave demanded. "I know it wasn't easy, but you always had a home. You always had food on the table. You never slept outside in the pouring rain. You never had some fucking pervert shoving your face into the ground."

Mercy stared past his shoulder. The first time Dave had told her about the sexual abuse he'd suffered as a child, she'd been racked with grief. The second and third time she had cried along with him. Then the fourth and fifth and even the hundredth time, she'd done whatever he'd asked to help him out of that dark place, whether it was cooking or cleaning or something in the bedroom. Something that hurt. Something that made her feel dirty and small. Anything that would make him feel better.

And then Mercy had realized that what had happened to Dave when he was a child didn't matter. What mattered was the hell he put her through now that he was an adult.

His need was the bottomless hole in the quicksand.

She said, "There's no use in having this conversation. My mind is made up."

"Seriously? You're not even gonna talk about it? You're just gonna fuck over your own child?"

"It's not me that's gonna fuck him over, Dave!" Mercy didn't care if guests could hear her. "You're the one I'm worried about."

"Me? What the hell am I gonna do?"

"You're gonna take his money."

"Bullshit."

"I've seen what you do when you've got a little cash in your pocket. You couldn't even hold on to that thousand bucks Papa gave you for more than a day."

"I told you I bought materials!"

"Who's bullshitting now?" Mercy asked. "You're never gonna be happy with a million dollars. You're gonna waste it on cars and football games and parties and buying rounds at the bar and being the big man around town and none of that's gonna change your life. It's not gonna make you a better person. It won't erase what happened to you when you were little. And you're gonna want more because that's what you do, Dave. You take and you take and you don't give a shit that it leaves a person empty."

"That's a fucking nasty thing to say." He shook his head as he started to walk away, but then he circled back, demanding, "You tell me a time I raised a hand to that boy."

"You don't have to hit him. You just wear him down. You can't help it. It's who you are. You're still trying to do it to that poor man in cottage ten. All your life, you make everybody feel so goddam little cause that's the only way you can make yourself feel big."

"You shut your fucking mouth." His hands snaked out, clamping around her throat. Her back was jammed against the tree. The breath was knocked out of her chest. This was what happened when Mercy's pity ran out. Dave found other ways to make her care.

"You listen to me, you goddam bitch."

Mercy had learned long ago not to leave marks on his face or hands. She clawed at his chest, digging her fingernails into the flesh, desperate for release.

"You listening?" He tightened his grip. "You think you're so goddam smart? You got me all figured out?"

Mercy's feet kicked out. She saw literal stars.

Dave said, "You need to think about who gets Jon's proxy if you die. How're you gonna stop the sale going through lying dead in your grave?"

Mercy's lungs started to shake. His angry, bloated face was swimming in front of her eyes. She was going to lose consciousness. Maybe die. For just a moment, she wanted to. It would be so easy to give in this final time. To let Dave have his money. To let Jon ruin his life. To let Fish find his way off the mountain. Papa and Bitty would be relieved. Delilah would be ecstatic. No one would miss Mercy. There wouldn't even be a faded photo on the family wall.

"Fucking bitch." Dave loosened his grip before she passed out. The look of disgust on his face said it all. He was already blaming Mercy for making it get this bad. "I ain't never stole from nobody I love. Never. And fuck you for saying that."

Mercy sank to the ground as he stomped through the forest. She listened to his angry rantings, waiting for them to fade away before she dared move again. She touched underneath her eyes, but she felt no tears. She leaned her head back against the tree. Looked up at the trees. Sunlight strobed through the leaves.

There were times early on when Dave would apologize for hurting her. Then he'd transitioned into his half-ass apology stage, where he mouthed the words, yet somehow ended up blameless. Now, he was unwavering in his confidence that it was Mercy who brought out the meanness in him. Mr. Laid-Back Dave. Mr. Easy-Going Dave. Mr. Life-of-the-Party Dave. No one realized that the Dave they saw was the show. The real Dave, the true Dave, was the one who'd just tried to strangle the life out of her.

And the real Mercy was the one who'd wanted him to.

She touched her neck, checking for tender spots. That was definitely going to bruise. Excuses flooded her brain. Maybe a horse-roping accident. Fell on the handlebars of a bike. Slipped getting out of a canoe. Got caught up in fishing line. There were dozens of explanations at her fingertips. All she had to do was look in the mirror tomorrow morning and pick the one that matched the angry blue marks.

Mercy struggled to get to her feet. She coughed into her hand. Blood dotted her palm. Dave had really done a number on her. She picked her way back to the path, playing a sort of game where she thought back through all of the times he'd hurt her. There were countless slaps and punches. Mostly he was quick about it. He'd strike out, then retreat. Rarely, he would keep on her like a boxer refusing to hear the bell. There had only been two times he'd choked her completely out, both within a month of each other, both because of the divorce.

She'd caught Dave cheating on her. Then cheating on her again. Then cheating on her again, because the thing with Dave was, he took getting away with something once as permission to do it more. Looking back, Mercy didn't even believe that he was in love with any of the women. Or even attracted to them. Some were way older. Some were out of shape or had half a dozen kids or were incredibly unpleasant people. One wrecked his truck. The truck that Bitty had paid for. One stole from him. Another left him holding a bag of weed when the cops knocked on the door of his trailer.

What Dave liked about cheating wasn't the sex. God knew his pecker was hit or miss. What he loved was the act of cheating. Skulking around. Texting secret messages into his burner phone. Swiping through dating apps. Lying about where he was going, when he would be back, who he was with. Knowing that Mercy would be humiliated. Knowing the women he'd roped in were dumb enough to think Dave would leave Mercy and marry them. Knowing that he could fuck around and let everybody find out.

Knowing that Mercy would still take him back.

Sure, she always made him work for it, but Dave got off on that part, too. Pretending that he had changed. Crying his crocodile tears. The drama of all the late-night calls. The constant texting. Showing up with flowers and a romantic playlist and a poem he'd written on the back of a bar napkin. Begging and pleading and scraping and bowing and cooking and cleaning and showing a sudden interest in parenting Jon and being saccharine sweet until Mercy took him back.

Then a month later, beating the shit out of her for dropping her keys too loudly on the kitchen table.

Strangulation was a giant red flag. At least that was what Mercy had read online. When a man put his hands around a woman's neck, that woman was six times more likely to suffer serious violence or die by homicide.

The first time he'd strangled her was the first time Mercy had asked him for a divorce. Asked him, not told him, like she needed his permission. Dave had exploded. Squeezed her neck so hard she'd felt the cartilage move. She'd passed out cold in their trailer, woken up covered in her own piss.

The second time was when she'd told him she'd found a little apartment for her and Jon in town. Mercy couldn't remember what happened next, other than that she'd really thought she was going to die. Time had been lost. She didn't know where she was. How she'd gotten there. Then she'd realized she was in the tiny apartment. Jon was sobbing in the next room. Mercy had rushed to his crib. He was red-faced, covered in snot. His diaper was full. He was terrified.

Sometimes, Mercy could still feel his little arms desperately clinging to her. His tiny body shaking as he wailed. Mercy had soothed him, held him all night, made everything okay. Jon's helplessness had motivated her to finally break away from Dave. She had filed for divorce the next morning. Left the apartment and moved back into the lodge. She hadn't done it for herself. She hadn't snapped because of Dave's constant humiliations or the fear of broken bones or even death, but because she finally understood that if she died, Jon would have no one.

Mercy had to break the pattern for real this time. She would block the sale. She would do whatever it took to keep Dave from wearing down her son. Papa would die eventually. Bitty hopefully didn't have much longer. Mercy would not doom Jon to a lifetime of drowning in quicksand.

As if on cue, Mercy heard Jon's loping walk around the Loop. His arms were out, hands floating along the tops of bushes like an airplane's wings. She watched him in silence. He used to walk the same way when he was little. Mercy could remember how excited he used to get seeing her on the path. He would run into her arms and she would lift him into the air, and now she was lucky if he acknowledged her existence.

He dropped his arms to his sides when she stepped onto the path. He said, "I went down to the shed to help Fish with the canoes, but he told me he's got it. Cottage ten is checked in."

Mercy's brain immediately went to another task she could assign him, but she stopped herself. "What're they like?"

"The woman's nice," Jon said. "The guy's kind of scary."

"Maybe don't flirt with his wife."

Jon flashed a sheepish smile. "She had a lot of questions about the property."

"You answered them all?"

"Yep." Jon crossed his arms. "I told her to look for Bitty at supper if she wanted to know more."

Mercy felt herself nodding. There were a lot of things she had changed from Papa's time, but no son of hers was going to sound ignorant about the land they were standing on.

He asked, "Anything else?"

Mercy thought about Dave again. He had a pattern after their fights. He'd go to the bar, drink up his anger. It was tomorrow she had to worry about. There was no way he wouldn't find Jon and tell him about the investors. No doubt Mercy would be the villain of his story.

She said, "Let's go down to the lookout bench. I want you to sit down with me for a minute."

"Don't you got work to do?"

"We both do," she told him, but she walked down the trail toward the lookout bench anyway. Jon followed from a distance. Mercy touched her fingers to her neck. She hoped that he couldn't see any marks. She hated the look Jon gave her when Dave snapped. Part recrimination, part pity. Any concern had left long ago. She guessed it was like watching someone run head-first into a wall, get up, then run head-first into the wall again.

He wasn't wrong.

"Okay." Mercy sat on the bench. She patted the space beside her. "Let's do this."

Jon slumped down at the opposite end, his hands deep in the pockets of his shorts. He'd turned sixteen last month, and almost overnight, puberty had finally caught up with him. The sudden hit of hormones acted like a pendulum. One minute he was full of swagger and flirting with a guest's wife, the next minute he looked like a lost little boy. He reminded Mercy so much of Dave that she was momentarily at a loss for words.

Then the surly teenager reared his head. "Why are you looking at me all weird?"

Mercy opened her mouth, then closed it. She wanted more time. There was an uneasy peace between them right now. Instead of ruining it by lecturing Jon about vaping or not cleaning his room or all the usual stuff she nagged him about, she looked out at the view. The parade of greens, the surface of the Shallows gently rippling from the wind. In the fall, you could sit in this same spot and watch the leaves turn, all the color draining down from the peaks. She had to save this place for Jon. It wasn't just his future that would be secured here. It was his life.

She said, "I forget sometimes how pretty it all is."

Jon didn't offer an opinion. They both knew he would be perfectly happy living in a windowless box in town. He had Dave's habit of blaming other people for his sense of isolation. Both of them could be in a room full of people and still feel alone. Being honest, Mercy often felt the same way.

She told Jon, "Aunt Delilah is at the house."

He looked at her, but he didn't say anything.

"I want you to remember, no matter what happened when you were a baby, Delilah loves you. That's why she went to court. She wanted to keep you for herself."

Jon stared into the distance. Mercy had never spoken a bad word about Delilah. The only good lesson she had learned from Dave was that the person yapping all the time and being an asshole rarely got sympathy. Which was why Dave only showed his monster side to Mercy.

Jon asked, "That's her Subaru on the parking pad?"

Mercy felt like a fool. Obviously, Jon had seen Delilah's car.

You couldn't keep a secret around here. "I think Papa and Bitty have been talking to her. That's why she drove up."

"I don't want to live with her." Jon glanced at Mercy before looking away again. "If she's here for that—I'm not leaving. Not for her, anyway."

Mercy had used up all of her tears a long time ago, but she felt a profound sadness at the certainty in his voice. He was trying to take care of his mother. This might be the last time he did that for a while. Maybe ever.

He asked, "What does she want?"

Mercy's throat hurt so bad she felt like she was swallowing nails. "You need to find Papa. He's going to tell you what's going on."

"Why don't you tell me?"

"Because—" Mercy struggled to explain herself. This wasn't cowardice. It would be so easy to shape Jon's view to her own thinking. But Mercy knew that she would be as bad as Dave if she manipulated her son. God knew she could do it. Even at sixteen, Jon was still too pliable. He was full of hormones and gullible as hell. She could talk him into walking off a cliff if she put her mind to it. Dave would absolutely destroy him.

"Mom?" Jon said. "Why won't you tell me yourself?"

"Because you need to hear the other side from somebody who wants it."

He smirked. "You're talking weird."

"Let me know when you wanna hear my side, okay? I'll be as honest with you as I can. But you need to hear it from Papa first. All right?"

Mercy waited for his nod. Then she looked into his clear blue eyes and felt like somebody had reached their hands inside of her chest and ripped her heart into two pieces.

That was Dave's doing. He was going to take another part of Mercy, the most precious part, and she would never get it back.

Jon was staring at her. "You okay?"

"Yep," she said. "The woman in cottage seven wants a bottle of whiskey. Can you get that for her?"

"Sure." Jon stood up. "Which kind?"

"The most expensive kind. And ask her if she wants more

69

tomorrow." Mercy stood up, too. "Then I want you to take the rest of the night off. I'll handle the clean-up after supper."

The toothy smile returned, and he was like her little boy again. "For real?"

"For real." Mercy drank in his excitement. She wanted to hold on to this moment as long as she could. "You've been doing a really good job around here, baby. I'm proud of you."

His smile was better than any drug she'd ever injected. Mercy had to compliment him more, to give him a chance to be a kid more. She was about to destroy her entire family. She had to break the asshole McAlpine cycle, too.

She said, "No matter what happens, remember that I love you, baby. Never forget that. You're the best thing that's ever happened to me, and I just fucking love you so much."

"Mom," he groaned.

But then he wrapped his arms around her, and Mercy felt like she was walking on air.

It lasted about two seconds before Jon broke away. She watched him trot up the trail, resisting the urge to call him back.

Mercy turned around before he disappeared. She let herself take a few seconds to collect herself before she got back to work. She went left at the split and walked along the curve of the lake. She could smell the fresh scent of the water alongside a musty, woodsy undertone.

They did a campfire every Saturday night by the Shallows to give the guests one last hurrah. S'mores and hot chocolate and Fish strumming his mandolin because obviously Fish was the type of sensitive soul who played the mandolin. Guests loved it. Honestly, Mercy did, too. She liked seeing the smiles on their faces and knowing that she was part of the reason they were happy. As the mother of a teenage son, as the ex-wife of an abusive alcoholic, as the daughter of a cruel son-of-a-bitch and a cold and distant mother, she had to take her wins where she could find them.

Mercy looked out over the water. She wondered how Papa would explain the investors to Jon. Would he paint Mercy in a bad light? Would he scream and curse her name? Had she unwittingly done some stealthy manipulation? The person being an asshole rarely got sympathy. Jon would want to protect her, even if he didn't agree with her.

There was nothing she could do now but wait for him to find her.

Working would make that time go by faster. She took out her notepad. She would check on the honeymooners on her way back up the hill. She would fix the toilet herself. She would have to talk to the kitchen. She made a mark in the back for the bottle of whiskey Jon was delivering to cottage seven. She had a feeling the dentist would drop some serious dough before she checked out on Sunday. No reason Monica shouldn't have the top shelf bottles with her platinum Amex. Papa was a teetotaler. He had never pushed liquor sales. The small batch whiskeys Mercy had promoted in the last year were almost solely responsible for the jump in profit.

Mercy tucked her pad back in her pocket as she walked down the terraced path. She saw Fish by the equipment shed. He was hosing out the canoes. Mercy's heart was pained at the sight of her brother on his knees. Fish was so earnest and true. He was the oldest child, but Papa had always treated him like an after-thought. Then Dave had come along and Bitty had made it clear who she really thought of as her son. It was no wonder he'd chosen to basically disappear.

She was about to call his name when Chuck came out of the equipment shed. His shirt was off. His face and chest were so red that they looked sunburned. He was carrying a piece of flattened out aluminum foil in one hand and a lighter in the other. The flame sparked. Smoke wafted off the foil. As Mercy watched, he held it up to Fish. Fish fanned the smoke toward his face, taking a deep breath.

"Mercy?" Chuck said.

"Dumbasses," she hissed, turning back around.

"Mercy?" Fish called. "Mercy, please don't—"

The sound of her feet running up the trail drowned out what-ever else he had to say. She couldn't believe her stupid brother. This was exactly what she'd warned him about during the family meeting. He wasn't even bothering to hide it anymore. What if she'd been a guest? Jon had just been down at the shed. What if he'd come over the trail and seen the two of them cooking like that? How the hell would they explain that away?

Mercy kept going straight, bypassing the fork in toward the Loop. She didn't slow her pace until she was on the other side of the boathouse. She wiped the sweat off her face. Wondered how the day could get any worse. She looked at her watch. She had an hour before she had to help with dinner prep. She still hadn't talked to the kitchen about Chuck's stupid peanut allergy.

"Christ," she whispered. It was too much. Instead of heading back up the slope, she sank down onto the rocky shore. She forced out a long breath. Her senses keyed into nature on every side. The rustling leaves. The gentle waves. The smell of last night's campfire. The warmth of the sun overhead.

She shushed out another breath.

This was her place of peace. The Shallows was like an invisible anchor that kept her tethered to the land. She couldn't give this up. No one would ever love it the way she did.

Mercy watched the floating dock shift back and forth. She had also sought refuge here so many times. Papa hated the water, refused to learn how to swim. When he was on one of his tears, Mercy would swim out to the floating dock to get away from him. Sometimes, she would fall asleep under the stars. Sometimes, Fish would join her. Later, Dave did, too, but for different reasons.

Mercy felt her head shaking. She didn't want to think about the bad stuff. Her brother had taught her how to swim here. He'd taught Dave how to tread water because Dave was too scared to stick his head below the surface. Mercy had shown Jon the best place to dive off the floating dock, the spot where the water was deepest, the spot where you could quietly slip away if guests showed up. When Jon was younger, they would come here on Sunday mornings. He would talk to her about school or girls or things he wanted to do with his life.

God knew he never opened up to her like that anymore, but Jon was a good kid. He wasn't setting the world on fire at school, and he wasn't popular by any stretch, but compared to his parents, he was pretty much thriving. All Mercy wanted was for him to be happy.

She wanted that more than anything in the world.

Jon would eventually find his people. It might take some time, but it would happen. He was kind. Mercy had no idea where he'd gotten that from. Sure, he had a quick temper like Dave. He made bad decisions like Mercy. But he doted on his grandmother. He only complained a little when Mercy put him to work. Of course he was bored up here. Every kid was bored up here. Twelve-year-old Mercy hadn't started skimming from the liquor bottles because her life was so damn exciting.

"Fuck," she breathed. Her brain wouldn't stop going to the bad places.

She forced the switch to come on, mindlessly staring up at the impossibly blue sky until the sun shifted toward the range. She closed her eyelids against the burning light. The white dot left its memory in her retinas. She watched the color turn darker, almost navy. Then it scrolled into a word. Looping cursive. Arcing across Landry Peterson's heart.

Gabbie.

The guests in cottage five had made their reservation under the name Gordon Wylie. A copy of Gordon's driver's license was on file for the booking. Gordon's credit card had pre-paid the deposit, was used to secure the bill. Gordon's license plate was on the Lexus at the trailhead. Gordon's home address was on the shipping labels for their suitcases.

Landry's name only appeared once on the registration, as the second guest. His employer was the same as Gordon's: Wylie App Co. In retrospect, it sounded like something out of Looney Toons. For all Mercy knew, the name Landry was fake. The lodge only verified the person who was responsible for the bill. They took it on faith that people were honest about their jobs, their interests, their experience with horses and rock climbing and rafting.

Which meant that Landry Peterson could be anybody. He could be a covert lover. A longtime friend with benefits. A work colleague who was looking for something more. Or he could be related to the young woman that Mercy had killed seventeen years ago.

Her name had been Gabriella, but her family had called her *Gabbie.*

4

Sara sat on the edge of the bed and let herself cry. She was so overwhelmed by emotion that she actually sobbed. There had been so much stress leading up to the wedding. They'd had to postpone the ceremony by a month so she could get the cast off her broken wrist. She'd had to cancel orders and move around schedules and juggle work projects and postpone cases. Then there was the circus act of juggling cousins and aunts and uncles and making sure everyone had a hotel reservation and a car and food they would like and places they could go because some of them had flown across the ocean and had decided to stay for the week and wanted to know what they could do and see and Sara was apparently their personal Lonely Planet guide.

Her sister and mother had helped, and Will had done more than his fair share, but Sara had never been so relieved to have something over.

She looked down at the rings on her finger. She took a deep, calming breath. Sara deserved an Academy Award for not losing it this morning when Will had said they would start their honeymoon trip after taking a hike. Two hours away. In the mountains. When the airport was twenty minutes from his house.

Their house.

She had tried not to fret about it. Not while they were loading up their backpacks. Not when they got into the car. Not when they left the city limits. Not when they parked at the trailhead. Will was in charge of the honeymoon. Sara had to let him be in charge of it. But then they'd stopped for lunch in a field and she'd noticed that time was slipping away and she'd panicked that he was going to surprise her with some sort of camping situation.

Sara hated camping. Despised would be a better word. The only reason she had endured Girl Scouts was because she had been driven to earn all the badges.

Which was the story of Sara's life. She had always pushed herself to the extreme. She'd graduated a year early from high school. Raced through undergrad. Battled to the top of her class in medical school. Gone balls to the walls during her residency. Then there was pediatrics practice, her transition to becoming a full-time medical examiner. She had always used her education in service to other people. To take care of children in a rural area and then at a public hospital. To give family members of crime victims some closure. And she'd looked after her little sister along the way. Taken care of her parents. Offered companionship to her aunt Bella. Supported her first husband. Grieved his death. Worked so hard to build something meaningful with Will. Survived his toxic ex-wife's intrusions. Navigated his weird relationship with his boss. Became close friends with his partner. Fallen in love with his dog.

When Sara looked back at her life, what she saw was a woman who was constantly moving forward, always making sure that everyone was okay.

Until now.

Sara looked at her open suitcase. Will had downloaded all of her books on her iPad. He'd updated the podcasts on her phone. Her sister had packed exactly what she needed down to the right toiletries and hairbrush. Her father had included one of his hand-tied fishing lures and a list of very bad dad jokes. Her aunt had donated a large straw hat to protect Sara's ghostly pale skin from the sun. Her mother had given her a small pocket Bible, which had felt a bit overbearing at first, but then Sara had realized that a page was bookmarked. Her mother had used a light pencil mark to highlight a section from Ruth 1:16:

> . . . *for whither thou goest, I will go; and where thou lodgest, I will lodge: thy people shall be my people . . . thy God will be my God.*

Reading the passage had sent Sara over the edge. Her mother had perfectly captured Sara's feelings for Will. She would go wherever he took her. She would lie with him wherever he chose. She would treat his family of choice as her own. She would've even pretended to like camping if that's what it came down to. She was totally and completely devoted.

Which was how weeping had given way to crying, crying had given way to sobbing, and she had sunk down onto the bed like an overwhelmed Victorian. Sara couldn't help it. Everything was too perfect. The wonderful wedding ceremony. This beautiful lodge. The gifts from her family. The thoughtfulness Will had put into everything. He'd even asked for her favorite yogurt to be put in the small fridge in the kitchen. Sara had never felt so well-cared for in her life.

"Come on," she chided herself. Falling apart time was over. Will would be back soon.

She found the box of tissues on the back of the toilet so she could blow her nose. There was a small selection of bath salts by the deep soaking tub. For Will's sake, she chose the least perfumy one before turning on the tub faucet. She checked herself in the mirror. Her skin was red and blotchy. Her nose was practically glowing. Her eyes were bloodshot. Will was going to come back from the main house expecting steamy bathtub sex and find her looking like an escaped lunatic.

Sara blew her nose. She let her hair down because she knew that Will liked it that way. Then she went to the bedroom and finished unpacking their clothes. Her little sister hadn't been completely altruistic. Tessa had jokingly packed a sex toy inside the bottom of the suitcase. Sara was zipping it back in the bag when she heard a loud voice outside the front window.

"Paul!" a man called. "Would you wait the hell up?"

Sara walked into the front room. The windows were open. She stayed in the shadows as she watched two men arguing on the path below. They were older, very fit and clearly frustrated.

"Gordon, I don't care what you think," Paul said. "It's the right thing to do."

"The right thing to do?" Gordon asked. "Since when do you care about the right thing?"

"Since I saw how she fucking lives!" Paul yelled. "It's not okay!"

"Hon." Gordon wrapped his hands around the man's arms. "You've got to let it go."

Paul slipped out of his grasp. He started jogging down the path toward the lake.

Gordon ran after him, yelling "Paul!"

Sara pulled the sheers closed on the window. That was interesting. On the hike in, Keisha had said that the app guys were named Gordon and Landry. Sara wondered if Paul was another guest or someone who worked at the lodge. Then she made herself stop wondering because she wasn't here to figure other people out. She was here to have steamy bathtub sex with her husband. *Husband.*

Sara felt herself smiling as she walked back into the bathroom. She had seen the look on Will's face when she'd called him her husband for the first time. It had matched the absolute delight she'd felt when he'd called her his wife.

She looked out the large picture window behind the tub. No sign of Gordon and Paul. The cottage was at a much higher elevation than the path. She couldn't even see the lake. The view was trees and more trees. She checked the water temperature, which was just right. The tub was going to be full a lot faster than she'd anticipated. Sara was a plumber's daughter. She knew her way around water flow. She also knew her husband. She might just manage to distract him from the fact that she'd been crying if Will found her nude and waiting. Which was exactly what happened when he walked into the bathroom five minutes later.

Will dropped the pillow he was holding. "What's wrong?"

Sara lay back in the tub. "Get in."

He glanced out the window. He was shy about his body. Where Sara saw the lean muscle and sinew, the contour of his gorgeous abs, his beautiful, strong arms, Will only saw the scars he'd carried since childhood. The puckered, round cigarette burns. The hook of a wire hanger. The skin graft where the ripped tissue had been too damaged to heal.

Sara's eyes started to sting from tears again. She wanted to go back in time and murder every single person who had ever hurt him.

"You okay?" Will asked.

She nodded. "Just enjoying the view."

Will didn't stop to test the temperature. He slipped into the tub across from her. They almost didn't fit. His knees were several inches above the rim of the tub. Sara shifted around so she could rest her head on his chest. Will wrapped his arms around her. They both looked out at the treetops. There was a mist hovering over the mountain range. She liked the idea of listening to the rain on the tin roof.

She said, "I have a confession."

He pressed his lips to the top of her head.

"I got a little overwhelmed by everything."

"Bad overwhelmed?"

"Good overwhelmed." She looked up at him. "Happy overwhelmed."

Will nodded. She gave him a soft kiss before resting her head on his chest again. There was room in this conversation for him to speak. She could tell he had been feeling slightly overwhelmed, too. Though Will was more likely to go for a ten-mile run up the side of a cliff than sit on the bed and cry.

He asked, "Did your sister pack everything you need?"

"Including a ten-inch, bright pink dildo."

Will was quiet for a second. "I guess we could try it out if you wanted something smaller?"

Sara laughed as he pulled her closer. There was a complete absence of sound inside the marble bathroom. Not even a drop of water came from the faucet. Sara listened to the steady rhythm of Will's breathing. She closed her eyes. She lay in his arms until the water started to cool. She hadn't planned on falling asleep, but that's exactly what happened. When she came to, the mist of rain had slowly moved across the mountain.

She took a deep breath and sighed it out. "We should go do something, right?"

"Maybe." Will started slowly stroking her arm. She resisted the urge to purr like a cat. He said, "I have a confession."

Sara couldn't tell if he was joking or not. "What is it?"

"There's a guy here at the lodge who lived at the children's home when I was there."

The information was so unexpected that Sara needed a second to process it. Will rarely mentioned people from the home. She looked up at him, asking, "Who?"

"His name is Dave," Will said. "He was all right in the beginning. Then something happened. He changed. Kids started calling him the Jackal. I dunno, maybe he came up with the name himself. Dave was always giving people nicknames."

Sara rested her head back on his chest. She listened to the slow beat of his heart.

He said, "We were friends for a while. Dave was in the same classes as me. Remedial stuff. I thought we got along pretty well."

She knew that Will had only been in remedial classes because of his dyslexia. He hadn't been diagnosed until college. He still treated it like a shameful secret. "What happened to him?"

"He was sent to live with a really bad foster family. They gamed the system. Made up all kinds of things that were wrong with Dave so they'd get more money for treatment. And then he started getting infections. So . . ."

Sara listened to Will's voice trail off. Recurrent urinary infections in children could often be a sign of sexual abuse.

"They took him out of the placement, but Dave came back mean. Only, I didn't realize it at first. He still pretended like we were friends. I kept hearing all these bad things about him, but everybody said bad things about everybody else. We were all screwed up."

Sara felt the rise and fall of his chest.

"He started trying to bully me. Picking fights. I wanted to punch him a few times, but it wouldn't have been fair. He was smaller, younger than me. I could've really hurt him." Will continued stroking her arm. "Then he started going around with Angie, which—I'm not an idiot. It's not like he dragged her into the basement. She was with a lot of guys. It made her feel like she had some control over her life. I guess Dave was that way, too. It hit me different when Angie did it with him, though. Like I said, I thought he was my friend, then he turned on me. And she knew that and did it anyway. It was a bad situation."

Sara could not begin to understand the warped dynamics between Will and his ex-wife. The only good thing she could say about the woman was that she was gone.

"Dave kept messing around with her. He made sure I knew about it, kept rubbing it in my face. It's like he wanted me to beat him up. Like it would prove something if he could break me." Will was silent for a long while. "Dave's the one who started calling me Trashcan."

Sara felt her heart sinking. She couldn't imagine what it was like for Will to run into this awful man right after his wedding, to have every bad memory about his childhood dredged up. The nickname in particular would've been like a kick to the teeth. Over the last few days, Will had made some passing jokes about his side of the aisle being empty, but Sara had seen the truth in his eyes. He was missing his mother. Her last act of love toward her child was to place him in a trash can so that he would be safe. Then this loathsome asshole had turned that fact into a means of torture.

"Dave tried to apologize," Will said. "On the trail just now."

She looked up again in surprise. "What did he say?"

"It wasn't a real apology." Will gave a dry laugh, though nothing about the situation was funny. "He said, 'Come on, Trashcan. Don't look at me like that. I'll apologize if it'll help you get over it.'"

"What a fucker," Sara whispered. "What did you say?"

"I started counting down from ten." Will shrugged. "I can't tell you whether or not I was actually going to hit him, but he scampered off when I got to eight, so we'll never know."

She felt her head shaking. Part of her wished that he'd pummeled the prick into the dirt.

"I'm sorry this happened," Will said. "I promise I won't let it get in the way of our honeymoon."

"Nothing's going to get in the way." Sara thought of an addendum to her mother's Bible verse. Will's enemies were her enemies. Dave better pray he didn't run into Sara this week. "Is he a guest?"

"I think he's an employee. Maintenance, by the way he was dressed." Will kept stroking her arm. "It's funny, because Dave ran away from the home a few years before I aged out. The cops interviewed all of us, and I told them he was probably up here. Dave loved the camp. Tried to go every year. I used to help him with the Bible verses. He'd read them out loud so many times that I'd memorize them. He'd practice with me on the bus, during PE, study hall. If he'd put half that effort into school, he sure wouldn't've been stuck with the slow kids like me."

Sara pressed her finger to his lips. He was not slow.

Will took her hand and kissed her palm. "Are we finished with confessions?"

"I have one more."

He laughed. "Okay."

She sat up so that they could look at each other. "There's a trail on the map called Little Deer. It leads to the back side of the lake."

"Jon said that *awinita* is the Cherokee word for fawn, which is a little deer."

"Do you think the trail leads to the campsite?"

"Let's find out."

5

SIX HOURS BEFORE THE MURDER

The kitchen staff was doing its usual mad dash to prepare for dinner service when Mercy walked in. She darted out of the way, barely missing a stack of plates that was piled over the dishwasher's head. She caught Alejandro's eye. He gave her a quick nod that everything was okay.

Still, she asked him, "You got the message about the peanut allergy?"

He nodded again, this time with a tilt of his chin that said she should leave.

Mercy didn't take it personally. She was content to let him work. Their last cook was a handsy old coot with a bad oxy habit who'd been arrested for trafficking the week after Papa's accident. Alejandro was a young Puerto Rican chef fresh out of the Atlanta Culinary School. Mercy had offered him carte blanche over the kitchen if he could start the next day. The guests loved him. The two townie kids who worked the kitchen seemed enthralled. She just didn't know how much longer he'd be content to cook bland white-people-spicy up in the hills.

She pushed open the door to the dining room. A sudden wave of nausea sent her stomach into a spin. Mercy braced her hand against the door. Her brain kept pushing down all the stress, but her body kept reminding her that it was there. She opened her mouth to draw in a deep breath, then got back to work.

Mercy went around the table, adjusting a spoon here, a knife there. The light caught a water stain on one of the glasses. She used her shirt tail to wipe it off as she scanned the room. Two long tables bisected the space. During Papa's time, there had only been bench seating, but Mercy had splurged on proper chairs. People drank more when they could sit back. She'd also invested in speakers to play soft music and lighting that could be dimmed to set the mood, both of which Papa hated, but there wasn't much he could do about it because he couldn't work the controls.

She returned the glass, adjusted another fork, moved a candelabra to center it on the table. She silently counted place settings. Frank and Monica, Sara and Will, Landry and Gordon, Drew and Keisha. Sydney and Max, the investors, were down with the family. Chuck was by Fish so they could sulk together. Delilah had been put at the end like an afterthought, which seemed appropriate. Mercy knew that Jon wouldn't show his face. Not only because he'd probably talked to Papa about the investors by now, but because Mercy had foolishly given him the night off. Alejandro didn't do dishes and the townies liked to be off the mountain by eight-thirty at the latest. Mercy would be up until midnight cleaning and doing breakfast prep.

She looked at her watch. Cocktail service would start soon. She walked onto the deck. Another upgrade after Papa's accident. She'd had Dave enlarge the viewing platform that the boards cantilevered over the cliff. He'd had to get help with the supports, him and his buddies drinking beer while they dangled from ropes over a fifty-foot drop into the ravine. He'd finished off the project by wrapping string lights around the railings. There were bench seats and ledges for drinks and it was actually perfect if you didn't know he'd been six months late and charged her three times what he'd quoted.

Silently, Mercy let her eyes scan the bottles of liquor on the bar. Their exotic labels showed well in the early evening sunlight. Under Papa, the lodge had only offered a house wine with the taste and consistency of Smucker's. Now, they sold whiskey sours and gin and tonics for ridiculous amounts of money. Mercy had always suspected their level of guests would pay for Tito's and Macallan. What she hadn't anticipated was that the lodge could bring in almost as much from liquor sales as they could from the rack rate.

Penny, another townie, was behind the bar getting things ready. She was older than the rest of the staff, time-worn and no-nonsense. Mercy had known her for years, dating back to when Penny started cleaning rooms in high school. They had both partied their asses off during those days, then both hit sobriety the hard way. Fortunately, Penny didn't need to drink to know what tasted good. She had an encyclopedic knowledge of obscure cocktails that thrilled guests and encouraged them to order more.

Mercy asked her, "Going good?"

"It's going." Penny looked up from slicing limes when voices echoed down the trail. Then she looked at her watch and frowned.

Mercy was not surprised to see that Monica and Frank had shown up early for cocktails. At least the dentist could hold her liquor. Monica wasn't loud or obnoxious, just eerily silent. Mercy had been around her share of drunks, and the quiet ones were usually the worst. Not because they could turn nasty or unpredictable. Because they were on a mission to drink themselves to death. Frank was annoying, but Mercy didn't see that he was drink-yourself-to-death bad.

Then again, people thought the same thing about Dave.

"Welcome!" Mercy plastered on a smile when they reached the deck. "Everything good?"

Frank smiled back. "It's fantastic. We're so glad we came."

Monica had gone straight to the bar. She tapped a bottle, telling Penny, "Double, neat."

Mercy felt her mouth fill with saliva as Penny opened the bottle of WhistlePig Estate Oak. She told herself the sudden longing was because her throat still felt raw from where Dave had strangled her. A little sip of rye would soothe the pain. Which was exactly what she'd told herself the last time she'd slipped, only that was with corn mash.

Monica scooped up the glass and pounded down half the contents. Mercy couldn't begin to know what kind of high-flying life you needed to live in order to get drunk at $20 a pour. After the second glass, you couldn't taste it anyway.

The crunch of gravel under Papa's chair announced his arrival.

Bitty was pushing him with her usual scowl on her face. A man and woman walked on either side of the chair. They had to be the investors. Both were probably in their late fifties, but were rich enough to be Atlanta Forties. Max was dressed in jeans and a black T-shirt. The cut of both made him look like a million bucks. Sydney was wearing the same, but where he had on HOKAs, she was sporting a well-worn pair of leather riding boots. Her bleached blonde hair was pulled into a high ponytail on top of her head. She had cheeks as sharp as glass. Her shoulders were back. Her breasts were up. Her chin was lifted.

Mercy pegged her for a true horsewoman. You didn't get that posture from slumping around the shopping mall. The woman probably had a stable full of warmbloods and a full-time trainer on her estate in Buckhead. If you were paying somebody ten grand a month to teach a bunch of $200,000 ponies how to do-si-do, twelve million bucks for a second or third home was not going to worry you.

Bitty tried to catch Mercy's eye. Her mother's snarled face had a look of intense disapproval. Bitty was clearly still mad about the meeting. She liked things to go smoothly. She had always served as Papa's fixer, guilting them all into subservience and often into forgiveness.

Mercy couldn't handle her mother right now. She went back into the dining room. Her stomach pitched again. She let herself feel just a little bit of grief. Mercy had been half-hoping Jon would be loping behind Papa's chair. That her son would ask Mercy for her reasons, that they would talk it through, that Jon would understand he had more of a future here with the family business. That he would not outright hate her, or at least agree to disagree. But there was no Jon. Just her mother's scornful look.

Mercy was going to lose everybody before this night was over. Jon was not like Dave. His temper simmered before it exploded, and once it was out there, it took days, sometimes weeks, for him to reset to normal. Or at least a new normal, because Jon collected his grievances like trading cards.

There was a soft click. Mercy looked up. Bitty was gently closing the dining-room door. Her mother did everything with a deliberate quiet, whether it was cooking an egg or walking across the floor. She could sneak up on you like a ghost. Or Death, depending on her mood.

Her mood right now was firmly in the latter category. She told Mercy, "Papa's here with the investors. I know you've got your feelings, but you need to put on your best face."

"You mean my ugly fucking face?" Mercy saw her flinch, but she was only quoting her father. "Why should I be nice to them?"

"Because you're not gonna do all that stuff you were talking about. You're just not."

Mercy looked down at her mother. Bitty had her hands tucked into her narrow waist. Her cheeks were flushed. With her cherubic face and petite build, she could be mistaken for a theatrical child.

Mercy said, "I'm not bluffing, Mother. I'm going to ruin every single one of you if you try to push this sale through."

"You most certainly are not." Bitty impatiently stamped her foot, but even then, it was more like a shuffle. "Stop this foolishness."

Mercy was about to laugh in her face, but she thought of a question. "Do you want to sell this place?"

"Your father told you—"

"I'm asking what *you* want to do, Mother. I know that doesn't happen often, that you get a say." Mercy waited, but her mother didn't answer. She repeated the question, "Do you want to sell this place?"

Bitty's lips pressed into a tight line.

"This is our home." Mercy tried to appeal to a sense of fairness. "Grandaddy always said we aren't owners—we're stewards of the land. You and Papa had your time. It's not fair to make decisions for the next generation that won't affect your lives."

Bitty kept silent, but some of the anger had left her eyes.

"We've poured our lives into this place." Mercy indicated the dining hall. "I helped put the nails in these boards when I was ten. Dave built that deck people are out there drinking on. Jon's been on his knees cleaning that kitchen. Fish caught some of the food they're cooking right now. I've eaten almost every dinner of my life on this mountaintop. So has Jon. So has Fish. Do you want to take that away from us?"

"Christopher said he doesn't care."

"He said he doesn't want to get in the middle of it," Mercy corrected. "That's different from not caring. That's the opposite of not caring."

"You've devastated Jon. He wouldn't even come to supper."

Mercy's hand went to her heart. "Is he okay?"

"No, he's not," Bitty said. "Poor baby. All I could do is hold him while he cried."

Mercy's throat tightened, and the sharp, sudden pain caused by Dave's hands served to steel her spine. "I'm Jon's mother. I know what's best for him."

Bitty huffed a disingenuous laugh. She'd always tried to act more like a friend than a grandmother to Jon. "He doesn't talk to you like he talks to me. He has dreams. He wants to do things with his life."

"So did I," Mercy said. "You told me if I left, I could never come back."

"You were pregnant," Bitty said. "Fifteen years old. Do you know how embarrassing that was for me and Papa?"

"Do you know how hard it was for me?"

"Then you should've kept your legs closed," Bitty snapped. "You always push things too far, Mercy. Dave said the same thing about you. You're just going too far."

"You talked to Dave?"

"Yes, I talked to Dave. I had Jon crying on one shoulder and Dave on the other. He's torn up about all of this, Mercy. He needs that money. He owes people."

"Money won't change that," Mercy said. "He'll just end up owing different people."

"This time is different." Bitty had been reading from that same script for over a decade. "Dave wants to change. The money will give him the opportunity to do better."

Mercy felt her head shaking. Bitty had buckets of grace where Dave was concerned. There was an endless number of corners he could turn. Meanwhile, Mercy had been forced to endure a full year of monthly piss tests before her mother would let her have unsupervised time alone with Jon.

Bitty said, "Dave wants us to get a house down the hill where we can all live together."

Mercy laughed. Sneaky fucking Dave locking down Bitty and Papa's share of the sale, too. She'd give it a year before he was dipping into their retirement funds.

"He said we'd find something big, something all one level so Papa doesn't have to sleep in the dining room, with a pool for Jon so he can bring his friends over. The boy's lonely up here," Bitty said. "Dave can make a good life for us and Jon. And you, too, if you weren't so blasted stubborn."

Mercy laughed. "Why do I feel any surprise that you're taking Dave's side? I'm just as gullible as you are."

"He's still my baby, no matter how much you've twisted that around in your head. I've never treated him any different from you and Christopher."

"Except for all the constant love and affection."

"Stop feeling sorry for yourself." Bitty quietly stamped her foot again. "Papa was going to tell you this tonight, but no matter what happens with the investors, you're fired."

For the second time that day, Mercy felt gut punched. "You can't fire me."

"You're going against the family," Bitty said. "Where are you gonna live? Not in my house, no ma'am."

"Mother."

"Don't you *Mother* me," Bitty said. "Jon will stay, but you're out of here by the end of the week."

"You're not keeping my son."

"How are you going to support him? You don't have a dime to your name." Bitty's chin tilted up in arrogance. "Let's see how far you get down the mountain looking for a job with a murder charge hanging over your head."

Mercy got in her face. "Let's see how far your bony ass gets in prison."

Bitty reared back, stunned.

"You think I don't know what you've been up to?" There was something so intensely satisfying about the show of fear in her mother's eyes. Mercy wanted more. "Try me, old woman. I can call the cops any time."

"Listen up, girl." Bitty jabbed her finger in Mercy's face. "You keep up these threats, somebody's gonna put a knife in your back."

"I think my mother just did."

"When I come for somebody, I look them in the eye." She glared at Mercy. "You have until Sunday."

Bitty turned on her heel and left through the door. The fact that she departed without making a sound was far worse than any stomping and slamming. There would be no apologies or take-backs. Her mother had meant what she'd said.

Mercy was fired. She had a week to vacate the house.

The realization hit her like a blow to the head. Mercy sank down into a chair. She felt dizzy. Her hands trembled. Her palm left a sweaty streak on the table. Could they fire her? Papa was the trustee, but most everything else came down to a vote. Mercy couldn't count on Dave. Fish would stick his head in the sand. Mercy had no bank account, no money except for the two tens in her pocket, and that was from petty cash.

"Rough day?"

Mercy didn't have to turn around to know who'd asked the question. Her aunt's voice hadn't changed in the last thirteen years. It made a cruel kind of sense that Delilah had chosen now to come out of the shadows.

Mercy asked, "What do you want, you dried up old—"

"Cunt?" Delilah sat across from her. "Maybe I've got the depth, but certainly not the warmth."

Mercy stared at her aunt. Time had done nothing to alter Papa's older sister. She still looked like exactly what she was: an old hippie who made soap in her garage. Her long gray hair was braided down to her ass. She wore a simple cotton shift that could've been made from a flour sack. Her hands were calloused and scarred from soap making. There was a deep gouge in her bicep that had healed like a piece of wadded up burlap.

Her face was still kind. That was the hard part. Mercy couldn't reconcile the Delilah she'd grown up loving with the monster she'd ended up hating. Which was basically how Mercy felt about everybody in her life right now.

Except for Jon.

Delilah said, "It's startling when you think about the valiant stories that have been passed down about this old place. As if the entire area wasn't a staging ground for genocide. Did you know that the original fish camp was built by a Confederate soldier who went AWOL after the Battle of Chickamauga?"

Mercy didn't know the AWOL part, but she knew the place was founded after the Civil War. Family history had it that the first Cecil McAlpine was a conscientious objector who'd fled up to the mountains with an escaped lady's maid.

"Forget the romantic rigamarole," Delilah said. "That whole Lost Widow story is a steaming pile of horse shit. Captain Cecil brought an enslaved woman up here with him. The idiot thought they were in love. She saw it more as kidnapping and rape. She slit his throat in the middle of the night and ran off with all the family silver. He almost died. But you know McAlpines are hard to kill."

Mercy knew that last part for sure. "Do you think telling me that my ancestors were disgusting human beings is going to shock me into selling? You know I've met my father, right?"

"Oh, I have." Delilah pointed to the rough patch of skin on her bicep. "This wasn't from a riding accident. Your father swung an ax at me when I told him that I wanted to run the lodge. I hit the ground so hard that it broke my jaw."

Mercy bit her lip to keep from reacting. She was intimately familiar with that bit of truth. She had been hiding in the old barn behind the paddock when the attack had happened. Mercy had never told anyone what she'd witnessed. Not even Dave.

"Cecil put me in the hospital for a week. Lost part of the muscle in my arm. They had to wire my jaw shut. Hartshorne didn't bother trying to take a statement. I couldn't talk for two months." Delilah's words were brutal, but her smile was soft. "Go ahead and make the joke, Mercy. I know you want to."

Mercy swallowed the lump in her throat. "What's the point of this? Are you telling me to walk away like you did, before I get hurt?"

Delilah acknowledged the truth with another smile. "It's a lot of money."

Mercy felt her stomach fill with acid again. She was so damn tired of fighting. "What do you want, Dee?"

Delilah touched the side of her own face. "I see your scar healed better than mine."

90

Mercy looked away. Her own scar was still an open wound. It was carved into her soul like the name that was carved into that gravestone down at the cemetery.

Gabriella.

Delilah asked, "Why do you think your father left me out of the family meeting?"

Mercy was too exhausted for puzzles. "I don't know."

"Mercy, think about the question. You were always the smartest one up here. At least after I left."

It was her lilting tone that cut into Mercy—so soothing, so familiar. They'd been close before everything went to shit. As a child, Mercy would stay with Delilah during the summers. Delilah would send her letters and postcards from her travels. She was the first person Mercy had told she was pregnant. She was the only person who was with Mercy when Jon was born. Mercy had been handcuffed to the hospital bed because she was under arrest. Delilah had helped her cradle Jon to her bare chest so that she could nurse him.

And then she had tried to take him away for ever.

Mercy said, "You tried to steal my son from me."

"I won't apologize for what happened. I was doing what I thought was best for Jon."

"Taking him away from his mother."

"You were in and out of jail, in and out of rehab, then that awful thing happened with Gabbie. They barely managed to sew your face back together. You could've just as easily ended up dead yourself."

"Dave was—"

"Worthless," Delilah finished. "Mercy-love, I have never been your enemy."

Mercy snorted out a laugh. All she had these days were enemies.

"I secreted myself in the sitting room while Cecil was conducting the family meeting." Delilah didn't have to say that the walls in the house were thin. She would've heard everything, including Mercy's threats. "My girl, you're playing a dangerous game."

"It's the only game I know how to play."

"You would really send them to jail? Humiliate them? Destroy them?"

"Look at what they're trying to do to me."

"I'll grant you that. They've never been easy on you. Bitty would choose Dave over either one of her own children."

"Are you trying to cheer me up?"

"I'm trying to talk to you like an adult."

Mercy was overwhelmed with the desire to do something childish. That was the stupid side of her, the one that would torch a bridge while she was running across it.

"Aren't you tired?" Delilah asked. "Battling all these people. People who will never give you what you need."

"What do I need?"

"Safety."

Mercy's chest went tight. She'd had enough gut punches today, but the word hit her like a sledgehammer. Safety was the one thing she had never felt. There was always the fear that Papa would explode. That Bitty would do something spiteful. That Fish would abandon her. That Dave would—shit, it wasn't even worth going through the list because Dave did everything *except* make her feel safe. Even Jon didn't bring her a sense of peace. Mercy was always terrified that he would turn on her like the others had. That she would lose him. That she would always be alone.

She had lived her entire life waiting for the next punch.

"Sweetheart." Without warning, Delilah reached across the table and held on to Mercy's hand. "Talk to me."

Mercy looked down at their hands. This was where Delilah had aged. Sunspots. Scars from heating lye and oils. Callouses from packing and unpacking wooden molds. Delilah was too sharp. Too clever. This wasn't quicksand Mercy was running in. It was water set to boil.

Mercy crossed her arms as she leaned back in her chair. Delilah had been back on the property less than a day and already she was making Mercy feel raw and vulnerable. "Why did Papa leave you out of the family meeting?"

"Because I told him you have my vote. Whatever you want to do, I'll support."

Mercy shook her head again. This was some kind of trick. No one ever supported her, especially Delilah. "You're the one playing games now."

"There's no game on my part, Mercy. Per the rules of the trust, I still get copies of the financials. Based on what I can see, you've kept this place going through some very hard times. On a personal level, you've managed to right yourself." Delilah shrugged. "At my age, I would much prefer to walk away with the money, but I'm not going to punish you for turning your life around. You've got my support. I'll vote against the sale."

The word *support* grated on her like a bed of nails. Delilah wasn't here to offer support. She always had ulterior motives. Mercy was too tired to see them now, or maybe she was just fucking exhausted by her lying, hateful family.

She said the first words that came into her head. "I don't need your fucking support."

"Is that so?" Delilah looked amused, which was even more infuriating.

"Yeah, that's *so*." Mercy put a hard edge on the last word. Her hand ached to smack that smirk off Delilah's face. "You can stick your support up your ass."

"I see you haven't lost that famous Mercy Temper." Delilah still looked amused. "Is this wise?"

"You wanna know what's wise? Staying out of my fucking business."

"I'm trying to help you, Mercy. Why are you like this?"

"Figure it out yourself, Dee. You're the smartest one up here."

The walk across the room felt magnificent, like the most rewarding *go fuck yourself* ever. Warm air embraced Mercy as she pushed open the double doors. She took in the crowd. The deck was packed with people. Chuck was huddled with Fish, who wouldn't look at her when she tried to catch his eye. Papa was at the center of a group, giving them some bullshit story about seven generations of McAlpines loving each other and the land. Jon was still nowhere to be seen. He was probably eating a frozen dinner in his room. Or thinking about all the empty promises Dave had shot out of his ass about a giant house in town with a swimming pool and one big happy family that didn't include his fucking mother.

Mercy felt a sudden unease come over her body. She grabbed on to the railing. Reality hit her like a hammer to the skull. What the hell was wrong with her, storming out of the dining hall like that? Delilah's vote would've meant that Mercy only had to peel off one more person from Papa's side. And here Mercy was, fucking herself over for a single, fleeting moment of pleasure. It was the same bad decision-making that kept her going back to Dave. How many times did she have to keep throwing herself into brick walls before she realized that she could stop fucking hurting herself?

She touched her fingers to her bruised throat. Swallowed the spit that had flooded into her mouth. Ignored the flop sweat dripping down her back. The famous Mercy Temper. More like the famous Mercy Insanity. She willed her hands to stop shaking. She had to banish the conversation from her mind. Banish Delilah. Banish Dave. Her family. None of them mattered right now. She just had to get through dinner.

Mercy was still the manager here. At least until Sunday. She checked on the guests. Monica was sitting off to the side with a glass in her hand. Frank was standing close to Sara, who was politely smiling at Papa's yarn about a distant McAlpine wrestling a bear. Keisha was showing Drew a water spot on her glass. Fucking caterers. Let them deal with hard water and stoned townies who always rolled in half an hour late.

She looked for the other guests. Her stomach flipped when she saw Landry and Gordon coming down the trail. They were the last to arrive. Their heads were bent in private conversation. The investors were looking out over the ravine, probably discussing how many timeshares they could sell. Mercy hoped someone would toss them over the railing. She did another scan, searching for Will Trent. She had missed him at first. He was off in the corner, kneeling down to pet one of the cats. He still looked dick drunk, which meant Dave was the last thing on his mind.

Mercy should be so lucky.

"Hey there Mercy Mac." Chuck rested his hand on her arm. "If I could—"

"Don't touch me!" Mercy hadn't realized she'd shouted until everyone was looking at her. She shook her head at Chuck, forcing a laugh, saying, "Sorry. Sorry. You just scared me, silly."

Chuck looked confused as Mercy rubbed his arm. She never touched him. Avoided it at all costs.

"You're really packing on the muscle there, Chuck." She asked the crowd, "Does anyone want a refill?"

Monica held up a finger. Frank pushed down her hand.

"So, anyway, the bear," Papa said. "Legend goes he ended up running a cigar store in North Carolina."

There were some polite chuckles that broke the tension. Mercy used that as cover to walk toward the bar, which was fifteen feet away but felt like fifteen hundred yards. She turned the bottles, lining up the faded labels, silently longing for the taste of any or all of them in the back of her throat.

Penny whispered, "You all right, girl?"

"Hell no," she whispered back. "Lighten the pour on that one lady. She's gonna collapse at the table."

"If I put any more water in her glass, it's gonna look like a urine sample."

Mercy glanced back at Monica. The woman's eyes were vacant. "She won't notice."

"Mercy," Papa called. "Come meet this nice couple from Atlanta."

Her skin crawled at his jovial tone. This was the Papa that everyone adored. Mercy had loved watching this version of her father when she was a kid. Then she had started wondering why he couldn't be that same cheerful, charming man to his own family.

The circle parted as she walked toward him. The investors stood on either side of his chair. Bitty was behind him. She silently touched the corner of her mouth, coaxing Mercy to smile.

Mercy did just that, plastering a fake grin on her face. "Hey, y'all. Welcome to the mountain. I hope you'uns got everythin' ya need."

Papa's nostrils flared at her hillbilly accent, but he continued the introductions. "Sydney Flynn and Max Brouwer, this is Mercy. She's been running the place while we look for someone more qualified to take over."

Mercy felt her smile falter. He hadn't even told them that she was his daughter. "That's right. My daddy took quite a tumble down the mountain. It can be mighty dangerous up here."

Sydney said, "Sometimes nature wins."

Mercy should've guessed a horse lover would have a death wish. "I'm guessin' by your boots you know your way around a stable."

Sydney sparked to life. "Do you ride?"

"Oh, lordy, not me. My grandpappy always said horses are either homicidal or suicidal." Mercy realized that every single guest had booked a horse-riding adventure. "Unless they're really broken in. We only use therapy horses. They're used to working with kids. Max, do you ride?"

"God, no. I'm a lawyer. I don't ride horses." He looked up from his phone. Papa's no Wi-Fi rule for guests apparently had exceptions. "I just write the checks for them."

Sydney gave the shrill laugh of a kept woman. "Mercy, you'll have to show me around the property. I'd love to see more of the land inside the conservation easement. We've got some aerial shots of the pastures, but I want to look at them from the ground. Stick my hands in the soil. You know how it is. The earth has to speak to you."

Mercy held her tongue as she nodded. "I think my brother has you booked for fly fishing tomorrow morning."

"Fishing," Max said. "That's more my style. You can't fall off a boat and break your neck."

"You can, actually." Fish had come out of nowhere. "When I was in college—"

"All right," Papa said. "Let's get inside for dinner, folks. It smells like the chef has prepared another one of his delicious meals."

Mercy made her jaw relax so she didn't break her teeth. Papa had done nothing but complain about Alejandro's cooking from the moment the man had stepped foot in the kitchen.

She hung back while the guests followed Papa into the dining room. She caught a sympathetic smile from Will as he took up the rear. She guessed he knew what it felt like to be publicly shit on. There was no telling what kind of hell Dave had put him through at the children's home. She was glad to see at least one person had managed to shake off his foulness.

"Merce." Fish was leaning against the railing. He looked down at his glass, spinning the dregs of soda. "What was that about?"

The shock of confronting Bitty and pissing off Delilah had worn off. Now the panic was kicking in. "They fired me. Gave me until Sunday to leave."

Fish didn't look surprised, which meant that he already knew, and judging by his silence, and the entire history of their lives together, he hadn't said a damn thing to defend her.

Mercy said, "Thanks a lot, brother."

"Maybe it's for the best. Aren't you tired of this place?"

"Are you?"

He shrugged with one shoulder. "Max says they'll keep me on."

Mercy let her eyes close for a moment. Today was just one betrayal after the other. When she opened her eyes, Fish had knelt down to pet the cat.

"It's a good way out for me, Mercy." Fish looked up at her as he scratched behind the cat's ears. "You know I've never had a head for business. They're gonna close the lodge. Turn it into a family compound. Build out space for the horses. I'm going to be the land manager. I'll finally get to use my degree."

Mercy felt an overwhelming sense of sadness. He was talking like it was already done. "So you're good with a bunch of rich people keeping all of this land for themselves? Making the creeks and streams private? Basically owning the Shallows?"

Fish shrugged, looking back at the cat. "Rich people are the only ones who use it now."

She could only think of one way to get through to him. "Please, Christopher. I need you to be strong for Jon."

"Jon's going to be fine."

"Do you really think so?" she asked. "You know for a fact how Dave gets around money. He's like a shark smelling blood in the water. He's already spun some crazy ass dream about how he's gonna buy a house for Papa and Bitty to live in. Jon, too."

Fish rubbed the cat's belly too hard and got a swat in return. He stood up, but he looked over Mercy's shoulder because he couldn't look her in the eye. "Maybe that wouldn't be so bad. Dave loves Bitty. He'll always take care of her. Jon's always had a special connection with her, too. You know that she adores him. Papa can't hurt anybody from that chair. Living together could give them a fresh start. Dave's always wanted a family. That's why he came up here in the first place—to be somewhere he belongs."

Mercy wondered why her brother didn't think she deserved that, too. "Dave can't help himself. Look at what he's done to me. I can't even get a checking account. He'll scam them all out of their money and leave them high and dry."

"They'll be dead before that happens."

The truth felt more cold-blooded coming from her gentle brother. "What about Jon?"

"He's young," Fish said, like that made it easier. "And I need to think about myself for a change. It'd be nice to just do my job every day and not have all this family drama or the weight of the business. Plus, I can start giving back. Maybe set up a charity."

She couldn't listen to his hopey-dopey delusions anymore. "Are you forgetting what I said at the family meeting? I'm not going to let this place get stolen out from under me. You think I won't testify about what I saw at the shed today with you and Chuck? I'll have the feds come down on your ass so quick you won't even know what's happening until you're sitting in a jail cell."

"You're not going to do that." Fish looked her directly in the eye, which was the most chilling thing that had happened to her today. His gaze was unwavering, his mouth set. She had never seen her brother look so sure of anything in his life. "You told us that all your shit's already out there. That you've got nothing to lose. We both know there's something I could take away from you."

"Like what?"

"The rest of your life."

6

FIVE HOURS BEFORE THE MURDER

Sara leaned into Will as he rested his arm across the back of her chair. She looked up at his handsome face, trying not to melt like a boy-crazy teenager. She could still smell the scented bath salts on his skin. He was wearing a slate blue button-down shirt that was open at the collar. The sleeves were long and the temperature in the room was a bit warm. She saw a drop of sweat in his suprasternal notch, and the only thing that kept her from being a complete geek for referring to the indentation in his neck by its anatomical name was her desire to explore it with her tongue.

He stroked her arm with his fingers. Sara resisted the urge to close her eyes. She was feeling tired from the long day, and they had to get up at the crack of dawn tomorrow for yoga, then a hike, then paddle boarding. All of which sounded fun, but staying in bed all day would've been fun, too.

She listened to Drew tell Will about what to expect on the hike, the packed lunches and the panoramic views. She could tell Will was still feeling disappointed about the campsite. Not that they were sure whether they'd actually found it. None of the McAlpines they'd asked during cocktails had been particularly interested in confirming or denying its location. Christopher had feigned ignorance. Cecil had launched into another big fish tale. Even Bitty, who was supposed to be the family historian, had quickly changed the subject.

They would try their luck with the Little Deer trail again tomorrow afternoon. There hadn't been much time for exploring today because they'd wasted a good hour doing exactly the thing that Sara hated about camping, which was getting sweaty and stomping through thick underbrush, then having to check each other for ticks. Eventually, they'd stumbled upon an overgrown clearing with a large circle of rocks. Will had joked about finding a witches' coven. Sara guessed by the beer cans and cigarette butts that they'd discovered a make-out spot for teenagers.

More likely, they'd found the site of an old campfire circle. Which meant that the campsite had to be close by. The kids at the children's home had talked about bunk houses and a chow hall and sneaking around the back of the counselors' cottages at night to spy on them. Many years had passed since Will had heard those stories, but still, there would be foundations or remnants of the buildings. Things that were carried up a mountain generally didn't get carried back down.

Sara dipped back into the conversation just as Will asked Drew, "What did the two of you do this afternoon?"

"Oh, you know. This and that." He elbowed Keisha, who was making a point of looking at the spots on her water glass. Drew gave her a firm shake of his head, urging her to let it drop, then he asked Will, "How's the honeymoon?"

"Great," Will said. "What year did you two meet each other?"

Sara unfolded her cloth napkin on her lap, hiding her smile as Drew provided not just the year, but the actual date and location. Will was trying to be better about small talk, but no matter what he said, he always sounded like a cop soliciting an alibi.

Drew said, "I took her to the home game against Tuskegee."

Will said, "The stadium is off of Joseph Lowery Boulevard, right?"

"You know the campus?" Drew sounded impressed by the open-ended question designed to verify facts. "They were just breaking ground on RAYPAC."

"The concert hall?" Will asked. "What did that look like?"

Sara let her eyes and ears wander toward Gordon, who was sitting on her left. She tried to pick up on the conversation he was having with the man beside him. Unfortunately, their voices were too low. Of all the guests, the two men were the ones who struck Sara as the most mysterious. At cocktails, they had introduced themselves as Gordon and Landry, but Sara had heard the two of them on the path earlier and she'd distinctly heard Gordon call Landry by the name Paul. She didn't know what they were up to, but she imagined Will would get to the bottom of it once he started interrogating them about whether they were in the vicinity of cottage ten between the hours of four and four-thirty in the afternoon.

She tuned back into his conversation with the caterers.

"Who else was present?" Will asked Keisha, which was a perfectly normal question about a couple's first date.

Sara dipped out again and looked down at Monica, who was listing beside Frank. Sara had purposefully not counted the drinks. At least after two. The woman was nearly in a stupor. Frank had to prop her up with his arm. He was an annoying man, but he seemed to be concerned about his wife. The same could not be said for the two late arrivals. Sydney and Max were seated closer to the head of the table. The man had his head buried in his phone, which was interesting considering the Wi-Fi restrictions. The woman kept flipping her ponytail back like a horse swatting flies.

"Twelve in all," she was telling a very disinterested Gordon. "Four Appaloosa, a Dutch warmblood, and the rest are Trakehners. They're the youngest, but—"

Sara blocked her out. She liked horses, but not enough to make them her entire personality.

Will squeezed her shoulder to check in with her.

She leaned over to whisper in his ear. "Did you find the killer yet?"

He whispered back, "It was Chuck in the dining hall with the breadstick."

Sara let her gaze glance over Chuck, who was devouring a breadstick. He had a gallon water jug on the table beside him because no one trusted their kidneys anymore. Christopher, the fishing guide, was on his left. They both looked miserable. Chuck probably had good reason. Mercy had practically bitten his head off. She'd tried to cover for it, but clearly, he made her uncomfortable. Even Sara had picked up on his creepy vibe, and she hadn't said anything other than hello to the man.

She didn't get the same read off Christopher McAlpine, who appeared to be as shy as he was awkward. He was seated beside his strangely cold mother, whose lips were puckered into a frown. Bitty saw her son reach for another piece of bread and slapped his hand away like he was still a child. He put his hands in his lap, stared down at the table. The only family member who seemed to be enjoying the dinner was the man at the head of the table. He'd probably compelled them to attend. He clearly loved being the center of attention. The guests seemed enthralled by his stories, but Sara couldn't help but think he was the type of self-righteous blowhard who would cancel the prom and make dancing illegal.

Cecil McAlpine had a shock of gray hair and ruggedly hand-some features. Most everyone called him Papa. Sara guessed by the fresh scars on his face and arms that he'd suffered a cata-strophic accident within the last few years. In the context of bad accidents, he'd at least had some luck. The phrenic nerve, which controls the diaphragm, is formed from C-3, 4 and 5 nerve roots. Damage in that area would require spending the rest of your life on a ventilator. If you survived the initial injury.

She watched Cecil lift his ring finger on his left hand, indicating to his wife that he wanted a sip of water. He had offered Will and Sara a strong handshake with his right hand when they'd arrived for cocktails, but that had clearly zapped his strength.

Cecil finished drinking, then told Landry/Paul, "The spring that feeds the lake originates up the McAlpine pass. Follow Lost Widow Trail down to the bottom of the lake. The creek is about a fifteen-minute walk from there. Follow it for about twelve miles. That's a good hike straight up the side of the mountain. You can see the peak from the lookout bench on the way back to the lake."

"Keesh," Drew whispered hoarsely. "Let it go."

Sara could tell they were arguing about the water-spotted glass. She politely turned away, catching another conversation at the opposite end of the table. Cecil's sister, a crunchy granola type in a tie-dye dress, was telling Frank, "People think I'm a lesbian because I wear Birkenstocks, but I always tell them I'm a lesbian because I love having sex with women."

"Me, too!" Frank barked out a laugh. He raised his glass of water in a toast.

Sara shared a smile with Will. They were stuck too far away. The aunt seemed like the only fun one at the table. Sara guessed from the scars on her hands and forearms that she worked with chemicals. There was a much larger scar on her bicep that looked like an ax had taken a chunk out of her arm. She probably worked on a farm with heavy machinery. Sara could easily picture her with a corncob pipe and a pack of herding dogs.

"Hey." Will lowered his voice again. "What kind of name is Bitty?"

"It's a nickname." Sara knew that Will's dyslexia made his understanding of certain wordplay difficult. "Probably a variation on itty bitty. Because she's so small."

He nodded. She could tell the explanation had made him think about Dave, the purveyor of nicknames. Both of them had been glad the nasty prick hadn't shown up at cocktails. Sara didn't want Dave's shadow to extend into their night. She placed her hand on Will's thigh. Felt the muscle tense. She hoped this dinner didn't drag on. There were better things to eat.

"Here we go!" Mercy came out of the kitchen with a platter in each hand. Two teenage boys followed her with more platters and sauce bowls. "The starters tonight are a selection of empanadas, papas rellenas, and the chef's famous tostones, made from a recipe perfected by his mother back in Puerto Rico."

There were lots of oohs and ahhs as the dishes were placed along the center of the table. Sara expected Will to be panicked, but the man who thought honey mustard was too exotic seemed surprisingly okay.

She asked, "Have you tried Puerto Rican food before?"

"No, but I looked up the sample menu on their website." He pointed to the different offerings. "Meat inside of fried bread. Meat inside of fried potatoes. Fried green plantains, which are actually bananas, which are technically a fruit, but it doesn't count because they're fried twice."

Sara laughed, but she was secretly pleased. He really had chosen this place for her, too.

Mercy went around the table filling water glasses. She leaned down between Chuck and her brother. Sara watched Mercy's jaw tighten as Chuck mumbled something. She was the embodiment of a woman whose skin was crawling. There had to be some history there.

Sara turned away. She was determined not to get wrapped up in other people's problems.

"Mercy," Keisha said. "You mind swapping out our glasses?"

Drew looked annoyed. "It's okay, really."

"No problem." Mercy's jaw tightened even more, but she managed to twist her lips into a smile. "Be right back."

Water splashed onto the table as she picked up the two glasses and walked back into the kitchen. Drew and Keisha exchanged sharp looks. Sara guessed caterers were just as incapable of turning off their picky catering brains as medical examiners and detectives. And plumbers' daughters. The glasses were clean. The spots came from the mineral deposits in hard water.

"Monica," Frank said, but quietly. He was loading her plate with fried food, trying to get something into her stomach. "Remember the sorullitos we had in San Juan at that rooftop bar overlooking the port?"

Monica's eyes seemed to come into focus as she looked at Frank. "We had ice cream."

"We did." He held her hand to his mouth for a kiss. "Then we tried to dance the salsa."

Monica's expression softened as she looked at her husband. "You tried. I failed."

"You've never failed at anything."

Sara felt a lump in her throat as they stared into each other's eyes. There was something so poignant between them. Maybe she had misjudged the couple. Either way, it felt like an intrusion to watch. She looked up at Will. He had noticed, too. He was also waiting for her to start eating so that he could.

Sara picked up her fork. She speared an empanada. Her stomach grumbled, and she realized she was ravenous. She'd have to be careful not to get too full because she was not going to be the woman who went into a food coma the first night of her honeymoon.

"Mom!" Jon burst through the doors. "Where are you?"

They had all turned at the racket. Jon didn't walk so much as stagger across the room. His face was bloated and sweaty. Sara would guess he'd had almost as much to drink tonight as Monica.

"Mom!" he bellowed. "Mom!"

"Jon?" Mercy rushed out of the kitchen. She held a glass of water in each hand. She saw the state of her son but kept her cool. "Baby, come into the kitchen."

"No!" he yelled. "I'm not a fucking baby! You tell me the reasons! Now!"

His words were so slurred that Sara could barely understand him. She saw Will turn his chair from the table in case Jon lost his balance.

"Jon." Mercy shook her head in a warning. "We'll do this later."

"The fuck we will!" He walked toward his mother, his finger pointing in the air. "You wanna ruin everything. Dad has it planned out so we can all be together. Without you. I don't wanna be with you. I wanna live with Bitty in a house with a swimming pool."

Sara was shocked when Bitty made a noise that sounded almost like triumph.

Mercy had heard it, too. She glanced back at her mother, then told her son, "Jon, I'm—"

"Why do you ruin everything?" He grabbed her arms, shaking her so hard that one of the glasses slipped from her hand and shattered onto the stone floor. "Why do you gotta be such a bitch all the time?"

"Hey." Will had stood up when Jon had grabbed his mother. He walked over, telling the boy. "Let's go outside."

Jon spun around, screaming, "Fuck off, Trashcan!"

Will looked stunned. Sara felt the same. How did this kid know about the terrible name? And why was he screaming it now?

"I said fuck off!" Jon tried to shove him away, but Will didn't move. Jon tried again. "Fuck!"

"Jon." Mercy's hand was trembling so hard that the water sloshed in the remaining glass. "I love you, and I'm—"

"I hate you," Jon said, and the fact that he hadn't yelled the words felt far more devastating than his previous outbursts. "I wish you were fucking dead."

He walked out, slamming the door behind him. The sound was like a sonic boom. No one spoke. No one moved. Mercy was frozen.

Then Cecil said, "Look at what you did, Mercy."

Mercy bit her lip. She looked so stricken that Sara felt a sympathetic flush in her own face.

Bitty *tsk*ed her tongue. "Mercy, for godsakes, clean up that glass before you hurt anybody else."

Will knelt down before Mercy did. He took the handkerchief out of his back pocket and used it to hold broken shards from the water glass. Mercy shakily knelt alongside him. The scar on her face practically glowed with humiliation. The room was so quiet that Sara could hear the pieces of broken glass clicking together.

"I'm so sorry," Mercy told Will.

He said, "Don't worry. I break things all the time."

Mercy's laugh was cut off by a gulp.

"I say." Chuck put on a funny voice. "Apple doesn't fall far from the ye olde tree."

Christopher said nothing. He reached for another breadstick. He took a noisy bite. Sara could not imagine the rage she would feel if someone said anything even remotely bad about her little sister, but the man just chewed like a useless fool.

In fact, they were all staring at Mercy as if she were inside a tent at an old carnival freak show.

Sara addressed the table. "We should probably eat this delicious food before it gets cold."

"That's a good idea." Frank was likely used to ignoring drunken outbursts. He added, "I was just reminding Monica of a trip we took to Puerto Rico a few years back. They have a type of salsa that's different from the Brazilian *samba*."

Sara played along, "In what way?"

"Shit," Mercy hissed. She had cut open her thumb on the glass. Blood dripped onto the floor. Even from a distance, Sara could tell the wound was deep.

Sara automatically stood up to help, asking, "Is there a first aid kit in the kitchen?"

"I'm fine, I—" Mercy's uninjured hand covered her mouth. She was going to be sick.

Cecil muttered, "For chrissake."

Sara wrapped her cloth napkin tightly around Mercy's thumb to help stop the bleeding. She left the rest of the broken glass to Will and guided Mercy into the kitchen.

One of the young waiters looked up, then quickly returned to preparing the plates. The other was intently loading the Hobart. The chef was the only one who seemed to care about Mercy. He looked up from the stove, his eyes tracking her across the room. His brow was furrowed in concern, but he stayed silent.

"I'm okay," Mercy told him. Then she nodded to Sara. "It's back here."

Sara followed her toward a bathroom that looked like it served as a pass-through to a cramped office. There was an electric typewriter on the metal desk. Papers were stacked all over the floor. There was no telephone. The only nod to modernity was a closed laptop sitting on top of a stack of accounting ledgers.

"Sorry for the mess." Mercy reached underneath a row of hooks that held jackets for colder weather. "I don't wanna ruin your night. You can just hand me down that first aid kit and get back to supper."

Sara had no intention of leaving this poor woman bleeding in the bathroom. She was reaching for the kit on the wall when she heard Mercy retch. The toilet lid popped up. Mercy was on her knees when a stream of bile came up. She hacked a few more times before sitting back on her heels.

"Fuck." Mercy wiped her mouth with the back of her good hand. "I'm sorry."

Sara asked, "May I look at your thumb?"

"I'm all right. Please, go enjoy your supper. I can handle this."

As if to prove her point, she grabbed the first aid kit and sat down on the toilet. Sara watched as Mercy tried to open the case with one hand. It was clear that she was used to doing everything by herself. It was also clear that she couldn't maneuver this particular situation on her own.

"May I?" Sara waited for Mercy's reluctant nod before she took the case and snapped it open on the floor. She found the usual assortment of bandages along with emergency fluids, three suture packs, and two Stop the Bleed kits—a tourniquet, wound packing gauze, hemostatic dressings. There was also a vial of lidocaine, which wasn't strictly legal for a kitchen first aid kit, but she imagined they were used to doing their own triage this far from civilization.

She told Mercy, "Let me see your thumb."

Mercy didn't move. She stared blankly at the first aid supplies as if she were lost in a memory. "My father used to be the one who gave people stitches if they needed them."

Sara could hear the sadness in her voice. Cecil McAlpine's days of having the dexterity to patch someone up were over. Still, it was hard to feel sorry for the man. Sara couldn't imagine her own father ever talking to her the way Cecil had spoken to Mercy. Particularly in front of strangers. And her mother would've snatched the beating heart out of anyone who dared say a word against either of her daughters.

She told Mercy, "I'm sorry."

"Not your fault." Mercy's tone was clipped. "Do you mind opening that roll of dressing for me? I don't know how it works, but it'll stop the bleeding."

"It's coated with a hemostatic agent to absorb the water content from blood and promote clotting."

"I forgot you're a chemistry teacher."

"About that," Sara felt her face redden again. She hated outing herself as a liar, but she wasn't going to subject Mercy to battle dressing. "I'm a medical doctor. Will and I decided to keep our professions quiet."

Mercy didn't seem fazed by the dishonesty. "What's he do? Basketball player? Tight end?"

"No, he's an agent with the Georgia Bureau of Investigation." Sara washed her hands at the sink as Mercy took her time absorbing the news. "I'm sorry we lied. We didn't want to—"

"Don't worry about it," Mercy said. "Considering what just happened, I'm in no position to judge."

Sara adjusted the temperature of the water. In the harsh overhead light, she could see three red marks slashing the left side of Mercy's neck. They were fresh, probably no more than a few hours old. The bruising would be more pronounced in a few days.

She told Mercy, "Let's flush out your wound in case there's any glass."

Mercy stuck her hand under the faucet. She didn't even flinch, though the pain must've been significant. She was obviously used to being hurt.

Sara took the opportunity to study the red marks on Mercy's throat. Both sides showed damage. Sara imagined if she wrapped her hands around the woman's neck, the lines would match her fingers. She had done the same thing many times with patients on her autopsy table. Strangulation was a common feature in domestic violence-related homicide.

"Look," Mercy said. "Before you keep on helping me, you should know that Dave's my ex. He's Jon's father. And he's obviously the jackass that told Jon your husband was called Trashcan a million years ago. Dave does petty shit like that all the time."

Sara took in the information in stride. "Is Dave the one who strangled you?"

Mercy slowly turned off the faucet, not answering.

"That could explain your nausea. Did you pass out?"

Mercy shook her head.

"Are you having difficulty breathing?" Mercy kept shaking her head. "Any changes in vision? Dizziness? Problems remembering things?"

"I wish I couldn't remember things."

Sara asked, "Do you mind if I examine your neck?"

Mercy sat back on the toilet. She tilted up her chin by way of agreement. The cartilage was aligned. The hyoid bone was intact. The red marks were prominent and swollen. The pressure on her carotids combined with the compression of her trachea could've easily led to her death. The only thing more dangerous was a chokehold.

Sara guessed that Mercy was aware of how close she'd come to dying, and she knew that lecturing a victim of domestic violence had never stopped a future act of domestic violence. All that Sara could do was let the woman know that she wasn't alone.

She said, "Everything seems okay. You're going to have some bad bruising. I want you to find me if at any time you feel like something's wrong. Night or day, all right? I don't care what I'm doing. This could be serious."

Mercy looked skeptical. "Did your husband tell you the real story about Dave?"

"He told me."

"Dave gave him the nickname."

"I know."

"There's probably other shit that—"

"I honestly don't care," Sara said. "You're not your ex-husband."

"No," Mercy said, looking down at the floor. "But I'm the dumbass who keeps taking him back."

Sara gave her a moment to collect herself. She opened the suture kit. Laid out the gauze, the lidocaine, a small syringe. When she glanced up at Mercy, she could tell the woman was ready.

Sara said, "Hold your hand over the sink."

Again, Mercy didn't flinch when Sara poured iodine into the wound. The cut was deep. Mercy had been handling food. The shard of glass had been on the floor. Any one of these things could lead to an infection. Normally, Sara would've given Mercy a script for antibiotics just in case, but she would have to make do with a warning. "If you feel feverish or see any red marks, or experience unusual pain—"

"I know," Mercy said. "There's a doctor in town I can follow up with."

Sara could tell by the tone of her voice that she had no intention of following up. Again, she spared the woman a lecture. One thing that Sara had learned from working in the emergency department in Atlanta's only public hospital was that you could treat the injury if not the disease.

Mercy said, "Let's get this over with."

She was compliant as Sara draped paper towels across Mercy's lap. Then she put a drape from the first aid kit on top of that. Sara washed her hands again. Then used the hand sanitizer.

"He seems nice," Mercy said. "Your husband."

Sara shook out her hands to dry. "He is."

"Do you . . ." Mercy's voice trailed off as she gathered her thoughts. "Does he make you feel safe?"

"Completely." Sara looked up at Mercy's face. The woman didn't seem like the type who easily showed her emotions, but her expression was one of profound sadness.

"I'm glad for you." Mercy's tone was wistful. "I don't think I've ever felt safe around anybody in my life."

Sara couldn't find a response, but Mercy didn't seem to want one.

"Did you marry your father?"

Sara almost laughed at the question. It sounded like neo-Freudian hokum, but this wasn't the first time she'd heard the turn of phrase. "I remember when I was in college, I got so angry when my aunt told me that girls always marry their fathers."

"Was she right?"

Sara thought about it as she slipped on the nitrile gloves. Will and her father were both tall, though her father had lost his lankiness. They were both frugal, if frugal meant spending countless minutes scraping the last ounce of the peanut butter out of the jar. Will wasn't one for dad jokes, but he had the same self-deprecating sense of humor as her father. He was more likely to fix a broken chair or patch a wall himself than call a handyman. He was also more likely to stand up when everyone else stayed seated.

"Yes," Sara admitted. "I married my father."

"Me, too."

Sara gathered she wasn't thinking of Cecil McAlpine's good traits, but there was no way to follow up. Mercy went quiet, lost in her own thoughts as she stared down at her injured thumb. Sara drew lidocaine into the syringe. If Mercy noticed the pain from the injections, she didn't say. Sara guessed if you spent your day dealing with bruises and strangulation, a needle piercing your flesh was a small inconvenience by comparison.

Still, Sara made quick work of closing the wound. She dropped in four sutures, spacing them close together. Mercy already had one scar on her face that likely served as a reminder of a bad time. Sara didn't want her looking down at her thumb and remembering another.

Sara recited the usual precautions as she wrapped the gauze. "Keep it dry for a week. Tylenol as needed for pain. I'd like to look at it again before I check out."

"I don't think I'll be here. My mother just fired me." Mercy gave a sudden, surprised laugh. "You know, I hated this place for such a long time, but now all I do is love it. I can't imagine living anywhere else. It's in my soul."

Sara had to remind herself not to wade into their personal business. "I know it seems bad now, but things are usually better in the morning."

"I doubt I'll make it that long." Mercy was smiling, but there was nothing humorous about what she said. "There's hardly a person on this mountain right now who doesn't want to kill me."

7

ONE HOUR BEFORE THE MURDER

Sara rolled over in bed to find Will's side empty. She looked for the clock, but there was nothing on the bedside table except his phone. They had both been too troubled by what had happened at dinner to do anything more entertaining than falling asleep to a podcast about Big Foot in the North Georgia mountains.

"Will?" She listened, but there was no sound. The cottage was quiet enough that she knew he wasn't inside.

Sara found the light cotton dress she'd worn to dinner on the floor. She walked into the living room. Her knee banged the edge of the couch. She muttered a curse in the darkness. She went to the open window and checked the porch. The gently swaying hammock was empty. The temperature had cooled down. There was a feeling of a coming rainstorm in the air. She craned her neck to see down the path to the lake. In the soft glow of the moonlight, she spotted Will sitting on a bench that overlooked the mountain range. His arms were spread out along the back. He was staring off into the distance.

She slipped on her shoes before carefully navigating down the stone stairs. Sandals probably weren't a good idea this late at night. She could step on something venomous or twist her ankle. Still, she didn't turn back to get her hiking boots. She felt drawn to Will. He had been quiet after dinner, reflective. They were both a bit shell-shocked by the scene between Mercy and her family.

Sara was again reminded of how fortunate she'd been to have a loving, close family. She'd grown up thinking that was the norm, but life had taught her that she'd gotten the luck of the draw.

Will looked up when he heard Sara on the path.

She asked, "Do you want some time alone?"

"No."

He wrapped his arm around her as she sat down. Sara leaned into him. His body felt solid and reassuring. She thought about Mercy's question—*does he make you feel safe?* Except for her father, Sara had never been so sure of a man in her life. It bothered her that Mercy had never felt that way. As far as Sara was concerned, it fell under the category of fundamental human needs.

Will said, "Feels like it's going to rain."

"Whatever will we do with all that free time stuck inside our cottage?"

Will laughed, his fingers tickling her arm. But the smile quickly faded as he stared out into the night. "I've been thinking a lot about my mother."

Sara sat up so that she could look at him. Will kept his head turned away, but she could tell by the way his jaw had clenched that this was hard for him.

She said, "Tell me."

He took in a deep breath, like he was about to put his head under water. "When I was a kid, I used to wonder what my life would've been like if she'd lived."

She rested her hand on his shoulder.

"I had this idea that we would've been happy. That life would've been easier. School would've been easier. Friendships. Girlfriends. Everything." His jaw tightened again. "But now, I look back and—she struggled with her addictions. She had her own demons. She could've OD'd or ended up in prison. She would've been a single mother with an abusive ex. So maybe I would've ended up in state care anyway. But at least I would've known her."

Sara felt an overwhelming sadness that he'd never had the chance.

"It was nice to have Amanda and Faith at the wedding," he said, referring to his boss and partner, who were the closest thing he had to family. "But I just wonder."

Sara could only nod. She had no frame of reference for what he was going through. She could only listen and let him know that she was there.

"She loves him," Will said. "Mercy and Jon. It's obvious she loves him."

"It is."

"The fucking Jackal."

"You never found out what happened to him after he ran away from the home?"

"Nothing." Will shook his head. "Obviously, he found his way up here, managed to survive, managed to get married and have a kid. That's what I don't get, you know? That life, being a father, having a wife and kid, that's the kind of life he always wanted. Even when we were kids, he used to talk about how being part of a family would solve all of his problems. And here he is with everything he wanted, and he's fucked it all up. The way he treats Mercy is unconscionable, but Jon clearly needs him. Dave's still his father."

Sara had never met the man, but she didn't think Dave was much of anything. She also didn't know whether he was still at the lodge. Normally, Sara would never break a patient's confidence, but Mercy was a victim of domestic violence and Will was a law enforcement officer. The fact that Mercy was talking as if she felt like her life was in danger had pushed Sara into thinking she had a duty to report. She hadn't considered the impact the information would have on Will. Dave's violent tendencies were literally causing him to lose sleep.

"The part that really makes me angry," Will said. "What Dave went through—it was bad. Worse than what I went through. But the terror, the unrelenting fear—those memories live inside of your body no matter how much your life changes for the better. And Dave's turning around and doing the same damn thing to the person he's supposed to love."

"Patterns are hard to break."

"But he knows what that feels like. To be scared all the time. To not know when you're gonna get hurt. You can't eat. You can't sleep. You just walk around with a rock in your stomach all the time. And the only thing good about being hurt is you know that you've got a few hours, maybe a few days, before they'll hurt you again."

Sara felt tears well into her eyes.

He asked, "Does it bother you?"

Sara wanted to know what he was really asking. "Does what bother me?"

"That I don't have a family."

"My love, I'm your family." She turned his head so that he would look at her. "I will go where you go. I will stay where you stay. Your people are my people, and my people are yours."

"You've got a lot more people than I do." He forced an awkward grin onto his face. "And some of them are really weird."

Sara grinned back. She had seen this before. His coping mechanism during the rare times he talked about his childhood was to always retreat into humor. "Who's weird?"

"The woman with the feathered hat, for one."

"Aunt Clementine," Sara provided. "She has an outstanding warrant for stealing chickens."

Will chuckled. "I'm glad you didn't tell Amanda. She would've loved to arrest someone at my wedding."

Sara had seen the emotion on Amanda's face when Will had asked her to dance. There was no way she would've ruined the moment. "I told you my aunt Bella's second husband died by suicide. Shot himself in the head. Twice."

The awkwardness had left his smile. "I can't decide if you're joking about that."

Sara looked into his eyes. The moonlight picked out the flecks of gray inside the blue. "I have a confession."

He smiled. "What?"

"I really want to have hot lake sex with you."

He stood up. "The lake is this way."

They held hands as they walked down the path, stopping along the way to kiss. Sara leaned against his shoulder, matching his pace. The absolute silence on the mountain made her feel like they were the only two people on earth. When she'd thought about her honeymoon, this was what Sara had imagined. The full moon glowing in the sky. The fresh air. The safe feeling of Will beside her. The glorious prospect of uninterrupted, unrushed time to be with each other.

She heard the lake before they reached it, the gentle slap of waves against the rocky shore. Up close, there was something breathtaking about the Shallows. The water was cast in an almost neon blue. The trees curved around the bend like a protective wall. Sara could see a floating dock several yards out. There was a diving board and a sunbathing platform. She had grown up on a lake, and it made her happy to be close to the water. She kicked off her sandals. She slipped out of her dress.

"Oh," Will said. "No underwear?"

"Hard to have hot lake sex unless you're naked."

Will glanced around. He clearly didn't relish the idea of public nudity. "It seems like a bad idea to jump into something you can't see in the middle of the night when no one knows where you are."

"Let's live dangerously."

"Maybe we should—"

Sara cupped him between the legs and gave him a deep kiss. Then she walked into the water. She suppressed a shiver at the sudden drop in temperature. Even though it was the middle of summer, the melt in the Appalachians had come late. There was something bracing about the chill as she swam toward the floating dock.

She turned onto her back to check on Will, asking, "Are you coming in?"

Will didn't answer, but he rolled off his socks. Then started to unbutton his pants.

"Whoa," she said. "A little more slowly, please."

Will made a show of pushing down his pants. Then he moved his hips as he unbuttoned his shirt. Sara gave out a whoop of encouragement. The water didn't seem so chilly anymore. She adored his body. His muscles looked like they had been carved from a slab of marble. He had the sexiest legs that any man had a right to. Before she could really drink him in, Will did the same thing she had, walking straight into the water. Sara could tell by his clenched teeth that the temperature had surprised him. She would have to work to warm him up. She pulled him close, resting her hands on his strong shoulders.

He said, "Hey."

"Hey." Sara smoothed back his hair. "Have you ever been in a lake before?"

"Not by choice. Are you sure the water's safe?"

"Copperheads are usually more active at dusk." She could see his eyes widen in alarm. He'd grown up in Atlanta, where most of the snakes were under the capitol dome. "We're probably too far north for cottonmouths."

He glanced around nervously, as if he'd be able to see a cottonmouth before it was too late.

"I have a confession," Sara said. "I told Mercy we lied to her."

"I figured. Is she gonna be okay?"

"Probably." Sara was still worried Mercy's thumb would get infected, but there was nothing she could do about that. "Jon seems like a good kid. It's hard being a teenager."

"There's something to be said for growing up in an orphanage."

She pressed her finger to his lips, then tried to distract him. "Look up."

Will looked up. Sara looked at Will. The muscles on his neck stood out. She saw his suprasternal notch. Which brought her back to dinner. Which unfortunately brought her back to Mercy.

She said, "Places like this, you scratch a little bit under the surface and all sorts of bad things come out."

Will gave her a careful look.

"I know what you're going to say: this is why we lied."

Will raised an eyebrow, but he spared her the *I-told-you-so*.

"Hey," she said, because they had spent enough of their night talking about the McAlpines. "I have another confession."

He started smiling again. "What's your confession?"

"I can't get enough of you." Sara licked her tongue into the notch on his neck, then kissed her way up. She let her teeth graze his skin. The water temperature became a non-issue. Will reached between her legs. The feel of his touch made her moan. She reached down to return the favor.

Then a blood-curdling scream echoed across the water.

"Will?" Sara clutched him by instinct. "What was that?"

He took her hand, scanning the area as they waded back to shore.

Neither of them spoke. Will passed Sara her dress. She turned it around, looking for the end. She was still hearing the scream echo in her head, trying to figure out where it had come from. Mercy seemed like the most likely source, but she hadn't been the only person upset tonight.

Sara went through the others, starting with the caterers. "The fighting couple at dinner. The dentist was wasted. The IT guy was—"

"What about the single guy?" Will pulled on his pants. "The one who kept needling Mercy?"

"Chuck." Sara had watched the creepy man staring at Mercy over dinner. He seemed to revel in her discomfort. "The lawyer was obnoxious. How did he get on the Wi-Fi?"

"His horse-obsessed wife annoyed everybody." Will shoved his feet into his boots. "The lying app guys are up to something."

Sara had told him about the weird Landry/Paul name change. "What about the Jackal?"

Will's face went stony.

Sara slid on her sandals. "Babe? Are you—"

"Ready?"

Will didn't give her a chance to answer. He went ahead of her up the path. They passed the cottage, then veered left onto the Loop. She could feel him making an effort to match his pace to hers. Sara would've normally broken into a run, but her sandals made that impossible.

He finally stopped, turning to her. "Is it okay if—"

"Go. I'll catch up." Sara watched him run into the dense forest. He was bypassing the Loop, making a straight line toward the main house, which made sense because that was where the only light was coming from.

Sara turned back toward the lake. From the map, there had been three sections, one tiered larger than the next like a wedding cake. She could've sworn the scream came from the bottom layer, at the opposite end of the Shallows. Or maybe it wasn't a scream. Maybe an owl had plucked a rabbit from the forest floor. Or a mountain lion had squared off with a raccoon.

"Stop," Sara chided herself.

This was insanity. They'd darted off without a plan. It wasn't like Sara could run around waking people up because she might have heard a scream. There had been enough drama at the lodge tonight. The problem was likely Will and Sara. Neither one of them could turn off their brains from work. There was nothing for her to do but continue up to the main house. She would sit on the porch stairs and wait for Will to join her. Maybe one of the fluffy cats would keep her company.

Sara was grateful for the low voltage lighting along the trail as she made her way up to the house. She couldn't tell if the walk felt longer or shorter this time. There were no landmarks to pick out. She didn't have a watch. Time seemed to stand still. Sara listened to the sounds of the forest. Crickets chirped, creatures scattered. A breeze rustled her dress. The promise of rain was heavy in the air. Sara picked up the pace.

Another few minutes passed before she saw the porch light glowing from the main house. She was about fifty yards away when she noticed a figure coming down the stairs. The moon had gone behind some clouds. The pitch black dueled with the weak light bulb, creating a monstrous shape. Sara chastised herself for feeling afraid. She had to stop listening to Big Foot podcasts before she fell asleep. The shape was a man carrying a backpack.

She was about to call out when he stumbled across the compound, fell to his knees and started vomiting.

The sour smell of alcohol wafted through the air. Sara had a split-second where she considered turning around, finding Will, and going on with her night, but she couldn't quite bring herself to look the other way. Particularly because she had a sinking suspicion that the monstrous figure was actually a troubled teenager.

She tried, "Jon?"

"What?" He stumbled, grabbing his backpack as he tried to stand. "Go away."

"Are you all right?" Sara could barely see him, but he was clearly not all right. He was swaying back and forth like a windsock. "Why don't we sit down on the porch?"

"No." He took a step back. Then another. "Fuck off."

"I will," she said. "But let's find your mom first. I'm sure she wants to—"

"Help!"

Sara felt her heart freeze inside of her chest. She turned toward the sound. There was no mistaking it had come from the back part of the lake.

"Please!"

The front door had slammed closed by the time she turned back toward Jon. Sara didn't have time for a drunk kid. She was more worried about Will. She knew that he would go directly toward the screaming woman.

She had no choice but to take off her sandals. She lifted the hem of her dress and started running across the compound. Her brain furiously tried to figure out the best route. At cocktails, Cecil had mentioned Lost Widow Trail led to the bottom of the lake. Sara vaguely recalled seeing it marked on the map. She ran around the Loop, bypassing the trail to the dining hall. She couldn't find any markings for Lost Widow. All she could do was take off into the forest.

Pine needles drove into the soles of her bare feet. Briars pulled at her dress. Sara blocked the worst of the damage with her arms. This wasn't a sprint. She had to pace herself. Judging by the map, the bottom of the lake was quite a distance from the compound. She slowed to a jog, even as she was considering all the things she should've done first. Locate a first aid kit. Put on her hiking boots. Alert the family, because Jon was drunk and a kid and he'd probably passed out in his room.

Poor Mercy. Her family would not come running. They had been so horrible to her at dinner. The way her mother had snapped at her. The disgusted look on her father's face. Her brother's pathetic silence. Sara should've talked to Mercy more. She should've pressed the woman on her fears that she wouldn't make it to see the morning.

"Sara!"

Will's voice was like a hand squeezing around her chest.

"Get Jon! Hurry!"

She stumbled to a stop. Sara had never heard him sound so raw. She turned back toward the direction she'd come. There was no telling how much time had passed since she'd talked to Jon outside the house. She knew that Will was close. She also knew

121

that mindlessly running back to the compound was not what Jon needed.

Something very bad had happened to Mercy. Will wasn't thinking straight. Mercy would not want her son to see her in distress. If Dave had gotten to her, if he had really hurt her, then there was no way Sara would let Jon have that memory etched into his brain.

"Sara!" Will yelled again.

The sound of his need set her off again, this time with purpose. She ran full-out, tucking her arms into her body. The closer she got, the more the air thickened with smoke. The terrain dropped precipitously. Sara went into a controlled slide. She lost her balance at the last minute, nearly tumbling the rest of the way. The wind was knocked out of her, but she could finally see a clearing. She pushed herself up. Started running again. Saw the moonlight tracing the spine of a sawhorse, outlining the tools scattered on the ground, a generator, a table saw, then finally the lake.

The smoke blackened the space in front of her. Sara ran at a crouch along the curving, rocky terrain. There were three rustic cottages. The last one burned so hot that she could feel the heat on her skin. Smoke furled like a flag as the wind shifted back. Sara took another step closer. The ground was wet. She could smell the blood before she realized what she was standing in. The familiar copper penny smell that she'd lived with most of her adult life.

"Please," Will said.

Sara turned. A trail of blood led to the lake. Will was on his knees leaning over a prone body in the water. Sara recognized Mercy by her lavender-colored shoes.

"Mercy," Will sobbed. "Don't leave him. You can't leave him."

Sara walked toward her husband. She had never seen him cry this way before. He was more than distraught. He was utterly devastated.

She knelt down on the other side of the body. Gently rested her fingers on Mercy's wrist. There was no pulse. The skin was nearly frigid from the water. Sara looked at Mercy's face. The scar was nothing more than a white line. The woman's eyes stared lifelessly at the menagerie of stars. Will had tried to cover her with his shirt, but there was no obscuring the violence. Mercy had sustained multiple stab wounds, some of them so deep that they had probably shattered bone. The volume of blood was so great that Sara's dress wicked up the red in the water.

She had to clear her throat before she could speak. "Will?"

He didn't seem to register that Sara was there.

"Please," he begged Mercy. "Please."

He laced together his fingers and placed his palms over Mercy's chest. Sara couldn't find it in her heart to stop him. She had coded so many patients in her career. She knew what death looked like. She knew when a patient had already crossed over. She also knew that she had to let Will try.

He leaned over Mercy. Put his full weight into her chest.

She watched his hands press down.

It happened so fast that initially, Sara didn't understand what she was seeing. Then she'd realized a piece of sharp metal had sliced into Will's hand.

"Stop!" she yelled, grabbing his hands, pinning them in place. "Don't move. You'll cut the nerves."

Will looked up at Sara, his expression the same that he would offer a stranger.

"Will." Sara tightened her grip. "The knife is inside her chest. You can't move your hand, okay?"

"Is Jon—is he coming?"

"He's back at the house. He's okay."

"Mercy wanted me to tell him that—that she loves him. That she forgives him for the fight." Will was shaking with grief. "She said that she wanted him to know it's okay."

"You can tell him all of that." Sara wanted to wipe away his tears, but she was afraid he would rip out the knife if she let him go. "We need to help you first, okay? There's some important nerves in this part of your hand. They help you feel objects. A basketball. Or a gun. Or me."

Slowly, he came back to himself. He stared down at the long blade that had impaled the webbing between his thumb and index finger.

Will didn't panic. He said, "Tell me what to do."

Sara let out a shallow breath of relief. "I'm going to take away my hands so I can make an assessment, all right?"

She saw Will's throat work, but he nodded.

Sara gently let him go. She studied the injury. She was grateful for the moonlight, but it wasn't enough. Shadows crisscrossed the scene—from the passing smoke, from the trees, from Will, from the knife. Sara pinched the tip of the blade between her thumb and index finger. She tested it to see how tightly it was embedded inside Mercy's body. The firm resistance told her that the knife had somehow wedged between the vertebra or sternum. There was no way to pull it out except by force.

In any other situation, Sara would've stabilized Will's hand to the blade so that a surgeon could remove it in a controlled setting. They didn't have that luxury. Mercy was partially submerged in water. The pressure from Will was the only thing keeping her body from shifting with the waves. They were God only knew how far from a hospital, let alone an EMT. Even with all of the help in the world, they would be ill-advised to try to carry both Mercy's body and Will out of the forest with his hand pinned to her chest. Not to mention the risk of having a living person pinned to a dead body. The bacteria from decomposition could set up a life-threatening infection.

She would have to do it here.

Will was on Mercy's left side. The knife was sticking out of the right side of her chest, otherwise it would've been in her heart, which would have precluded attempting CPR. Will's fingers were still laced together, but the damage was limited to his right hand. The angled tip of the knife had pierced the web between his thumb and index finger. Roughly three inches of the serrated blade was showing. She estimated it was half an inch wide and razor sharp. The killer had probably taken it from the family kitchen or the dining hall. Her hope was that most of the important structures in Will's hand had been spared—there wasn't much going on in the thenar web—but Sara wasn't taking any chances.

She called out the anatomy for her sake as much as Will's, "The thenar muscles are innervated by the median nerve, here. The radial nerve provides sensation to the back of the hand from the thumb to the middle finger, here and here. I need to make sure they're intact."

"Okay." His expression had turned stoic. He wanted this over with. "How do you check for that?"

"I'm going to touch your fingers around the outside, and you need to tell me if the sensation is normal or if something feels off."

She could see the concern in his face as he nodded.

Sara lightly traced her finger along the outside edges of his thumb. Then she did the same with his index finger. Will didn't offer any feedback. His silence was maddening. "Will?"

"It's normal. I think."

Sara felt some of her anxiety lessen. "I can't get the blade out of the body. I'm going to lift your hand off the blade, but I need you to relax the muscles in your arms, keep your elbows soft, and let me do all the work. Don't try to help me, okay?"

He nodded. "Okay."

Sara held his thumb steady as she slipped the tips of her fingers underneath his palm. As slowly as she could, she started to lift upward.

Will hissed in air between his teeth.

Sara continued lifting until she had finally cleared the blade.

Will let out a long breath. Even though he was free, he kept his hand in the same position, fingers splayed, hovering in the air above the body. He looked at his palm. The shock had worn off. He was feeling everything now, realizing what had happened. He moved his thumb. Flexed his fingers. Blood dripped from the wound, but it was more of a trickle than a spray, which indicated that the arteries were intact.

"Thank God," Sara said. "We should go to the hospital so they can look at this. There could be damage we're not seeing. You're caught up on your Tdap, but the wound needs to be thoroughly cleaned out. We can find someone to take us down the access road and drive back to Atlanta."

"No," Will said. "I don't have time for that. Mercy wasn't just stabbed. She was butchered. Whoever did this was frenzied, angry, out of control. The only way you hate somebody that much is if you know them."

"Will, you need to go to the hospital."

"I need to find Dave."

8

Will followed Sara into the dining hall. The lights were off, but someone had left the music playing. He put out his arm to stop her from going toward the kitchen. Dave could be hiding out. He could have another knife.

Will went in first. He hoped that Dave had another knife. Will could take the murdering asshole with one hand. He'd spent nearly ten years at the children's home holding himself back, but they weren't kids anymore. He kicked open the kitchen door. Turned on the overhead lights. He could see clear back to the bathroom and into the office beyond.

Empty.

He scanned the knives hanging on the wall and sticking out of the butcher's block. "Doesn't look like any are missing."

Sara didn't seem to care about identifying the murder weapon. She headed toward the bathroom.

Will asked, "Is there a phone in the office?"

"No." She pulled the first aid kit off the wall. "Wash both of your hands at the sink. You're covered in blood."

Will looked down. He'd forgotten that he'd used his shirt to cover Mercy. His bare chest was coated in red. Crimson lake water had stained his navy cargo pants, leaving darker splotches like a dalmatian. He turned on the kitchen faucet, saying, "We need to call local police, get together a search party. If Dave's on foot, he could be halfway down the mountain by now. We're wasting time."

"We're not doing anything until I stop the bleeding." Sara opened the first aid kit on the kitchen counter. She squirted a liberal amount of dishwashing soap in her hands, then scrubbed at his forearms to get them clean. "Tell me why you're so certain that Dave killed Mercy."

Will hadn't been expecting the question because it seemed obvious that Dave was guilty as hell. "You told me he already tried to strangle Mercy once today."

"But he wasn't at dinner. We didn't see him anywhere in the woods or on the trails." Sara grabbed a dishtowel and started cleaning the blood off his stomach. "Less than two hours ago, Mercy's exact words were, 'There's hardly a person on this mountain right now who doesn't want to kill me.'"

"You told me she walked that back. Tried to pretend like she was joking."

"And then she was murdered," Sara said. "You're focusing on Dave for the obvious reason, but it could've been someone else."

"Like who?"

"How about the guy who introduced himself as Landry but his partner called him Paul?"

"What does that have to do with Mercy?"

Instead of answering, she told him, "This is going to hurt."

Will clenched his jaw as she poured disinfectant into his open wound.

"The pain will get worse before it gets better," she warned. "How about Chuck? Mercy clearly wanted nothing to do with him. Even after she basically told him to fuck off, he kept staring at her like a stalker."

Will was about to answer when she pinched some gauze around the webbing between his thumb and finger. It felt like she'd lit a match to gunpowder. "Jesus, what is that?"

"QuickClot," she said. "It can cause cutaneous burns, but it'll stop the bleeding. I need to hold pressure for a few minutes. You've got maybe twenty-four hours before it has to come off. Or you can go to the hospital and have the wound properly taken care of."

Will could tell from her clipped tone which choice she wanted him to make. "Sara, you know I can't walk away from this."

"I know."

She kept a steady pressure on the bandage. Neither of them

spoke, but they were each thinking their own thoughts. She was probably running through all the ways his hand could get infected or nerves could be damaged or whatever medical thing she was most concerned about. He was thinking about Dave with a singular intensity that took his mind away from the fact that his hand felt like it was exploding from the inside.

"Just another minute." Sara was watching the second hand move around the clock on the wall.

Will watched her to pass the time. She was as sweaty and disheveled as he was. He picked a twig out of her hair. She was barefooted. Mercy's blood in the water had turned Sara's sage-colored cotton dress into a tie-dye version that reminded him of the outfit Mercy's aunt had worn at dinner.

Thinking about the aunt made him think about the rest of Mercy's family. Will had been so focused on tracking down Dave that he hadn't considered what needed to happen first. As of right now, he had no authority in the investigation. At best, he was a witness, at worst, he was just a placeholder until the local sheriff arrived.

It might take a while for the man to reach the lodge. Will would have to do the death notification. Jon would have to be told that his mother had been murdered. The kid would probably want to see her body. Mercy couldn't be left floating in the water, so Will and Sara had managed to carry her into the second cottage. They had barred the door with some of the lumber scattered around the worksite so that an animal couldn't get to her. The coming rain meant the crime scene would be destroyed anyway.

"Cecil's disability presumably takes him off the list." Sara was still going through alternative suspects. "Jon was with me."

"Why was Jon with you?"

"He was still drunk. I think he was trying to run away." Sara kept the bandage on his hand while she opened a pack of gauze. "There was obviously tension between Mercy and her brother. And her mother. God, they were all so awful to her at dinner."

Will knew she was trying to help, but this wasn't a complicated case. "The cabin was set on fire, probably to cover the crime scene. Her jeans were pulled down, probably because she was assaulted. She was dragged to the water, probably so she would drown. Bonus points for washing away any DNA. The attack was frenzied. The killer was angry, uncontrolled, violent. Sometimes, the obvious is obvious for a reason."

"And sometimes, an investigator can develop tunnel vision at the start of a case that ends up leading him in the wrong direction."

"I know you're not questioning my skills."

"I'm always on your side," she said. "But I'm giving you a check on the situation. You understandably hate Dave."

"Tell me how he's not the prime suspect."

Sara didn't have an immediate answer. "Look at us. Look at our clothes. Whoever killed Mercy would've been covered in blood."

"That's why the clock's ticking," Will said. "The crime scene is basically useless. We've got the blade inside Mercy's chest, but we don't know where the broken handle is. I don't want to give Dave a second longer to destroy the evidence, but I'm going to have to wait for the sheriff to get here. He'll have to organize a manhunt and formally start the investigation. I'm not sure how I'd get out of this place anyway. I don't have a legal justification to confiscate a vehicle."

Sara started wrapping his hand with a compression bandage. "We need to find a phone. Or the Wi-Fi password."

"We need more than that. I've got emergency SOS on my phone. All you have to do is find a clear signal. It uses satellites to send a text and location to emergency services and specified contacts."

"Amanda."

"She'll be able to talk her way into the investigation," Will said. The GBI wasn't allowed to take over a case. They had to be asked by the locals or ordered in by the governor. "We're in Dillon County. The sheriff's probably dealt with one murder his entire career. We need arson experts, forensics, a complete autopsy. If the manhunt stretches into tomorrow, we'll have to coordinate with marshal services in case Dave's crossed state lines. The sheriff won't have any of that in his budget. He'll be grateful when Amanda shows up."

"I'll get your phone from the cottage and send out the text."

Sara tied off the bandage. "Go ring the bell at the main house. That will bring everyone out."

"Unless it's not Dave," he allowed. "Then we'll know pretty fast if someone else is involved. They'll either be covered in blood, or they won't come out. Or they'll have the broken knife handle hidden somewhere. We'll need to search all the cottages and the main house."

"Are you allowed to do that?"

"Exigent circumstances. The killer escaped from the scene. There could be other victims. Are you ready?"

"Wait a second." Sara went back to the bathroom and brought out a white jacket that probably belonged to the chef. "Put this on. I'll bring you something from the cottage to change into."

She helped him into the jacket. It was so tight across the shoulders that Sara struggled with the buttons. The thick material gaped open at the bottom, but there was nothing to be done about it. She knelt down and tied the lace on his boot. Will remembered that she was still barefooted. He took his socks out of his pocket and offered them to her.

"Thank you." Sara's eyes stayed on his as she put them on. "Promise me you'll be careful."

He wasn't worried about himself. It occurred to Will that he was sending his wife to their cottage, the farthest cottage from the main compound, alone at night with a killer on the loose. "Maybe I should come with you."

"No. Go do your job." She pressed her lips to his cheek for a second longer than usual. "The family will probably want to make sure Mercy isn't alone all night. Tell them I'll sit with the body until she can be removed."

Will touched his hand to her face. Her compassion was one of the many reasons why he loved her.

He said, "Let's go."

They split up when the Chow Trail hit the Loop. The clouds had shifted with the coming rain, obscuring the full moon. Will felt all of his senses on alert. It was so dark that Dave could be standing ten feet in front of him and Will would have no idea. He picked up the pace, jogging toward the house, ignoring the tweak in his ankle. The burning pain in his hand got pushed down on the list of things he had to worry about.

Sara was right about considering other possible suspects, but not for the reasons she'd stated. One day, Will was going to be called to testify about this night in front of a jury. He was going to make sure he could honestly say he'd considered other suspects. There were going to be no mistakes in this investigation that a defense attorney could use to pry apart a conviction. Will owed that to Mercy.

He especially owed that to Jon.

The wooden post with the ancient-looking bell on top was a few feet from the main house. Will felt like a lifetime had passed since he'd stood by the porch stairs eating brownies and potato chips. The day flashed before his eyes, but instead of the things he'd thought he'd remember from his honeymoon—Sara's smile, the hike to the lodge, holding her in his arms while she fell asleep in the bathtub—he was remembering all the points of tension that had spoked out from Mercy McAlpine on the day she had been brutally murdered.

Dave had strangled her. Chuck had enraged her. Keisha had pissed her off about the water glasses. Jon had humiliated her in front of a crowd. Cecil had been cruel. Bitty had been frosty. Christopher had been cowardly. The horse-crazy woman had clearly pissed off Mercy when she'd asked for a tour of the pastures. The chef had stayed inside the kitchen when Jon had caused a scene. Maybe the lying app guys were hiding something from Mercy. Maybe the dentist or the IT guy or the bartender or—

Will didn't have time for maybes. He reached for the rope and pulled. The sound the bell made was more like a clang than a ring. He yanked the rope a few more times. The noise was obscene in the silence, but what had happened to Mercy at the lake was the definition of depraved.

He was reaching for the rope again when lights started to come on. First inside the main house. The curtain twitched in one of the windows on the top floor. Will saw Bitty dressed in her robe, scowling as she looked down. Another second-story light came on, this one in the far back corner. There was a popping noise as floodlights sparked on around the perimeter of the compound. Will hadn't noticed the fixtures in the trees during the daytime, but he was grateful for them now because he could see the layout of the entire area.

The windows in two of the cottages were glowing like every lamp had been switched on. He saw Gordon come onto his porch. The man was wearing black bikini briefs and nothing else. Landry/Paul was nowhere to be seen. Two cottages away, Chuck stumbled down the stairs wearing a yellow bathrobe with a rubber duck pattern. He cinched the terry cloth material closed, but not before Will saw that he was naked underneath.

The lights clicked on in another cottage. Will expected to see Keisha and Drew, but Frank opened the door in a white undershirt and boxers. He adjusted his glasses. He looked startled to find Will. He asked, "Is everything okay?"

Will was about to answer when he heard the door to the main house groan open.

"Who's out there?" Cecil McAlpine's chair rolled onto the porch. He was shirtless. Deep scars crisscrossed his chest. They were straight slashes, like he'd lain on pieces of sharp metal. "Bitty? Who rang the bell?"

"I have no idea." Bitty stood behind her husband, face twisted by anxiety as she tightened the sash on her dark red robe. She asked Will, "What the hell is going on?"

Will raised his voice. "I need everyone outside."

"Why?" Cecil demanded. "Who the hell are you to tell us what to do?"

"I'm a special agent with the Georgia Bureau of Investigation," Will announced. "I need everyone outside right now."

"Special agent, huh?" Gordon glanced back into his cottage before he casually walked down the stairs.

Still no Landry.

"I'm sorry." Frank had stayed put on the porch. "Monica's out of it. She had a bit too much to drink and—"

"Bring her out here." Will started walking toward Gordon's cottage. "Where's Paul?"

"In the shower." Gordon didn't correct him on the name. "What are you—"

Will pushed open the door. The cottage was smaller than his and Sara's, but basically the same layout. Will heard the shower turn off. He called, "Paul?"

A voice said, "Yeah?"

Will took that as all the confirmation he needed that the two men had lied about Paul's name. He walked into the bathroom. Paul was reaching for a towel. He glanced at Will, then did a double-take, probably because of the small chef's jacket. His mouth went into a smirk. He asked, "Did you get bored with your vanilla wife?"

Will looked at his watch. 1:06 in the morning. Not the usual time for a shower. He saw Paul's clothes piled onto the floor. He used the toe of his boot to move them apart. No blood. No broken knife handle.

"Is there a reason you're in my bathroom looking like you just left a Taylor Swift concert?" Paul was drying his hair with the towel. Will could see a tattoo on his chest, an ornate flowery design around a looping script. Paul clocked that he'd noticed. He draped the towel over his shoulder, covering the word. "I'm not generally into the strong, silent type, but I could make an exception."

"Get dressed and come outside."

Will's bad feeling about Paul just got worse. He glanced around the bedroom, then the living room on his way out. No bloody clothes. No broken knife handle.

More people had assembled while he was inside the cottage. As Will crossed the compound, he saw Cecil's chair at the top of the main stairs. Christopher was standing beside Chuck, also in a yellow patterned bathrobe, this one with fish. They were all tracking him with their eyes, taking in the dark stains on his cargo pants, the tight-fitting chef's jacket.

No one asked any questions. The only sound came from Frank, who made a tutting noise as he helped Monica sit down on the bottom stair. She was wearing what looked like a black silk slip, and was so drunk that her head kept lolling to the side. Sydney, the horse lady, was with her husband, Max. They were still wearing the matching jeans and T-shirts they'd had on at dinner, but Sydney was in flip-flops instead of her riding boots. Of all the people assembled, the wealthy couple looked the most agitated. Will didn't know if it was guilt or privilege that made them wary of being called out of bed in the middle of the night.

"Are you going to explain yourself?" Gordon was leaning against the bell post, still dressed in only his briefs. Paul was slowly making his way across the compound. He'd put on a pair of boxers and a white T-shirt. The smirk had left his face. He looked like he was worried.

Will turned at the sound of footsteps on the family's front porch. Jon walked down the stairs with none of his earlier bravado. His hair was wet. Another late-night shower, probably to sober up. The kid was dressed in pajamas, no shoes. His face was bloated. His eyes were glassy.

Will asked, "Where's Keisha and Drew?"

"They're in three." Chuck pointed to the cottage that lined up to the corner of the front porch. The windows were closed, curtains drawn. No lights were on.

Will asked Chuck, "Is there a phone inside the house?"

"Yes, in the kitchen."

"Go inside. Call the sheriff. Tell him a GBI agent asked you to report a code one-twenty-two, needs immediate assistance."

Will didn't hang around to explain himself. He jogged toward cottage three. Every step brought him a feeling of dread. Again, he thought about his conversation with Sara in the kitchen. Had Will developed tunnel vision? Was Mercy's attack a random event? The lodge was in the foothills of the Appalachian Trail, which stretched 2,000 miles up the eastern seaboard from Georgia to Maine. At least ten murders had taken place on the trail since they started recording them. Rapes and other crimes were rare, but not uncommon. That Will knew of, at least two serial killers had stalked victims on the trail. The Olympic bomber had spent four years hiding in these woods. It was exactly like Sara had said: scratch a little bit under the surface and all sorts of bad things came out.

Will made his footsteps heavy on the stairs to cottage three. Like the other cabins, there was no lock. He threw open the door so hard that it banged against the wall.

"Jesus Christ!" Keisha screamed. She sat up straight in bed, blindly reaching for her husband. She shoved up her pink eye mask. "Will! What the fuck?"

Drew moaned. He was pinned under the octopus of a sleep apnea mask. The machine was making a loud mechanical sound that competed with a spinning box fan by the bed. He pushed the mask away, asking, "What's wrong?"

"I need you both outside. Now."

Will left, silently running through the count, trying to see who was missing. The group was still assembled by the stairs. Chuck was in the house calling the cops. Sara was hopefully on the trail heading back this way. He asked Christopher, "Where's the kitchen staff?"

He provided, "They go home at night. They're usually off the mountain by eight-thirty."

"Did you see them leave?"

"Why does that matter?"

Will squinted at the parking pad. Three vehicles. "Who drives the—"

"Enough of your questions," Bitty said. "Why didn't you tell us you're a police officer? Your registration form said you're a mechanic. Which one is it?"

Will ignored her, asking Christopher, "Where's Delilah?"

"Up here." She was leaning out of a window on the second floor. "Do I really have to come down?"

"What the hell, man?" Drew strode toward Will with an aggressive look on his face. He and Keisha were dressed in matching blue pajamas. The man's previously friendly face was filled with a simmering anger. "You got no right scaring the shit out of my wife like that."

"Hold up," Keisha said. "Where's Sara? Is she okay?"

"She's fine," Will told her. "There's been a—"

"I called the sheriff." Chuck trotted down the stairs. "He said it'd take fifteen or twenty minutes to get up here. I couldn't offer any details. I told him you're a cop and gave him the code and said that he needs to hurry."

"You're a cop?" Drew's anger kicked up several notches. "You told me you work on cars, man. What the fuck is going on?"

Will was about to answer when Delilah walked onto the porch. She asked the only question that should matter right now—

"Where's Mercy?"

Will's eyes found Jon. He was sitting on the stairs a few treads up from Monica. Bitty was standing beside him. She was so small that his shoulder came up to her waist. She kept his head pinned to her hip with a fiercely protective arm. With his curly hair slicked back, Jon looked young and vulnerable, more like a boy than a man. Will wanted to take him aside, to gently explain to him what had happened, to assure him that he would find the monster who had taken his mother away from him.

But how could he tell this child that the monster was probably his own father?

"Please," Delilah said. "Where's Mercy?"

Will swallowed down his emotions. The best thing for Jon right now was for Will to do his job. "There's no easy way to say this."

"Oh, no." Delilah's hand went to her mouth. She had already figured it out. "No-no-no."

"What?" Cecil demanded. "For godsakes, spit it out!"

"Mercy's dead." Will ignored the gasps from the guests. He was watching Jon as he delivered the news. The kid was stuck somewhere between shock and disbelief. Either way, it hadn't hit him yet. Maybe in a few years Jon would remember this moment and wonder why he had felt paralyzed sitting there with his head pressed against his grandmother's side. The recriminations would flood in—he should've demanded answers and screamed and howled over the loss.

For now, all that Will could offer him were details. "I found Mercy down by the water. There are three buildings—"

"The bachelor cottages." Christopher turned toward the lake. "What's that smell? Is there a fire? Was she in a fire?"

"No," Will said. "There was a fire, but the flames burned themselves out."

"Did she drown?" Christopher's tone was hard to decipher. He spoke with an odd air of detachment. "Mercy's a good swimmer. I taught her in the Shallows when she was four years old."

"She didn't drown," Will said. "She sustained multiple injuries."

"Injuries?" Christopher's tone was still flat. "What kind of injuries?"

"Hush," Bitty said. "Let the man speak."

Will debated how much to give away in front of all the guests, but the family had a right to know. "I saw stab wounds. Her death will be ruled a homicide."

"Stabbed . . . ?" Delilah clutched the railing to keep herself upright. "Oh, my Lord. Poor Mercy."

"Homicide?" Chuck repeated. "You mean she was murdered?"

"Yes, you idiot," Cecil answered. "You don't get stabbed multiple times by accident."

"Poor baby." Bitty wasn't talking about Mercy. She pulled Jon closer, pressing her lips to the top of his head. He clutched at her in anguish. His face had disappeared into the material of her robe, but Will could make out his muffled sobs. "You'll be okay, my sweet boy. I'm here."

Will kept addressing his words toward the family: "We secured her body inside one of the cottages. Sara has offered to sit with her until she can be removed."

"This is awful." Keisha had started to cry. "Why would anyone want to hurt Mercy?"

Drew pulled her close, but he still managed to pin Will with a look of unbridled hatred.

Will tuned him out. He was more interested in the family. He'd expected a collective sense of grief, but as he studied each person, he saw nothing even close. Christopher's earlier detachment was still visible on his downturned face. Cecil's expression was one of a man who'd been incredibly inconvenienced. Delilah had her back to Will, so he had no clue what she was thinking. Bitty was understandably focused on Jon, but the woman had shed no tears for her daughter, even as her grandson shook with grief beside her.

The thing that struck Will the most was that none of them had any questions. He had done countless death notifications. Families wanted to know: *Who did it? How did it happen? Did she suffer? When could they see her body? Was he sure it was her? Could this be a mistake? Was he absolutely certain? Had he*

137

caught the murderer? Why wasn't he out catching the murderer? What was going to happen next? How long would it take? Would they seek the death penalty? When could they bury her body? Why had this happened? For godsakes, why?

"You assholes." Delilah's bedroom slippers thumped on the boards as she slowly walked down the stairs. She was talking to her family. "Which one of you did this?"

Will watched her stop in front of Bitty. The aunt's anger had sparked like lightning. Her lower lip trembled. Tears streamed from her eyes.

"You." She jammed her finger in Bitty's face. "Did you do it? I heard you threaten Mercy before dinner."

Chuck barked a nervous laugh.

Delilah turned on him. "Shut your filthy mouth, you disgusting pervert. We all saw you pawing at Mercy. What was that about? And you, you feckless pantywaist."

Christopher didn't look up, but it was clear he knew Delilah was talking to him.

Delilah said, "Don't think I'm not on to you, *Fishtopher*."

Cecil said, "Dammit, Dee, stop this bullshit. We all know who did this."

"Don't you dare." Bitty's voice was soft, but it carried weight. "We don't know at all."

"For fucksakes." Delilah's hands were on her hips as she loomed over Bitty. "Why are you always protecting that worthless piece of shit? Didn't you just hear the man? Your daughter has been murdered! Stabbed multiple times! Your own flesh and blood! Don't you care?"

"Like you care?" Bitty demanded. "You've been gone for thirteen years and suddenly you know everything about it?"

"I know about you, you goddam—"

"That's enough." Will had to get them separated before they tore each other apart. "You should each go back to your bedrooms. Guests, please go back to your cottages."

Cecil said, "Who put you in charge?"

"The state of Georgia. I'm standing in until the sheriff arrives." Will addressed the group. "I'm going to need to get statements from all of you."

"Fuck no." Drew turned toward Bitty, saying, "Ma'am, sorry for your loss, but we'll be gone when the sun comes up. You can ship our bags back home. Charge our credit card. Forget about that other business. Do whatever you want up here. We don't care."

"Drew," Will tried. "I need a witness statement, that's all."

"Oh hell no," Drew said. "I don't have to answer your questions. I know my rights. As a matter of fact, you don't say shit to me or my wife from now on, Mr. Police Officer. You think I haven't seen this *Dateline* before? It's the people who look like us who end up going down for shit they had nothing to do with."

Drew dragged Keisha back toward their cottage before Will could think of a reason to stop them. The door slammed so loudly that it sounded like a shotgun going off.

No one spoke. Will looked down the trail that led to cottage ten. The low lights showed the path was empty. He shouldn't have let Sara go off on her own. This was taking too long.

"Officer?" Max, the wealthy lawyer from Buckhead, waited for Will's attention. "While Syd and I firmly back the blue, we'll also decline to be interviewed."

Will had to stop this. "You're all witnesses. No one has been designated a suspect. I need statements about what happened at dinner, and where everyone was after dinner."

"What do you mean 'where everyone was'?" This question came from Paul. His eyes shifted toward Gordon. "Are you asking us for alibis?"

Will scrambled to keep them from bolting. "Jon told us someone walks the Loop at eight in the morning and ten at night. Maybe they saw something."

"It was Mercy," Christopher said. "She was on the ten o'clock loop this week. I was on the eight."

Will remembered Jon telling them the details, but he wanted to keep them talking. "What does that look like? Do you knock on doors?"

"No," Christopher said. "People flag us down if they need anything. Or they leave notes on the stairs. There's a rock you place over the paper to keep it from blowing away."

"Look." Monica had temporarily revived. She was pointing at

their cottage. "We left a note under a rock on our porch around nine o'clock. It's gone."

Will guessed that was confirmation of life. "Did Mercy bring the thing you asked for?"

"No," Frank glanced at Monica.

Will assumed from the look the request had been for more alcohol. "Did anyone see Mercy after ten o'clock?"

No one answered.

"Did anyone hear any screams or shouts for help?"

Again, he was met with silence.

"I hate to interrupt again," Max said, though he wasn't interrupting anything. "But Syd and I need to get back into town."

Sydney said, "Horses have to be fed and watered."

Will would've expected a better excuse, but there was no point in challenging them. Legally, they couldn't be compelled to talk, let alone stick around.

"Cecil, Bitty." Max turned to the McAlpine family. "We're both so sorry about your daughter. It was a lovely evening spoiled by an unspeakable tragedy. We understand your family needs time to grieve."

Cecil didn't look like he wanted time for anything. "We're still ready to go forward. Now more than ever."

"Sure," Max said, not sounding sure at all.

Sydney added, "We'll hold your family in our thoughts and prayers."

The pair walked off shoulder-to-shoulder. Will wondered what Cecil was ready to go forward with. The Buckhead couple had gotten special treatment from the beginning. The Wi-Fi password was the least of it. Will assumed the $150,000 Mercedes Benz G550 parked between an ancient Chevy and a dirty Subaru meant they'd been allowed to bypass the hike into the lodge.

"Fuck this," Gordon said. "I need a drink."

He headed back toward his cottage. Paul joined him, but not before glancing back at Will. The look sent up a red flag. In the bathroom, Paul had clearly noticed the blood on Will's pants, but hadn't been fazed. Now, he was visibly nervous. Obviously, the news of Mercy's death had changed his demeanor. Figuring out why would have to wait until Will was sure the property was secure.

Six of the cottages were occupied, which left four empty. Dave could be hiding in any of them. Will silently debated the pro of checking them versus the con of giving the family time to regroup. His gut told him to stay put. There was something deeply wrong with how they were behaving. Paul wasn't the only person making him suspicious. Maybe Sara had a point about tunnel vision.

"Excuse me, Will?" Frank and Monica were the only guests remaining. "I don't care that you lied about being a cop. It's lucky that you were here. And Monica and I don't have anything to hide. What do you want to know?"

Will wasn't going to start with Frank and Monica. "Could you both return to your cottage? I need to speak to the family first. There are some private details we need to address."

"Oh, right." Frank helped Monica stand. The woman could barely walk on her own. "Just give a knock when you're ready. We'll do whatever we can to help."

Will saw that none of the McAlpines had moved. No one would look at him. No one had started in on the questions. Except for Delilah, no one had expressed a hint of grief. The air felt heavy with calculations.

"Will?"

Sara had finally joined them. Will was relieved to see that she was safe, but he was also relieved to have some assistance. He jogged toward her so they could have some privacy away from the McAlpines. She had changed into a T-shirt and jeans. She was carrying one of his button-down shirts under her arm.

She handed him his phone, then passed him the shirt. "It took a while to get a signal, but I sent the text and got a confirmation. Everyone's been notified. How's your hand?"

His hand felt like it was caught in a bear trap. "I need you to get the family inside and babysit them while I check the other cottages. Don't let them get their stories straight. The sheriff should be here soon. See if there's a missing knife in the kitchen. If you get a chance, Paul has a tattoo on his chest. I want to know what it says."

"Got it." Sara walked ahead of him toward the house. She addressed the family using her professional tone. "I'm very sorry for your loss. I know this is a traumatic time for all of you. Let's go inside. Maybe I can answer some of your questions."

Bitty was the first to speak. "Are you a cop, too?"

"I'm a doctor and a medical examiner with the Georgia Bureau of Investigation."

"You're a couple of liars is what you are." Bitty seemed even more concerned than Drew that they were both law enforcement. Will watched her grab Jon by the arm and drag him back into the house. Christopher took over pushing Cecil's chair. Chuck quickly followed. Only Delilah hung back. Will needed her to go inside. If Dave was hiding in one of the empty cottages, he could be armed with a knife or a gun. Will didn't want to risk Delilah getting caught in the crossfire. Or being taken hostage.

He placed his shirt on the stairs, then slipped his phone into his pocket. He put his hand to his chest to help with the pain. Delilah was watching him carefully. She hadn't gone inside with the family.

He asked, "Did you have something to tell me?"

She clearly had a lot to say, but she dragged it out, pulling a tissue from her pocket, sniffing, wiping her eyes. He didn't think it was for show. She was truly shaken by Mercy's death. Unless you were Meryl Streep, you couldn't fake that kind of despair.

Finally, she asked, "Did she suffer?"

Will kept his answer neutral, "I got there at the end."

"You're sure—" her voice caught. "You're sure she's gone?"

Will nodded. "Sara pronounced her at the scene."

Delilah dabbed at her eyes with the tissue. "I've stayed away from this godforsaken place for over a decade, and the second I'm back, I'm mired in their bullshit."

He got the feeling she was referring to more than the murder. Will double clicked the button on the side of his iPhone to start his recording app. "What bullshit are you mired in?"

"More than is dreamt of in your philosophy, Horatio."

"Let's skip the Shakespeare," Will said. "I'm an investigator. I need facts."

"Here's one," she said. "Every person inside of that house is going to lie to you. I'm the only one who's going to tell you the truth."

In Will's experience, the least honest people were the ones who went out of their way to announce that they were being honest, but he was eager to hear the aunt's version of the truth. "Run it down for me, Delilah. Who has a motive?"

"Who doesn't?" Delilah asked. "Those rich jackasses from Atlanta—they're here to buy the lodge. There has to be a family vote to approve the sale. Twelve million dollars split seven ways. Mercy gets two votes, her own as well as Jon's, because he's still a minor. She told the family in no uncertain terms that she wouldn't let the sale happen."

Will felt some of his calculations start to shift. "When was this?"

"During the family meeting at noon today. I hid in the sitting room to listen because I'm nosey and I love drama. Finally, it pays off." Delilah took another tissue from her pocket to wipe her nose. "Cecil tried to browbeat Mercy into voting to sell, but she turned on him. Turned on all of them, really. Mercy said she wasn't going to let them take the lodge from her. Or Jon. That she would ruin every one of them if it came to that. She told them if she lost this place, she was going to take them all down with her. And she meant it. I could tell from her tone that she meant it."

Will found himself recalculating again. Money motives were at the root of most crimes. Twelve million bucks was a lot of motive. "What did she threaten to do?"

"Expose their secrets."

"Do you know their secrets?"

"If I did, I would tell you all of them. My brother is an abusive asshole, I'll give you that much, but his days of hurting people are over. Physically, at least." Delilah glanced back at the house. "Mercy's threats had more teeth, if you catch what I mean. She said some of them could go to prison. Some of them would never get their reputations back. I wish I could remember more of the details. At my age, I'm lucky I can still find my way home, but those are the two things that stuck."

Will recalled something she'd said earlier. "You told Bitty you overheard her threatening Mercy before dinner."

"She fired her, is what Bitty did." Delilah angrily shook her head. "Then, she told Mercy if she didn't vote to sell the lodge, she'd end up with a knife in her back."

That felt like a remarkable coincidence. But Bitty was small. She couldn't drag Mercy to the lake. At least not without help. "What about Dave?"

"Greedy bastard." Her mouth twisted in disgust. "He was voting to sell, too."

That hadn't been the question Will was asking, but now he wanted to know, "Why does Dave get a vote?"

"Cecil and Bitty legally adopted him twenty-odd years ago, which unfortunately means he's part of the family trust. If you're in the trust, you get a vote."

Will needed another moment to reset, but for personal reasons. Dave hadn't just gotten one family. He'd gotten two. "How did the adoption come about?"

"They found him slinking around the campgrounds like a feral cat. Cecil wanted to hand him over to the sheriff, but Bitty took a shine to him. She's normally a cold fish, but Bitty's got a very unhealthy relationship with that boy. She comes down on Mercy like a ton of bricks, she treats Christopher like a red-headed stepchild. Meanwhile, Dave can do no wrong. I dare say she's the same way with Jon, probably because he's the spitting image of his father. They all act like this is perfectly normal, by the way."

Will didn't question her about the fact that Dave was the equivalent of a half-uncle to his own son. He was uniquely qualified to understand the strange relationships that came out of the foster care system.

Instead, he asked, "What about Christopher? You called him something else."

"Fishtopher. It's a nickname Dave gave him. I was trying to be an asshole because he used to hate the name, but I guess he's gotten used to it. That's how Dave works. He wears you down until you just let him do what he wants to do."

Will tried to steer her away from Dave. "Would Christopher hurt Mercy?"

"Who knows?" she asked. "He's always been reclusive. Not eccentric-reclusive, more like serial-killer-collecting-women's-panties-reclusive. And Chuck—they seem like two peas in a pod, lurking around the woods doing God knows what."

"You said you haven't been here in over a decade. How do you know they lurk around?"

"I spotted them colluding near the woodpile when I drove up to the house this morning. Faces close together, shooting furtive looks. They saw my car and Chuck scampered off like a startled squirrel, while Christopher ducked down as if the tall grass could make him invisible. Something was definitely up." She sniffed again. "Then, after the family meeting, I saw both of them back in that same spot with their heads together again."

Will would need to add the woodpile to his list of areas to search. "Are they in a relationship?"

"You mean are they like the two exhibitionists in cottage five?" She gave a vacant laugh. "Christopher should be so lucky. He's had terrible luck with women. His high school girlfriend got pregnant by another boy. Then that awful business happened with Gabbie."

"Who's Gabbie?"

"Just another girl he lost. It was a long time ago. He never really dated after that. At least not that I know about. Then again, it's not like I've been kept in the loop."

Will felt a drop of water hit his head. The rain was coming, but he stood there in the open waiting for her to speak.

She said, "Listen, Dave is probably your best bet. They all had a reason to want her dead, but Dave used to beat the hell out of Mercy. Broken bones. Bruises. No one ever said or did anything to stop it. Except for me, and a lot of good that did. You can't change people by telling them they're wrong. They have to come to it themselves. And I guess—I guess this means she never will."

Will saw her throat work. Fresh tears welled into her eyes. He asked, "What about you? Did you have a reason to want Mercy dead?"

"Are you asking for a motive?" She let out a heavy sigh. "I was glad Mercy finally had her life on track. I even offered to help her block the sale of the lodge, but Mercy's proud. *Was* proud. Jesus, she was so young. I don't even know what to say to Jon. He never had a father, and now to lose his mother like this . . ."

Will tested her honesty. "What are those people inside the house going to tell me when I ask them whether or not you have a motive?"

"Oh, they'll definitely throw me under the bus." Delilah shoved the folded tissue back into her pocket. "They'll say that I wanted revenge because Mercy stole Jon away from me. I raised him from the day he was born until he was three, nearly four, years old. Mercy sued to get permanent custody restored in January 2011. This was a year after the car accident."

Will guessed, "That's how she got the scar on her face?"

Delilah nodded. "I gather it put the fear of God into her. Made her re-examine her life, decide to grow up a bit. I was dubious. Heroin is a hell of a monkey to have on your back. Her sobriety felt tenuous to me. The custody battle was akin to a street fight. Dragged on for half a year. We tore each other apart. I was heartbroken when she won. Told her on the courthouse steps that I hoped she died. She cut me entirely out of Jon's life. I wrote letters, tried to call. Bitty stopped me at every turn, but I'm sure Mercy knew she was doing it. So, that's my motive. If you believe it took me thirteen years to snap."

"Where was Dave in all this?"

"Mercy was with him. Then she wasn't. Then she was. Then she was in the hospital, and it was over. Then she was out of the hospital, and it was back on." Delilah rolled her eyes in exasperation. "Dave never attended any supervised visitations. Too drunk or stoned, I assumed. Or terrified of me. Which he should've been. If that was Dave lying dead at the lake right now, you'd rightly put me at the top of your list."

"What's going to happen to Jon now?"

"I have no idea. He doesn't really know me anymore. I think it's probably best he stays with Cecil and Bitty. They're the lesser of the evils. He's lost his mother. He'll lose his father if there's any justice. Jon needs things to stay as familiar as possible. Maybe one day I can have a relationship with him, but that's what I want. Right now is about what Jon needs."

Will wondered if that was her real answer or the one that she thought made her look good. "Where were you tonight between ten and midnight?"

She arched an eyebrow, but answered, "I read in my room until around nine-thirty or ten. No alibi. I was asleep in bed when the bell started to clang. You get to my age, moisture is a stranger. I've got a bladder like a steel trap."

Will heard a car. The sheriff had finally arrived. The brown car pulled into the parking pad just as Sydney and Max were rolling their suitcases toward the Mercedes. If they noticed the sheriff, they didn't react. They were too busy getting the hell out of here. Will thought it said a lot about the couple that they hadn't offered to give anyone else a ride back into town.

Delilah let out a disgusted groan when the sheriff got out of the car. They both watched him reach back to grab a large umbrella.

Delilah mumbled, "Never fear, Biscuits is here."

"Biscuits?"

"Nickname." She looked up at Will. "Agent whatever-your-name-is, I don't know you from Adam's housecat, but I wouldn't trust that man as far as I can throw him. And I'm pretty damn good at throwing things."

Will felt more rain drops hit the top of his head as he watched the sheriff walk across the compound. The man was probably five-eight, and slightly pudgy underneath his brown sheriff's uniform. The fit wasn't flattering to anyone, but the sheriff looked particularly uncomfortable in the tight pants and stiff collar. He was also in no hurry. He stopped to open his umbrella when the rain started to come down in earnest. Will picked up his folded shirt and jogged up the stairs. He dropped it in a rocking chair. He waited with Delilah under the cover of the porch.

The sheriff slowly climbed the stairs, then stood at the top looking out at the compound while he shook out his umbrella. He leaned it against the house by the front door. He looked up at Will.

"Sheriff." Will had to shout over the shush of rain on the metal roof. "I'm Will Trent with the GBI."

"Douglas Hartshorne." Instead of asking Will for the rundown, he scowled at Delilah. "You show up after thirteen years on the night Mercy gets stabbed to death. What about that?"

Will didn't let Delilah answer. "How do you know she was stabbed?"

His smile had an arrogant quality. "Bitty called me on the road."

"How surprising." Delilah told Will, "They call her Bitty because she's got fools like him wrapped around her bitty finger."

The sheriff ignored her, asking Will, "Where's the body?"

Delilah said, "Down by the bachelor cottages."

"Did I ask you?"

"For godsakes, Biscuits. It's not like you're going to do a thorough investigation."

"Don't call me Biscuits," he shouted. "And if I was you, Delilah, I'd shut the hell up. You're the only one up here with a history of stabbing people."

"It was a goddam fork." Delilah explained to Will, "This was back before Jon was born. Mercy was living in my garage. I caught her trying to steal my car."

The sheriff countered, "So you say."

Will felt his teeth grit as they continued to bicker. This bullshit was burning through time they didn't have. The sheriff seemed more focused on scoring points than the fact that he had a murder on his hands. Will looked at his watch. Even if Amanda woke up to read the emergency text, it would take her a minimum of two hours to drive up from Atlanta.

"Go fuck yourself." Delilah walked down the stairs, oblivious to the pouring rain. "I'm going to go sit with my niece."

"Don't touch anything," the sheriff called.

She raised a middle finger to let him know what she thought about the order.

The sheriff told Will, "Some things don't get better with age."

Will needed this man to focus on what mattered. "Should I call you Sheriff or—"

"Everybody calls me Biscuits."

Will's teeth gritted again. No one in this place went by their actual name.

Still, he ran down the last two hours for the sheriff. "Roughly around midnight tonight, I was at the lake with my wife. We heard three screams. The first was about ten minutes apart from the second two, which were closer together. I ran through the woods and located the area with the three bachelor cottages. The last one was on fire. Mercy was located at the lake shore. Her upper body was in the water, but her feet were on dry land. I discovered that she was stabbed multiple times. Blood loss was severe. We spoke, but her only concern was Jon, her son. I wasn't able to get any information about her attacker. I tried to administer CPR, but the blade of the knife was still inside of her chest. It subsequently pierced my hand. The handle must have broken off during the attack. I was unable to locate it at the scene. There doesn't seem to be any missing knives in the commercial kitchen. We should check the family kitchen and all of the cottages. As soon as the sun comes up, we can begin a grid search. I recommend starting at the main compound and moving in the direction of the crime scene. Do you have any questions?"

"Nah, you covered everything. That was a damn good briefing. Gonna need to run it down one more time for the coroner. The roads are getting dicey. Shouldn't be more than another half hour." Biscuits looked down at Will's bandaged hand. "I was wondering what happened to your paw."

Will wanted to shake some urgency into the man. Mercy was dead. Her son was in the house grieving. "I can take you to see the body."

"She'll still be dead when the rain passes and the sun comes up." Biscuits looked out at the compound again. "Delilah ain't wrong about nothing to investigate. Mercy's got an ex. Dave McAlpine. Long story on how they all got the same name, but them two have been beating on each other since they were teenagers. My baby sister used to see 'em walloping on each other back in high school. What happened this time was, they took it too far and she ended up dead."

Will had to take a slow breath before he responded. It sounded a hell of a lot like the sheriff was blaming Mercy for being a murder victim. "My boss—"

"Wagner? Is that her name?" He didn't wait for confirmation. "She offered to send some of her field agents to take over, but I told her to cool her jets. Dave will show up eventually."

Amanda didn't have a cool setting on her jets. "We should search Mercy's room."

"Who's the 'we' here, fella?" Biscuits was smiling, but not really. "My county, my case."

Will knew he was right. "I'd like to volunteer to help look for Dave."

"Don't waste your time. I already had my deputy swing by his trailer and all the bars he hangs out at. He ain't around. Probably sleeping it off in a ditch somewhere."

Will pivoted. "He might be hiding in one of the empty cottages. I don't have my weapon, but I can give you backup for the search."

"Don't bother," Biscuits said. "Dave ain't allowed up here after six. Papa banned him from the compound a while back. The only reason he's been up this last month is to work on the bachelor cottages."

Will wondered if the man understood the words coming out of his own mouth. Dave was a murder suspect. He wasn't sticking to a curfew. Will tried another angle, asking, "What kind of vehicle does he drive?"

"He ain't allowed to drive. DUI. I think he's gotta woman brings him up and down the mountain. Dave's real good at talking people into doing things for him."

Will waited for the man to suggest they speak to this woman, or consider other possible places to search, or even the fact that Dave could still drive without a license, but Biscuits seemed content to watch the rain come down.

"Whelp." The man turned back to Will. "I should probably go in and check on Bitty. Been a hard couple of years for the poor little gal."

Will kept his mouth shut and made himself accept the obvious. The sheriff was too close to the family. He was blinded by their same disregard for Mercy's life. He wasn't interested in searching for the main suspect or collecting evidence or even talking to witnesses.

Not that the possible witnesses were going to help. Two of them had already driven away in their Mercedes. Two more had refused to be interviewed. Two were acting suspicious while they walked around in their underwear. Two of the least important ones were eager to help. One was an enigma wrapped up in a duck bathrobe. The victim's immediate family was behaving like a stranger had died. Add to that the fact that part of the murder weapon was missing. Their prime suspect was in the wind. The body had been partially submerged in water. The cabin had been burned to the ground. The rest of the crime scene was at this very moment being washed away.

Maybe Biscuits was right about Dave showing up eventually. The sheriff was clearly relying on a rural jury's belief that cops were the good guys who only arrested people if they were guilty, but Dave wasn't a typical defendant. He would know how to manipulate the jury. He would put on a vigorous defense. Will wasn't going to let a man called Biscuits be the reason Dave got away with murder. Neither was he going to stand around with his thumb up his ass while he waited for the next bad thing to happen.

"Will?" Sara had opened the front door. "Jon left a note on his bed. He ran away."

Dear Jon—

It's probably stupid to be writing you a letter I'm not even sure you're ever gonna read, but here I am doing it. People in AA say it's good to put your thoughts down on paper. I started doing that when I was twelve but I stopped cause Dave got ahold of my diary and made fun. I shouldn't of let him take that from me, but people been taking things from me my whole life. I guess what made me start back writing is I want some kind of record in case something bad ever happens to me. What I'm gonna tell you first is this. Today I filed court papers to get you back so I can start being what I should of been from the get-go. Your mama.

Delilah doesn't have a lot of money, but she told me to my face that she would spend every last dime she had just to hold on to you. She's got her reasons and I won't go into them. One day you'll learn the story of my ugly face and understand why she hates me so much. Why everybody does, I guess. And you got it written down right here that I never said it ain't for no reason.

I've pretty much fucked up every day of my eighteen years on this planet except for one, and that's the day I gave birth to you. I'm trying to unfuck my life right now by getting you back. I'm sorry for my cursing. Your grandma Bitty would be on my ass about it, but I'm talking to you like a man cause you're not gonna read this when you're still a boy.

I gave you up. That's the truth. I was going through withdrawal and chained to a hospital bed cause I was under arrest for driving drunk again. Delilah was there and it don't cost me nothing to admit I was glad to see her. The doctor wouldn't give me any pain medication cause I was a junkie. The cop

152

wouldn't loosen the handcuff, that's the kind of asshole he was. It's not like I could run off with a baby coming out of me, but this is the world you were born into.

I guess you could say it's a world I created for myself, and you wouldn't be wrong. That's why I gave you up to Delilah that day. I wasn't thinking about you or how lonely I would be without you. I was thinking about where I was gonna get my drink on or find some pills to hold me over until I could score, and that's the honest truth. When I was a kid, I started drinking to drown away my demons but what I did was create a prison for myself trapped with the demons inside.

But that is over for real now. I been a whole six months without anything and that's a fact. I've stopped partying and I'm even going to night classes to get my GED so when you're in school you can't say nothing about me not finishing as an excuse for you to drop out. Your daddy's been giving me hell for spending all that time studying when I should be taking care of him, but I'm trying to change my life. I'm trying to make things better for you cause you are worth it. He'll see that one day. He just doesn't know you like I do.

I guess this letter seems like I'm being hard on your daddy. I'm not gonna say anything bad about him but one thing. I know in my heart that he's gonna take money from Delilah to turn on me in the custody case. It's just his way because there ain't never enough money or enough love in the world that are ever gonna be enough for him. And I'm pretty sure the rest of my family will turn on me, too, but not for money, just for making things easy on themselves. It's not that they for real hate me. At least I don't think so. It's just that they all tend to go to ground when things are messy, like rabbits burrowing deep into a hole. It's for survival, not out of spite. At least that's what I'm holding on to, cause if I took it personal, I don't think I'd be able to get out of bed every morning.

That's what I'm doing now. Getting out of bed every morning. Showing up at the motel down the mountain to clean rooms. Same thing I've been doing at the lodge for as long as I can remember, but nobody whipping me if I do it too slow. And nobody telling me the roof over my head and food on the table is my only reward for hard work.

The motel don't pay much, but if I manage to keep saving, it'll be enough one day to get us a little apartment to live in. I'm not gonna raise you in your daddy's trailer down the holler where half the world drops by every night to party. You and me are gonna live in town and you're gonna see the world. Or at least more of the world than what I did.

This is the first time in my life I've had cash money in my pocket that belongs to me. I was always having to beg Papa or Bitty for change so I could buy a pack of gum or go to a movie. And then your daddy made me beg. But now I don't have to beg nobody. I just work at the motel and they pay me and that's a honest living. Even your daddy can't take that away. Lord knows he tries. If he knew how much I was really making, I wouldn't have a dime.

Like I told you, I'm not saying your daddy is a bad man, but what I will tell you is that even though he wasn't born into us, he's a McAlpine, sure enough. Maybe even worse, cause he's got different skins he slips in to depending on what he needs to get out of somebody. You'll have to decide for yourself when you're grown up whether that's a problem. You're a McAlpine, too, so who knows? You might end up exactly like all the rest of them.

Baby, if that's what happens, I will still love you. No matter what you do or if Delilah wins and I have to accept that spending two hours with you at the community center every other weekend is all I'm ever gonna get, I will always be there. I don't even care if you end up being the worst McAlpine in the bunch. Even worse than me, a person with blood on her hands. I'm always gonna forgive you, and I'm always gonna stand up for you. I will never be a rabbit hiding in a hole. At least not where you're concerned. The skin you see on me, even the ugly parts, maybe especially the ugly parts, is the same skin through to my heart.

I love you forever,
Mama

9

Sara read aloud from the brief note that Jon had left on his bed. "'I need some time. Don't come looking for me.'"

"Well, damn," the sheriff said. "Maybe he'll find Dave and save us the trouble."

She watched the side of Will's jaw jut out like a shard of glass. Sara assumed he was having as bizarre a time on the porch with the sheriff as she'd had inside the house with Mercy's cold, calculating family. None of them seemed affected by her death. All they had talked about, screamed about, railed about, was money.

Sara asked the sheriff, "Do you think Jon went to see Mercy?"

"Didn't mention it in his note," the man said, as if a sixteen-year-old could be relied upon to write down his intentions. "Old truck's still over yonder. Jon would'a passed through here if he was on foot. The trail to the bachelor cottages is way down thataway."

Sara tried, "Does he have a girlfriend? Someone in town he might—"

"Boy's about as popular as a snake in a sleeping bag. We'll hear soon enough if somebody spots him in town. The hike will take him a couple of hours, and that's after the rain clears. No way he'd take a bike out in this weather. End up like Papa tumbling down a cliff."

Nothing he said brought her any relief, but Sara felt like she might as well shout at the rain as try to get the sheriff to show concern for a missing child.

Will told Sara, "If he went to see Mercy, Delilah will be there. She wanted to sit with the body."

Sara felt her eyes sting with the threat of tears. At least someone actually cared.

"Ma'am, I'm Douglas Hartshorne, by the way." The sheriff held out his hand. "You can call me Biscuits."

"Sara Linton." His hand felt weak and clammy when Sara shook it. She glanced at Will, who looked like he wanted to throw the man over the side of the railing. It made no sense that the two law enforcement officers were standing on the porch talking while Mercy lay brutally murdered down by the lake. They should be searching for Dave, taking witness statements, arranging for Mercy's body to be cared for. She could tell by the way Will had his left hand clenched that the lack of momentum was causing him more pain than the wound in his right hand.

She couldn't give up. She asked the sheriff, "Is it possible Jon will try to take revenge on Dave?"

Biscuits shrugged. "Note don't say anything about revenge."

Sara tried yet again, "He's still a minor who lost his mother to a brutal murder. We should look for him."

Will said, "I can help search."

"Nah, the boy was raised in these woods. He'll be fine. Thank you kindly for the offer anyways. I got it from here on out." Biscuits started for the door, but then he seemed to remember Sara. He tipped his hat to her. "Ma'am."

Will and Sara were both speechless as Biscuits gently closed the door behind him. Will nodded for Sara to move toward the corner of the porch. They could only stare at each other. Neither one of them could articulate their feelings.

Finally, Will said, "Come here."

Sara buried her face in his chest as his arms wrapped around her. She felt her body let go of a tiny bit of the anguish she'd been carrying since they'd left the lake. She wanted to cry for Mercy, to yell at her family, to find Dave, to bring back Jon, to feel like she had actually done something on behalf of the dead woman lying inside an abandoned old cottage.

"I'm sorry," Will said. "This isn't much of a honeymoon for you."

"For us," she said, because this was meant to be a special week for him, too. "What can we do now? Tell me how to help."

Will seemed reluctant to let her go. Sara leaned against one of the posts. The late hour had suddenly caught up with her. They both stared at each other again. The only sound was the rain gushing off the roof and slapping the hard ground.

Will asked, "What happened inside?"

"I volunteered to make coffee so I could search the kitchen. If there's a missing knife, I couldn't tell. It looks like they've been hoarding cutlery since the lodge opened. We'll have to find the broken handle before we can try for a match."

"I'm sure Biscuits will get right on it." He rested his injured hand against his chest. Now that the adrenaline had burned off, the pain was probably making itself known.

He asked, "When did Bitty talk to the sheriff?"

Sara felt the surprise register on her face. "I didn't see her on the phone. Probably when I was in the kitchen."

"There was nothing you could've done about it anyway." Will moved his hand higher, like he could put it out of reach of the burning. "I need to find Dave. He could still be on the property."

The thought of him going after Dave injured and without backup sent a chill through her spine. "He could have another weapon."

"If he's still hanging around up here, he wants to get caught."

"Not by you."

"What is it you're always saying? Life makes you pay for your personality?"

Sara felt her throat tighten. "The sheriff—"

"Isn't going to help," Will said. "He told me the coroner should be here in thirty minutes. Maybe they'll treat this murder with some urgency. Did you get anything at all from the family?"

"They were worried about the guests who are leaving and the ones who are due here on Thursday. Could they keep the deposits? Would people still come? Who was going to order the food and handle the staff and book the guides?" Sara still could not believe none of them had said anything about Mercy. "Then things got really heated when they started talking about the investors."

"You know about the sale?"

"I gathered the details from the screaming match over who would get Jon's proxy vote, particularly if Dave is arrested." She crossed her arms. She felt a strange kind of vulnerability on Mercy's behalf. "Somewhere in the middle of it, Jon disappeared upstairs. I tried to follow him, but Bitty said to give him time."

"That's what his note said—that he needed time."

Sara remembered, "I got onto the Wi-Fi. Open your phone so I can share the connection."

Will tapped in his code with his thumb. Fortunately, he was left-handed, so at least he still had dexterity. Sara made sure he was on the network before retrieving his shirt from the rocking chair. She started to unbutton the ridiculously tight chef's jacket.

Will said, "You know I can do that."

"I know." Sara helped him out of the jacket. He made it clear he was humoring her when she held open the arms so he could dress. Her hands felt clumsy on the buttons. The events of the night had left her shaken. She did the last button, then pressed her hand to his heart. There were a lot of things she could've said to keep him from leaving, but Sara knew above all else that Will wanted to get to work.

So did Sara.

Not many people had cared about Mercy when she was alive, but there were at least two people who cared very much that she was dead.

"You'll need these." She took his earbuds out of her pants pocket and slid them into his. Will could read, but not quickly. It was easier for him to use the text-to-speech app on his phone. "I texted you the names of the kitchen staff along with their phone numbers. I managed to get them off a list taped by the kitchen door. They should come through when your messages load."

He was looking out toward the parking pad. He was ready to go. "I'll start with the cottages, then I want to check that wood-pile. Delilah told me Christopher and Chuck were hanging around there earlier. Could be there's a hiding place."

"I can talk to Gordon and Landry, try to figure out what that tattoo means."

"Landry answered to the name Paul, so that's what you should call him until he gives a better explanation." Will pointed to one of the cottages. The lights were on. "The guys are over there.

Drew and Keisha are there, but they're refusing to talk. Not that I think they'd have much to say. I doubt they could hear anything inside their cottage. It was basically a wind tunnel. They're really upset we lied to them about who we are."

Sara felt an ache over their lost week. She knew that Will had liked Drew, and she had been looking forward to spending time with Keisha.

He said, "There was something odd that Drew said to Bitty before they stormed off. Something along the lines of, 'forget that other business. Do what you like up here.'"

"Maybe they had a complaint about their cottage?"

"Maybe." He continued through the rundown. "Monica and Frank are there. Chuck came out of there. Max and Sydney were there. They already left."

"Great," Sara said. The crime scene was washed out and the witnesses were disappearing along with it. "What a shitshow. Does anyone care that Mercy's dead?"

"Delilah does. As least I think she does." He looked down at his phone. His messages had started to load. "According to her, Christopher had a few failed relationships. One woman got pregnant by another guy and left him, another woman was lost. I don't know if that means dead or disappeared or if it even matters. People hide things for their own reasons."

Sara felt a lightbulb clicking on in her head, but not about Christopher's love life. "The argument the app guys had on the trail outside our cottage."

"What about it?"

"Paul said, 'I don't care what you think. It's the right thing to do,' then Gordon said, 'Since when do you care about the right thing,' then Paul said, 'Since I saw how she fucking lives.'"

Will was giving her his undivided attention. "She, meaning Mercy?"

"There are only two women living at this place, and the other one is Bitty."

He scratched his jaw. "Did Gordon have a response?"

Sara closed her eyes, trying to recall. The two men had spent perhaps fifteen seconds arguing in front of the cottage before walking down the trail. "I think Gordon said, 'You've got to let it go.' Then Paul walked down toward the lake, and I couldn't hear anything else."

"Why would Paul care how Mercy is living?"

"It sounded like he resented it."

The screen on Will's phone lit up. He looked down. "Faith dropped me a pin half an hour ago. She's on seventy-five, about to hit five-seventy-five."

Sara felt a total disconnect between the happy honeymooner who'd made the same car trip yesterday and the woman in the middle of a murder investigation now. "She probably has two more hours until she gets here."

"My plan is to have Dave in custody by then so she can do the interrogation."

"You're still sure it's him?"

"We can talk about who else it could be, or I can go find Dave and settle it once and for all."

Sara got the feeling that Will had more things to settle than he was letting on. "What about the sheriff? He made it clear he doesn't want our help."

"Amanda wouldn't be sending Faith if she didn't have a plan." Will's phone went back into his pocket. "I need you in the house while I check the empty cottages."

Sara couldn't go back into the depressing house. "I'll talk to Gordon and Paul. Maybe I can figure out what's going on there. Do you remember anything about the tattoo?"

"Lots of flowers, a butterfly, a curly script, definitely a word. Arced around his chest here." He touched his hand over his heart. "He put on a T-shirt before he came out. I don't know if that means he didn't want anyone else to see it or maybe he was just putting on a shirt because that's what you do when you get out of the shower."

This was the frustrating part of an investigation. People lied. They hid things. They kept their secrets. They shared others. And sometimes none of it had anything to do with the crime you were trying to solve.

Sara told him, "I'll see what I can find out."

Will nodded, but he didn't move. He was really going to wait until she was safely inside cottage five.

Sara borrowed the large umbrella leaning up against the side of the house. Her hiking boots were waterproof, but there was no stopping the rain from splashing against her legs. By the time she reached the small, covered porch, her pants were soaked from the knees down. So much for the water-resistant material. She folded the umbrella, then knocked on the door.

It was hard to tell if there was any sound inside the cottage over the white noise of rain. Fortunately, Sara didn't have to wait long before Gordon answered the door. He was wearing black briefs and fuzzy slippers.

Instead of asking Sara why she was here or what she wanted, he flung open the door, saying, "Misery loves company."

"Welcome to our sad little party," Paul called from his place on the couch. He was wearing boxers and a white T-shirt. His bare feet rested on the coffee table. "We're just sitting around in our underwear getting hammered."

Sara tried to play along. "Reminds me of college."

Gordon laughed as he walked into the kitchen. "Grab a seat."

Sara chose one of the deep club chairs. The cottage was smaller than her own, with the same style furniture. She could see through to the bedroom. There were no suitcases laid out on the bed, which she took as a sign that they weren't planning to leave. Or maybe they had different priorities. There was an open bottle of bourbon on the coffee table. Two empty glasses were beside it. The bottle was half full.

Gordon put a third glass on the table. "What a fucking night. Morning. Fuck, the sun will be up soon."

Sara could feel Paul studying her.

He asked, "Married to a cop, huh?"

"Yes." Sara wasn't going to lie anymore. "I work for the state, too. I'm a medical examiner."

"I could not touch a dead body." Gordon scooped up the bourbon from the coffee table. "This stuff tastes like turpentine, but you wouldn't know it from the price."

Sara recognized the upscale label. She couldn't remember the last time she'd had a hard drink. Will had an aversion to alcohol that dated back to his childhood. Sara had become a teetotaler by default.

Paul said, "It's the altitude, right? Changes your taste buds."

"Hon, that's on airplanes." Gordon sloshed doubles into all three glasses. "We can't be thirty thousand feet up right now."

Paul asked, "What's the elevation here?"

He was looking at Sara when he asked the question, so she provided, "We're about twenty-three hundred feet above sea level."

"Thank God we're not going to get hit by a plane. That would be the cherry on top of this shit sundae." Gordon handed Sara her glass. "What does a medical examiner do? Is that like what's her name who was in that show?"

"What show?" Paul asked.

"The one with the hair. We heard her on *Mountain Stage*. And then she was on *Madam Secretary*."

Paul snapped his fingers. "*Crossing Jordan*."

"That's the one." Gordon downed half of his glass. "Kathryn Hahn was in that. We love her."

Sara assumed their original question had gotten lost. She took a sip of bourbon and tried not to blanch. Calling it turpentine was a compliment.

"Right?" Paul had noticed her reaction. "You've got to hold it in your mouth to get past the gag reflex."

Gordon snorted at the double entendre. "I guess there's none of that for the honeymooners tonight."

"What's Agent McSexy up to?" Paul asked. "Doesn't look like anyone's interested in giving him a statement."

Sara felt a heat wash over her body as she thought about Will searching for Dave on his own. "Did either of you see Mercy after dinner tonight?"

"Oh, cop questions," Gordon said. "Shouldn't you read us our Miranda Rights first?"

Sara had no obligation to read them anything. "I'm not a police officer. I can't arrest you."

She left out the part about how she could give testimony as a witness to anything they said.

Gordon volunteered, "Paul saw her."

Sara guessed that meant the Landry ruse was well and truly over. "Where was she?"

"Right outside our place. This was roughly around ten-thirty.

I just happened to be looking out the window." Paul held his glass to his mouth but didn't drink. "Mercy strolled along for a bit, then went up the stairs to Frank and Monica's."

"Monica was probably asking for more booze," Gordon supplied. "Frank said she left a note on the porch."

Paul said, "Not sure how she managed to hold a pen. That bitch was pickled."

"To Monica's liver," Gordon raised his glass in a toast.

Sara pretended to take another drink. She thought it was interesting that Paul knew where Mercy had gone. You couldn't see Frank and Monica's cottage from their windows. You had to actually walk onto the porch, which meant he had been tracking Mercy's progress.

"So," Gordon said. "What'd she look like?"

Sara shook her head. "Who?"

"Mercy," Gordon said. "She was stabbed to death, right?"

"Pretty gruesome," Paul said. "I bet she was terrified."

Sara looked down at her glass. The two men were treating this like a reality show.

Paul asked, "Do you know if our hike is still on for tomorrow?"

"Hon," Gordon said. "That's a bit ruthless."

"It's also valid. We paid a fuckton of money to get up here." He looked at Sara. "Any idea?"

"You'll have to ask the family." Sara couldn't keep up the pretense any longer. She returned her glass to the table. "Paul, Will told me he saw the tattoo on your chest."

Paul's laugh sounded forced. "Don't worry, sweetheart. He's totally into you."

Sara wasn't worried. "I've learned in my job that every tattoo has a story. What's yours?"

"Oh, it's a stupid one," he said. "A little too much tequila. A little too much melancholy."

Sara looked at Gordon. He shrugged. "I'm not a tattoo person. I hate needles. What about you? Any tramp stamps you want to tell us about?"

"None." She tried to come at this from a different angle. "Have you guys been at the lodge before?"

"First time," Gordon said. "Not sure we'll be repeat customers."

"I dunno, hon. We could probably get a deal if we book right now." Paul reached for the bourbon as he sat up on the couch. He poured another double, then asked Sara, "You want more?"

"She's barely touched the first one." Gordon reached out his hand. "May I?"

Sara watched Gordon dump her glass into his.

She asked, "What about Mercy?"

Paul slowly sat back.

Gordon asked, "What about her?"

"It seemed like you knew her. Or at least knew of her." She said this to Paul. "And like you weren't happy to find her living a nice life up here at the lodge."

Sara caught a flash of something in Paul's eyes, but she couldn't tell if it was anger or fear.

Gordon said, "She was a strange bird, don't you think? A bit rough around the edges."

"And what about that scar on her face?" Paul asked. "I bet that could tell you a story, too."

"I wouldn't want to hear it," Gordon said. "The whole family is a bit suss if you ask me. The mother reminds me of that girl from that movie, but her hair was dark, not stringy white like a witch's pubes."

Paul asked, "Samara from *The Ring*?"

"Yes, but with an evil child's voice." Gordon looked at Sara. "Have you seen it?"

Sara wouldn't let them sidetrack her. "So you'd never met Mercy before you checked in?"

Gordon answered, "I can honestly say today was the first time that I ever laid eyes on the poor woman."

"That was yesterday," Paul said. "It's already tomorrow."

Sara pressed a little harder. "Why did you lie about your name?"

"We were just having a little fun," Gordon said. "Like you and Will, right? You lied, too."

Sara couldn't argue with that logic. This was one of the many reasons she hated lying.

"Let's have a toast." Paul raised his glass. "To all the liars on the mountaintop. May they not all share the same fate."

Sara knew it was pointless to ask if he was including Mercy in their liars' club. She watched Paul's throat work as he drank the entire contents of his glass. He slammed it down on the coffee table for good measure. The sound echoed in the silence. No one spoke. Sara could hear a dripping sound outside. The rain had passed for now. She hoped that Will had kept his bandage dry. She hoped that he wasn't lying on his back with a knife sticking out of his chest.

She was about to take her leave when Gordon broke the tension with a loud yawn.

He said, "I'd better go to bed before I turn into a pumpkin."

Sara stood. "Thanks for the drink."

There were no pleasant goodbyes, just a pointed silence as Sara left the cottage. She looked up at the sky. The full moon had moved toward the ridgeline. Only a few clouds remained. Sara left the umbrella on the porch and walked down the stairs. She scanned the compound looking for Will. The floodlights were still blazing, but there was only so far they could reach.

Movement near the parking pad caught her eye. No false Big Foot sightings this time. She recognized Will by his shape. His back was to her. Both his hands were down at his sides. She assumed his bandage was soaking wet. There was no sign of Dave, which shouldn't have brought her any relief, but it did anyway. She thought Will must have been looking at the woodpile Delilah had mentioned, but then a set of headlights broke through the darkness.

Sara put up her hand to block the light. Not a car, but a dark-colored sprinter van. She assumed the coroner had arrived. She hoped the man would be glad to have a state medical examiner already on scene, but considering the unexpected reactions Sara had witnessed tonight, she wasn't taking anything for granted. At the very least, she hoped the coroner knew the limitations of his job.

People often confused the role of medical examiner with that of a county coroner. Only the former position required a medical doctor. The latter could be, and tended to be, anything but. Which was unfortunate, because county coroners were the gatekeepers of death. They were in charge of overseeing the collection of evidence and officially ruling whether or not a death was suspicious enough to ask the state medical examiner to perform an autopsy.

The state of Georgia was the first to recognize the office of coroner in its 1777 constitution. The position was elected, and there were only a few requirements to run for office: candidates must be at least twenty-five years of age, registered to vote in the county in which they were running, have no felonies on their record and have a high school diploma.

One coroner out of the state's 154 counties was an actual physician. The rest were funeral directors, farmers, retirees, pastors, and in one case, a motor-boat repairman. The position paid $1200 a year and required the coroner to be on call 24/7. Sometimes, you got what you paid for. Which was how a suicide could be ruled a homicide and an act of domestic violence could be coded as a slip-and-fall.

Sara's hiking boots snicked against the mud as she walked toward the parking pad. The driver's side door opened. She was surprised to see a woman get out. She was even more surprised to see the woman was dressed in coveralls and a trucker hat. Sara had been expecting a funeral director because of the van. The floodlights caught the logo on the back panel. Moushey Heating and Air. Sara felt her stomach grip itself into a fist.

"Yeah," the woman was saying to Will. "Biscuits told me y'all were trying to horn in on the case."

Sara had to bite her lip to keep her mouth closed.

"Don't worry," the woman had clocked her expression. "Multiple stab wounds, right? Gonna say homicide is an easy call on that one. State's gonna get the body eventually. No harm in starting out with you here. I'm Nadine Moushey, Dillon County coroner. You're Dr. Linton?"

"Sara." The woman had an uncomfortably firm grip. "What have you been told?"

"Mercy was stabbed to death, probably Dave did it. Heard it's your honeymoon, too?"

Sara felt Will's surprise. He still didn't know how small towns worked. Every person within fifty miles probably knew about the murder by now.

Nadine said, "That sucks big time. Though if I'm looking back at my honeymoon, probably would've been lucky if somebody had killed the bastard."

Will said, "It seems like you know the victim and the main suspect."

"My little brother went to school with Mercy. I knew Dave from hanging out at the Tastee Freeze. He's always been a violent prick. Mercy had her troubles, but she was okay. Not mean like the rest of 'em. Which was to her detriment, I guess. You don't wanna be dropped into a snake pit unless you've got the sharpest fangs."

Will asked, "Is there anyone other than Dave who would want Mercy dead?"

"I was thinking on that the whole drive up," Nadine said. "I haven't run across Mercy since Papa's accident a year and a half ago, and then I only saw her once at the hospital. Town's a hard place for her. She mostly stays up the mountain. Place is real isolated. Not a lot for folks to gossip about if you're not mixing it up in town a little."

Sara asked, "What about the scar on her face?"

"Car accident. Drunk driving. Hit a guard rail. Metal split up the middle, pretty much sliced off one side of her face. There's a long, sad story behind that, but Biscuits can tell you the nitty gritty. It was his pa, Sheriff Hartshorne, who handled it, but Biscuits worked the scene, too. The families have always been close."

Sara wasn't surprised by the information. It helped explain why Biscuits was in no hurry.

"The sheriff told me Dave's license got revoked off a DUI," Will said. "He mentioned that Dave has a female driver who brings him up to the lodge and back so that he can work."

Nadine gave a belly laugh. "That female would be Bitty. Dave's burned about every woman in the tri-county area. Nobody would get out of bed for him. Or in bed, if you ask me. I've already raised two boys. Don't want to take care of another. What happened to your hand, you don't mind my asking?"

Will looked down at his bandaged hand. "You didn't hear about the murder weapon?"

Sara supplied, "Will attempted CPR. He didn't realize that the knife blade was broken off inside Mercy's chest."

Will said, "Locating the knife handle should be a priority. I didn't see anything laying around when I searched the cottages for Dave, but it's worth a more thorough search."

"Fuck me, that's grim. Let's head on down while we're talking." Nadine reached into her van and pulled out a flashlight and a toolbox. "First light's not for another couple'a three hours. We got more rain coming mid-morning, but I'm not gonna try to bring her out until the sun's up. For now, let's see what's the what."

Nadine walked ahead with the flashlight. She kept the beam pointed at the ground, illuminating a few yards at a time. Will waited until they were on the bottom part of the Loop Trail to start briefing the coroner on the events of the evening. The fight at dinner. The screams in the night. Finding Mercy clinging to the last seconds of her life on the lake shore.

Hearing it all said aloud put Sara at the scene again. She silently added her own perspective. Rushing through the forest. Desperate to find Will. Finding him kneeling over Mercy. The look of anguish on his face. He'd been so overcome with grief that he hadn't even noticed Sara, let alone the blade sticking out of his right hand.

The memory threatened to bring tears again. When the two of them had been standing alone on the McAlpines' front porch, Sara had been so relieved to feel his arms around her, but now she realized that Will had probably needed comfort, too.

She reached down to hold his left hand as they started down a winding path. Sara had seen Lost Widow Trail clearly marked on the map, but her logical brain had failed her when she'd dashed off into the woods, barefooted and panicked by the sound of Will's pleas for help.

The terrain started to drop precipitously. The trail meandered back and forth as they spiraled down. The path wasn't as well maintained as the Loop. Nadine mumbled a curse when a low-hanging branch knocked back her hat. She raised the flashlight higher to keep it from happening again. They went single file as they zigzagged down into the ravine below the dining hall. The string lights around the railing were off. Sara guessed the staff had left shortly after dinner. She tried not to think about standing on the observation deck with Will. It felt like a lifetime ago.

Will slowed his pace as the trail widened. Sara hung back, too. She knew he wanted to know what had happened with the app guys. If they were even app guys. Both men had proven they were adept liars.

But then, so had Sara and Will.

She kept her voice low, telling him, "Paul saw Mercy walking to Frank and Monica's porch around ten-thirty."

"He didn't think to mention that before?"

"He didn't mention a lot of things," Sara said. "I couldn't get anything out of him about the tattoo, why he gave a fake name, whether or not they knew Mercy, or what the argument on the trail was about. I don't think it was just the alcohol. They came across as incredibly blasé about everything."

"Fits the theme of the night." Will cupped her elbow as they walked down a particularly steep slope. "I didn't find anything in the woodpile. No sign of Dave in the cottages. No broken knife handle. No bloody clothes. We're already three hours into this. Dave's probably crossed state lines by now."

"Did you talk to Amanda?"

"She didn't pick up."

Sara looked up at him. Amanda always picked up when Will called. "What about Faith?"

"She got behind a pile-up on the interstate. It'll be another hour minimum before they can clear out the accident and open the road back up."

Sara bit her lip so hard she tasted blood. There was no way she would be able to persuade Will to wait for Faith now. Once they turned Mercy's body over to Nadine, he was going to find a way to get a car and drive down the mountain to find Dave.

"Nadine," Sara called. She couldn't change Will's mind, but she could at least do her job. "How long have you been the county coroner?"

"Three years," Nadine said. "My dad used to do it, but old guy problems caught up with him. Congestive heart failure, kidney failure, COPD."

Sara was familiar with the trio of co-morbidities. "I'm sorry."

"Don't be. He had his fun earning it." Nadine stopped to face them. "Y'all are probably used to a bit of anonymity down there in Atlanta, but up here, you should know, everybody knows everybody's business."

Neither Will nor Sara told her that at least one of them knew small towns very well.

"Thing is, it's boring as shit up here, and when you're young, you get into things." Nadine leaned her hand against a tree. She had clearly been thinking about this on the hike down. "The thing about Mercy is, she was wilder than all of us put together. Knocking back booze. Taking pills. Shooting dope. Stealing shit from the store. Breaking car windows. TP-ing houses. Egging the school. You name a petty crime, she was part of it."

Sara tried to square the troubled woman she'd spoken to in the kitchen bathroom with the wild picture Nadine was painting. It wasn't a hard connection to make.

"Y'all know how parents will say their kid is good, they're just hanging around with the wrong people? That was Mercy. She was the wrong people for every kid in town." Nadine shrugged. "Maybe they were right back then, but that ain't how it was now. The thing about small towns is, you're basically born into Elmer's glue. Whatever your reputation is when you're a kid, that's how folks are gonna think about you for the rest of your life. So even though Mercy cleaned herself up, started doing right by Jon, turned this place around when her daddy tumbled himself down a cliff, Mercy was still stuck in that Elmer's glue. You following me?"

Sara nodded. She knew exactly what the woman was saying. Her own little sister had enjoyed an active sex life in high school that still earned her sideways glances, even after Tessa had married, given birth to a beautiful daughter, and served as a missionary overseas.

"Anyway, I'm guessing that was a question you had about why folks aren't more torn up about her murder," Nadine finished. "They think Mercy deserved it."

Will said, "That's exactly what I picked up on from the sheriff."

"Yeah, well, you'd think a man who's been called Biscuits for nearly twenty years of his miserable life would understand that people can change." Nadine did not sound like a fan of the sheriff.

"Dave gave him the nickname in high school. Poor sap was a real roly-poly back then. Dave said his belly was popping out of the top of his pants like a can of biscuits."

Nadine turned back down the trail. Sara watched her flashlight dance across the trees. They walked in silence for another five minutes until they reached a terraced area. Nadine went first, then turned around to offer the benefit of her flashlight.

She said, "Watch out, the going's tricky."

Sara felt Will's hand at the small of her back as she carefully walked down. The wind had shifted, bringing a smokey scent from the burned out cottage. She could feel a mist on her skin. The temperature had dropped from the rainstorm. The cooler air was pulling condensation off the surface of the lake.

"I heard Dave was fixing up the old cottages," Nadine said. "Looks like he was doing his usual bang-up job."

Sara watched Nadine's flashlight bounce over the sawhorses and discarded tools, the empty beer cans, smoked-down joints and cigarette butts. Having learned quite a bit about Dave McAlpine, she was not surprised he'd trashed his own worksite. Men like that only knew how to take. They never considered what they were leaving for others.

"Hello?" a tense voice called. "Who's there?"

"Delilah," Will said. "It's Agent Trent. I'm here with the coroner and—"

"Nadine." Delilah had been sitting on the stairs that led up to the second cottage. She stood up when they approached, wiping dirt from the back of her pajama bottoms. "You took over for Bubba."

"I'm out all hours fixing busted compressors anyway," Nadine said. "I'm real sorry about Mercy."

"So am I." Delilah used a tissue to dab under her nose. She asked Will, "Have you found Dave?"

"I searched the empty cottages. He's not there." Will glanced around the area. "Have you seen Jon? He ran away."

"God," Delilah breathed. "Can things get any worse? Why did he run away? Did he leave a note?"

"Yes," Sara answered. "He said he needed time and that we shouldn't try to find him."

Delilah shook her head. "I have no idea where he'd go. Is Dave still living in the same trailer park?"

"Yep," Nadine answered. "My granny lives across the way. I told her to keep an eye out for Dave. I'm sure she's sitting up in her chair by the window. She watches that place like it's one of her shows on TV. If she sees Jon, she'll call me."

"Thank you." Delilah's fingers played with the collar of her pajama top. "I was hoping Dave would show up here. I would gladly drown him in the water."

"Wouldn't be much of a loss, but you probably won't get the chance," Nadine said. "Those bully-bitchy types, they kill their wives, then they usually kill themselves. Am I right, doctor?"

Sara couldn't say that she was completely wrong. "It happens."

Will didn't seem happy with the prospect of Dave committing suicide. He clearly wanted to drag him away in handcuffs. Maybe he was right. Everyone was treating it as a foregone conclusion that Dave had killed Mercy.

"Whelp," Nadine said. "Might not be a good idea to yap in front of a cop about how you want to murder somebody who might wind up dead. Should we get started?"

Will took her down to the shore. Sara stayed back with Delilah because they didn't need another set of footprints on the already compromised scene. She tried to conjure up any memory of what the ground had looked like when she'd first arrived. The moon had been partially obstructed by clouds, but still offered a spray of light.

There had been a large pool of blood at the base of the stairs. More blood had puddled into the drag marks that made a straight line toward the shore. Blood had turned the water red as Mercy's life had drained away. Her underwear and jeans had been pulled down. She had likely been assaulted before she was stabbed. There had been too many wounds to count.

Sara mentally prepared herself for the autopsy. Mercy had been strangled earlier in the day by Dave. She had accidentally sliced open her thumb on a broken piece of glass during dinner. Sara imagined there would be multiple signs of injuries past and present. Mercy had told Sara that she had married her father. Sara assumed that meant that Dave was not the first man to abuse her.

She turned to look at the closed cottage door. The body had already started to decompose. There was the familiar odor of bacteria breaking down flesh. The door was still barred with the two-by-four Will had taken from a pile of lumber by the worksite. They had laid Mercy's body in the center of the room. There was nothing to cover her but Will's bloodied shirt. Sara had resisted the need to make her more presentable—smooth back her tangled, wet hair. Close her eyelids. Straighten her clothes. Pull up her torn underwear and jeans. Mercy McAlpine had been a complicated, troubled, and vibrant woman. She deserved respect, even if it only came in death. But every centimeter of her body could bear witness to the person who'd murdered her.

Delilah said, "I should've fought harder to stay in her life."

Sara turned to look at the woman. Delilah gripped the tissue in her hand. Her tears flowed unabated.

"After I lost custody of Jon, I told myself that I walked away because he needed stability. I didn't want him to feel pulled between me and Mercy." Delilah looked out at the lake. "In truth, it was my pride. The custody battle turned deeply personal. It stopped being about Jon and started being about winning. My ego couldn't accept the loss. Not to Mercy. I saw her as a worthless junkie. If I'd only given her time to prove that she was more than that, I could've been a port in the storm. Mercy needed that. She always needed that."

"I'm sorry that things ended badly." Sara spoke carefully, not wanting to pick at a fresh wound. "It's a lot to take on, the raising of someone else's child. You must've been close to Mercy when Jon was born."

"I was the first person to hold him," she said. "Mercy was carted off to jail the day after he was born. The nurse put him in my arms and I . . . I had no idea what to do."

Sara heard no bitterness in her dry laugh.

"I had to stop by Walmart on my way home. I had an infant in one hand and a cart in the other. Thank God some woman saw me looking perplexed and helped me figure out what I needed. I spent the entire first night reading message boards about how to take care of a baby. I never planned on raising a child. Didn't want to. Jon was—he is a gift. I have never loved anyone as much as I loved that boy. Still do, actually. Haven't seen him in thirteen years, but there's a giant hole in my heart where he belongs."

Sara could tell the loss was weighing on Delilah, but she still had questions. "Jon's grandparents didn't want to take him?"

Delilah gave a sharp laugh. "Bitty told me I should leave him outside the fire station. Which is something, considering Dave was abandoned by his own mother at a fire station."

Sara had seen evidence of Bitty's cold-bloodedness toward her own daughter, but this was an unconscionable thing to say about an infant.

"It's strange, isn't it?" Delilah asked. "You hear all this talk about the sanctity of motherhood, but Bitty has always hated babies. Particularly her own. She would let Mercy and Christopher sit around in their own shit and piss. I tried to intervene, but Cecil made it clear I wasn't to interfere."

Sara hadn't thought it was possible to be more disgusted with Mercy's family. "You lived here when Christopher and Mercy were babies?"

"Until Cecil chased me off," Delilah said. "One of my many regrets was not taking Mercy when I had the chance. Bitty would've gladly handed her over. She's one of those women who says she gets along better with men because she doesn't like other women, but the truth of the matter is other women can't stand being around her."

Sara was very familiar with the pick-me type. "You seem convinced that Dave is guilty."

"What was it Drew said? I've seen this *Dateline* before? It's always the husband. Or the ex-husband. Or the boyfriend. And in the case of Dave, my only surprise is that he took so long to get to this point. He was always an angry, violent little thug. He blamed Mercy for everything bad in his life when the fact is, she was honestly the only good." She folded the tissue before wiping her nose again. "Besides, who else could it be?"

Sara didn't know, but she had to ask, "Do any of the guests seem familiar to you?"

"No, but I haven't been here in a really long while," Delilah said. "If you're asking my opinion, the caterers were nice, but not as easy-going as I like. I didn't talk much to the two app guys.

They're not my kind of gay. The investors, well, not my kind of assholes. Monica and Frank were lovely, though. We talked about travel and music and wine."

Sara must have looked surprised, because Delilah laughed.

"Monica should be forgiven for being so deep in her cups. They lost a child last year."

Sara felt a tinge of guilt for her ungenerous thoughts. "How awful."

"Yes, it's wrenching to lose a child," Delilah said. "It wasn't the same when I lost Jon, but to have something taken from you that's so precious . . ."

Sara listened to her voice trail off. She could see Will walking toward the burned-out cottage with Nadine. They were deep in conversation. Sara was relieved to see that the coroner, at least, was taking the investigation seriously.

Delilah picked up where she had left off. "The thing about losing a child is that it either tears a couple apart or it brings them closer together. I blew up a twenty-six-year relationship when Jon was taken away from me. She was the love of my life. It was my own damn fault, but I would certainly like the chance to go back and do things differently."

"Sara?" Will waved her over. "Come see this."

Sara couldn't think of a way to keep Delilah from following her, but at least the woman kept her distance. Nadine was shining her flashlight onto the charred remains of the third cottage. One wall was still standing, but most of the roof was gone. Smoke wafted off the chunks of charred wood that had fallen through what was left of the floor. Even with the deluge of rain, Sara could still feel heat coming off the rubble.

Will pointed to a pile of debris in the back corner. "Do you see it?"

Sara could see it.

There were several types of backpacks on the market, ranging from the style that every child carried to school to the ones designed for serious hikers. The second category tended to offer features specifically designed for outdoor use. Some were extra lightweight for day hikes or climbing. Others had internal frames to keep them rigid for heavier loads. Still others had external metal frames that could be expanded in order to carry larger items such as tents and bedrolls.

Every variation was constructed with nylon, a material that was rated by denier, a unit of density based on the length and weight of the fiber. The closest corollary would be the thread count in sheets. The higher the denier, the more durable the fabric. Add to that the various coatings that were meant to make the material weather resistant, weatherproof, and sometimes, if a silicone and fiberglass mixture was used, fire resistant.

Which was apparently the case with the backpack in the corner of the burned-out cottage.

10

Will used the camera on his phone to document the placement and style of the backpack. It looked functional and expensive, like the type of equipment a real hiker would carry. There were three zippers, all closed: one for the main compartment, one for a smaller section in the front, and another for a pocket at the bottom. The material looked stretched to the limit. He could see two sharp corners pressing against the nylon that indicated a box or a heavy book was inside. The rain had stripped away some of the black soot from the fire. The nylon was lavender in color, almost identical to the shade of Mercy's Nikes.

Delilah came closer. "I saw that same bag in the house earlier."

Will asked, "Where was it?"

"Upstairs," she said. "Mercy's bedroom door was open. I saw it leaned against her dresser drawers. It didn't look that full, though. All of the zippers were open."

Will looked at Sara. They knew what *should* be done. The backpack was a valuable piece of evidence, but it was sitting among other valuable evidence. The arson investigator would want to take photos, comb through the debris, collect samples, run tests, search for accelerant, because something had clearly been used to make sure the cottage burned. Will had been inside while it was blazing. Fire didn't spread like that on its own.

Nadine offered her flashlight to Will, asking, "Can you hold on to this for me?"

He pointed the light downward while Nadine opened the heavy-looking toolbox she'd carried to the scene. She retrieved a

177

pair of gloves. Then she reached into the back pocket of her coveralls for a pair of needle-nose pliers.

He trailed her with the beam of the flashlight. Thankfully, she didn't trample through the smoldering remnants of the fire. She walked around to the back. She reached over toward the lavender backpack. With a delicate precision, she grasped the metal pull tag of the zipper between the pliers and gently tugged. The bag opened up around two inches before the teeth caught.

Will angled up the light so she could have a better look inside.

Nadine said, "Looks like there's a notebook, some clothes, women's toiletries. She was going somewhere."

Sara asked, "What kind of notebook?"

"Composition type that kids take to school." She turned her head to get a different angle. "The cover looks like it's plastic. Melted from the heat. The bottom is full of water. Rain must've found its way in through the zipper. Pages are soaked together like glue."

Will asked, "Can you read anything?"

"Nope," she said. "And I'm not gonna try. We need somebody a lot smarter than me to handle that thing without destroying the pages."

Will had dealt with this kind of evidence before. The lab would need days to process the notebook. To make matters worse, the flashlight had picked out a burned plastic and metal carcass beside the backpack.

Nadine saw it, too. "Looks like an older-model iPhone. That thing is toast. Shine the light under there."

Will followed the spot she pointed to. He saw the remnants of a charred metal gas can. Dave had probably used it to fill the generator, then he'd used it to burn away the crime scene after murdering his wife.

Sara asked Delilah, "Do you know if Mercy said anything about leaving?"

"Bitty gave her until Sunday to get off the mountain. I don't know where she would go, especially in the middle of the night. Mercy's an experienced hiker. This time of year, we've got young male black bears looking to establish territory. You don't want to accidentally cross one."

Nadine said, "No offense, Dee, but Mercy wasn't known for her logic. Half the time she landed herself in hot water, it was because she flew off the handle and did something stupid."

Sara weighed in. "Mercy wasn't angry after the fight with Jon. She was worried. According to Paul, she made the ten o'clock rounds and picked up Monica's request from her front porch around ten-thirty. He didn't mention that she was acting strange. Even without that, I don't believe Mercy would head off in the night and leave Jon with things unsaid."

"No," Delilah said. "I don't believe she would, either. But why come here? There's no plumbing or electricity. She might as well stay at the house. God knows those people know how to glare at each other in angry silence."

They all looked at the backpack as if it could offer up an explanation.

Nadine said the obvious. "This is a hotel, people. If Mercy was sick of her family, she'd stay in one of the guest cottages."

Will offered, "Some of the beds were unmade when I searched the empty cottages. I figured they hadn't been cleaned from the previous guests."

"Penny's the cleaner. She's also the bartender. Might be worth asking her the question." Nadine looked up at Will. "You were searching the cottages for Dave?"

"I could've told you that was a waste of time," Delilah said. "Dave would be too afraid to stay in a cottage. My brother would tar his ass."

Will didn't point out that her brother couldn't leave his own house without assistance. "If Dave wanted to get out of here fast without being seen, he wouldn't go back to the main compound. He could follow the creek and eventually hit the McAlpine Trail, right?"

"Theoretically," Delilah said. "Lost Widow Creek is too deep to cross at the lake. You have to get past the big waterfall, and then it's still rough going. Might as well go another two hundred yards and cross on the stone footbridge at the mini waterfall. It's more like a white water section than Niagara Falls. From there, you can make a straight line down through the woods and pick up the McAlpine Trail. You'd be down the mountain in three or four hours. Unless a bear stopped you first."

179

"I dunno," Nadine said. "I don't see Dave going for a hike when the family truck's right by the house. He's been known to jack a vehicle or two when it suits him."

Will had been so sure of who Dave was as a kid that he hadn't thought to ask about his criminal record as an adult. "Has he ever been inside?"

"Early and often," Nadine said. "Dave's been in and out of county lock-up for DUIs, thieving, that kind of thing, but he's never landed himself in Big Boy prison, as far as I know."

Will could guess why Dave had never been sentenced to a state facility, but he tried to be careful. "The McAlpines are close to the sheriff's family."

"Bingo," Nadine said. "If you wanna know what to worry about, Dave's specialty is bar fights. He gets wasted, then he starts needling at people, only when they snap, he's ready with a switch-blade."

"A switchblade?" Sara's voice went up in alarm. "Has he stabbed someone before?"

"Stabbed a leg once, slashed a couple of arms. Opened up one guy's chest to the bone," Nadine said. "People round here don't blink much over a bar fight. Dave took his licks. He gave some out. Nobody died. None of 'em pressed charges. That's a Saturday night."

Delilah said, "I thought Dave only picked on women."

"You're still seeing him as that stray pup looking for a home," Nadine said. "Dave's grown into his badness. All those demons he carried up from Atlanta have gotten older and meaner. Not sure how he's gonna wriggle out of this one, if that's any conso-lation. Murder is murder. That's a life sentence. Should be the death penalty, but he plays the poor battered orphan card better than most."

"I'll believe it when he's behind bars," Delilah said. "He's always been slippery as a snake. Ever since he slithered up the mountain. Cecil should've left him at that old campsite to rot."

Will knew that everything they were saying about Dave was true, but he couldn't help but feel defensive hearing them talk about abandoning a thirteen-year-old kid. He tried to catch Sara's eye, but she was studying the backpack.

"My God, that's where he's hiding!" Delilah exclaimed. "Camp Awinita. Dave used to sleep there when things got bad at the house. I'm sure he's there now."

Will felt like an idiot for not thinking of the campsite sooner. "How long will it take to get there?"

"You look like a sturdy man. It'll take you fifty minutes, maybe an hour. Go past the Shallows, then loop around to the back section of the middle part of the lake. The camp is a forty-five-degree angle from the diving platform, give or take."

"We were in that area before dinner," Will said. "We found a circle of rocks, like an old campfire."

"That's the bead circle for the Camp Fire Girls. It's roughly four hundred yards from the campgrounds, give or take. Too many Boy Scouts were sneaking over in the middle of the night, so they pushed it farther out. What you need to do is stay on the forty-five-degree angle from the diving platform. You'll find some bunkhouses that have been standing since the 1920s. I'm sure they're still there. Dave's bound to be in one of them." Delilah's hands were on her hips. "If you give me a moment to change, I'll take you right to it."

Will said, "That's not happening."

"I agree," Nadine chimed in. "We've already got one woman stabbed to death."

"Actually," Delilah said. "Now that I'm thinking about it, a canoe would be quicker."

Will liked the idea of sneaking up on Dave from the water. "There's a trail to the equipment shed, right?"

"Take Old Bachelor, just past the sawhorses. Go left on the Loop Trail, then back down at the fork toward the lake. The shed's tucked behind some pines."

"I'll go with you," Sara volunteered.

Will was about to shut her down, but then he remembered he only had one good hand. He told Sara, "You have to stay in the boat."

"Understood."

They started to leave, but Nadine was suddenly blocking his way.

"Hold up there, big guy. I've been happy letting you two kids tag along up till now, but Biscuits made it real clear he's not turning over the investigating. You can have the body, but the GBI doesn't have any authorization to be hunting down a murder suspect in Dillon County."

"You're right," Will said. "Tell the sheriff my wife and I are prepared to make our statements when he finds the time. For now, we're heading back to our cottage."

Nadine knew he was full of shit, but she had the sense to stop blocking his way. She stepped aside with a heavy sigh.

Delilah said, "Good luck."

Will followed Sara. She used the flashlight to supplement the changeable moonlight. Instead of following Delilah's directions toward the trail, she kept to the lake shore, probably because the route was more of a direct path to the shed. Will tried to plot out how they would handle the canoe. He could probably use the heel of his injured hand as a fulcrum, then pull back with his good hand, which meant the bulk of the work would need to come from his biceps and shoulders. He tested his bandaged hand. The fingers could move if he ignored the searing pain.

"Do you want my opinion?" Sara asked.

Will hadn't thought that her opinion was any different from his. "What's wrong?"

"There's nothing wrong," she said, sounding like a lot was wrong. "My opinion, if you're interested, is that you should wait for Faith."

Will had waited around long enough. "I told you she hit a traffic jam. If Dave's at the campsite—"

"You're unarmed. You're injured. You're soaking wet from the rain. Your bandage is filthy. You're probably setting up an infection. You're clearly in tremendous pain. You don't have authorization, and you have never paddled a canoe in your life."

Will chose the easiest point to knock down. "I can figure out how to paddle a canoe."

Sara used the light to find a way past the rocky shore. He caught the set look to her face. She was angrier than he'd thought.

"Sara, what do you want me to do?"

Her head started shaking as she splashed through the shallow water. "Nothing."

Will didn't have an argument for *nothing*. What he knew was that Sara was incredibly, consistently logical. She didn't get upset without reason. He silently scrolled back through the conversation at the crime scene. Sara had gone quiet when Nadine had told them that Dave carried a switchblade. And that he had used it on other men.

He studied her stiff back as she picked her way across a rocky incline. Her movements were jerky, like the anxiety was trying to punch its way out of her body.

He said, "Sara."

"You need both hands to perform a forward stroke in a canoe," she lectured. "Your dominant hand is the control hand. It goes on the top of the paddle at the palm grip. Your stroke hand goes on the shaft. You have to be able to stroke the paddle through the water while you push down and twist the control if you want to keep the canoe straight. Can you twist and stroke with both of your hands?"

"I like it better when you do it."

Sara swung around on him. "I do, too, babe. Let's go back to the cottage and bang one out."

He grinned. "Is this a trick?"

She whispered a filthy curse, then continued her forward momentum.

Will wasn't one to break a long silence. He also wasn't going to argue with her. He kept his mouth closed as they slogged through a dense patch of brush. Sara's sudden burst of anger wasn't the only thing making the hike uncomfortable. He was sweating. The blister on his foot was rearing its ugly head. His hand was still throbbing with every heartbeat. He tried to tighten the bandage. Water dripped from the gauze.

Sara said, "You need to listen to me."

"I'm listening, but I don't know what you're trying to say."

"I'm saying that I'm going to have to paddle the boat by myself to the other side of the lake so we don't go around in circles for the rest of our natural lives."

"At least we'll be together."

She stopped again, turning to face him. There was not even a hint of a smile on her lips. "He carries a switchblade. He cut a man's chest to the bone. Do I have to tell you what organs are in your chest?"

He knew better than to joke this time. "No."

"What you're thinking now—that Dave is pathetic, that he's a loser. All of that's probably true. But he's also a violent criminal. He's not going to want to go back to jail. According to you and everybody else up here, he's already got one murder on his conscience. Adding another isn't going to faze him."

Will could hear the naked fear in her voice. Now he got it. Her first husband had been a cop. The man had underestimated a suspect and ended up dead because of it. There was no good way for Will to tell her that same fate wasn't going to fall on him. He was built differently. He had spent the first eighteen years of his life expecting people to do brutal and violent things, then the subsequent years doing everything he could to stop them.

She reached for his good hand, holding so tightly that he could feel the bones shift.

"My love," she said. "I know what your job is, that you make these life and death choices almost every day, but you need to understand that it's not just your life anymore, and it's not just your death. It's *my* life. It's *my* death."

Will traced his thumb along her wedding band. There had to be a way for them to both get what they wanted. "Sara—"

"I'm not trying to change you. I'm just telling you I'm scared."

Will tried to split it down the middle. "How about this: once I have Dave in custody, I'll go to the hospital with you. A place up here, not down in Atlanta. And you can take care of my hand and Faith can get a confession out of Dave and that will be the end of it."

"How about we do all of that, then you help me look for Jon?"

"That sounds reasonable." Will readily accepted the bargain. He had not forgotten the promise he'd made to Mercy. There were things that Jon needed to hear. "What now?"

Sara looked out over the water. Will followed her gaze. They were close to the equipment shed. Moonlight bathed the diving board on the floating dock.

She said, "I'm not sure how long it will take me to get us across. Twenty minutes? Thirty? I haven't paddled a canoe since Girl Scouts."

Will guessed back then she hadn't been dragging the dead weight of a grown man who couldn't hold a paddle. On the return trip, there would hopefully be two grown men. Which brought its own problems. Will's water attack fantasy hadn't gone past taking Dave down. He would have to hike the murderer out of the campsite rather than bring him back across the water. There was no way he was going to have Sara in a boat with Dave.

He said, "I want to check the shed to see if there's any rope."

Sara didn't ask him what the rope was for. She retreated into silence as they resumed the hike, which was somehow worse than when she was yelling at him. He tried to think of something to say that would make her less worried, but Will had learned the hard way that telling a woman not to feel something was not the best way to stop her from feeling that thing. In fact, it tended to make her furious on top of feeling that thing.

Fortunately, the journey didn't take that much longer. Sara's flashlight caught the canoes first, all stored upside-down on a rack. The equipment shed was roughly the size of a two-car garage. The double doors had a serious latch considering the place was so isolated. The spring-loaded chain-grip slide bolt had a foot-long metal bar that had to be flipped over to release the latch. A spring safety latch looped through the end of the bar, pinning it to a hasp lock on the door.

By way of explanation, Sara said, "Bears can open doors, too."

Will let her twist open the hasp, then he took over pushing the metal bar. The mechanism was tight. He had to put his shoulder into it, but finally, the doors swung open. Will caught a weird mixture of wood smoke and fish.

Sara coughed at the smell, waving her hand in front of her face as she walked into the shed. She found the light switch on the wall. The fluorescent bulbs revealed a neatly ordered workshop. Tools were outlined with blue tape on a pegboard. Fishing poles were on hooks. Nets and baskets lined an entire wall. There was a stone countertop with a sink and well-used cutting board. Two sets of scissors and four knives of varying lengths were hanging from a magnetic strip. All but one of the blades was slim and non-serrated.

Will was a gun guy, not a knife guy. He asked Sara, "Is anything missing?"

"Not that I can tell. It's a standard set for cleaning fish." Sara pointed them out from first to last. "Bait knife. Boning knife. Fillet knife. Chunk knife. Dressing scissors. Line snip."

Will didn't see any rope. He started opening drawers. Everything was arranged in sections. Nothing was loose. He recognized some of the fasteners from his own garage, but assumed they weren't used on cars. He found what he needed in the last drawer. Whoever was in charge of the shed was too thorough not to have the basics: a roll of duct tape and heavy-duty zip ties.

The ties were neatly bound together with a bungee strap. Will couldn't bind them back with one hand. He felt guilty leaving the ties loose in the drawer, but there were more important things to worry about. Six of the larger ties went into his back pocket. He shoved the roll of tape into a deeper pocket in the leg of his cargo pants.

He was shutting the drawer when he thought about the knives on the wall. Will took the smallest one, the bait knife, and tucked it down the side of his boot. He didn't know how sharp the blade was, but anything could puncture a lung if you rammed it hard enough into a man's chest.

"What's this?" Sara asked. She had cupped her hands around her eyes as she tried to see through the slats in the back wall. "Looks mechanical. Maybe a generator?"

"We'll check with the family." Will found a padlock underneath some hanging metal baskets. He pulled at the hasp, but it was firmly in place. "Bears?"

"Guests, probably. There's no internet or TV. I imagine a lot of late-night drinking goes on. Help me with this." Sara had located the paddles. They were high up to the ceiling, hanging like shotguns on a rack. "The blue one looks like the right size."

Will was surprised by the light weight when he lifted the paddle off the hook.

She said, "Bring two in case one gets lost in the water. I'll get the life jackets."

Will didn't think it was a good idea to wear bright orange as they approached the campsite, but he wasn't going to fight that battle.

Outside the shed, he followed Sara's lead flipping one of the canoes off the rack. There was nothing for Will to do but stand by as she maneuvered the paddles into the hull and tossed in the life jackets. She pointed out the carrying handles around the gunwale, told him where to stand, how to lift. She went silent again as they carried the canoe to the lake. Will tried not to pick up on her anxiety. He had to focus his mind on one singular purpose: bringing Dave to justice.

Sara kept the splashing to a minimum as she walked into the shallow water. Will lowered the boat when she told him to. She lined up the back end so that it was anchored in the mud. He was about to get in when Sara stopped him.

"Hold still." She helped him into one of the life jackets, then made sure the clips were secure. Then she leaned down and held the boat steady so that he could get in.

Will felt needlessly fussed over, but climbing in with one hand was harder than he'd anticipated. He sat on the bench at the rear of the boat. His weight lifted up the bow. Sara's weight only brought it down slightly when she climbed in. She didn't sit on the other bench. She got on her knees and used the paddle to push them out onto the water. She started off using shallow strokes until they'd put some distance between themselves and the shore.

By the time they reached open water, Sara had established a steady rhythm. When it came time to leave the Shallows and navigate into the larger part of the lake, she shifted from one side of the canoe to the other to make the turn. Will tried to keep an idea of where the diving platform was as the boat glided across the expanse. The equipment shed disappeared from sight. Then the shoreline. Soon, all he could see was darkness and all he could hear was the paddle working and the sound of Sara's breathing.

The moon peered around the clouds as they reached the middle of the lake. Will took the opportunity to check the bandage around his hand. Sara was right that the gauze was dirty, and probably also right about the infection. If someone had told Will there was a chunk of white-hot coal inside the web between his finger and thumb, he would've believed them. The burning slightly lessened when he lifted his hand to chest level, resting it on the edge of the life vest.

He reached down to his boot, checking on the bait knife. The handle was thick enough to keep the blade from sliding down to his ankle. He pulled out the knife, testing the motion. He hoped like hell Dave wasn't tracking their progress across the water. Will wanted the knife to be a surprise if things went sideways. The neon orange vests felt like they were glowing. He scanned the horizon, searching for the shore. It came into view slowly. First some lighter patches among the blackness, then he could make out rocks, then eventually what looked like a sandy beach.

Sara glanced back at him. She didn't have to say it. A sandy beach meant they had found the campgrounds. It was in bad shape. Will saw the remnants of a rotted-out dock, a partially submerged boat launch. A rope dangled from a towering oak tree, but the wooden seat that had turned it into a swing had dropped into the water long ago. There was something haunting about the place. Will wasn't one to believe in ghosts, but he had always trusted his gut, and his gut was telling him that bad things had happened here.

The canoe started to slow. Sara reversed the strokes as they approached the beach. Up close, he could see weeds growing through the sand. Broken bottles. Cigarette butts. The edge of the boat made a grinding sound as it banked onto the shore. Will unclipped his life vest and let it drop. Again, he thought about the bait knife in his boot, but this time it was in relation to leaving Sara unprotected. The best thing to do was send her back to the shed. He could hike to the lodge with or without Dave.

"No." She had a bad habit of reading his mind. "I'll wait for you ten yards out."

Will got out of the boat before she told him she was going to supervise the search. Nobody would've called his dismount graceful. He tried to keep the splashing to a minimum as he righted himself onto solid ground. Then he used the steel toe of his boot to give Sara a firm push back onto the water.

He waited until she started working the paddle before he scanned the forest. First light had yet to break, but the terrain was more visible than it had been when they'd left the equipment shed. He turned to find Sara again. She was paddling backward, keeping her eyes trained on Will. He thought about watching her swim toward the floating dock in the Shallows only a few hours ago. She was doing the backstroke, inviting him to join her. Will had felt such elation that his heart had turned into a butterfly.

And across the water, Dave was raping and stabbing the mother of his child.

Will turned away from the canoe and walked into the woods. He tried to get his bearings. Nothing looked familiar from their earlier search for the campsite. It wasn't just the lack of light. Before, they had approached from the back end of the Shallows. They'd stopped when they'd reached the circle of rocks. Will slipped his phone out of his pocket and tapped open the compass app as he headed in what he hoped was the right direction.

The forest was dense and overgrown, more so than the uncleared areas around the lodge. Using his flashlight app would be tantamount to lighting a beacon. He turned down the brightness on his screen as he followed the compass. After a while, Will realized that he didn't need it. There was the musty scent of smoke in the air. Fresh, like a campfire burning, but with a revolting undertone of cigarettes.

Dave.

Will didn't immediately move toward the target. He stood absolutely still, focusing on regulating his breathing and quieting his mind. Any worries about Sara, the pain in his hand, even Dave, were pushed to the side. The only thing he thought about was the person who truly mattered.

Mercy McAlpine.

Only a few hours ago, Will had found the woman clinging to the last few moments of her life. She had known it was the end. Refused to let Will go for help. He was on his knees in the water, begging Mercy to tell him who was responsible for the attack, but she had shaken her head like none of it mattered. And she was right. In those final moments, none of it really did matter. The only person she cared about was the person she had brought into the world.

Will silently repeated the message he would relay to Jon—

Your mother wants you to get away from here. She said you can't stay. She wanted you to know it's okay. That she loves you so much. That she forgives you for the argument. I promise you that you're going to be okay.

Will continued forward at a deliberate pace, careful not to step on any fallen branches or piles of leaves that might alert Dave to his presence. As he got closer, the silence of the forest was broken by the soft beat of "1979" by the Smashing Pumpkins. The music was turned down low, but it offered enough cover for Will to move more freely toward the source.

He altered his trajectory, approaching Dave from the side. He saw the outline of a few bunkhouses. All one story, rough-hewn, raised two feet in the air on what looked like telephone poles. There were four houses clustered together in a half circle. Will peered into the windows, scanning the interiors to make sure Dave was alone. In the last bunkhouse, he saw a sleeping bag, some boxes of cereal, cartons of cigarettes and cases of beer. Dave had planned on being here for a while. Will wondered if that would help him build a case for premeditation. There was a difference between a spur of the moment murder and one where you carefully planned your escape ahead of time.

Will kept himself low as he carefully approached his target. The fire Dave had built wasn't blazing, but it was generous enough to illuminate his immediate surroundings. He'd also done Will the courtesy of bringing a Coleman lantern that was giving off upwards to eight hundred lumens, the rough equivalent of a sixty-watt light bulb.

Dave had always been afraid of the dark.

The large, circular clearing wasn't as overgrown as the rest of the grounds. Boulders cropped up around a fire pit. Stumps of trees had been placed for seating. There was a grilling rack that swung out over the pit. Will knew there were more clusters of bunkhouses, more fire pits, scattered around the campsite. Back at the children's home, he had heard stories about nightly marshmallow roasts and impromptu singalongs and scary stories. Those days were long gone. There was an eerie feeling about the circle, more like a place of sacrifice than a place of joy.

Will found a spot behind a large water oak to crouch down.

Dave was leaning against a felled log that was about four feet long and maybe eighteen inches in diameter. Will debated strategies. Surprise Dave from the rear? Jump him before he could think to act? Will needed more information.

He carefully moved forward, knees bent, muscles tensed in case Dave turned around. The smell of smoke thickened. The recent rain had made the wood smolder. As Will got closer, he caught a familiar metallic clicking sound. A thumb quickly rotating a friction wheel, the wheel meant to create a spark that ignites the gas from butane, the gas meant to feed a flame that lit the end of a cigarette.

He heard the metallic click again, then again, then again.

It was just like Dave to keep trying a lighter that was clearly empty. He kept flicking the wheel, hoping to pry out one more spark.

Finally, Dave gave up, mumbling, "Fuck, man."

The fact that he had a fire source two feet in front of him didn't give Dave any ideas. Even after he tossed the plastic lighter into the fire. The ensuing spit of flames made Dave throw up his hands to protect his face. Will took the distraction as his chance to close the distance between them. Dave slapped the melted plastic off his forearms. The pain didn't seem to register. It didn't take Sherlock Holmes to figure out why.

Crushed beer cans littered the ground. Will stopped counting after ten. He didn't bother cataloguing the spent joints and cigarette butts, which were all smoked down to the filters. A fishing pole was leaning against an overturned log. The grill had been swiveled out. Stray bits of charred meat were glued to the grate. Dave had used the surface of a tree stump to prepare the fish. Decapitated heads, tails and bones rotted in a pool of dark blood. A long, slender boning knife rested beside a six-pack of beer.

Will calculated that the curved seven-inch blade was easily within Dave's reach. If the man heard a twig snap or the rustling of leaves or even got a bad feeling that someone was coming up behind him, all he had to do was reach out to the tree stump and he was armed with a lethal weapon.

The question was, did Will meet him with his own knife? Will had the element of surprise. He wasn't drunk or stoned. Normally,

Will could confidently predict that he could have Dave pinned to the ground before the man knew what hit him.

Normally, Will had two working hands.

"1979" faded into the blasting guitar of "Tales of a Scorched Earth." Will took the opportunity to reposition himself again. He wasn't going to sneak up on Dave. He was going to approach from the front like he'd followed the trail around the Shallows and ended up here. Hopefully, Dave was too wasted to realize that the meeting wasn't a coincidence.

The time for being stealthy had passed. Will spotted a downed branch on the forest floor. He lifted his foot and stepped on it. The steel-toe boot sounded like an aluminum bat cracking open a gourd. For good measure, Will let out a loud curse. Then he tapped his phone to turn on the flashlight.

By the time Will looked back up, Dave already had the boning knife in his hand. He tapped his phone to pause the song. He stood slowly, scanning the forest with beady eyes.

Will took a few more noisy steps, waving around his phone like he was a caveman who didn't understand how light worked.

"Who's there?" Dave brandished the knife. He'd changed clothes since Will had seen him on the Loop Trail. His jeans were bleach-stained and torn. A bloody hand had swiped across his yellow T-shirt. He slashed the sharp blade through the air, demanding, "Show yourself."

"Shit." Will filled his tone with disgust. "What the fuck are you doing out here, Dave?"

Dave smirked, but he kept the knife raised. "What're *you* doing here, Trashcan?"

"Looking for the campsite. Not that it's your fucking business."

Dave huffed a laugh. He finally lowered the knife. "You're fucking pathetic, man."

Will stepped into the clearing so that Dave could see him. "Just tell me how to get out of here and I'll leave."

"Go back the way you came, dumbass."

"You think I didn't try that already?" Will kept walking toward him. "I've been out in these goddam woods for over an hour."

"You wouldn't see me leaving that sexy little redhead alone." Dave's wet lips twisted into a smirk. "What was her name again?"

"If I ever hear you say it, I'll punch it out of your mouth through the back of your skull."

"Shit," he said, but he backed down easily enough. "Just go left up to the rock circle, then hook a right around the lake, then left back up to the Loop Trail."

Will was a second too late figuring out Dave hadn't backed down at all. Telling a dyslexic to go left then right was the equivalent of telling him to go fuck himself.

Dave started chuckling as he took his place back in front of the fire. He leaned against the felled log, returned the boning knife to its place on the tree stump. Will could tell he expected that to be the end of it. Dave had spent a lifetime getting things wrong. The only question was, at what point did Will tell the man that he was a special agent with the GBI? Technically, nothing that Dave said before that moment, even if he outright confessed to killing Mercy, could be used against him in court. If Will was going to do this right, he had to establish a rapport, then slowly lead Dave into the truth.

He asked, "You got any beer left?"

Dave raised an eyebrow in surprise. The Will he knew from his childhood wasn't a drinker. "When'd you get hair on your balls?"

Will knew how to play this game. "After your mom sucked them dry."

Dave laughed, reaching back to twist a beer off the six-pack. "Pull up a chair."

Will wanted to keep some distance between them. Rather than sitting in front of the fire alongside Dave, he leaned his back against a boulder. He rested his phone beside his bad hand. He bent his knee to keep the bait knife in his boot close to his good hand. He had to be prepared if Dave decided to put up a fight.

Dave didn't seem like he was thinking about fighting. He was too busy looking for ways to be an asshole. He could've tossed the can of beer to Will, but he spiraled it like a football.

Will caught it in one hand. He opened it one-handed, too, making sure the spray hit the fire.

Dave nodded, clearly impressed. "What happened to your hand? You get a little too rough with your lady? She looks like a biter."

Will held back the response that wanted to come. He had to put it all aside—the sense of betrayal and fury that still festered from their childhoods. The disgust over what kind of man Dave had turned out to be. The brutal way he had murdered his wife. The fact that he had abandoned his son to pick up the pieces.

Instead, Will held up his bandaged hand, saying, "Cut it on a piece of broken glass at dinner."

"Who patched you up? Was it Papa?" Dave clearly enjoyed the cruelty of the joke. He stared into the fire with a smug grin on his face. His hand went under his shirt as he scratched his belly. Will could see deep gouges where someone had scratched him. There was another scratch on the side of his neck. By all evidence, he had recently been in a violent altercation.

Will placed the can of beer on the ground beside his boot. He rested his hand beside it, making sure the bait knife was in reach. The best-case scenario would leave it tucked inside his sock. A lot of cops thought the way you met violence was with violence. Will wasn't one of those cops. He wasn't here to punish Dave. He was going to do far worse than that. He wanted to arrest him. To put him in jail. To make him suffer through the stress and helplessness of being a defendant in a criminal trial. To let him have that boundless sense of hope that he might possibly get away with it. To see the crushing look on his face when he realized that he hadn't. To know that he would have to scramble and claw every day for the rest of his life because inside the prison walls, men like Dave were always at the bottom of the pyramid.

And none of that took into account the death penalty.

Dave let out a pained sigh to fill the silence. He picked up a stick. Stoked the fire. He kept glancing over at Will, waiting for him to say something.

Will wasn't going to say something.

Dave waited less than a minute before he let out another pained sigh. "You keep up with anybody from back then?"

Will shook his head, though he knew a lot of their former housemates had ended up in prison or in the ground.

"What happened to Angie?"

"I don't know." Will felt his hands wanting to clench into fists, but he kept both of them resting on the ground. "We were married a few years. Didn't work out."

"She fuck around on you?"

Will knew Dave already had the answer. "What about you and Mercy?"

"Shit." Dave poked at the fire until it sparked. "She never ran around on me. Had it too good at home."

Will forced out a laugh. "Sure."

"Believe whatever you want, Trashcan. I'm the one what left her. Got tired of her bullshit. All she ever does is complain about this place, then she gets a chance to leave, and . . ."

Will waited for him to say more, but Dave dropped the stick and grabbed a fresh beer. He didn't speak again until the can was drained and laying crushed on the ground.

"They had to close this place down. Too many counselors diddling the kiddies."

Will shouldn't have been surprised. This wasn't the first time the idyllic setting he'd imagined as a child had been spoiled by a predator.

Dave asked, "Why'd you come up here, Trashcan? You never wanted to see the camp when we was kids. You were better at memorizing them Bible verses than I ever was."

Will shrugged. He wasn't going to tell Dave the truth, but he needed to come up with a believable story. He remembered what Delilah had said about the circle of rocks. "My wife used to come here when she was in the Camp Fire Girls. She wanted to see it again."

"You married a Camp Fire Girl? Does she still got the uniform?" He snorted a laugh. "Jesus Christ, how is it fucking Trashcan's living in a porn movie while I'm lucky if I find poon that ain't stretched out like a gummy bear?"

Will steered the conversation back to Mercy. "Your ex gave you a son. That's something."

Dave opened another beer.

Will said, "Jon seems like a nice kid. Mercy did a good job with him."

"Wasn't all her doing." Dave slurped foam off the top of the can. He hadn't downed it like the previous one. He was pacing himself now. "Jon always knows where to find me. He's gonna make a fine man one day. Good lookin' too. Probably catching OPP like his daddy at that age."

Will ignored the dig, which was clearly meant to invoke Angie. "You ever think you'd end up married?"

"Shit no." Dave's laugh was filled with a tinge of bitterness. "Being honest, I thought I'd be dead by now. It's dumb luck I made it up here from Atlanta without some pervert picking me up on the side of the road and trafficking me to Florida."

Will knew he was trying to brag about running away. "You hitched?"

"Sure did."

"It's not a bad place to hide out." Will made a show of looking around the campsite. "When you disappeared, I told them this was where you'd go."

"Yeah, well." Dave cocked back his elbow on the log.

Will tried not to react. Dave had managed to position his hand closer to the knife. Whether this was intentional or not remained to be seen.

Dave said, "I knew who I was the first time I came up here on that church bus, you know? Like, I could fish and hunt and feed myself. Didn't need nobody looking after me. I wasn't built for living in a city. I was a rat down there. I'm a mountain lion up here. Do what I want. Say what I want. Smoke what I want. Drink what I want. Nobody can fuck with me."

It sounded great until you understood his freedom came at a price that Mercy had paid. "You were lucky the McAlpines took you in."

"There were good days and bad days," Dave said, always teasing out a bad story. "Bitty, she's an angel. But Papa? Shit, he's a mean motherfucker. Used to beat the hell outta me with his leather belt."

Will was not surprised to hear that Cecil McAlpine had been physically abusive.

"He didn't care if the belt slipped and I got whacked with the buckle. I used to get these big welts all over my ass and down my legs. Couldn't wear shorts cause I didn't want the teachers to see. All I needed was them dragging me back to Atlanta."

"They could've placed you up here."

"Didn't want it," he said. "Bitty needed the money from the state just to put food on the table. I couldn't abandon her, especially to him."

Will was familiar with an abused child's need to help everyone but themselves.

"Anyways." Dave gave a practiced shrug. "What about you, Trash? What happened when I left your pathetic ass?"

"I aged out of the system. Turned eighteen, got a hundred dollars and a bus ticket. Ended up at the Salvation Army."

Dave hissed air between his teeth. He probably thought he knew how bad things could get for an unaccompanied teenager sleeping in a homeless shelter.

He did not know.

Dave asked, "Then what?"

Will skirted the truth, which was that he'd ended up sleeping on the street, then sleeping in a jail cell. "I managed to figure it out. Put myself through college. Got a job."

"College?" He huffed a laugh. "How'd you manage that with barely being able to read?"

"Hard work," Will said. "Sink or swim, right?"

"You're damn right about that. All that bad shit we went through when we was little, it made us survivors."

Will didn't like his tone of shared camaraderie, but Dave was a murder suspect. He could use whatever tone he wanted so long as he ended up confessing. Will asked, "The McAlpines didn't have a problem with you hooking up with Mercy?"

"Hell yeah they did. Papa used a fucking chain on me when she wound up pregnant. Kicked me off the mountain. Her, too." Dave's raspy chuckle turned into a cough. "I took care of Mercy, though. Made sure she was clean when Jon was born. Helped Delilah get him settled in. Gave her whatever money I could spare to help."

Will knew for a fact that he was lying. "You didn't want to raise him yourself?"

"Shit. What do I know about taking care of no baby?"

Will figured if you were man enough to make a baby, you should be man enough to figure out how to take care of one.

Dave asked, "You got kids?"

"No." Sara wasn't capable, and Will knew too many terrible things that could happen to a child. "Seems like there's still a lot of bad blood between Mercy and her family."

"You think?" Dave knocked back the rest of his beer. He crushed the can, then dropped it with the others. "It's hard this far up the mountain. You're isolated. Not much to do. You got rich, stuck-up bitches expecting you to wipe their skinny, tight asses. Papa pushing you around. Taking you to the barn to beat the fire outta your ass cause you didn't put the towels in the right place."

Will knew Dave wasn't just venting. He was looking for a gold medal in the Abused Kids Olympics. "Sounds pretty bad."

"It sure as hell was," Dave said. "You and me learned the hard way you just gotta count the minutes until it's over, right? They'll get tired eventually."

Will looked into the fire. He was cutting a little too close.

"This is why we lie," Dave said. "You tell this shit to a normal person, they can't take it."

Will kept his eyes on the flames. He couldn't find the words to change the subject.

"You tell your wife all that shit you been through?"

Will shook his head, but that wasn't completely true. He had told Sara some things, but he would never tell her all the things.

"What's it like?" Dave waited for Will to look up. "Your wife, she's normal, right? What's that like?"

Will could not bring Sara into this moment.

"Don't think I could be with a normal woman," Dave admitted. "Mercy, she came to me damaged. I knew what to do with that. But fuck, a Camp Fire Girl? And a schoolteacher? How the hell do you even make that work?"

Will shook his head again, but in truth, things had been hard with Sara at first. He'd kept waiting for the games, the emotional manipulation. He couldn't accept that she would listen to him and try to understand instead of collecting his secrets like razor blades she could use to slice him open later on.

"She's smokin' hot. I'll give you that. But hell, I couldn't be with somebody that perfect. Does she even fart?"

Will couldn't stop himself from laughing, but he didn't answer.

"Gotta be a gentleman, huh?" Dave reached for his pack of cigarettes. "That's the other part I couldn't swing. I need a gal knows how to scream when I grab her by the hair."

Will pretended to drink from his can of beer. His words had put Will back at the lake shore by the bachelor cottages. The way Mercy's hair had spread out in the water. Blood had swirled around her body like dye. She had clutched Will's shirt collar, keeping him beside her instead of letting him find help.

Jon.

Will put both his hands back on the ground, anchoring himself. "Why'd you come find me on the trail yesterday?"

Dave shrugged as he dug around for another lighter in his pocket. "I don't know, man. I do shit and I look back at it and I can't tell you why."

"You asked me if I was still carrying around a grudge against you."

"And?"

"I honestly never thought about you after you ran away."

"That's good, Trash, cause I never thought about you, neither."

"To be honest, I would've totally forgotten about you again." Will tested the waters. "Except for what you did to Mercy."

Dave didn't react at first. He shook the lighter. The flame caught. He touched it to the tip of the cigarette. He blew a jet of smoke in Will's direction.

He asked, "Did you follow me?"

Will had only seen Dave once before Mercy's death. He was waiting for Will on the Loop Trail. Will had given him to the count of ten to leave. "You mean, did I follow you after you ran off with your tail between your legs?"

"I didn't run off, dumbfuck. I chose to walk away."

Will said nothing, but it made sense that Dave would slink away from Will, then find Mercy to take out his anger on.

"Shit, I know you followed me, you pathetic asshole," Dave said. "I sure as hell know Mercy didn't tell nobody. She's a lot of things, but she ain't no snitch."

Will noticed he was still talking about Mercy in the present tense. "You sure about that?"

"Hell yeah I'm sure." Dave smoked. He was nervous. "What do you think you saw?"

Will assumed he was worried about the strangulation. "I saw you choke her."

"She didn't pass out," he said, as if that was a defense. "She fell against the tree, then her ass hit the ground. I had nothing to do with that. Her legs give out. That's all."

Will stared his credulity into him.

"Look, dude, whatever you think you saw, that's between me and her." Dave threw his hand in the air, then rested it in his lap. He flicked the cigarette end, knocking off the ash. "Why are you even asking? You sound like a fucking cop."

Will guessed now was as good a time as any to give him the news. "I am, actually."

"You *am* what?"

"I'm a special agent with the Georgia Bureau of Investigation."

Smoke puffed out of his mouth as he laughed. Then he stopped laughing. "For real?"

"Yep," Will said. "That's what got me through college. I wanted to help people. Kids like us. Women like Mercy."

"That's bullshit, man." Dave pointed at him with his cigarette. "Ain't no cop ever helped kids like us. Look at what you're doing here now, asking me about some private shit that happened a couple'a three hours ago. Ain't no way Mercy filed a report. You're just all up in my business cause that's what you fuckers do."

Will slowly moved his injured hand across the ground until he felt the edge of his phone. "You're right. Mercy didn't file a report. I can't arrest you for strangling her."

"Damn right you can't."

"But if you wanted to admit to abusing your wife, I'd be happy to take your confession."

Dave laughed again. "Sure, man, give it your best shot."

Will forced his thumb to double click the button on the side of his phone, turning on the recording app. "Dave McAlpine, you have the right to remain silent. Anything you say or do can be used against you in a court of law."

Dave laughed again. "Yeah, I'm gonna be silent."

"You have the right to an attorney."

"Cain't afford no attorney."

"If you can't afford an attorney, one will be provided for you by the courts."

"Or the courts can suck my fat dick."

"With these rights in mind, are you willing to talk to me?"

"Sure, dude, let's talk about the weather. Rain passed real quick, but we're gonna get more. Let's talk about the good ol' days at the children's home. Let's talk about that tight little snatch you got up at your cottage. Why you down here dickin' around with ol' Dave when you could be pounding it into that throat goat?"

"I know you strangled Mercy on the trail this afternoon."

"So what? Mercy likes being roughed up every now and then. And there ain't no way in hell she's gonna turn me in for it." Dave sounded smugly confident. "Stay the fuck out of my business or you're gonna figure out real soon what kind of man I grew up to be."

Will wasn't satisfied with getting Dave admitting to domestic violence. He wanted more. "Tell me what happened tonight."

"What about tonight?"

"Where were you?"

Dave smoked his cigarette, but something had changed. He had talked to enough cops to know when one was asking him for an alibi.

Will said, "Where were you, Dave?"

"Why? What happened tonight?"

"You tell me."

"Shit." He sucked on the cigarette. "Something bad went down, didn't it? You weren't just wandering around out here like a dumbass. What are we talking about? State crime, right? Drug deal go bad? You on to some traffickers?"

Will said nothing.

"That's why it's you and not fucking Biscuits." Dave sucked down to the filter. "Fucking bullshit, man."

Will still said nothing.

"What now?" Dave said. "You think you're gonna take me in, motherfucker? With your one hand and your bullshit story about seeing me strangle my wife?"

"Mercy isn't your wife anymore."

"She's mine, you fucking piece of shit. Mercy belongs to me. I can do whatever the fuck I want to her."

"What'd you do to her, Dave?"

"None of your goddam business. This is some bullshit." He flicked his cigarette into the fire. He didn't yank another beer off the pack. He didn't rest his hand in his lap. He leaned back again, resting his elbow on the log, putting the boning knife within easy reach.

This time, the movement was clearly deliberate.

Dave tried to pretend that it wasn't. "Get outta here with your bullshit."

"Why don't you get out of here with me?"

Dave snorted again. He wiped his nose with his arm, but it was only an excuse to put himself closer to the boning knife.

Will ignored the searing pain in his injured hand as he gripped it into a fist. He used his good hand to push up the leg of his pants so the handle of the bait knife was out in the open.

Dave said nothing. He just licked his lips, eager to get things started. This was what he'd been wanting from the second he'd spotted Will on the Loop Trail. In truth, maybe Will had wanted it, too.

They both stood up at the same time.

The first mistake people made in a knife fight was that they worried too much about the knife. Which was fair. Being stabbed hurt like hell. Belly wounds could put a clock over your grave. A straight shot to the heart could send you there quicker.

The second mistake people made in a knife fight was the same mistake most people made in any type of fight. They assumed it would be fair. Or at least that the other person would play fair.

Dave had been in his share of knife fights. He clearly knew the two mistakes. He kept the boning knife straight out in front of him while he reached for the switchblade in his back pocket. His plan was clever enough. Distract Will with one knife while he plunged in the other.

Fortunately, Will had his own clever plan. He knew that Dave's primary concern was the bait knife. He wasn't thinking about Will's injured hand. He hadn't noticed that Will had grabbed a handful of dirt. Which was why he was so surprised when Will slashed it into his face.

"Fuck!" Dave staggered back. He dropped the boning knife, but muscle memory kept his dominant hand in play.

Nadine had been wrong about the switchblade, which only required the push of a button to release the blade. Dave carried a butterfly knife. It served as both a lethal weapon and a distraction. Two metal handles folded like a clamshell around the sharp, narrow blade. Opening it with one hand required a quick figure-eight movement of the wrist. You pinched the safe handle with your thumb and fingers while you flipped the latched handle over your knuckles. Then you rotated the safe handle, swung the latch handle over your knuckles again, flipped it back home, and you ended up wielding a ten-inch-long knife.

Will didn't give a shit about the knife.

He swung back his leg and drove his steel-toe boot straight up into Dave's groin.

January 16, 2014

Dear Jon—

I've had you back with me for three years now, which means there are gonna be more years of us being together than years that we were apart. I know it's been a long time since I wrote you a letter, but maybe it'll be easier if I tell myself it's only going to be once a year, especially since it seems like January is the month my life always gets turned upside-down. I'm choosing January sixteenth because that's what I think of as your gotcha day. I'm gonna be honest and tell you I got that phrase from Aunt Delilah. She's got a ton of dogs and who knows when their actual birthdays are, but she calls the day they came to live with her their gotcha day. So three years ago is your gotcha day, the day I brought you back to the mountaintop to live with me so I could be your full-time mother.

Not that you're a stray dog, but I was just thinking about it because this morning I was missing her. I know that's stupid to say since Delilah's the one that took you from me to begin with, and I had to fight something fierce to get you back, but Delilah was always the one I ran to when things got bad. And things are really bad now.

The truth is, not a day goes by that I don't think about drinking and drugging, but then I think about you and our lives together and I don't do it. The thing is, something bad happened with your daddy over the holidays and before I knew it, I was at the liquor store buying a bottle of Jack. Couldn't even wait to get home. I just popped the top in the parking lot and nearly downed the whole thing in a couple of gulps. It's funny how you don't even taste it after a while. You just feel the burn and then your head swims and I'm not ashamed to say it's

204

been so long since I got my drink on that I threw it right back up.

There was a time maybe when things were bad enough that I'd get that alcohol back in me one way or another, but that wasn't this time. I threw the bottle in the trash. Then I sat in the car a long while and thought about what brought me there.

Your daddy almost killed me is the plain way of saying it. It was New Year's Eve and he threw himself a big party and smoked a lot of meth, which he's done before but this musta been a bad batch. He was like a possessed devil and it scared the shit out of me. He was tearing around trashing the trailer and I was yelling back at him, which I probably shouldn't of done, but baby I'm so damn tired.

Your daddy isn't a bad man, but he can do some bad things. He'll get a little money in his pocket and bet it on a hail Mary or party all week and then it's gone. Then he'll blame me for not stopping him from blowing through all his money. Then he'll bug me until I give up whatever cash I got stashed away, even if it means we can't buy groceries or keep the power turned on, and none of this is the worst of it, cause on top of it all he's been cheating on me.

I mean he's cheated on me before, but this time he chose a girl I work with. Who I thought was my friend. Not a friend like Gabbie, but a friend anyway that I could talk to and pass the time with. The both of them thought they were so damn clever sneaking around right under my nose, but I could tell something was going on. I just held my tongue because your daddy was only doing it to hurt me, and God knows we've been here before, but I wasn't up for going through the same thing again where he cheats on me then begs me to come back and then once I'm back he cheats again.

What he did this time was, he made sure he was fucking her in one of the motel rooms I was assigned to clean. The schedule is on our fridge he sees every time he gets himself a beer, is how I know he knew. She knew, too, because her name is on the damn schedule. And there they both were fucking up a storm in that very room when I walked in with a bunch of towels and sheets in my hands. I know your daddy was expecting me to blow my top, but I didn't. I just didn't have it in me to say anything. I ain't never seen him so shocked as when I just backed out of that room and shut the door like it didn't matter.

And being honest, it didn't.

I told you this has happened before with the cheating, but it was only this time that I could see things had changed. And when I say changed, I mean inside me. You'll see that as you get older sometimes you can look back and see a pattern. The pattern with your daddy was, he cheats, I find out, there's a blow-up and a beat down and then he turns sweet in case I get any ideas about leaving. This time, we skipped the blow-up and the beating and went straight to your daddy being sweet. Taking out the trash, picking his clothes up off the floor, even cranking my car in the morning so it'd be warmed up for me. One day I caught him singing to you and it was real pretty but it stopped as soon as I left the room.

See, I didn't give him the reaction he wanted, which was to throw myself at his feet and beg him to stay. I don't know what it is about your daddy that's so broken inside, and it's hard to explain, but what he wants most in the world is for people to get desperate enough that all they got left is to cling to him.

And then when they're clinging, he hates them for it.

What kept me going this time was I promised myself that you and me would be out of that godforsaken trailer by the end of January. But I wasn't gonna be a sneak about it. Sneaking is your daddy's territory. I thought about this a lot, and I had it set in my mind that the right thing to do was to tell him we were leaving instead of packing up all our shit and moving out while he was gone. Anyway, it wasn't like I could really get away from him since we live in the same damn town. Also, there's you. I can't stand being around him anymore, but Dave is still your daddy, and I'm not gonna take you away from him no matter what terrible things he does to me.

Anyway, he'll tell you I was a bitch for leaving him, but I want you to know I didn't plan on being a bitch. I wanted to keep it civil. So I brought him a beer and sat him down on the couch and said that he needed to listen to me cause I had something important to say.

He was dead quiet right up until I mentioned the apartment in town. I guess that's when it got real for him, and also looking back I think that's when he realized I hadn't told him about all the money. He asked me how much the deposit was, did it come furnished, where I'd park, did you have your own room, that kind of thing. Which I stupidly at the time took to mean he wanted to make sure it was safe for you and me. I made a point of promising him that he could come by and see you whenever he wanted. I said a couple or three times how important he is to you, that I always want you to have your daddy in your life. Which is true, because I'm saying the same thing to you in this letter.

What he wanted to know next was about child support and that kind of thing, which honest to God I hadn't even considered. Ain't no judge alive who can get money out of Dave's pocket. He'll either go to prison or his grave before he parts with a penny, even for somebody he loves. Even if that somebody is you. Anyway, he was real calm through all of it, smoking and nodding and drinking and not saying much more than those questions, then when I went quiet, he asked me if I was finished talking. I said yes. He put out his cigarette. And then he went fucking nuts.

I'm not gonna lie. I was expecting him to punish me, so I was prepared for the beat down that was coming. Your daddy ain't creative when it comes to hurting me, but there are a couple things he's never done before that he did that night. One was he pulled out his knife. The other was he choked me.

Now when I read back through that, it makes it sound like he was gonna use his knife on me. That ain't true. He was gonna use it on himself. And while I sure as hell don't want to be married to him anymore, I don't want your daddy to die, especially by his own hand. The Lord turned his back on me a long while ago, but I know for damn sure he doesn't forgive people who take their own lives and I would never wish eternal hell on your daddy.

That's why I nearly lost it when I saw that blade draw blood from his neck. I was on my knees on the floor begging him not to do it. He kept saying he loved me, that I was the only person on earth who made him feel like he belonged, and that he lost so much at the children's home and I was the only one who could make it up to him.

I don't know if any of this is true, but what I do know is we were both crying our eyes out by the time he finally put the knife down on the coffee table. All we could do was hold each other for a good long while. I would've said anything to stop him from killing himself. I kept telling him I loved him, that I would never leave him, that we would always be a family.

After that part was over, we both sat on the couch just staring at the wall, so exhausted from our own emotions, but then he says to me, "I'm glad you're not leaving," and that part I could not abide, because I was even more sure after that emotional display that I had to go. What I said was I would always be there for him. That I will always love him, and that I just wanted him to be happy.

Then I guess the mistake I made was I shoulda just left it at that, but I had to open my stupid mouth and tell him that I wanted to be happy, too, and there was no way either of us would ever be really happy while we were still together.

I have never seen your daddy move as fast as he did then. Both his hands went around my neck. The scary thing was, he wasn't even yelling. I've never heard him be so quiet. He was just watching me, his eyes all bugged out as he strangled me. I felt like he wanted to kill me. And maybe he thought he did kill me. I don't wanna be woo-woo about this, cause I'm not psychic or anything, but I would swear to you on a stack of Bibles that even after I passed out, I knew what was going on.

The closest I can come to describing it is, I was hovering up by the ceiling, and I looked down and saw myself lying there on that ugly green carpet that I could never get clean. I remember feeling embarrassed because my pants were wet like I'd pissed myself, which ain't happened in a good long while, not since I gave up the drink and drugs. Anyway, your daddy was still choking me out while I watched from the ceiling.

Then he gave me one last shove and stood up. Instead of leaving out the door, he just stared down at me.

And stared. And stared.

It was the look on his face that struck me most, cause there was no expression. Just a few minutes before, he was sobbing and all emotional threatening to kill himself, and then he went to nothing. Absolutely nothing. And it come to me that this was maybe the first time I've really seen him for who he is. That the crying Dave or the laughing Dave or the high Dave or the angry Dave or even the Dave who pretends he loves me ain't the Dave that he is at all.

The real Dave is empty inside.

I don't know what all those foster parents took from him, or the PE teacher who abused him, but they dug down so deep into his soul that there was nothing else left. Sure as shit nothing was left for me. Being honest, I don't even know if he's got anything in there for you.

I'm gonna be real with you, it shook me seeing him like that. More so than losing my breath, which was something I've been terrified of since I was little. And that made me wonder what else Dave's been hiding.

God knows he loves your grandma Bitty something fierce, but did he ever really love me? Did he ever care? In his own way, he gave me time to figure it out. He's in jail now on account of getting into another bar fight after he finished with me. Which is what he deserves, but still I'm worried about him. Jail is a hard place for men like your daddy. He has a habit of pissing people off. And I'm really scared of him getting out if you want to know the whole truth. I'm scared of that empty man who was looking down at me like a fly he'd just pulled the wings off of.

And all that makes me worry about you, baby. You know there's nothing you could do that I wouldn't forgive, but your daddy ain't happy being the way he is. Nobody could be happy with that. He's so empty the only thing that fills him up is getting emotions off other people. Sometimes that's good when he's buying rounds and being the big man around town. Sometimes that's bad when he's smoking meth and tearing up his trailer. And sometimes it's really bad when he's choking me so hard that I'm thinking I'm gonna die. And then I'm looking at his face and what I'm seeing is that the only thing he has ever enjoyed in his life is shifting his misery onto other people.

Lord, this is a dark tale of a man. Maybe you will never see that side of him. I hope that you never do, because it's like staring into the mouth of hell. Your daddy can do whatever he wants to me, but he ain't never, ever, gonna raise a hand to you. But I'm not gonna be the kind of ex-wife who turns her child against his father, neither. If you end up thinking he's a bad man, it's gonna be because you saw it for yourself with your own two eyes.

So I'm gonna end this letter by telling you three good things about your daddy.

One is, I know this is gross and I've been saying from the beginning that it ain't true, but your daddy is family to me. He ain't like your uncle Fish in that he's like a brother, but he's close to that, and I'm not gonna deny it to you of all people.

Two is, he can still make me laugh. That might not sound like a lot, but I haven't had much joy in my life, which is why it's so hard for me to let him go. Me and Dave didn't start out like this. There was a time when your daddy was everything to me. It was him I ran to when Papa came after me. It was him I confided in. Him I wanted to please. He was so much older than me and had been through so much bad shit that I felt like he understood me. I never even really wanted him. I just wanted him to want me. But don't go feeling sorry for your daddy. He knew what was up and he was fine with it. Even happy with it. I hope you don't ever have to feel that for yourself, where you're in a situation where you'd rather be tolerated than loved.

Anyway, that's enough about that.

Three is, your daddy saved my life when I got into that car accident. I know that sounds dramatic, but he really did save me. Visited me in the hospital. Held my hand. Told me I was still pretty when we both knew that wasn't never gonna be the truth. Said it wasn't my fault when we both knew that wasn't true, either. I've only ever seen him treat one other person that gentle, and that's Bitty. Honestly, I think I've been chasing that version of Dave ever since. Anyway, I don't want to dig too far into that part in my misery, but let's just say your daddy stepped up.

So that's what I want you to know about him, especially that third thing. And that's probably why a part of me will always love him, even though I'm pretty sure that one day he's gonna kill me.

I love you forever,

Mama

11

Faith Mitchell stared at the clock on the wall.

5:54 in the morning.

Exhaustion had slammed into her body like a tank that was on fire. She had been fueled by a sense of urgency as she'd battled her way through horrendous traffic to get here, but all of that had come to a screeching halt inside the waiting room of the Dillon County Sheriff's Office.

The front door had been unlocked, but no one was at reception. No one had answered her knock on the locked glass partition or appeared when she rang the bell. No cruisers were parked in the empty lot. No one was answering the phone.

For the millionth time, she looked at her watch, which was twenty-two seconds ahead of the clock on the wall. Faith stood on the chair to move the second hand forward. If someone was watching her through the security camera in the corner, she hoped that they would call the police.

No such luck.

Douglas "Biscuits" Hartshorne had told Faith to meet him at the station, but that had been twenty-three minutes ago. He hadn't returned multiple calls and texts. Will's phone was either out of range or his battery had died. Sara's went straight to voicemail. No one was answering the phone at the McAlpine Family Lodge. According to their website, the only way into the place was to hike up a mountain, which sounded like a punishment that was meted out to the Von Trapp children before Maria showed up with her guitar.

All that Faith could do was pace back and forth across the

room. She wasn't actually sure what her job was at the moment. Her one phone call with Will had been staticky because of the torrential downpour, but he'd given her enough information to know that a bad thing had happened because of a bad guy. Faith had listened to the audio files he'd texted her during the never-ending drive up to the mountains, and from what Faith could tell, it sounded like Will had pretty much wrapped up the case.

The first recording was like backstory for the worst episode of *Full House* ever. Delilah had offered the rundown on Mercy McAlpine's shitty relations, from her abusive father to her cold mother to her weird brother to her brother's even weirder friend. Then there was the gross stuff about Dave and Mercy, which wasn't exactly incest but wasn't exactly *not* incest. Then Sheriff Biscuits had ambled in after the commercial break expressing zero fucks about a brutally murdered woman and her missing teenaged son. The only pertinent information Faith had learned from the entire conversation was Will's very thorough rundown of how exactly he'd come across the body of Mercy McAlpine. And ended up with a knife in his hand for his trouble.

The second recording was like an episode of *24*, but as if Jack Bauer was actually required to follow the Constitution he had sworn to protect. It started with Will reading Dave McAlpine his Miranda Rights, then Dave admitting to strangling his wife earlier in the day, then a stand-off that led to a scuffle wherein—if Faith knew her partner—Will had kicked Dave so hard in the nuts that the man had projectile vomited.

A warning on this last part would've been nice. Faith had heard it in Dolby digital surround sound from the speakers inside her Mini. She'd been stuck in traffic in the middle of nowhere in the pitch dark in the pissing rain and had to open her door so that she could dry heave onto the pavement.

She looked at the clock again.

5:55.

One more minute down. There couldn't be that many more to go. She dug around in her purse for some trail mix. Her head was aching like she had a low-grade hangover, which made sense considering a handful of hours ago, she had been blissfully living the life of a woman who was not expected to participate in any form of adulting.

In fact, Faith had been enjoying a cold beer in the shower when her phone had made a funny noise. The triple chirping was like a bird perched on her bathroom basin. Her first thought was that her twenty-two-year-old son was too old to be messing with her ringtones. Her second thought put her into a full-on sweat even though she was standing under a stream of water. Her two-year-old daughter had figured out how to change the phone settings. Faith's digital life would never be safe again. A virtual walk of shame flashed in front of her eyes: the selfies, the sexting, the random dick pics that she had absolutely solicited. Faith had nearly dropped her shower beer as she'd bolted out from behind the curtain.

The text was so alien that she had stared at the screen like she had never seen words before.

EMERGENCY SOS REPORT
Crime
INFORMATION SENT
Emergency Questionnaire
Current Location

Lather, rinse, repeat: her first thought was of Jeremy, who was on an ill-advised road trip to Washington DC, if *ill-advised* meant his mother did not want him doing it. Her second thought was of Emma, who was on her first sleepover with a close friend. Which was why Faith's heart was in her throat as she'd scrolled past the response from the satellite relay. Of all the things she had been expecting to read, from a mass shooting to a catastrophic accident to a terrorist attack, what she'd read was so unexpected that she wondered if it was some kind of phishing scam.

GBI special agent Will Trent requesting immediate assistance with murder investigation.

Faith had actually looked at herself in the mirror to check if she was having another crazy work dream. Two days ago, she had danced her ass off at Will and Sara's wedding. They were supposed to be on their honeymoon. There shouldn't be a murder, let alone an investigation, let alone a satellite text for assistance. Faith was so out of it that she had literally jumped when her phone had started to ring. Then she was perturbed that the Caller ID showed her boss, exactly who you wanted to talk to when you were staring at your naked self in your bathroom mirror with a beer in your hand at quarter past one in the morning.

Amanda hadn't bothered with an *I'm sorry to bother you on your week off* like a normal human being who cared about other human beings. All she had given Faith was an order—

"I want you out the door in ten minutes."

Faith had opened her mouth to respond, but Amanda had already ended the call. There was nothing to do but wash the soap off her body and frantically search for some work clothes in the Mount Everest of dirty laundry piled around her washing machine.

And here she was five hours later doing fuck all.

Faith looked at the clock again. She'd shaved off another minute.

She thought of all the things she could be doing right now. Laundry, for one, because her shirt was gamey. Drinking another shower beer. Rearranging her spice cabinet while she listened to NSYNC as loud as she wanted. Playing Grand Theft Auto without having to explain her indiscriminate killing. Not worrying whether Emma was scared about sleeping in a different bed. Not worrying that Emma was loving sleeping in a different bed. Not worrying that Jeremy was on a road trip to tour Quantico in hopes of joining the FBI. Not worrying that the FBI agent who was driving him there happened to be the man Faith was sleeping with, and that they'd been going at it hot and heavy for eight months and Faith still couldn't bring herself to call him anything other than the man she was sleeping with.

And that was just her problems for the right now. Faith had planned on using her week-long holiday to give her sainted mother a break from babysitting Emma. And to remind her daughter that she actually had a mother. Faith had overscheduled the time like she was cramming for a test, booking an afternoon tea at the

Four Seasons, signing up for face-painting lessons and pottery painting lessons, buying tickets to the Center for the Puppetry arts, downloading a kid's audio tour of the botanical gardens, looking into trapeze lessons, trying to find—

Her phone started to ring.

"Thank God," Faith shouted into the empty room. This was not a good time to be trapped with her own thoughts. "Mitchell."

"Why are you at the sheriff's office?" Amanda demanded.

Faith suppressed a curse. She wasn't happy that Amanda could track her phone. "The sheriff told me to meet him at the station."

"He's at the hospital with the suspect." Amanda's tone of voice indicated this was a well-known fact. "It's directly across the street. Why are you dawdling?"

Yet again Faith opened her mouth to respond just as Amanda ended the call.

She grabbed her purse and left the cramped waiting room. Pink clouds tinted the sky. Twilight had finally broken. The street lights were powering down. She took a deep breath of morning air as she picked her way across the railroad tracks that bisected the small downtown area. The city of Ridgeville was not much to write home about. A one-story, 1950s strip mall stretched from one end of the block to the other and was filled with tourist-trappy businesses like antique shops and candle stores.

Ridgeville Medical was two stories of cinder block and glass, the tallest building as far as the eye could see. The parking lot was filled with pick-up trucks and cars that were older than Faith's son. She spotted the sheriff's cruiser by the front door.

"Faith."

"Fuck!" Faith jumped so hard she almost dropped her purse. Amanda had come out of nowhere.

"Watch your language," Amanda said. "It's not professional."

Faith guessed this was her origin story for saying *fuck* the rest of her life.

"What took you so long?"

"I was trapped behind an accident for two hours. How did you get past?"

"How did you not?"

Amanda's phone buzzed. She showed Faith the top of her head

as she looked down at the screen. Her perfectly coifed salt and pepper hair was spiraled into its usual helmet. There was nary a wrinkle on her skirt and matching blazer. Her thumbs were a blur as she responded to a text that would be one of the thousands she received today. Amanda was a deputy director at the GBI, responsible for hundreds of employees, fifteen regional offices, six drug enforcement offices, and over a half dozen specialized units that were active in all 159 of Georgia's counties.

Which begged the question from Faith, "What are you doing here? You know I can handle this."

Amanda's phone went into her jacket pocket. "The sheriff's name is Douglas Hartshorne. His father was on the job for fifty years until a stroke forced him into retirement four years ago. Junior ran unopposed for the office. He seems to have inherited his father's dislike of the agency. I was given a hard no when I offered to take over the case."

"They call him Biscuits," Faith supplied. "Which is good, because I keep wanting to say Douglath like Mr. Dink."

"Do I look like a person who would enjoy that reference?"

Amanda looked like a person who was walking into the hospital. Faith followed her into the waiting room, which was packed with misery. All of the chairs were filled. People were leaning against the walls as they silently prayed for their names to be called. Faith had a flashback to her own early morning jaunts to the emergency department with her children. Jeremy had been the type of baby who could scream his way into a high fever. Fortunately, Emma had come along around the time Will had met Sara. There was something to be said for having a pediatrician as a close friend.

Which reminded Faith, "Where's Sara?"

"She's in lockstep with Will, as usual."

Not exactly an answer, but Faith was over trying to poke that bear. Plus, Amanda was already opening the door to the back, despite the sign that warned STAFF ONLY.

They were met with even more misery. Patients were parked on gurneys along the hallway, but Faith didn't see any nurses or doctors. They were probably behind the closed-off curtained areas that served as rooms. She could hear Amanda's kitten heels stabbing the laminate tiles over the staccato of heart monitors and respirators. Faith silently tried to puzzle out why Amanda had driven two hours at oh-dark-thirty to come to a podunk town for an already-solved murder case that was well below her paygrade. Hell, it was even below Faith's paltry paygrade. The GBI only stepped in after an investigation went sideways, and even then, their services had to be requested. Biscuits had made it clear he wasn't interested.

Amanda stopped at the empty nurses' station and tapped the bell. The ring barely registered over the sounds of moaning and machinery.

Faith asked, "Why are you really here?"

Amanda was on her phone again. "Will is supposed to be on his honeymoon. I'm not going to let this job suck the life out of him."

Faith suppressed a whiny *what about me?* Amanda had always had a stealthy connection to Will. She'd been working patrol with the Atlanta Police Department when she'd found baby Will in a trash can. Until recently, he'd had no idea that Amanda's invisible hand had been guiding him his entire life. Faith was dying to know more than the bullet points, but neither one of them were given to sharing deep, dark secrets, and Sara was annoyingly loyal to her husband.

Amanda looked up from her phone. "Do you like Dave for the murder?"

Faith hadn't considered the question because it seemed so obvious. "He admitted to strangling Mercy. He didn't offer an alibi. The aunt documented a long history of domestic violence. He was hiding in the woods. He resisted arrest. If you can call ten seconds of machismo and thirty seconds of vomiting resisting."

"The family seems strangely unaffected by the loss."

Faith guessed that meant Amanda had listened to Will's audio files, too. Faith had spent so much time listening to them in the car that she'd practically memorized some of Delilah's observations. "The aunt says there's a solid money motivation. She described Mercy's brother as serial-killer-collecting-women's-panties-reclusive. She called her own brother an abusive asshole. She said her sister-in-law was a cold fish. And that Bitty threatened to put a knife in Mercy's back a few hours before she had a knife broken off in her back."

"Delilah also said something about the exhibitionists in cottage five."

Faith had wanted to know more about that part, too, but only because she was as nosey as Delilah. "Chuck sounds like he'd be interesting to talk to. He's close to the brother. He might know some secrets. Then there's the rich assholes who were trying to buy the lodge."

"We'll never get to them. They'll have lawyers on top of lawyers," Amanda said. "How many guests are staying at the lodge?"

"I'm not sure. The website says they don't allow more than twenty total guests at a time. If you like being outside and sweating, the place looks fantastic. I couldn't find out how much it costs, but I'm assuming eleventy billion dollars. Will must've spent an entire year's pay on that place."

"Another reason to keep him out of this," Amanda said. "I want you to handle the interview with Dave. He was transported here by ambulance. Sara wanted to rule out testicular torsion."

Faith knew it wasn't funny, but she found it a little funny. "What code should I use for that in the report? Eighty-eight?"

Amanda walked straight past Faith. She had spotted Sara at the end of the hallway. Once again, Faith found herself skipping to catch up. Sara was wearing a short-sleeved T-shirt and cargo pants. Her hair was piled onto the top of her head. She looked exhausted as she squeezed Faith's arm.

"Faith, I'm so sorry you got pulled into this. I know you had your whole week planned out with Emma."

"She'll be fine," Amanda said, because toddlers were super chill about unexpected changes. "Where's Will?"

"Getting cleaned up in the bathroom. I had him soak his hand in a dilute Betadine solution before he was stitched up. The blade missed the nerves, but I'm still worried about infection."

Amanda asked, "And Dave?"

"His epididymis took the brunt of the blow. That's a coiled tube attached to the posterior side of the testicles that sperm travels through during the ejaculatory process."

Amanda looked annoyed. She hated medical speak. "Dr. Linton, in plain terms."

"His balls are bruised in the back. He'll need to rest, elevate and ice, but he should be fine in a week."

Since Faith was going to be interviewing Dave, she asked, "Is he on any pain medication?"

"His doctor gave him Tylenol. It's not my call, but I would've prescribed Tramadol, a round of ibuprofen for the swelling, and something for the nausea. The spermatic cord loops from the testicles through the inguinal canal into the abdomen, then back behind the bladder to attach to the urethra at the prostate gland, and finally the urethra goes out to the penis. Which is a long way of saying that Dave experienced a horrific trauma. Then again—" She shrugged. "That's what he gets for threatening Will with a butterfly knife."

Faith smelled another criminal charge. "Where's the knife?"

"Will gave it to the sheriff." Sara knew what she was thinking. "The blade is under twelve inches, so it's legal."

Amanda said, "Not if he was carrying it concealed with the purpose of using it for offense."

Faith countered, "That's only a misdemeanor, but if we can tie it back to the murder—"

"Dr. Linton," Amanda interrupted. "Where is Dave now?"

"He was admitted overnight for observation. The sheriff's in the room with him. I should add that Dave was wearing a shirt that had a bloody handprint on the front. The sheriff is logging the clothes and personal items into evidence. He should also be taking photos of the scratches on Dave's torso and neck. The local coroner's name is Nadine Moushey. She's already put in an official request for the GBI to handle Mercy's autopsy." Sara looked at her watch. "Nadine should be retrieving Mercy's body from the cottage soon. She told me to meet her downstairs in the morgue at eight."

Amanda said, "I've alerted the SAC overseeing region eight that she needs to oversee transporting the body to headquarters."

"Are you saying I should step back?"

"Is your input entirely necessary?"

"Do you mean, should a board-certified medical examiner who

saw the victim *in situ* offer her expert opinion during a preliminary physical exam?"

"You've developed the habit of asking questions rather than giving answers."

"Have I?"

Amanda's expression was unreadable. She was technically Sara's boss, but Sara had always treated her more as a colleague. And now because of Will, Amanda was in some ways Sara's mother-in-law, but also not.

Faith broke the stand-off. "Is there anything else we should know?"

Sara said, "There was a backpack at the crime scene. Delilah identified it as belonging to Mercy. Fortunately, the nylon was coated with a fire-resistant chemical. The contents could be interesting. Mercy packed some toiletries and clothes, plus a notebook."

Faith's second wind stirred. "What kind of notebook?"

"Composition, something a kid would take to school."

"Did you read it?"

"The pages were soaked, so it'll have to go to the lab for processing. I'm more interested in where Mercy was going. It was the middle of the night. She'd had a very public blow-up with her son earlier in the evening. Why was she leaving? Where was she going? How did she end up at the lake? Nadine pointed out that there were plenty of empty cottages if Mercy needed a break from her family."

"How many?" Faith asked.

"The number is irrelevant," Amanda said. "Focus on getting a confession out of Dave. That's how we wrap this up quickly. Correct, Dr. Linton?"

"The Dave part, at least." Sara looked at her watch again. "Delilah should be outside by now. We're going to look for Jon."

Amanda asked, "Does that seem like a good way to spend your honeymoon?"

"Yes."

Amanda kept her eyes on Sara for a moment longer, then turned and walked away. "Faith?"

Faith guessed that was her cue that they were leaving. She pumped her fist in solidarity with Sara before jogging to catch up again. She told Amanda, "You have to know Sara's not going to let a teenager who just lost his mother disappear off the grid."

"Jeremy was self-sufficient by the age of sixteen."

Jeremy had eaten so much cheese at the age of sixteen that Faith had been forced to seek medical intervention. "Teenage boys aren't as resilient as you think."

Amanda bypassed the elevators and took the stairs. Her mouth was set in a tight line. Faith wondered if she was thinking about Will at that age, but then she reminded herself there was no use trying to get inside Amanda's head. She tried to focus her brain on interviewing Dave instead.

During the two hours she'd been parked on the interstate, Faith had taken the time to look up David Harold McAlpine's criminal record. His juvenile file was sealed, but there were plenty of charges on his adult sheet, all of them the types of crimes you'd expect from an addict who beats his wife. Dave had been in and out of jail for various offenses, from bar fights to stealing cars to boosting baby formula to drunk driving to domestic violence. Very few of the charges had stuck, which was curious, but unsurprising.

Like Amanda, like Faith's own mother, Faith had started her career as a beat cop with the Atlanta Police Department. She knew how to read between the lines of a rap sheet. The explanation behind the repeated failures to prosecute DV charges successfully was obvious—Mercy had refused to testify. The curious lack of serious consequences on the other offenses pointed to a man who indiscriminately snitched on his fellow inmates in order to get his ass out of jail or keep himself from going to Big Boy prison.

That's where the unsurprising part came in. A lot of men who beat on their wives were remarkably petty cowards.

Amanda pushed open the door at the top of the stairs. Faith joined her a few seconds later. The hallway lights were dimmed. There was no one manning the nurses' station across from the elevator. Faith saw a board on the wall that listed patient names and nurse assignments. There were ten rooms, all full, but only one nurse.

"Dave McAlpine," Faith read. "Room eight. What are the odds?"

They both turned when the elevator doors opened. Will was wearing a button-down plaid shirt and a pair of scrubs that were too short for his long legs. Faith could see his black socks peeking out of the tops of his boots. He was cradling his bandaged right hand to his chest. There were tiny scrapes on his neck and face.

Amanda gave him her usual warm welcome. "Why are you dressed like a surgeon in a Ska band?"

Will said, "Dave vomited all over my pants."

"Yeah he did." Faith saved the high-five for later. "Sara told us you smashed his balls into his bladder."

Amanda gave a short sigh. "I'll go inform the sheriff that he will welcome our assistance on this investigation."

"Good luck," Will said. "He's been adamant about keeping the case."

"I imagine he's also adamant about not wanting every business in his county scrutinized for undocumented workers and child labor violations."

Faith watched Amanda walk away, which was the theme of her morning. She told Will, "I'm handling the interrogation. Anything I should know?"

"I placed him under arrest for assault and resisting. Biscuits agreed not to say anything about the murder, so as far as I know, Dave doesn't know we found the body. His biggest concern is he thinks I saw him strangle Mercy on the trail yesterday."

"Dude thinks you'd just stand there while he strangled a woman?" Faith liked a gullible suspect. "Sounds like I might be home in time to drive Emma to Clown Camp."

"I wouldn't count on it," Will said. "Don't underestimate Dave. He puts on a stupid hillbilly act, but he's manipulative, cunning, and cruel."

Faith was having a hard time getting a read off what Will was trying to tell her. "His sheet is littered with idiot crimes. The worst sentence he ever got was half a nickel in county lock-up for grand theft auto. The judge gave him work-release."

"He's a snitch."

"Exactly. Snitches don't tend to be criminal masterminds, and he's gotten caught a lot of times for somebody you're calling cunning. What am I missing?"

"That I know him." Will looked down at his bandaged hand. "Dave was at the children's home when I was there. He ran away when he was thirteen. He came up here. There's an old campground. It's a long story, but Dave will probably bring it up that we have a history, so you should be ready for it."

Faith felt like her eyebrows were going to disappear into her scalp. Now it was making sense. "What else?"

"He used to bully me," Will said. "Nothing physical, but he was an asshole. We called him the Jackal."

Faith couldn't imagine Will being bullied. Setting aside that he was a giant, there was the age difference. "Dave's four years younger than you. How did that work?"

"He's not four years younger than me. Where did you get that?"

"His criminal sheet. His birthday's all over the place."

Will shook his head with something like disgust. "He's two years younger than me. The McAlpines must've aged him down."

"What does that mean?"

"It's not as easy to do now because everything's digitized, but back then, not every kid showed up with a valid birth certificate. Foster parents could petition the court to change a kid's age. If the kid was shitty, they'd age him up so he'd be out of the system sooner. If he was easy, or if he was receiving enhanced benefits, then they would age him down so the money kept rolling in."

Faith felt sick to her stomach. "What's an enhanced benefit?"

"More problems, more money. Maybe the kid's got emotional issues or he's experienced sexual assault and needs therapy, which means you've got to drive him to appointments and maybe he's more of a handful at home, so the state gives you more money for your trouble."

"Jesus Christ." Faith couldn't keep the catch out of her voice. She had no idea whether any of this had happened to Will. Just the thought of it made her incredibly sad. "So Dave was a troubled kid?"

"He was sexually assaulted by a PE teacher in elementary school. It lasted a few years." Will shrugged it off, but the violation was horrifying. "He'll try to use it for pity. Let him talk, but just be aware that he knows what it's like to be helpless, and he grew up to be the type of man who beat his wife for years and eventually raped and murdered her."

Faith could hear the anger in his voice. He really hated this guy. "Does Amanda know that you know Dave?"

Will's jaw clenched, which was his way of saying yes. It also went a long way toward explaining why Amanda had driven two hours to get here. And why she wanted Will as far away from this case as possible.

For Faith's part, she had more questions. "Dave's a grown man. Why did he stay up here with the McAlpines if they exploited his troubled childhood for money?"

Will shrugged again. "Before he ran away, Dave had a suicide attempt that landed him a psych hold. Once you're in a facility, it's hard to get out. On the facility side, there's a money incentive to keep the kid in treatment. On the kid side, you feel really angry and suicidal because you're locked down in a psych ward, which kind of wags the dog. They kept Dave locked up for six months. He was back at the home less than a week before he bolted. The McAlpines had their problems, but I can see where he felt like they saved him. He definitely would've been sent back to Atlanta without the adoption."

Faith stored all of this away in her heart so she could cry about it later. "A thirteen-year-old boy knows he's not eleven. The judge would've asked him."

"I told you he's sneaky," Will said. "Dave was always lying about stupid things. Stealing people's stuff or breaking it because he was jealous you had something he didn't. He was one of those kids who always kept a running tally. Like, you got an extra handful of tater tots at lunch so I should get an extra handful at dinner."

Faith knew the type. She also knew how hard it was for Will to talk about his childhood. "Tater tots are delicious."

"I'm really hungry."

Faith rooted around in her purse for a candy bar. "I take it you want something with nuts?"

Will grinned as she handed him a Snickers bar. "By the way, Sara wasn't a hundred percent on Dave being the murderer."

This was new information. "Okay. But you are?"

"I absolutely am. But Sara's gut is usually pretty good. So." Will ripped open the wrapper with his teeth. "The last witness to see Mercy before she died had her outside cottage seven around 10:30."

Faith found her notebook and pen. "Talk me through the timeline."

Will had already shoved half the Snickers bar into his mouth. He chewed twice, then swallowed, then said, "Sara and I were at the lake. I looked at my watch before I got in. It was 11:06. I'd guess it was around 11:30 that we heard the first scream."

"More like a howl?"

"Correct," Will said. "We couldn't tell which direction it came from, but we thought probably the compound. That's where the house and most of the cottages are. Sara and I walked together for a bit, then we split up so I could take a more direct route. I ran through the forest. Then I stopped because I thought it was stupid, right? We heard a howl in the mountains and we ran into the woods. I decided to go find Sara. That's when I heard the second scream. I'd ballpark the time between the howl and the first scream at around ten minutes."

Faith started writing again. "Mercy screamed a word—*help*."

"Right. Then she screamed *please*. There was a much shorter gap between the second and third scream, maybe a second or two. But it was clear they both came from the direction of the bachelor cottages by the lake."

"Bachelor cottages." Faith noted the name. "Is that where you were swimming?"

"No, we were at the opposite end. It's called the Shallows. The lake is really big. You need to get the map. The Shallows is on one end and the bachelor cottages are on the other. The compound is high above both, so basically I went up one side of a hill, then down the other side."

Faith really needed to see that map. "How long after the second and third scream did it take you to reach Mercy?"

Will shook his head and shrugged. "It's hard to say. I was amped up, surrounded by trees in the middle of the night, trying not to face plant. I wasn't paying attention to time. Maybe another ten minutes?"

"How long does it take to get from the compound to the bachelor cottages?"

"We took one of the trails down with the coroner to show her the crime scene. That was about twenty minutes, but we were walking as a group and sticking to the path." He shrugged again. "Maybe ten minutes?"

"You're just going to say everything took ten minutes?"

Will shrugged a third time, but told her, "Sara looked at my watch when she pronounced Mercy dead. It was exactly midnight."

Faith wrote that down. "So, ballpark, there was roughly twenty minutes between the howl at the compound and when you found Mercy in the water, but Mercy needed ten of those minutes to get from the howl point to the scream point where she died."

"Ten minutes is plenty of time to murder a woman, then set a cottage on fire. Especially if you had it all planned out in advance," Will said. "Then you stroll back around the lake to the old camp-site and wait for the local sheriff to botch the investigation."

"Are you sure the howler was the screamer?"

Will thought about it. "Yes. Same tone of voice. Also, who else would it be?"

"We're going to end up running around this entire property with stopwatches, aren't we?"

"Accurate."

He looked a hell of a lot happier about that than Faith was. "So why does Sara think Dave's not our guy?"

"The last time I laid eyes on Dave was around three in the afternoon. Sara talked to Mercy roughly four hours later. She saw bruising on Mercy's neck. Mercy said it was Dave who strangled her. But she seemed more concerned about her family coming after her, I guess over blocking the sale of the lodge. Mercy wasn't worried about Dave. In fact, she said that everybody on the mountain wanted her dead."

"Guests included?"

Will shrugged.

"I mean—" Faith tried not to get ahead of herself. She had always wanted to work a real-life locked-room mystery. "You've got a limited number of suspects trapped in a remote location. That's some *Scooby-Doo* shit."

"There were six family members at dinner—Papa and Bitty, Mercy and Christopher, Delilah and I guess you can throw in Chuck. Jon showed up before the first course, drunk off his ass and yelling at Mercy. Then there were the guests. Me and Sara, Landry and Gordon, Drew and Keisha, Frank and Monica. Also the investors—Sydney and Max. We were all packed in around a long dinner table."

Faith looked up from her notebook. "Were there candelabras on the table?"

He nodded. "And a chef and a bartender and two waiters."

"And Then There Were None."

He shoved the last of the Snickers into his mouth. "Heads-up."

Amanda was walking back toward them, the sheriff straggling behind her. Biscuits looked exactly how Faith had imagined when she'd heard his voice on the recording. A bit round, at least a decade older than her and several IQ points shorter. She could tell from the look on his pasty face that he'd reached the third stage of dealing with Amanda, skipping over anger and acceptance and going straight to sulking.

"Special Agent Faith Mitchell," Amanda introduced. "This is Sheriff Douglas Hartshorne. He's graciously agreed to let us take over the investigation."

Biscuits didn't look gracious. He looked pissed off. He told Faith, "I'm gonna be in the room when you talk to Dave."

Faith didn't want the company, but she gathered from Amanda's silence that she didn't have a choice. "Sheriff, has the suspect said anything about the crime?"

Biscuits shook his head. "He ain't talking."

"Did he ask for a lawyer?"

"Nope, and he's not gonna give you anything and it's not like we even need it. We already got the evidence to put him away. Blood on his shirt. Scratch marks. History of violence. Dave likes to use knives. Always carries one in his back pocket."

Faith asked, "Does he usually carry anything other than the butterfly knife?"

Biscuits clearly didn't like the question. "This is a local matter, oughta be handled locally."

Faith smiled. "Would you like to join me in room eight?"

Biscuits made a grand sweep with his arm in an *after you* gesture. He trailed Faith down the hall so closely that she could smell his sweat and aftershave.

He said, "Look, sweetheart, I know you're just following orders, but you need to understand something."

Faith stopped, turning to face him. "What's that?"

"You GBI agents, you go from the classroom to the conference room. You don't know what it's like to do street-level policing. This kind of murder, it's a real cop's bread and butter. I could'a told you twenty years ago one of 'em would'a ended up dead and the other would'a ended up in the back of a squad car."

Faith pretended like she hadn't spent ten years of her life on patrol before earning her slot on the Atlanta homicide squad. "Educate me."

"The McAlpines, they're a good family, but Mercy was always a handful. In and out of trouble. Drinking and drugging. Sleeping around. Girl was pregnant by the time she was fifteen."

Faith had been pregnant at fifteen, but she said, "Wow."

"Wow is right. Pretty much ruined Dave's life," Biscuits said. "Poor guy never managed to right himself after Jon was born. In and out of jail. Always getting into scrapes. Dave was battling his own demons even before Mercy got knocked up. Had a rough time of it in foster care. Got sexually assaulted by a teacher. It's a goddam miracle he ain't blown his brains out."

"Sounds like it," Faith said. "Should we go talk to him about the murder?"

She didn't wait for his answer. Faith pushed open the door to a short vestibule. Bathroom on the right. Sink and cabinet on the left. The lights were dimmed. She could hear the soft murmur of a television. The air was filled with the stale scent of a habitual smoker. A set of clothes was piled into the sink bowl. She saw an empty paper bag marked EVIDENCE on the counter. The sheriff had gone so far as to take out a pair of gloves, but he hadn't actually bagged and tagged the suspect's personal items: a pack of cigarettes, a bulging Velcro wallet, a tube of Chapstick and an Android phone.

Dave McAlpine muted the television when Faith turned up the lights. He didn't look worried about being under arrest or having two cops in his hospital room. He was reclining in bed with one arm over his head. His left wrist was handcuffed to the bed railing. His hospital gown had slipped off his shoulder. His lower half was covered by a sheet, but he must've been sitting on a pillow because his pelvis was rotated up like Magic Mike taking center stage.

If Biscuits looked exactly how she'd imagined from Will's recording, Dave McAlpine was the exact opposite. Faith had somehow framed him in her head as somewhere between Moriarty from Sherlock Holmes and Wyle E. Coyote. In person, Dave was handsome, but in a bedraggled, high-school-prom-king-gone-to-seed kind of way. He'd probably slept with every other woman in town and had a $20,000 gaming set-up inside his rented trailer. Which was to say, exactly Faith's type.

"Who's this?" Dave asked Biscuits.

"Special Agent Faith Mitchell." Faith flipped open her wallet to show him her credentials. "I'm with the Georgia Bureau of Investigation. I'm here to—"

"You're prettier in person." He nodded toward Faith's work photo. "I like your hair longer."

"He's right." Biscuits had craned his neck to look at the picture.

Faith flipped the wallet closed as she resisted the urge to shave her head. "Mr. McAlpine, I know my partner has already read you your rights."

"Shit, did Trashcan tell you we go way back?"

Faith chewed the tip of her tongue. She'd heard Will called this name before. The nastiness didn't lessen with repetition.

She said, "Special Agent Trent told me you were both at the children's home together."

Dave stuck his tongue into his cheek as he studied her. "Why's the GBI care about this anyway?"

Faith put the question back on him. "Tell me what *this* is."

He gave a husky, smoker's laugh. "Have you talked to Mercy yet? Cause there's no way in hell she dimed me out."

Faith let him lead the conversation. "You admitted to strangling her."

"Prove it," he said. "Trashcan's a shit witness. He's always had it out for me. Wait till my lawyer gets him on the stand."

Faith leaned against the wall. "Tell me about Mercy."

"What about her?"

"She was fifteen when she got pregnant. How old were you?"

Dave's eyes cut to Biscuits, then back to Faith. "Eighteen. Check my birth certificate."

"Which one?" Faith asked, because that math wasn't mathing. Dave had been twenty when he impregnated a fifteen-year-old, which meant that he'd committed statutory rape. "You know that everything is digitized now, right? All the old records are in the cloud."

Dave nervously scratched his chest. The gown slipped farther down his shoulder. Faith could see deep gouges where he'd been scratched.

Dave said, "Biscuits, go fetch that nurse for me. Tell her I need some goddam pain medication. My balls are on fucking fire."

Biscuits seemed confused. "I thought you wanted me to stay."

"Well, now I don't."

Biscuits huffed out his exasperation before taking his leave.

Faith waited for the door to close. "Must be nice having the local sheriff on a leash."

"Sure is." Dave reached under the bed sheet. He hissed air between his teeth as he pulled out an icepack and dropped it on the bedside table. "What are you looking for, darlin?"

"You tell me."

"I got no idea what happened last night." He pushed up the shoulder of his gown. "You let me outta here, I can ask around. I know a lot of people. Whatever went down that's big enough for the GBI to be interested—I figure that should be worth something."

"What would it be worth?"

"Well, one, taking this fucking handcuff off my wrist." He made the chain rattle against the bedrail. "And two, maybe you parting with some money. I figure a thousand to start. More if I can bring you a big arrest."

Faith asked, "What about Mercy?"

"Shit," he said. "Mercy doesn't know about anything that happens outside the lodge, and she's not going to talk to you anyway."

Faith noted the improvement in his grammar. The stupid hillbilly was gone. "It's hard for a woman to talk when she's been strangled."

"Is that what this is about?" he asked. "Is Mercy in the hospital?"

"Why would she be at the hospital?"

He sucked his teeth. "That's why you're here? Trashcan threw a shit fit after seeing me on the trail? Cause what happened was, I left Mercy exactly where she landed. That was around three in the afternoon. Talk to Trashcan. He can confirm it."

"What happened after you strangled Mercy?"

"Nothing," he said. "She was fine. Even told me to go fuck myself. That's how she talks to me. Always trying to push my buttons. But I left her alone. I didn't go back. So whatever happened to Mercy after that, she did it to herself."

"What do you think happened to her?"

"Hell, I don't know. Maybe she fell when she was walking back to the trail. She's done that before. Tripped and fell face-down in the woods. Caught her neck on a log so hard that she bruised her esophagus. Took a few hours for it to swell up, but she ended up driving herself to the emergency room saying she couldn't breathe. Ask the doctors. They'll have a record."

Faith's only surprise was that he couldn't come up with a better story. "When did this happen?"

"A while back. Jon was still little. It was right before I divorced her. Mercy will tell you herself she was overreacting. She could breathe fine. She just worked herself up into a panic. The doctors said she had some swelling in her throat. Like I said, she fell really hard on that log. It was an accident. Had nothing to do with me." Dave shrugged. "If the same thing happened again, that's on Mercy. Talk to her. I'm sure she'll tell you the same thing."

Faith was confused. Will had warned her not to underestimate Dave, but this was neither cunning nor clever. "Tell me where you went after you left Mercy on the trail."

"Bitty didn't have time to drive me back into town. I hiked down to the old campsite and got my drink on."

Faith silently weighed her options. This was getting them nowhere. She had to change tactics. "Mercy's dead."

"Shit," he laughed. "Right."

"I'm not lying," Faith assured him. "She's dead."

He held her gaze for a good long moment before looking away. Faith watched tears flood into his eyes. His hand went to his mouth.

"Dave?"

"Wh—" the word got tangled up in his throat. "When?"

"Around midnight last night."

"Did she—" Dave gulped. "Did she suffocate?"

Faith studied his profile. This was the cunning part. He was really good at this.

Dave asked, "Did she know that it was happening? That she was dying?"

"Yes," Faith said. "What did you do to her, Dave?"

"I—" His voice caught. "I strangled her. It was my fault. I choked her out too hard. She was gonna pass out, and I thought I pulled myself back in time but—Jesus. Oh, Jesus."

Faith pulled some tissues from the box and handed them over.

Dave blew his nose. "Did . . . did she suffer?"

Faith crossed her arms. "She knew what was happening."

"Oh, fuck! Fuck! What's wrong with me?" Dave put his head in his hand. The handcuff rattled against the railing as he cried. "Mercy Mac. What did I do to you? She was terrified of suffocating. Since we were kids, she always had these dreams where she couldn't breathe."

Faith tried to figure out where to go from here. She was used to long negotiations with suspects who parceled out the truth. Sometimes they put themselves in the vicinity of the scene as opposed to in the actual spot, or admitted to one part of the crime but not the other.

This was another thing entirely.

"Jon." Dave looked up at Faith. "Does he know what I did?"

Faith nodded.

"Fuck. He's never gonna forgive me." Dave's head went back

into his hand. "She tried to call me. I didn't see it come in cause I didn't have a signal up on the mountain. I could've saved her. Does Bitty know? I need to see Bitty. I gotta explain—"

"Wait," Faith said. "Go back. When did Mercy call you?"

"I don't know. I saw the messages when Biscuits took my phone away. They must'a loaded when we got down the hill."

Faith found Dave's Android on the sink by the door. She used the edge of her notebook to bump the screen on. There was at least half a dozen notifications, all time stamped, all but one with the same message:

MISSED CALL 10:47PM – Mercy Mac

MISSED CALL 11:10PM – Mercy Mac

MISSED CALL 11:12PM – Mercy Mac

MISSED CALL 11:14PM – Mercy Mac

MISSED CALL 11:19PM – Mercy Mac

MISSED CALL 11:22PM – Mercy Mac

Faith scrolled down to the last one.

VOICEMAIL 11:28PM – Mercy Mac

Faith flipped open her notebook. She looked at the timeline.

By Will's estimation, Mercy had howled at 11:30 PM, two minutes after she had left a voicemail for Dave. Faith stuck her notebook back in her pocket. She slipped on the sheriff's gloves before picking up Dave's phone and walking back to his bed.

She asked him, "You couldn't get a signal on your phone, but Mercy could?"

"There's Wi-Fi around the main house and at the dining hall, but you don't get cell coverage until you're halfway down the mountain." He wiped his eyes. "Can I listen to it? I wanna hear her voice."

Faith had assumed she'd have to file a warrant to hack the phone. "What's your password?"

"My gotcha day," he said. "Oh-eight-oh-four-ninety-two."

Faith traced the numbers into the lock. The phone opened. She felt an unwelcome shakiness as her finger hovered over the voicemail icon. Before she played it, she took out her own phone to record whatever the message said. Her hand was sweating inside the glove when she finally tapped *play*.

"*Dave!*" Mercy cried, almost hysterical. "*Dave! Oh my God, where are you? Please, please call me back. I can't believe—oh, God, I can't— Please call me. Please. I need you. I know you've never been there for me before, but I really need you now. I need your help, baby. Please c-call—*"

There was a muffled sound, like Mercy had pressed the phone to her chest. Her voice was heartbreaking. Faith felt a lump in her throat. The woman sounded so desperately alone.

"I failed her," Dave whispered. "She needed me, and I failed her."

Faith looked at the progress bar under the message. There were seven more seconds left. She listened to Mercy's soft cries as the bar got smaller and smaller.

"*What are you doing here?*"

Mercy's voice sounded different—angry, afraid.

"*Don't!*" she yelled. "*Dave will be here soon. I told him what happened. He's on his—*"

There was nothing more. The bar had reached the end.

"What happened?" Dave asked. "Did Mercy say what happened? Is there another message? A text?"

Faith stared at the phone. There was no other message. There was no other text. There was only the timestamped notifications and Mercy's last known recorded words.

"Please," Dave begged. "Tell me what this means."

Faith thought about what Delilah had told Will. The money motive. Her asshole brother. Her nasty sister-in-law. Mercy's serial killer vibes brother. His creepy friend. The guests. The chef. The bartender. The two waiters. The locked-room mystery.

She told Dave, "It means you didn't kill her."

12

Sara stood on the edge of the loading dock in the bowels of the hospital as she watched the rain pour down. The search for Jon had turned up nothing. They had checked his school, the trailer park where Dave lived, and a few hangouts that Delilah remembered from her days as a teenager. They were heading back up the mountain to check the lodge and search the old bunkhouses when black clouds started rolling in. Sara could only hope Jon had found a warm, dry place to shelter before the sky had broken open. Both she and Delilah had been adamant that they wouldn't let the weather stop them from searching, but then visibility had dropped, and thunder had shaken the air, and they had both decided to go back into town because it would do Jon no good if one or both of them were struck dead by lightning.

The weather app on Sara's phone was predicting the rain would not let up for another two hours. The deluge was unrelenting, sending creek water over the banks, spilling out of gutters, and turning the downtown corridor into a river. Delilah had gone home to feed her animals, but there was no telling whether she would make it back into town.

Sara looked at her watch. Mercy would be ready for her soon. The hospital's X-ray tech had told them it would take at least an hour to get through the backlog of living patients. Nadine had gone on a call to fix an air conditioner while Biscuits stayed with the body. Sara had been relieved when the sheriff had turned down her offer to spell him. She needed time to prepare herself mentally for the exam. The thought of seeing Mercy McAlpine lying on a table filled her with a familiar sense of dread.

In her previous life, Sara had been the county coroner for her small hometown. The morgue had been inside the basement of the local hospital, much as the one the Dillon County coroner used. Back in Sara's coroner days, the victims had been familiar if not personally known to her. That was how small towns worked. Everyone either knew each other or knew someone who did. The job of coroner was one of tremendous responsibility but could also be one of great sadness. Working for the state, Sara had lost sight of what it felt like to be personally connected to a victim.

A few hours ago, she had been stitching together Mercy's wounded thumb inside the bathroom at the back of the kitchen. The woman had looked washed out and beaten down. She had been worried about the argument with her son. She had been troubled by what was going on with her family. The last thing on her mind had been her ex-husband. Which made sense, considering what Faith had discovered. Sara wondered what Mercy would've thought to know that one of her last acts on earth was to give her abusive ex an alibi.

"You were right."

"I was." Sara turned to look at Will. She could tell from his expression that he was already beating himself up over the mistake. She wasn't going to pile on. "It wouldn't have changed anything. You still had to find Dave. He was the most obvious suspect. He checked the most boxes."

"You're being a lot nicer about it than Amanda was," he said. "The access road to the lodge is washed out. We can't get any cars in or out until the creek goes back into the bank. We need an off-road vehicle that can make it through the mud."

Sara caught the irritation in his voice. Will hated standing around. She saw his jawbone sticking out as he clenched his teeth. He moved his freshly bandaged hand to his chest. Elevating it above his heart would stop the throbbing, but the pain would continue to gnaw at him because Will refused to take anything stronger than Tylenol.

She asked, "How's the hand?"

"Better," he said, though the tightness in his shoulders told her otherwise. "Faith gave me a Snickers bar."

Sara hooked her arm through his. Her hand brushed against

the gun under his shirt. He was well and truly back on the job. She knew what was coming next. "How are you going to get back to the lodge?"

"We're waiting on the field office to bring some UTVs. That's the only way we can get up there."

Sara tried not to think of all the patients she'd seen with traumatic brain injuries from flipping their UTVs. "Are the phones and internet still working at the lodge?"

"For now," he said. "We've got satellite phones coming just in case. It's good that everybody's still stuck up there, though. No one knows that Dave has an alibi. Whoever killed Mercy is thinking that they got away with it."

"Who's still at the lodge?"

"Frank, for one. I'm not sure why, but he's taken it on himself to answer the main phone in the commercial kitchen. Drew and Keisha didn't make it out before the storm hit. Apparently, they're not too happy about that. The app guys don't seem interested in leaving. It sounds like Monica is sleeping it off. Chuck and the family are still there. Except for Delilah. The chef and the two waiters arrived at five this morning, which is their usual time. The bartender doesn't come in until noon. She's also the cleaner, so I want to talk to her about those unmade beds in the vacant cottages. Faith went to find her while we are waiting for the UTVs. She lives on the outskirts of town."

Sara wasn't surprised Faith had slipped out. She hated autopsies. "You didn't go with her?"

"Amanda told me to stay here and run background checks."

"How do you feel about that?"

"About how you'd think." He shrugged, but he was clearly annoyed. Will wasn't one to idle around while other people did things. "What about the forensics on Dave?"

"The presumptive test on the stain across the front of his shirt came back as non-human. I'm guessing from the smell that Dave used it to wipe his hand when he was cleaning fish. The scratch marks on his chest could've come from the earlier attack on Mercy. He admitted to strangling her. She would've fought back. He claims the scratch on his neck was self-inflicted. Mosquito bite. There's no way to tell if he's lying, so the mosquito scratch wins. Are you going to be able to hold him on anything?"

"I could bring charges for resisting arrest and threatening me with a knife. He could accuse me of excessive use of force and targeting him because of our past. Mutually assured destruction. He's free to walk out of here anytime he wants." Will shrugged it off, but she could tell he wasn't happy with the situation. "It's just another pile of shit Dave managed to skate through unscathed."

"If it's any consolation, walking is exceptionally difficult for him right now."

Will didn't seem consoled. He stared out at the rain. She didn't have to wait long for him to tell her what was really bothering him. "Amanda isn't happy we got caught up in this."

"I'm not happy, either," Sara admitted. "We weren't given much of a choice."

"We could go home."

She could feel Will studying her face, looking for a sign that she was wavering.

She said, "Jon is still missing, and you promised Mercy that you would tell her son that she forgives him."

"I did, but odds are that Jon will turn up eventually, and Faith already has her teeth in the case."

"She's always wanted to solve a locked-room mystery."

Will nodded, but he didn't say anything else. He was waiting for Sara to decide.

She felt to her back teeth that this was a marriage-defining moment. Her husband was placing an awful lot of power in her hands. Sara was not going to be the type of wife who abused it. "Let's get through the day, then you and I can make a decision together about what to do about tomorrow."

He nodded, then asked, "Tell me why you didn't think it was Dave."

Sara wasn't sure if there was exactly one thing. "Watching how Mercy's family treated her at dinner—I don't know. Looking back, it seems like they all had it in for her. They certainly didn't appear to be upset that she'd been murdered. Then there's the thing Mercy said about how some of the guests might have it out for her, too."

"Which guests do you think she was talking about?"

"It's weird that Landry gave a fake name, but who knows if there was a sinister reason. You and I lied about our occupations. Sometimes people lie because they want to lie."

"You didn't pick up Chuck's last name, did you?"

She shook her head. Sara had avoided talking to Chuck as much as possible.

"There was something Drew said before he and Keisha lawyered up," Will told her. "He was talking to Bitty and Cecil, and he said something like, 'Forget about that other business. Do what you want up here.'"

"What other business?"

"No idea, and he made it clear he's not talking to me."

Sara couldn't see either Keisha or Drew murdering anybody. But that was the thing about murderers. They didn't tend to announce themselves. "Mercy wasn't just stabbed once. She had multiple wounds. Her body is a classic example of overkill. The attacker must have known her very well."

"Drew and Keisha have stayed at the lodge twice before." Will shrugged. "Keisha pissed off Mercy at dinner asking for a new glass."

"That's hardly something you'd murder over." Sara added, "Then again, there are multiple crime documentaries about women who snap."

"I'll take that as a warning." Will was joking, but not for long. "Dave made the most sense. There must've been something that made you look in a different direction."

"I can't explain it other than a gut feeling. In my experience, someone who has been abused for any length of time knows when their lives are most at risk. When Mercy and I talked, Dave was barely a blip on her radar."

"His credit check didn't have a lot of surprises. His bank account is overdrawn by sixty dollars, he's got two credit cards in collections, his truck was repossessed, and he's drowning in medical debt."

"I'm sure everyone up here has medical debt."

"Not Mercy," he said. "As far as I can tell, she's never had a credit card, a car loan, a bank account. There's no record of her ever filing a tax return. She doesn't have a driver's license. She's never voted. She doesn't have a cell phone account or phone number in her name. No Facebook, Insta, TikTok or other social media accounts. She's not even on the website for the lodge. I've seen some wonky background checks before, but nothing like this. She's a digital ghost."

"Delilah said she was in a bad car accident. That's how she got the scar."

"Her criminal record is clean. I guess it helps if you're family friends with the local sheriff," Will said. "Which brings us to Mercy's parents. Cecil and Imogene McAlpine. There was a huge payout from the insurance company after Cecil's accident. They're both drawing social security. They've got around a million bucks in a private pension fund, another half million in a money market, a quarter of a million in index funds. Credit cards are paid off every month. No outstanding debt. The brother's in good shape, too. Christopher paid off his student loans one year ago. He's got a fishing license, driver's license, two credit cards and a bank account with over two hundred grand in it."

"Good God. He's only a few years older than Mercy."

"I guess it's easy to save money when you don't have to pay room and board, but Mercy's in the same boat he is. Why doesn't she have anything?"

"It sounds deliberate. Maybe they were using money to control her." Sara didn't want to think about how helpless Mercy had felt. "Was there cash in her backpack?"

"Just clothes and the notebook," Will said. "The arson investigator's processing it for evidence, then it's going to be turned over to the lab. The plastic cover on the notebook melted and the pages are soaked from the rain. If they're not careful, the whole thing could be lost. We have to wait it out, but I'd really like to know what Mercy wrote."

Sara shared his eagerness. Mercy had packed the notebook for a reason. "What about her phone?"

"The fire destroyed it, but we tracked the number through Dave's caller ID. She was using a VoIP provider. We're waiting for a sign-off on a warrant for the account. She probably used a pre-filled debit card to pay for it. If we can get the card number, we might find out if she was using it for other things."

Sara felt more anxious with every new detail of Mercy's claustrophobic life. "Did you find out anything about Delilah?"

"She owns her house, but it looks like her main source of income is an online candle-making business and whatever she gets from the family trust. Credit score's reasonable. Her car is almost paid off. She's got around thirty grand in a savings account, which is good, but she's not flush like the rest of the family."

"She's better off than Mercy."

"Yeah." Will rubbed his jaw as he watched a car slowly navigate a two-inch-deep puddle. His body was tensed, almost coiled. If the UTV didn't show up soon, he would probably climb back up the mountain trail on his own. "The chef came back clean. The waiters are teenagers."

Sara asked, "What's the plan?"

"We need to find that broken knife handle, but that's a needle in a haystack. Or a forest. I want to talk to every man who was at the lodge last night. Mercy was raped before she was murdered."

"We don't know for certain that she was raped. Her pants could've been taken down during the struggle." Sara had a job to do, too. She could only follow the science. "I'll note any signs of sexual trauma and do the swabs, and I'm sure whoever performs the autopsy will closely inspect the vaginal vault, but you know assault doesn't always present itself post-mortem."

"Don't say that to Amanda. She hates when you talk like a doctor."

"Why do you think I do it?" Sara knew that would get a smile out of him.

Unfortunately, it didn't last long this time, either.

"Where is this guy?" Will looked at his watch. "I have to get back up to the lodge and start asking questions. They've had too long to get their stories straight. I need Faith to help me pry them apart. I also want to find the guest registry so I can run the names."

"Do you think the McAlpines will make you get a warrant?"

He had a sly smile on his face. "I mentioned to Frank it might be a good thing for him to poke around the office."

"He'll expect a junior police badge before this is over with,"

Sara said. "Poor Mercy. She was basically a prisoner up there. No car. No money. No support. Completely alone."

"The chef's definitely at the top of my list. He had the most consistent interaction with Mercy."

Sara had noticed the way the chef's eyes had followed Mercy through the kitchen. "You think she wasn't so alone?"

"Maybe," Will said. "I'm going to talk to the waiters first, see if they noticed anything. The bartender's got four DUIs, but they're from the nineties. What is it with DUIs up here?"

"Small town. Not much else to do but get drunk and get in trouble."

"You grew up in a small town."

"I certainly did."

Will's attention was pulled toward the parking lot again. This time, he looked relieved.

The diesel engine of an F-350 rumbled over the downpour. The truck was hauling two Kawasaki Mule side-by-sides with all-terrain tires and GBI markings. Sara's stomach clenched at the thought of Will going back up the mountain. Someone at the lodge had brutally murdered Mercy McAlpine. They were likely feeling safe right now. Will was about to change that.

Sara needed something to do other than worry. She reached up to kiss his cheek. "I'm going in. Nadine is probably ready for me."

"Call me if anything comes up."

She watched Will jump off the loading dock and jog toward the truck. Through sheets of rain. With his injured hand hanging down. With his bandage getting wet again.

Sara made a mental note to track down some antibiotics as she went back into the building. The heavy metal door sealed out the storm. The sudden silence made her ears ring. She walked down the long corridor that led to the morgue. The overhead lights were flickering. Water had seeped under the laminate floor tiles. Equipment from the recently closed maternity ward lined the halls.

She assumed the hospital would be one of the many rural medical centers that closed before the end of the year. Staffing was in short supply. There was only one doctor and two nurses covering the entire emergency department. Double those numbers would've still been short. After medical school, Sara had gotten a tremendous sense of pride from serving her local community. Now, rural hospitals couldn't find staff, let alone keep them. Too much politics and too little sanity had them leaving in droves.

"Dr. Linton?" Amanda was waiting for her outside the closed door to the morgue. She had her phone in her hand and a frown on her face. "We should talk."

Sara braced herself for another battle. "If you're looking for an ally who can help you pull Will away from this case, then you're wasting your time."

"Being well-balanced does not mean carrying a chip on each shoulder."

Sara let her silence be her response.

"Very well," Amanda said. "Run down the victim for me."

Sara took a moment to switch on her work brain. "Mercy McAlpine, thirty-two-year-old Caucasian female. Found on her family property with multiple stab wounds to the chest, back, arms and neck. Her pants were pulled down, which could indicate sexual assault. The murder weapon was broken off inside her upper torso. She was found alive but did not offer any identifying information about her killer. She expired at approximately midnight."

"Was she wearing the same clothing you saw at dinner?"

Sara hadn't thought about it until now, but she answered, "Yes."

"What about everyone else? How were they dressed when you saw them after finding Mercy?"

Sara felt slow on the uptake. Amanda was obviously interviewing her as a witness. "Cecil was shirtless, wearing boxers. Bitty was in a dark red terrycloth robe. Christopher was wearing a bathrobe with fish on it. Chuck was wearing something similar, but with rubber ducks. Delilah was in green pajamas—pants and a button-down shirt. Frank was in boxers and an undershirt. Monica was in a black, knee-length negligée. I didn't see Drew and Keisha or Sydney and Max. The app guys were both in their underwear. Will caught Paul coming out of the shower."

"Paul is the one who was in the shower at one in the morning?"

"Yes," Sara answered. "For what it's worth, I don't think they're the early-to-bed types."

"Nothing struck you as suspicious? No one stood out?"

"I wouldn't call the family's reaction normal, but no."

"Run it down for me."

"Cold is the phrase that keeps coming to mind, but I can't say that I had a good impression of them even before they learned of Mercy's death." Sara tried to think back to the dinner. "The mother is very petite and defers to her husband. She piled on when her daughter was publicly humiliated. The brother is strange in that way that some men can't help but be strange. The father was clearly putting on a show for the guests, but I imagine he would've treated me much differently if he'd known I'm a doctor and not a high school chemistry teacher. He comes off as the type who only likes women in traditional roles from the last century."

"My father was like that," Amanda said. "He was so proud of me when I joined the force, but the minute I outranked him, he started tearing me down."

Sara would've missed the flash of sadness if she hadn't been looking directly at Amanda's face. "I'm sorry. That must've been hard."

"Well, he's dead now," Amanda said. "I need all of your observations documented in writing and sent via email. What's your plan for the body?"

"Uh—" Sara was used to these abrupt switches with Will, but Amanda could teach a master class. "Nadine will help me perform the physical exam. We'll collect any fingernail scrapings, fibers or hairs, blood, urine, any semen. They'll go to the lab for immediate analysis. The full autopsy will happen at headquarters tomorrow afternoon. The scheduling was moved up when I notified them that we no longer have a suspect in custody."

"Find me evidence to remedy that, Dr. Linton." Amanda opened the door.

Sara felt her eyes sting from the bright fluorescent lights. The morgue looked like every small-town hospital morgue built after the Second World War. Low ceilings. Yellow and brown tiles on the floors and walls. Lightboxes on the wall. Adjustable exam lights over the porcelain autopsy table. Stainless-steel sink with a long, attached counter. A computer and keyboard on a wooden school desk. A rolling stool and a mayo tray laid out with various tools for the physical exam. A cold room with twelve total refrigerated mortuary cabinets stacked four across and three high. Sara checked to make sure she had everything she needed for the physical exam: safety gear, camera, specimen tubes, collection bags, nail scrapers, tweezers, scissors, scalpels, slides, rape kit.

Amanda asked, "No luck finding the son?"

Sara shook her head. "Jon's probably hung over, sleeping it off. I'm going back out with the aunt after the exam to look for him."

"Tell him he's going to have to make a statement at some point. He could be valuable pinning down timeline, figuring out who was the last person to see Mercy alive," Amanda said. "Jon was with you when you heard the second and third scream, correct?"

"Correct," Sara said. "I saw him walk out of the house with a backpack. I imagine he was planning on running away. The fight with Mercy at dinner was intense."

"See what you can get out of the aunt while you're searching," Amanda said. "Delilah knows something."

"About the murder?"

"About the family," Amanda said. "You're not the only one on the team who gets gut feelings."

Before Sara could press her for more, the gears on the freight elevator started to make an ominous grinding sound. Water seeped under the bottom of the sliding doors.

Amanda said, "If you had to guess right now, who would be your prime suspect?"

Sara didn't need time to think. "Someone in the family. Mercy was blocking their payday from the sale."

"You sound like Will," Amanda said. "He loves a money motive."

"For good reasons. Outside of the family, I'd say it's Chuck. He's profoundly discomforting. The brother too, for that matter."

Amanda nodded before looking down at her phone.

Sara realized that she had been slow on the uptake again. Only now did it occur to her how strange it was that the deputy director was attending a preliminary external exam. The full autopsy where the body was opened up for examination would take place at headquarters and be performed by someone else on the team. Nothing probative would likely be found during Sara's external exam. She was only doing it to get a head start on collecting blood, urine and trace evidence that would be sent to the lab for processing. Mercy's body had been found partially submerged in water. The likelihood that Sara would find any information this morning that required immediate action was close to zero.

So why was the boss here?

The elevator doors groaned open before she had time to ask the question. More water poured out. Nadine stood on one side of a hospital gurney. Biscuits was on the other. Sara's gaze found the post-mortem bag. White vinyl, heat-sealed edges, a reinforced zipper with thick plastic teeth. The outline of Mercy's body was slight, as if she had managed to do in death what people had been trying to do to her for seemingly her entire life: make her disappear.

Sara let everything else fade away. She thought about the last time she'd seen Mercy alive. The woman had been embarrassed, but proud. She was used to doing everything for herself. Mercy had let Sara take care of her injured thumb. Now, Sara would help take care of her body.

Amanda said, "Sheriff Hartshorne, thank you for joining us."

Her pseudo-gracious tone didn't completely disarm him. "I have a right to be here."

"And you are welcome to exercise that right."

Sara ignored the dumbstruck look on the sheriff's face. She took the foot of the gurney and helped Nadine steer the body into the morgue. They worked together silently, shifting the body bag onto the porcelain table, rolling away the gurney. Next, they each geared up in gowns, respirators, face shields, safety glasses and exam gloves. Sara wasn't going to do a full autopsy, but Mercy had lain in the heat and humidity for hours. Her body had turned into a toxic brew of pathogens.

"Maybe we should put on masks, too," Biscuits said. "Lotta fentanyl up here. Mercy's got a long history of addiction. We could die just from breathing the fumes."

Sara looked at him. "That's not how fentanyl works."

He narrowed his eyes. "I've seen grown men taken down by that stuff."

"I've seen nurses accidentally spill it on their hands and laugh." Sara looked at Nadine. "Ready?"

Nadine gave her a nod before starting on the zipper.

In Sara's first years working as a coroner, body bags had been similar in design to sleeping bags with a gusset at the bottom. They were always made of black plastic and the zippers had been metal. Now, the bags were white and came in various materials and shapes depending on the application. Unlike the previous version, the industrial zippers formed a complete seal. The upgrades were well worth the extra cost. The white color helped in the visual identification of evidence. The waterproof aspect kept fluids from escaping. Both were needed in the case of Mercy McAlpine's corpse. She had been stabbed multiple times. Her bowel had been pierced. Some of her hollow organs had been opened. The body had entered the state of putrefaction where fluids had started to leak from every opening.

"Fuck!" Biscuits cupped both hands over his nose and mouth to block the smell. "Jesus Christ."

Sara helped Nadine free the top half of the bag. Biscuits opened the door and stood with his feet on the threshold. Amanda hadn't moved, but she started typing on her phone.

Sara steeled her composure before she turned her attention to the body.

Mercy had been left inside the bag and fully dressed for X-rays. It could be dangerous handling a corpse. Clothing could conceal weapons, needles, and other sharp objects. Or, in the case of Mercy, a knife lodged inside of her chest.

Will's shirt was still draped across her upper torso. The material was bunched up around the tip of the broken blade, which jutted from Mercy's breastplate like the fin of a shark. Blood and sinew had dried in ropes around the serrated edge. Sara imagined the X-ray would show the blade angled between the sternum and scapula. The killer had likely been right-handed. Hopefully, they would find fingerprints on the missing handle.

Sara let her gaze travel up and down the body. Mercy's eyes

were slit open, her corneas clouded. Her mouth was agape. Dried blood and debris patched her pale skin. Several shallow stab wounds had gouged out the flesh of her neck. The white of her right clavicle bone was exposed where the blade had flayed open the skin. The wounds in her lower back and upper thighs were weeping into the body bag. Every inch of exposed skin showed the brutality of her death.

"God bless her soul," Nadine whispered. "Nobody deserves this."

"No, they don't." Sara was not going to let herself feel helpless. She asked Nadine, "Do you record or transcribe?"

"I always feel funny talking into a recorder," Nadine said. "I usually just write things down."

Sara normally recorded, but she was mindful that this was Nadine's turf. "Could you take notes?"

"No problem." Nadine gathered the notebook and pen. She didn't wait for Sara's instruction to start writing. Sara read her block handwriting upside down. Nadine had noted the date, time, and location, then added Sara's name as well as Hartshorne's and her own. She asked Amanda, "Sorry, hon, but can you remind me of your name?"

Sara barely registered Amanda's response as she looked down at Mercy's ravaged body. Her jeans were still down at her ankles, but her bikini-style, dark purple underwear was pulled up around her hips. Dirt was caked into the waistband. Streaks of dirt traveled down her legs and caked into her jeans. There was a cluster of round scars on her upper left thigh. Sara recognized them as cigarette burns. Will had similar scars on his chest.

She felt her throat work at the thought of her husband. Her brain flashed up the memory of nuzzling his shoulder on the lookout bench. Back then, Sara had thought the worst thing that would happen on her honeymoon was watching Will struggle with thoughts of his lost mother.

Mercy was a lost mother, too. She had a sixteen-year-old son who deserved to know who had taken her away from him.

"All right." Nadine flipped to a fresh page in her notebook. "Ready."

Sara continued the external exam, calling out her findings.

Mercy's body had passed the peak stages of rigor mortis, but her limbs were still stiff. The muscles of her face had contracted, giving her the appearance of intense pain. Her upper body hadn't been submerged in the lake for long, but the skin at the back of her neck and shoulders was loose and mottled from the water. Her hair was tangled. There was a pink cast to her pale skin from the blood that had swirled into the water.

A flash popped. Nadine had started taking photographs. Sara helped her align rulers for scale. There was debris under Mercy's fingernails. A long scratch traced down the back of her right arm. Her right thumb was still bandaged where Sara had stitched up the cut from the broken water glass. Dark bloodstains indicated the sutures had torn free, likely during the attack. The red strangulation marks Sara had seen on Mercy's neck in the bathroom were more pronounced, but not enough time had elapsed before she died for bruises to appear.

Sara turned Mercy's right arm, checking the underside. Then she checked the right. The fingers and thumbs were curled, but Sara could see the palms. No slashes from the knife. No edema. Not even a cut. "She doesn't appear to have defensive wounds."

"It's just not showing up," Nadine said. "Mercy was a fighter. No way she'd just stand there and take it."

Sara wasn't going to disabuse her of the narrative. The fact was that no one knew how they would respond to an attack until they were attacked. "Her shoes tell us some of the story. Mercy was standing for part of the attack. The spray is from arterial blood. The spatter could be from the knife plunging in and out. There's dirt caked onto the tops around the toes. We saw drag marks from the cottage to the lake. Mercy was face-down when this happened. There's also dirt in the waistband of her underwear, on her knees, inside the folds of her jeans."

Nadine said, "Dirt looks like the same type as what's at the lake shore. I'll go back out later and collect samples for comparison."

Sara nodded as Nadine resumed photographing the findings. For several minutes, the only thing Sara could hear over the hum on the compressor on the refrigerated cabinets was the pop of the camera flash and Amanda typing on her phone.

When Nadine was finally finished, Sara helped her spread white butcher paper underneath the table. Then she picked up the magnifying glass from the tray. They worked in tandem going over every inch of Mercy's clothing in search of trace evidence. Sara found hair fibers, pieces of dirt and debris, all of which went into collection bags. Nadine was quietly efficient, labelling every piece of evidence, then making a notation on the evidence log indicating where it had been found.

The next step was exponentially more difficult than the previous ones. They had to remove Mercy's clothing. Nadine laid out fresh paper on the floor. Then she placed more paper on the long table by the sink so they could search the clothes again once they were removed.

Undressing a corpse was time-consuming and tedious, particularly when the body was still in rigor. Typically a human being had roughly the same amount of bacteria as cells. Most of the bacteria was in the intestines, where it was used to process nutrients. In life, the immune system kept the growth in check. In death, the bacteria took over, feeding on tissues, releasing methane and ammonia. These gases bloated the body, which in turn made the skin expand.

The material of Mercy's T-shirt was stretched so tight that their only choice was to cut it off. The underwire of her bra had to be pried away from her ribcage and left more than a half-centimeter deep divot under her breasts. Sara followed the seam on her underwear to cut it off. The waistband had left its mark. The thin material had to be picked away. Patches of skin came with it. Sara gently placed each strip onto the butcher paper like the pieces of a puzzle.

They couldn't remove the jeans without first taking off the shoes. Nadine untied the laces. Sara helped her remove the sneakers. The bands at the tops of Mercy's cotton athletic socks were loose, which made them easier to remove. Still, the material left a heavy cabled pattern in the skin. Removing the jeans was much more of a production. The material was thick and stiff from blood and other fluids that had dried. Sara carefully cut first one side, then the other, to take them off like a clam shell. Nadine carried the jeans over to the counter. She wrapped both halves in paper to prevent cross contamination.

They all stood silently as Nadine worked. No one was looking at the body. Sara could see the grim set to Amanda's face as she studied her phone. Biscuits was still in the doorway, but his head was turned as if he'd heard something at the end of the hall.

Sara felt her throat tighten as she studied the body. By her count, there were at least twenty visible stab wounds. The torso had received the brunt of the blows, but there was a gash in her left thigh, a gouge on the outside of her right arm. The blade had sunk to the hilt in some places, the skin imprinting with the outline of the missing handle.

The recent wounds weren't the only sign of damage.

Mercy's body revealed a lifetime of abuse. The scar on her face had drained of color, but it was no match for the other scars that riddled her skin. Deep, dark slash marks wrapped around her belly where she'd been whipped with something heavy and textured, probably a rope. Sara easily recognized the impression of a belt buckle imprinted on Mercy's hip. Her left thigh had been burned by an iron. She had multiple cigarette burns around the nipple of her right breast. There was a thin, straight slash bisecting her left wrist.

She asked Nadine, "Do you know of any suicide attempts?"

"More than a few." Biscuits had answered the question. "She had a couple of overdoses. That scar you're looking at is back from high school. Got into another knock-down with Dave. Cut her wrist open in the supply closet off the gym. Coach found her or she would'a bled out."

Sara looked to Nadine for confirmation. The woman had tears in her eyes. She nodded once, then picked up the camera to document the damage.

Again, Sara aligned the ruler for scale. She wondered how long it would take to stab a woman this many times. Twenty seconds? Thirty? There were more stab wounds on the back and legs. Whoever had murdered Mercy McAlpine had well and truly wanted her dead.

That he hadn't completely succeeded, that Mercy had still been alive after the cottage had been set on fire, after Will had run through the forest to find her, was a testament to her grit.

Nadine finally put down the camera. She took another deep breath to brace herself. She knew what was coming next.

The rape kit.

Nadine unsealed the cardboard box that contained everything needed to collect evidence from a sexual assault: sterile containers, swabs, syringes, glass slides, self-sealing envelopes, nail picks, labels, sterile water and saline, a plastic speculum, a comb. Sara could see her hands shaking as she laid each item out on the tray. Nadine used the back of her arm to wipe tears under her safety glasses. Sara's heart went out to the woman. She had been in Nadine's position many times before.

Sara asked, "Should we take a break?"

Nadine shook her head. "I'm not going to fail her this time."

Sara was carrying her own guilt about Mercy. Her brain kept taking her back to that moment in the bathroom off the kitchen. Mercy had told Sara that almost everyone on the mountain wanted to kill her. Sara had tried to press her, but when Mercy had pushed back, Sara had easily let it go.

Sara told Nadine, "Let's begin."

Because Mercy was still in rigor, they had to force her thighs apart. Sara took one leg. Nadine took the other. They pulled until the hip joints gave way with a terrible popping sound.

In the doorway, Biscuits cleared his throat.

Sara held a white square of cardboard below Mercy's pubis. She used the comb first, carefully pulling the teeth through pubic hair. Stray hairs, dirt, and other debris fell onto the paper. Sara was glad to see roots on some of the hairs. Roots meant DNA.

She passed the card and comb to Nadine so that she could seal both in a collection bag.

Next, Sara used several different lengths of swabs to check for semen on the insides of Mercy's thighs. Her rectum. Her lips. Nadine helped her force open the mouth. Again, there was a loud pop from the joint breaking apart. Sara adjusted the overhead light. She didn't see any contusions inside the mouth. She swabbed inside the cheeks, the tongue, the back of the throat.

The plastic speculum was sealed inside a wrapper. Nadine peeled the edges apart, offering the instrument to Sara. Again,

Sara adjusted the overhead light. She had to force the speculum into the canal. Nadine handed her swabs.

Sara said, "It looks like there's a trace amount of seminal fluid."

Biscuits cleared his throat again. "So she was raped."

"The fluid suggests sexual intercourse. I don't see any signs of edema or contusions."

Sara handed Nadine the last of the swabs to process. While she waited, Sara changed into fresh gloves. Her thoughts were on all of the men who'd been at the lodge last night. The chef. The two young waiters. Chuck. Frank. Drew. Gordon and Paul. Max, the investor. Even Mercy's brother, Christopher. Sara had sat at the dinner table surrounded by them. Any one of them could be the killer.

Nadine came back to the table. Sara drew blood from the heart into a large syringe. She used a twenty-five-gauge needle to take urine from the bladder. She handed the syringes over to Nadine for labeling. Then, she held a small piece of white cardboard under Mercy's fingers and used the wooden pick to clean out under her nails.

"This might be skin," Sara said. "She could've scraped her attacker."

"Good girl, Merce." Nadine sounded relieved. "I hope you made him bleed."

Sara hoped so, too. There would be a better chance of isolating DNA.

She was about to ask for Nadine's help to turn the body over when a phone buzzed.

Nadine said, "That's me. X-rays are probably uploaded."

Sara felt like they all needed a break. "Let's take a look."

Nadine was visibly relieved. She lowered her mask and took off her gloves as she walked toward the desk. Sara waited until the woman had logged into the computer to stand behind her. A few clicks brought Mercy's X-rays onto the screen. They were little more than thumbnails, but yet again, the history of abuse was writ large.

Sara was not surprised by the old fractures, but the number was substantial. Mercy's right femur had been fractured in two different places, but not at the same time. Some of the bones in her left hand looked like they had been deliberately hammered in two. Screws and plates were in multiple locations. The top of her skull and occipital bones had been fractured. Her nose. Her pelvis. Even her hyoid bone showed signs of an old injury.

Nadine picked up on this last one. She enlarged the image. "A snapped hyoid is a sign of strangulation. I didn't know you could live with it broken."

"It's a potentially life-threatening injury," Sara said. The bone was attached to the larynx and was involved in a lot of airway functions, from producing sound to coughing to breathing. "This looks like an isolated fracture to the greater horn. She could've been intubated or put on bed rest, depending on how she was presenting."

Amanda provided, "When Faith was interviewing Dave, he told her that Mercy drove herself to the hospital after a strangulation episode. She was having difficulty breathing and was admitted."

"I took that report," Biscuits called from the doorway. "Happened at least ten years ago. Mercy didn't say anything about being strangled. She told me she tripped over a log. Smashed into her neck."

Amanda gave Biscuits a pointed look. "So why were you called to take a report?"

Biscuits said nothing.

Sara went back to the X-rays, asking, "Can you show me this fracture?"

Nadine selected the image of the femur bone.

"I'd want a forensic radiologist to weigh in, but that looks decades old." She pointed to the faint line bisecting the lower half of the bone. "An adult fracture generally shows sharp edges, but if it's older, say dating back to childhood, the bone remodels and rounds out the edges."

Amanda asked, "Is that unusual?"

"Femur fractures in children tend to be shaft fractures. The femur is the strongest bone in the body, so it takes a high-energy collision to break it." Sara referred to the film. "Mercy suffered from a distal metaphyseal fracture. There's been a lot of debate about whether or not this kind of fracture indicates abuse, but the recent research isn't dispositive."

Biscuits asked, "What does that mean?"

Nadine said, "Cecil broke her leg when she was a baby."

"Hey now, she didn't say who did it," Biscuits countered. "Don't go blabbing stuff you can't back up with facts."

Nadine let out a long breath as she clicked open two more thumbnails. "This metal plate in her arm is from the car accident I told you about. And this one—see here where they had to reconstruct her pelvis? Good thing she'd already had Jon."

Sara stared at the abdominal X-ray. Mercy's pelvic bones were a stark white against the black, the vertebrae laddering up into the ribcage. The organs were in shadow. The faint outline of the small and large intestines. The liver. The spleen. The stomach. The ghostly blur of a small mass, maybe two inches long, showing early signs of ossification.

Sara had to clear her throat before she could speak. "Nadine, could you help me finish the rape exam before we turn her?"

Nadine looked confused, but she grabbed another pair of gloves before joining Sara at the table. "What do you need me to do?"

Sara didn't need her to do anything but revert to her comforting silence. There was an ultrasound machine in the hallway, but Sara wasn't going to ask for it with Biscuits in the room. Nadine had delivered a short lecture on Old Bachelor Trail about the glue that fixed life in a small town, but she had forgotten one very important lesson: there was no such thing as a secret.

Sara would have to use a pelvic exam to confirm what she had seen on the X-ray.

Mercy was pregnant.

13

"Fuckity-fuck-fuck." Faith tried not to bang her head against the steering wheel of her Mini. The storm had finally passed, but the gravel road had turned into a muddy nightmare. Rocks kept dinging into the side panels. The steering felt slippery. She looked up at the sky. The sun was brutal, like it wanted to suck back up as much water into the clouds as possible.

She had shot herself in the foot by volunteering to interview Penny Danvers, the cleaner and bartender at the lodge, but Faith hated autopsies. She attended them because it was her job, but every single part of the examination grossed her the hell out. She had never been able to get used to being around dead bodies. Which was how she'd ended up driving through the backroads of Bumfuck, North Georgia, instead of taking a victory lap for her excellent detective work interviewing Dave McAlpine.

She silently chastised herself. A better outcome would've been a confession or a giant clue that pointed to the killer so that Jon had closure. This wasn't a game of good guys vs. bad guys. Mercy had been a mother. Not just a mother, but a mother like Faith. They had both given birth to sons when they were barely more than children themselves. Faith had been lucky that her family had supported her. Without their strength holding her up, she could've just as easily ended up like Mercy McAlpine. Or maybe even trapped with a reprehensible abuser like Dave. Shitty men were like periods. Once you had your first one, your life was consumed by dread or panic over when it would show up again.

Faith glanced at the open notebook on the passenger's seat. Before she'd left the hospital, she'd worked with Will to incorporate Mercy's calls to Dave with Will's ballpark times about what he'd heard and from where. They'd managed to construct what was probably a close guess of the last hour and a half of Mercy McAlpine's life:

10:30: Seen making rounds (Paul: witness)

10:47, 11:10, 11:12, 11:14, 11:19, 11:22: Missed calls to Dave

11:28: Voicemail to Dave

11:30: First scream from compound (Howl)

11:40: Second scream from bachelor cottages (Help)

11:40: Third scream from bachelor cottages (Please)

11:50: Body discovered

Midnight: Death pronounced (Sara)

Faith was still not happy with the multiples of ten. She had to get up to that property and find that map. Her first goal was to establish the areas where the Wi-Fi worked so she could figure out where Mercy had been when the calls to Dave were made. From there, Faith could plot out the different possible routes Mercy could've taken to the bachelor cottages. Will might be off by as much as five minutes on either side, which didn't seem like a lot, but when you were building a murder case, every minute mattered.

At least Mercy had done them the favor of making so many calls. The voicemail had already been sent to the lab for sound analysis, but that would take at least a week to get back. Faith picked up her phone from the cup holder. She tapped the recording she'd made of Mercy's last message to Dave. The woman's voice sounded desperate as it echoed inside the Mini.

"*Dave! Dave! Oh my God, where are you? Please, please call me back. I can't believe—oh, God, I can't— Please call me. Please.*

I need you. I know you've never been there for me before, but I really need you now. I need your help, baby. Please c-call—"

Faith hadn't noticed before, but Mercy had started sobbing when she'd muffled the phone. In the car, Faith silently counted down the seven seconds of the woman's soft cries.

"What are you doing here? Don't! Dave will be here soon. I told him what happened. He's on his—"

Faith glanced down at her timeline. Thirty-two minutes later, Mercy was pronounced dead.

"What happened to you, Mercy?" Faith asked the empty car. "What was it that you couldn't believe?"

The woman had seen or heard something that terrified her enough to shove her clothes and notebook into the backpack to flee. She hadn't taken Jon, which meant whatever happened was only threatening to Mercy. Threatening enough that she needed Dave to show up for her after years of not being there. Threatening enough that she didn't go to her own family for help.

Faith's bet was that the bad thing had kicked off during the thirteen-minute gap between the first call to Dave and the frantic five missed calls that had started at the 11:10 mark. Mercy would've been inside the house at some point to pack her backpack. Faith wasn't sure what items she would take if she had to leave her house for ever, but chief among them would be the letter that her father had written to her before he'd died of pancreatic cancer. There was no way Mercy had taken the notebook unless it had incredible value.

And there was no way the lab would be done with the analysis in less than a week.

Dave will be here soon. I told him what happened.

Faith thought about all the times she had told a man that another man was on the way. Usually it happened when she was trying to enjoy a night out alone. There was always some dude who would sidle up to flirt. The only way to get rid of him was to make it clear that another man had already pissed on the fire hydrant he was sniffing.

Which brought Faith back to the locked-room mystery of it all. One of the tenets of the genre was that the person you didn't think did it had actually done it. Dave was so obvious that he practically had a neon arrow pointing at his head. The most dangerous time for a domestic abuse survivor was when she was leaving her abuser. The strangulation was a textbook sign of an escalation in violence. But being a reprehensible shitslug didn't make you a murderer. And Faith kept coming back to the voice-mail. Mercy wasn't telling Dave that Dave was on the way. There were only a handful of men at the lodge who could've caused Mercy to invoke his name.

Chuck. Frank. Drew. Max, the investor. Alejandro, the chef. Gregg and Ezra, the two waiters from town. Gordon and Paul, because you never knew. Christopher, because he and Mercy were basically raised inside a VC Andrews novel in the north Georgia mountains.

Faith let out a heavy sigh. She needed more information. Hopefully, Penny Danvers, the bartender and cleaner at the lodge, would be as insightful and talkative as Delilah had been on Will's recording. Hotel cleaners saw your character in its harshest light, and God only knew Faith had dropped a few truth-bombs on unsuspecting bartenders in her day. Which was probably not a rabbit hole she needed to go down right now. Instead, Faith focused on the never-ending gravel road. She glanced into her rear-view mirror. Then at the road. Then out the side windows. Everything looked the same.

"Fuck me."

She was completely and totally lost.

She slowed her car to look for signs of civilization. All she had seen in the last fifteen minutes were fields and cows and the occasional low-flying bird. Her GPS had told her to take a left at the fork in the road, but she was beginning to think it had lied. She checked her phone. No signal. Faith performed a three-point turn and headed back the way she'd come.

Somehow, the fields and cows and the occasional bird looked different on her way back. She rolled down both windows and listened for cars or a tractor or some indication that she was not the last woman on earth. All she heard was a stupid bird cawing. She turned the dial on the radio, expecting to hear either alien voices or the farm report, but she was rewarded with Dolly Parton singing "Purple Rain."

"Thank God," Faith whispered. At least something was still good in the world. The wind blew into the car, drying some of the sweat on her back. She heard her phone chirp. Faith looked down at the screen. The signal was back. She had two text messages.

Faith tapped in her code, telling herself it was okay to text and drive because the only person she could kill was herself. Which she almost did when she saw the text from her son.

He was at Quantico. He loved it there.

Faith had secretly been hoping that Jeremy would hate it. She did not want her son to be a cop. She did not want him to be an FBI agent. She did not want him to be a GBI agent. She wanted him to use his fancy degree from Georgia Tech and work in an office and wear a suit and make lots of money so when his mother crashed her car on the side of the road from texting and driving, she would wind up in a nice facility.

The other text was only marginally better. Faith's mother had sent a photo of Emma with her face painted like Pennywise, the clown from *It*. Faith would figure out later whether the homage was intentional. She sent back a bunch of hearts before dropping her phone in the cup holder.

"Fuck!" she screamed. A bird had nearly flown straight into her windshield. Faith turned the wheel and ended up bumping along the shoulder. She over-corrected. The car started to hydroplane. Everything slowed down. She knew that you turned into a skid when you were on ice, but did you do the same with mud? Did you wrench the wheel in the opposite direction or would that jackknife you into a ditch?

The answer came soon enough. The Mini morphed into Kristi Yamaguchi, twisting into a three-sixty, lifting up on two wheels, and gliding across the road until it landed in the opposite ditch.

The car gave a violent shudder as it settled into the gulley. Faith was too breathless to utter a curse, but she promised herself she would as soon as her asshole unclenched. There weren't a lot of ways this day could get any worse.

Then she got out of the car and saw her back wheel buried in two inches of mud.

"Mother—"

Faith put her fist to her mouth. She could handle this. She'd worked as a patrol officer. Her shifts had been routinely filled with helping dumbasses extricate their vehicles from ditches. She found her emergency kit in the trunk, which had blankets, food, water, an emergency radio, a flashlight and a collapsible shovel.

"Purple Rain" had reached its crescendo. She had to think Dolly Parton would appreciate an exasperated mother of two digging herself out of the mud in the middle of nowhere while she listened to the Prince cover. Faith's hands started to ache as she dug. She suffered through an entire Nickelback song clearing a path. For good measure, she grabbed handfuls of gravel and packed them at the base of the tire. She was splattered in mud by the time she was finished. She wiped her hands on her pants before getting back into the car.

She tapped the gas, praying for traction. The car inched forward, then rocked back. She kept at it, slowly rocking forward and back until her wheels found purchase on the gravel.

"You fucking queen," she told herself.

"Hell yeah."

"Fuck!" Faith jumped, banging her head on the sunroof. A woman was standing on the other side of the ditch. Her face was haggard, worn down by the hard sun and an equally hard life. A Bluetick hound was sitting beside her. She had a shotgun slung across her shoulders like a dangerous scarecrow. Her hands dangled from either end.

"Didn't think you could do it," the woman said. "Never met one of you city folks who could punch your way out of a wet paper bag."

Faith bought herself a moment to contain her freak-out by turning off the radio. She wondered how long the peanut gallery had been standing there. Long enough to see the Mini's Fulton County car tag, which identified her as a resident of Atlanta.

She told the woman, "I'm with the—"

"GBI," she said. "You're with that tall fella. Will, right? Married to Sara."

Faith guessed this woman was a witch. "I didn't catch your name."

"I didn't throw it." She lifted her chin in defiance. "Who you looking for?"

"You," Faith guessed. "Penny Danvers."

She gave a single nod. "Smarter than you look."

Faith ran her tongue along the back of her teeth. "Do you want a ride back to your place?"

"The dog, too?"

Faith didn't think her car could get any filthier. She reached over and pushed open the door. "I hope he likes Cheerios. My daughter likes to throw them at my head."

The dog waited for Penny to click her tongue before he jumped through the two front seats with his muddy paws, then promptly started hoovering the floor, which was the only good thing that had happened today. Penny got in the front. The door slammed. She braced the shotgun between her legs, the muzzle pointed at the roof. Another good thing. She could've pointed it at Faith.

"I'm two miles up on the left. Gets a little bumpy, so hang on," said the woman with the loaded shotgun who wasn't wearing her seat belt. "You'll see the barn before you see the house."

Faith put the gear in drive. Both windows were still down. She kept the speedometer at thirty so dust from the gravel road wouldn't choke them inside the car. And also because the dog smelled like a dog.

"So," Faith said. "Out hunting or—"

"Had a cayote take one of my chickens." Penny nodded at the radio, "Did you hear her cover of 'Stairway to Heaven'?"

Dolly Parton. The universal icebreaker. And a giant clue that Penny had been standing alongside the ditch for a hell of a lot longer than Faith had realized. She tried not to show her unease when she asked, "From *Halos and Horns* or from *Rockstar*?"

Penny chuckled. "Which one do you think?"

Faith couldn't begin to guess, and Penny didn't seem interested in volunteering. She had taken some bacon out of her pocket and was offering it to the dog. She saw Faith looking and offered her some bacon, too.

"I'm good," Faith said.

"Suit yourself." Penny took a bite, staring silently at the road as she chewed.

Faith was struggling to think of random facts about Dolly
Parton to break the ice when she silently reminded herself that
sometimes, it was better to keep your mouth shut. She let the
empty fields roll by. The cows. The occasional, low-flying, murder-
bird.

As promised, the road turned bumpy. Faith had to fight with
the steering wheel to keep from going into the ditch again. There
were potholes in the city, but these were more like crevasses. She
was grateful when she finally spotted the barn in the distance.
The thing was huge, bright red, and probably new because she
hadn't seen it on Google Earth. An American flag was painted on
the side that faced the road. Two horses swung up their heads to
watch the Mini pass.

Penny said, "We're patriots here. My father served in Nam."

Faith's brother was currently in the Air Force, but she said,
"I'm grateful for his service."

"We don't like having you Atlanta people all up in our business," Penny continued. "We got our own way of doing things.
You stay out of our lives. We'll stay out of yours."

Faith knew this woman was testing her. She also knew Georgia
would be Mississippi without metro Atlanta's tax dollars.
Everybody romanticized country living until they needed internet
and healthcare.

"It's up there." Penny pointed to the only driveway for thirty
miles like it was easy to miss. "On the left."

Faith slowed to make the turn down the long driveway. She
saw the name on the mailbox, and Penny's tribalism made a lot
more sense. "D. Hartshorne. That wouldn't be the sheriff?"

"Used to be," she said. "That's my daddy. He lives in the trailer
out back. We moved him there after his stroke cause he can't
handle stairs. Biscuits is my brother."

Faith treaded carefully. "Are you close?"

"You mean, did he tell me about Dave not being the one that
killed Mercy?"

Faith guessed she had her answer.

"If you're wondering, Biscuits called up to the lodge to tell
them, but he couldn't get through. Phone and internet finally
crapped out." She gave Faith a meaningful glance. "He's helping

the highway patrol clear an overturned chicken truck down in Ellijay. Asked me to let them know when I go in to work."

"Will you?"

"I dunno."

Faith couldn't control what Penny was going to do, but she could try to get as much information out of her as possible. "Biscuits told my partner that you used to see Mercy and Dave walloping on each other back in high school."

"Not much of a fair fight." Penny's jaw had cranked down so tight that her lips barely moved when she spoke. "Mercy could take a punch, I'll say that."

"Until she couldn't."

Penny gripped her hands around the shotgun, but clearly not because she wanted to use it. Her chin tilted down to her chest as they coasted toward the farmhouse. For the first time since the woman had announced herself on the road, she seemed vulnerable.

Faith wished like hell that Will was here. He could carry a silence longer than anybody she'd ever met. She had to bite her lip to keep herself from asking a question. They had almost reached the house by the time her effort paid off.

Penny said, "Mercy was a good person. That gets lost a lot of times, but it's true."

Faith pulled alongside a rusted Chevy truck. The house was as worn as Penny; paint peeling off bleached wood, rotted front porch, a swaybacked roof with missing shingles. There was another horse on the side of the house. He was tied to a post. His head dipped down into the water trough, but his eyes stayed on the car. Faith suppressed a shudder. She was terrified of horses.

"What you gotta know," Penny said, "is up here, girls get the message real early that whatever you get, that's what you deserve."

Faith didn't think that message was limited to any specific region.

"There was a big stink when Mercy got pregnant in high school. All kinds of phone calls and meetings. The pastor weighed in. Don't get me wrong, it's not like she was a good student, but she had a right to stay in school, and they wouldn't let her. Said she set a bad example. And maybe she did, but it still wasn't right how they treated her."

Faith chewed her bottom lip. She hadn't been stopped from entering ninth grade after she'd given birth to Jeremy, but everyone in the school had made it clear that they didn't want her there. She'd had to eat lunch in the library.

"Mercy was always wild, but the way that aunt stole her baby away was wrong. She's a lesbian. Did you hear?"

"I heard."

"Delilah's a wicked bitch. Got nothing to do with what she does in the bedroom. She's just wicked." Penny strangled the shotgun again. "She made Mercy jump through all kinds of hoops just to have visitation with her own child. It was wrong. Nobody stood up for Mercy. They all thought she was gonna fail, but she stayed off the liquor and heroin so she could get Jon back. That took real grit. Gotta admire her for battling those demons. Especially since she didn't get a lick of help."

"What about Dave?"

"Shit," Penny muttered. "He was working at the blue jean factory. That was a good job before they moved the whole thing to Mexico. He was rolling in dough, buying drinks down at the bar, living it up."

"What was Mercy doing?"

"Sucking dick on the corner so she could pay for a lawyer to get custody of Jon." Penny studied Faith carefully, looking for a reaction.

Faith didn't give her one. There wasn't one thing she would not do for her own children.

"The only job Mercy could get was at the motel, and the only reason that happened is the owner wanted to piss off Papa. Nobody else would hire her. She was poison down here. Papa made sure of that."

"You mean Cecil?"

"Yeah, her own damn daddy. All he ever did was punish her and punish her all of her damn life. I watched it happen. I've been cleaning rooms at the lodge since I was sixteen. Let me tell you this." Penny pointed her finger at Faith like this part was important. "Mercy took over the place after Papa had that bike accident, all right? And all I know is before Mercy was in charge, they could just about make payroll. Then she's running the place and they're hiring a fancy chef from Atlanta and another waiter from town and then Mercy tells me I can go to full-time cause they need a bartender for cocktail hour before supper. What do you think of that?"

"You tell me."

"Papa never understood that people wanna drink when they're on vacation. He served one glass each of that cheap-ass mulberry wine, and if guests wanted more, they had to pony up five dollars cash right then and there." She snorted a laugh. "Mercy brought in the top-shelf liquor, started advertising special cocktails, letting people run tabs. Some of those corporate retreats, they'll pay cash cause they don't want their bosses seeing they're basically alcoholics. Just do the math. At full capacity, they got twenty adults ordering enough hooch every night to justify a bartender."

Faith was excellent at math. Restaurants generally doubled the shelf price of liquor, but they bought it at wholesale pricing. Two cocktails a night times twenty people could net anywhere between four and six hundred dollars profit in a single day. And that didn't include wine sales and whatever they took back to their cottages.

"Mercy raised the rack rate twenty percent and nobody blinked an eye. She fixed up the bathrooms so you didn't get a fungus from taking a shower. She was bringing up high-dollar guests from Atlanta. Papa couldn't stand it." Penny looked back at the house. "Any other daddy would'a been proud, but Papa fucking hated her for it."

Faith wondered if Penny was offering up another suspect. "Cecil was badly injured after the bike accident, right?"

"Yeah, he can't get around no more, but he sure does run that hateful mouth of his." Penny's anger had leveled out. She let the shotgun rest against the dashboard. "I'm gonna be real with you, mostly cause you probably already run my record, but my license was permanently pulled."

Faith knew what she was really saying. Penny had gotten so many DUIs that a judge had passed down a lifetime ban.

"I know what you're thinking. Makes sense that an old drunk like me is a bartender. I've been sober for twelve years, so you can get off your high horse."

"That's not what I was thinking," Faith said. "Your father was still the sheriff twelve years ago. He had a lot of power. It must've been hard for him to not pull any strings to help you."

"You'd think so, right? But he loved it. Made sure I couldn't go anywhere without his permission. Had to beg him to take me to work. To the store. Or the doctor. Hell, I should thank him. Made me learn how to ride a horse."

Faith read between the lines again. "The only job you could get was at the lodge."

"You got it," Penny said. "Daddy had me up there so he could keep me under his thumb."

"He's friends with Cecil?"

"Those two bastards are cut from the same cloth." Her tone had turned bitter. "All him and Cecil ever cared about was being the motherfuckers in charge. Everybody thinks they're so great. Pillars of the community. But I'll tell you what, they get you under their thumb and . . ."

Faith waited for her to finish the *and*.

"They see a woman with high spirits—maybe she likes a drink, maybe she wants a little fun—and they tear her down to the ground. My daddy broke my mama so hard she ended up in an early grave. He tried to break me, too. Maybe he succeeded. I'm still here. Living in this shithole. Cooking his dinner. Wiping his bony ass."

Faith saw the haunted look in Penny's eyes as she stared at the house. The dog shifted in the back seat. He rested his snout on the console.

Penny's hand reached back to pet him as she continued, "You wanna know why the old men in this town are so angry? It's because they used to control everything. Who had to spread her legs. Who didn't. Who got the good jobs. Who couldn't earn an honest living. Who got to live in the good part of town and who got stuck on the wrong side of the tracks. Who could beat his wife. Who would go to prison for drinking and driving and who could end up in the mayor's office."

"And now?"

She huffed a laugh. "Now all they've got is Food Network and adult diapers."

Faith looked at Penny's worn face. Once you peeled away her posturing, there was a depressing level of defeat.

"Shit," Penny muttered. "No matter what I did, it was always gonna end up this way. Same with Mercy. Her daddy wrote the first page of her life before she had a chance to figure out her own story."

Faith let her continue to rant. She was normally all in for a good *men are assholes* session, but she had to find a way to re-center the conversation around the investigation. With Dave out of the picture, that left only a handful of suspects at the lodge who could've raped and murdered Mercy.

She waited for Penny to wind herself down before asking, "Was Mercy seeing anybody?"

"She barely ever left the mountain. Can't remember the last time she was down. Couldn't drive herself. Didn't like showing her face, especially after what she had to do to get Jon back. That old bitch that runs the candle shop spit in her face once, called her a whore. People down here got long memories."

"Mercy wasn't hooking up with anyone in town?"

"Hell no, that would'a gotten out on the front page of the newspaper. You can't keep nothing to yourself down here. Everybody's up in your business. Better off being a Happy Meal. Always come with a toy."

"What about the staff at the lodge? Was Mercy seeing someone there?"

"Don't eat where you shit. Alejandro's a tight ass and those two waiters don't have a pubic hair between 'em." Penny shrugged. "She might'a thrown a bone to a guest here and there."

Faith couldn't control her surprise.

Penny laughed. "A lotta those couples, they think being isolated at a luxury resort is gonna fix their marriage. Then the men give a look, maybe make a comment, and you know they're good for some fun."

Faith thought about Frank and Drew. Of the two men, Frank seemed like a prime target for a mountain quickie. "Where do they go?"

"Wherever they can be alone for five minutes." She fluttered her lips again. "Ten if you're lucky, then they slip back in bed with their wives."

Faith gathered she was speaking from experience. "Did Mercy ever have anything going on with Chuck?"

"Hell no. Poor little weirdo's been sweet on Mercy since Fish brought him home from college over Christmas break." She explained, "They call Christopher Fishtopher on account of he's obsessed with fish. Him and Chuck went to UGA together. Peas in a pod. Both of 'em are super geeky. Not a lot of luck with the ladies."

"I heard that Mercy yelled at Chuck during the cocktail party last night."

"She was nervy is all. Merce didn't tell me what was going on, but I could tell the family bullshit had her riled up more than usual. Chuck was in the wrong place at the wrong time. Which is his specialty, by the way. Always creeping up on people, especially women." Penny went to the obvious question. "If Chuck was a rapist, he would'a done raped Mercy a long time ago. And she would've sliced open his throat. I can promise you that."

Faith had worked her share of rape cases. No one knew how they would react. Her opinion was that whatever a victim did to survive was exactly what the victim should've done to survive.

"I'll tell you who Mercy was worried about," Penny said. "That guest, Monica, she was already off her ass when she showed up for cocktails. Lady tipped me twenty bucks cash money with her first drink. Told me to keep 'em coming, but I'm gonna be honest, I watered that shit down. Then Mercy told me to water it even more."

"What was she drinking?"

"Old Fashioneds with Uncle Nearest. Twenty-two bucks a pour."

"Holy hell." Faith readjusted her math on the liquor gains. The lodge could've been brushing up against a grand on some nights. "Anyone else drinking?"

"Just the normal amount. Husband didn't take a sip, though."

"Frank," Faith supplied. "Did he have any interactions with Mercy?"

"Not that I saw. Trust me, with what ended up happening, I would'a told Biscuits if I'd seen a dude trying to pull anything."

There was nothing left to ask about but the VC Andrews of it all. Faith tried to approach the subject carefully. "Did Fish ever hook up with any guests?"

Penny guffawed. "Only thing Fish could hook is trout."

Faith pulled a detail from Will's recording. "What about that awful business between Christopher and Gabbie?"

"Gabbie? Wow, that's a blast from the past. It's been a minute. I was still drinking when she died. So was Mercy, bless her heart."

Faith felt the hairs on the back of her neck go up. Delilah had made it out like another failed relationship for Christopher. "Do you remember Gabbie's last name?"

"Damn, this was years ago." Penny fluttered her lips in thought. "Can't remember, but she's a prime example of what I was talking about before. Gabbie come up from Atlanta to work at the lodge over the summer. Gorgeous as hell, full of life. Every man on that mountaintop was in love with her."

"Including Christopher?"

"Especially Christopher." She shook her head. "He was tore the hell up when she died. I'm still not sure he's over it. Took to his bed for weeks. Wouldn't eat. Couldn't sleep."

Faith was desperate to pepper her with questions, but she held back.

"Problem was, Gabbie noticed him," Penny said. "Fish's life, he's mostly invisible. Especially to women. And then comes Gabbie smiling and pretending to be interested in waterway management or whatever the hell he's yapping about at the dinner table. I mean, it's not his fault he can't read people. Gabbie was just being nice. You know how some men take kindness for interest."

Faith knew.

"The person Gabbie was real tight with was Mercy. They were close to the same age. Instant best friends, is what I'd call it, like within a day of meeting each other they were joined at the hip. Gotta admit, I was envious. Never had anybody that close to speak of. And they had all kinds of plans for when the summer was over. Gabbie's father owned a restaurant in Buckhead. Mercy was gonna move to Atlanta and wait tables and they were going to get an apartment together and make lots of money and live it up."

Faith could still hear the envy in Penny's voice.

"The two of 'em, they'd sneak out of the lodge almost every night. This was back when there'd be raves down at the old quarry. Stupidest location in the county to get wasted. The road out of there is twisted as a nun's twat. Drops straight down on either side, no guardrails until you hit the curve. They call the last mile Devil's Bend, cause you go down a hill and jerk into a corner like a roller coaster. I'd party with 'em sometimes, but something in my bones told me we'd all end up dead if we kept at it. Started my path to sobriety, especially after what happened."

"What happened?"

Penny hissed out a long sigh between her teeth. "Mercy drove her car straight off Devil's Bend. Dropped straight into the gorge. She got thrown through the front window, sliced off half her face, broke half her bones. Gabbie got crushed. Daddy said she had her feet up on the dashboard when it happened. Coroner told him her leg bones must'a pulverized her skull. Had to use dental records to identify her at the autopsy. Looked like somebody had taken a sledgehammer to her face."

Faith felt her stomach roil. She had worked those kinds of accidents.

"Say what you will about Cecil, but he kept Mercy out of prison. By all rights, she should'a been up on a manslaughter charge, at least. Bloodwork showed she was pumped full of dope when it happened. Mercy was still off her ass when Biscuits rode with her in the ambulance to the hospital. EMTs had to restrain her. He told me half her face was hanging off her skull and she was laughing like a hyena."

"Laughing?"

"Laughing," Penny confirmed. "She thought Biscuits was pranking her. Thought she was still at the lodge. That she'd OD'd and they were parked outside the house. EMTs heard her laughing, too, so word got around real quick. Ain't a person in this town you could'a put on a jury who wouldn't have convicted her at trial. But there wasn't a trial. Mercy basically walked. Which is another reason people in town hate her. They say she got away with murder."

Faith couldn't understand how that had happened. "Did she take a plea deal?"

"You're not hearing me. There was no deal to take. Mercy wasn't charged with nothing. Didn't even get a ticket. Voluntarily gave up her license. Never drove again as far as I know, but that was her choice, not a judge taking it away." Penny nodded, like she was agreeing with Faith's shock. "You were asking about abuse of power? That's what my daddy used it for, to put Mercy under Cecil's thumb for the rest of her living days."

Faith was dumbstruck. "She just got away with it? No consequences?"

"I mean, her face was a consequence. She told me every time she looked in a mirror, that scar reminded her of what a bad person she was. She was haunted by it. Never forgave herself. Maybe she shouldn't have."

Faith could not understand how any of this had happened. There were so many levers that had to be pulled in order for Mercy to escape criminal prosecution for vehicular homicide. And not just on the law enforcement side. The county had a prosecutor's office. A circuit judge. A mayor. A board of commissioners.

She guessed that Penny's tirade against the angry men who used to control this town was useful after all. Mercy hadn't been punished because they had all gotten together and decided that she wouldn't be punished.

"I guess the only good that came out of it is, that's when Mercy started trying to get sober," Penny said. "Took a few tries, but once her head was clear, all she could think about was Jon. She told me without him, she would'a walked into the lake and never come back out."

Faith didn't know how Mercy had stopped herself. The guilt of being responsible for her best friend's death must have been crushing.

"Being honest, I think sometimes Mercy would'a been better off serving her time in prison. The way Cecil and Bitty treated her was worse than anything could'a happened to her on the inside. It's bad enough when a stranger rips you down every day of your life, but when it's your own mama and daddy?"

Faith was surprised by her own feelings of sadness for Mercy McAlpine. She kept going back to something Penny had said— *Her daddy wrote the first page of her life before she had a chance to figure out her own story.* That wasn't entirely true. Cecil might have started it, but Dave continued the same abusive narrative, and yet another man had ended it. Faith didn't believe in fate, but it sounded like the woman hadn't stood a chance.

Her phone started to ring. The caller ID read GBI SAT.

She told Penny, "I need to get this."

Penny nodded, but she didn't get out of the car.

Faith pushed open the door. The sole of her boot sank into the mud. She tapped the phone. "Mitchell."

"Faith." Will's voice was faint over the satellite connection. "Can you talk?"

"Hold on." Faith squicked through the mud to get away from the car. Penny was openly watching her progress. The horse lifted its head as Faith walked past. His eyes followed her like a serial killer. She trudged out another few yards, then told Will, "Go ahead."

"Mercy was pregnant."

Faith's heart sank from the news. She could only think of Mercy. The woman couldn't catch a break. Then her detective brain took over, because this changed everything. There was no more dangerous time for a woman than during pregnancy. Homicide was the leading cause of maternal death in the United States.

"Faith?"

Faith heard the car door slam. Penny had gotten out. The dog was sitting at her feet. Faith kept her voice low, asking Will, "How far along?"

"Sara estimates twelve weeks."

Faith listened to the phone crackle in the silence. She turned her back to the car. "Did Mercy know?"

"Unclear," Will said. "For what it's worth, she didn't mention it to Sara."

"Penny told me Mercy's hooked up with guests before."

Will let the silence linger for another beat. "The road's completely washed out. We left another UTV for you back at the hospital. Find Sara and bring her up with you. She might be able to get Drew and Keisha to talk to her."

"You think Drew—"

"They've been to the lodge twice before," he reminded her. "Drew said something strange to Bitty this morning. Sara can fill you in."

"I'm heading back to the hospital now."

Faith ended the call. The horse snorted in her direction, even though she gave it a wide berth. Penny had the shotgun slung back over her shoulders. She was looking down at the ground.

Faith followed her line of sight. The Mini's back right tire was flat. "Fuck."

Penny asked, "You got a spare?"

"It's in my garage. My son took it out when he moved his band equipment." Faith hoped the FBI knew that Jeremy was a moron. She nodded to the Chevy truck. "Can I get a lift to the hospital? My partner needs me at the lodge."

"I don't drive, and that truck don't work, but Rascal's got plenty of gas."

"Rascal?"

Penny nodded toward the horse.

14

Will scanned the woods as he walked up the Loop Trail toward the main lodge. His injured hand was throbbing even though he held it to his chest in a permanent pledge of allegiance. The bandage had gotten wet again. He'd hosed himself down and changed into fresh pants while Kevin Rayman, the agent on loan from the GBI's North Georgia field office, was processing evidence from Mercy's bedroom.

Not that there was a lot to process. As with her financial situation, Mercy hadn't had much to her name. Her small closet was filled with utilitarian items. Nothing on hangers, just folded shirts, jeans, and outdoor attire. She had two pairs of worn sneakers and some expensive but old hiking boots. Will was struck by a familiar feeling. Every item of clothing he'd had as a kid had been donated by someone else. Mercy's clothes were faded and worn and in various sizes. He would've bet she hadn't bought them new.

In fact, nothing seemed new. Washed-out posters of O-Town, New Kids on the Block and the Jonas Brothers were on the walls. Some of Jon's childhood drawings were taped beside the door. Photographs documented the sixteen years of his life. School photos and some outdoor candids: Jon opening a stuffed giraffe at Christmas; Jon standing with Dave by a trailer; Jon lying on the couch where he'd fallen asleep with his phone resting against his chin.

Mercy's room seemed to have the only bookcase in the house. She had a snow globe from Gatlinburg, Tennessee, and at least fifty well-read romance paperbacks. Everything was dusted and tidy, which somehow made her meager belongings even more poignant. There were no secret papers hidden under her mattress. Her bedside drawer had what you would expect a woman to have. There was no bathroom connected to her room. Mercy shared the one at the end of the hall with the rest of her family. She hadn't taken her iPad when she'd packed to leave. The screen was locked. They would have to send it to the lab to try to break the code.

According to Sara, Mercy didn't have an IUD. They had no way of knowing if Mercy was even aware of the pregnancy. If she was taking birth control, the pills were probably in her backpack. Condoms didn't seem like the kind of thing a woman would grab if she was leaving in a hurry. The big questions remained: What had made her leave? Where was she planning on going? Why had she called Dave?

Will stopped on the trail and took his iPhone out of his pocket. He used the fingers of his injured hand to tap the screen, opening the recording of Mercy's voicemail to Dave. There was one section he kept coming back to.

I can't believe—oh, God, I can't— Please call me. Please. I need you.

Mercy's voice had a kind of hope tied up in desperation when she said the words *I need you*, like she was praying that this would be the one time that Dave didn't disappoint her.

Will returned his phone to his pocket and continued up the trail. He kept silently playing the message back in his head. He didn't understand how Dave had gotten here. Neither one of them had been given a choice about their shitty childhoods, but they had both decided what kind of men they would be. Will wasn't judging Dave for struggling with his demons. The alcohol and drugs made a certain kind of sense. But Dave had chosen to beat his wife, to strangle her, to terrorize her, to continually fail her.

That part was squarely on him.

Will silently berated himself for focusing on the wrong guy. He had to let go of being mad at Dave. Mercy's worthless ex-husband had been shunted to the periphery of the investigation. Identifying the killer, locating Jon; those were the only two things that Will needed to be worried about right now.

Sunlight bathed his face as he entered the main compound. Will adjusted the heavy satellite phone that was clipped to the back of his belt. He was wearing a paddle holster at his side. Amanda had loaned him her backup piece, a snub-nosed five-shot Smith and Wesson that was older than Will. He felt like an outlaw walking through town in an old Spaghetti Western. A curtain twitched in Drew and Keisha's cottage. Cecil glared at him from his wheelchair on the front porch. The two cats eyeballed him from their separate perches on the stairs. Paul was in the hammock outside his cottage. He had a book flat to his chest and a bottle of alcohol on the table. His mouth went into a smirk when he saw Will. He reached for the bottle and took a swig.

Will was going to let him stew for a bit longer. Paul was on his list of people to talk to, but he wasn't at the top. Interviews generally fell into two categories: confrontational or informational. The two waiters, Gregg and Ezra, were teenagers. They'd probably be a good source of information. Will wasn't sure where Alejandro would fall. Mercy was twelve weeks pregnant. Guests were in and out of the lodge. Will's primary focus was on the men who were consistently around Mercy.

Not to say that the other men at the compound weren't going to have their time in the barrel. The McAlpines had suspended all planned activities, but Chuck had gone fishing with Christopher as soon as the storm had passed. Drew was holed up inside cottage three with Keisha. Gordon seemed content to drink the day away with Paul. Frank was playing Columbo by way of the Hardy Boys.

Will was waiting for Amanda to come through with the warrant so that he could search the property for bloody clothes and the missing knife handle. The UTV carried a thermal printer in the lockbox that would hopefully work with the satellite phone so that Will could print the document and physically serve the warrant. The McAlpines had granted Will and Kevin access to Mercy's room, but he had a feeling they would push back on the rest of the place, especially considering they were still trying to hold on to paying guests.

Bitty had told Will in no uncertain terms that she and her husband were too overcome with grief to answer any questions.

Which was fair, but the woman hadn't seemed overcome with anything but anger. Sara had already searched the kitchen for the broken knife handle, so the house was low on his list. At some point, the lake might have to be dragged. That decision was above Will's paygrade. For now, the best use of his time was talking to people and trying to figure out who had a motive to murder Mercy.

Will scanned the trees, trying to figure out which way to go. Last night, they had gotten to dinner by following the bottom half of the Loop. Sara had led them to another trail down to the dining hall, but Will had honestly been paying more attention to Sara than the route.

Out of the corner of his eye, he saw the door to Frank's cottage crack open. A hand stuck out, waving Will over. He could see Frank hiding in the shadows, which would've been funny in any other circumstances. Will was literally out in the open. Everyone could see him crossing the compound toward cottage seven. He figured now was as good a time as any to interview Frank. Monica had been completely wasted last night. Frank could've easily slipped out for a tryst. He could've just as easily showered off Mercy's blood and slipped back into bed without his wife knowing.

Frank kept up the cloak and dagger as Will came up the stairs. The door cracked open wider. Inside, Will's eyes took a moment to adjust to the darkness. The curtains were drawn across the windows and French doors to the back. The door to the bedroom was closed. There was an odor of sickness in the air.

"I got the names you asked for," Frank handed Will a folded sheet of paper. "I found the guest registry in an office off the back of the kitchen."

Will opened the page. Thankfully, Frank had written in block letters, which made it easier for him to read. He tucked the note into his shirt pocket for later. For now, Frank was in the hot seat. "Thanks for helping me out. How did you get past the staff?"

"I threw a rich white guy tantrum and demanded to use the phone. Nobody told me it wasn't working." He sounded excited. "Anything else you need me to do, chief?"

"Yeah." Will was about to knock some air out of the guy's sails. "Did you hear anything last night?"

"Nothing, which is weird, because I have really good hearing. It's not like I got much sleep. I was up and down with Monica all night. If someone had yelled in this vicinity, I would've heard it."

Will's follow-up question was cut off by the sound of retching from behind the closed bedroom door. Frank tensed as they both listened. The retching stopped. The toilet flushed. The silence returned.

"She'll be okay." Frank's voice had the practiced cadence of a man who was used to making excuses for his alcoholic wife. "Have a seat."

Will was glad Frank was making this easy for him. The furniture was the same style as the couch and club chairs in Will and Sara's cottage, but it looked more worn. There was a stain on the carpet with a paper towel soaking up the dark liquid. That was where the smell was coming from. Will took the chair farthest away from it.

"What a day." Frank rubbed his face as he sank into the couch. He looked embarrassed. He also looked exhausted. His face was unshaven. His hair was uncombed. He'd clearly had a hard night even before Will had woken up the entire compound. "How's your hand?"

Will's hand was throbbing with every beat of his heart. "It's better, thanks."

"I keep thinking about Mercy at dinner last night. I wish that I had helped her, but I don't know what I could've done."

"There wasn't much anybody could do."

"Well, maybe?" Frank asked. "Like, I could've done what you did. Helped clean up the broken glass. Instead, I started talking about the food. I wish I hadn't done that, because I think it gave everyone permission to ignore what had just happened."

There was no practiced cadence to his voice now, but Will gathered his need to always smooth things over was a recurring dilemma.

"I want to do something now," Frank said. "Mercy's dead, and no one seems to care. You should've seen them all at breakfast. Gordon and Paul kept making dark jokes. Drew and Keisha would barely talk. Christopher and Chuck might as well have sealed themselves inside of an acrylic box. I tried to speak to Bitty and Cecil, but—do you get a bad vibe off of them?"

Will wasn't going to share his vibes. Frank was low on his list of suspects, but he was still on the list. "Did you tell me that you've been to the lodge before?"

"No, that was Drew and Keisha. Third time up here, can you believe it? Though I doubt they'll ever come back."

"You and Monica travel a lot. When was your last trip?"

"Oh, gosh, it must've been Italy. We went to Florence three months ago. Stayed two weeks. There was a lot of wine. Maybe that was a mistake on my part, but we've got to live, right?"

"Right." Will made a mental note to confirm the timeline, but it would let Frank off the hook for Mercy's pregnancy, if not the murder. "What were your impressions of Mercy?"

Frank leaned back on the couch with a heavy sigh. He seemed lost in thought for a moment. "My parents were both alcoholics. I don't know what it is about me, but I can pick up on it when someone is troubled. It's like a sixth sense."

Will understood. He had grown up surrounded by addicts. His first wife still had a passion for opioids. He was hyper-aware of anyone showing the same patterns.

"Anyway, that's what my Spidey-senses told me. That Mercy was troubled."

Monica coughed from the bedroom. Frank's head turned as he listened again. Will felt sorry for the man. It was an incredibly stressful way to live. Will still got inexplicably anxious if Sara's lips so much as touched a glass of wine.

Frank said, "Maybe that's why I kept such a wide berth. With Mercy, I mean. I didn't want to get tangled up in her drama. I guess I have enough on my hands. You know, Monica wasn't like this when our son was alive. She was funny and easy-going and she put up with me, which is saying a lot. I know I'm a handful. Nicholas was our shining ray of joy. Then the leukemia took him from us and . . . Our therapist says everyone handles grief in their own way. I really thought coming up here would give us a reset, you know? Believe it or not, before Nicholas died, Monica seldom drank. She liked an occasional margarita, but she knew about my parents, so . . ."

Will knew the compassionate thing to do was let the man talk. Frank was clearly alone inside of his wife's addiction. But this was a murder investigation, not therapy. He'd let Frank do some busy work, but that didn't take him off Will's list of suspects.

"Sorry." Frank's Spidey-sense picked up on Will's impatience. He stood up from the couch. "I know I talk too much. Thanks for listening. Let me know what I can—"

Monica coughed from the other room again. Will noticed the worry on Frank's face. The man had clearly seen a hangover before, but there was something that told Will this time was different.

He asked, "What's going on, Frank?"

Frank glanced back at the bedroom door, keeping his voice low. "Believe it or not, last night wasn't that bad. She had a lot, but not as much as usual."

"And?"

"I don't think it's an emergency, but—" Frank shrugged. "She keeps throwing up. I've gone through all the Coke in the fridge. I brought some toast from the kitchen. She can't keep anything down."

Will wished this conversation had happened twenty minutes ago. Sara had already left the hospital in the second UTV. "My wife is a doctor. I'll make sure she checks on Monica as soon as she gets here."

"I'd appreciate that." Frank was too relieved to ask how Sara had gone from being a chemistry teacher to a doctor. "Like I said, I don't think it's an emergency."

His minimizing cut at Will's better angels. He put his hand on Frank's shoulder. "We'll get her some help, Frank. I promise."

"Thanks." Frank gave an awkward smile. "I know it's crazy, but maybe you understand. I think you understand. I saw you and Sara together, and it reminded me, you know? She's worth fighting for. I really, really love my wife."

Will watched Frank's eyes fill with tears. He was saved coming up with something thoughtful to say when Monica coughed again. Her footsteps banged across the floor as she ran for the toilet.

"Excuse me." Frank disappeared into the bedroom.

Will didn't leave. He looked around. The couch and chairs. The coffee table. Frank had cleaned up. Nothing looked out of place. Will did a quick search, checking under the cushions, rifling the shelves and drawers in the tiny kitchen, because Frank seemed like a nice guy but he was also a lonely, grief-stricken husband who was looking to save his marriage—exactly the type of guest that Mercy had probably hooked up with before.

Frank had left the bedroom door ajar. Will used the toe of his boot to push it open the rest of the way. The room was empty. Frank was in the bathroom with Monica. Will stepped inside. Their clothes were still folded in their suitcases. He found a stack of books, mostly thrillers. The usual digital devices. The bed was unmade. The fitted sheet had soaked through with sweat. There was a used trash can on the floor by the bed.

No bloody clothes. No knife handle with the blade broken off.

Will backed out of the room. He looked at his watch. He wouldn't feel right until Sara was standing in front of him. At the very least, she could give him that look like he was an idiot for not taking pain medication for his hand.

Which was a valid look, but it wouldn't change the situation.

Cecil was still glaring when Will walked out of the cottage. Will spotted a sign with a plate and silverware beside an arrow. This had to be the Chow Trail. Will recognized the zigzag shape from last night. The crushed stone was flattened in parallel rows from Cecil's wheelchair.

Will put a zig between himself and the house before he looked at the guest list Frank had given him. He could easily make out some of the names, but that was only because he already knew them. The last names were a different story. He found a tree stump to sit on. He placed the paper on his lap, inserted his earbuds. He used his phone's camera to scan the names, then loaded the scan into his text-to-speech app.

Frank and Monica Johnson

Drew Conklin and Keisha Murray

Gordon Wylie and Landry Peterson

Sydney Flynn and Max Brouwer

Will set up a hot spot with the satellite phone and sent the list to Amanda so she could run background and criminal checks. The upload took almost a full minute. He waited until she had texted back a check mark that the information was received. Then he waited to see if she texted anything else. Half of him was relieved when the three dancing dots disappeared.

Amanda was extremely furious with him right now. More than usual, which said a lot. She had tried to take the case away from Will. Will had told her he would work it anyway. It had turned into a thing. All he could do was wait for that moment in the near future when she would shove her razor-sharp claws down his throat and rip out his intestines.

For now, he had a chef and two waiters to interview. Will folded up the list and stuck it back into his shirt pocket. He tucked his phone and earbuds back into his pants pocket. He clipped the satellite phone on his belt. He pressed his injured hand to his chest and resumed his trek.

The Chow Trail took another gradual curve before zigging back toward the dining hall. The design made sense considering Cecil's chair couldn't handle a sharp, downward slope, but Will would have to tell Faith to adjust her timeline. Mercy wouldn't have bothered with following the curves, especially if she was running for her life.

Will waited until he was standing on the viewing platform to look back up the trail. He thought he could see the roof of the main house. He went to the edge of the platform that overlooked the lake. The tops of trees obscured the shore, but the bachelor cottages were down there somewhere. He leaned over the railing and looked straight down. The drop was steep, but he imagined someone who'd grown up on this property would know how to get down quickly. Will had a feeling he was going to end up being the one sliding down the side of a cliff while Faith held the stopwatch.

He walked around the back of the building toward the kitchen, glancing through the window on his way. The chef was working at a commercial food mixer. The two waiters were carrying large black plastic bags of trash out the back door.

Will was about to go inside when the satellite phone vibrated on his belt.

He took a few steps away from the building before answering, "Trent."

"Are you still doing this?" Amanda asked.

He heard the clear warning in her prickly tone. "Yes, ma'am."

"Very well," she said. "I've been trying to reach a circuit judge up here who has phone service. Apparently, the storm took out the main transformers that service the northwestern part of the state, but I'll make the warrant happen. The dive team is currently searching for a body in Lake Rayburn. Let's keep that as an option of last resort. As you know, it's very expensive to search a lake, particularly one that deep, so I need you to find that knife handle quickly and on land."

"Understood."

"I located Gordon Wylie's marriage certificate. He's married to a man named Paul Ponticello."

"Anything on their sheets?"

"Nothing. Wylie owns a company that developed a stock market app. Ponticello is a plastic surgeon with an office in Buckhead."

Will imagined the men were not hurting for money. "What about the others?"

"Monica Johnson picked up a DUI six months ago."

"Makes sense. And Frank?"

"I found a death certificate for their child, twenty years old. Leukemia. Solid financial picture on both of them," Amanda said. "The same with all the others. Wealthy, educated professionals for the most part. Drew Conklin is the exception. He has a fifteen-year-old charge for aggravated assault."

The information surprised him. "Do you have details?"

"I'm tracking down the arrest report for the specifics. Conklin didn't serve time, so a plea deal was made."

"Do you know if a weapon was involved?"

"It wouldn't have been a firearm," Amanda said. "He would've gotten mandatory jail time."

"Could've been a knife."

"Do you like him for this?"

Will tried to put his personal feelings aside, but it was hard. He needed to know what *business* Drew had wanted to talk with

Bitty about. "It definitely moves him up to the top of my list, but I don't know."

"Kevin Rayman is a highly accomplished and decorated agent."

She was talking about the GBI field agent. "He's doing a great job up here."

"Faith is a dogged investigator."

"That doesn't sound like a compliment."

"Wilbur, you're supposed to be on your honeymoon. There will always be murder cases. You can't work them all. I will not let this job take over your life."

He was tired of hearing the same lecture. "No one cares that Mercy is dead, Amanda. They all abandoned her. Her parents haven't asked a single question. Her brother's literally gone fishing."

"She has a son who loves her."

"So did my mother."

Uncharacteristically, Amanda didn't have an immediate comeback.

In the silence, Will watched one of the waiters pushing a wheelbarrow loaded with trash bags up yet another trail. He assumed it was a shortcut to the house. Faith was definitely going to need the map. And her running shoes. Will's stride was twice as long as Mercy's. Faith would be the one who got to run around the forest.

"All right," Amanda finally said. "Let's get this closed quickly, Wilbur. And don't expect compensatory time. You've made it quite clear this is how you're choosing to spend your vacation days."

"Yes, ma'am." Will ended the call and clipped the phone back on his belt.

He glanced into the kitchen window. The chef had moved to the stove. Will walked around the octagon to the back of the building. The trail up to the house also went down toward the creek that fed the lake. Faith was going to have some choice words for him by the time the day was over.

A free-standing freezer was under a lean-to on the other side of the trail. The door to the kitchen was closed. The second waiter was still outside. He was stacking cans into a paper grocery sack.

His hair had fallen into his eyes. He looked younger than Jon, maybe fourteen years old.

"Shit!" The kid had seen Will and dropped the bag. Cans rolled in every direction. He scrambled to gather them, shooting Will furtive looks like a criminal caught in the act, which was obviously accurate. "Mister, I'm not—"

"It's all right." Will helped him with the cans. The kid hadn't taken much. Green beans, condensed milk, corn, black-eyed peas. Will knew what it was like to be desperate and hungry. He was never going to stop someone from stealing food.

The kid asked, "Are you gonna arrest me?"

Will wondered who had told him that Will was a cop. Probably everybody. "No, I'm not going to arrest you."

The kid seemed unconvinced as he packed cans back into the bag.

"You've got some good stuff here."

"The milk is for my baby sister," he said. "She's got a sweet tooth."

"Are you Ezra or Gregg?"

"I'm Gregg, sir."

"Gregg." Will handed him the last can. "Have you seen Jon?"

"No, sir. I heard he ran off. Delilah already asked me if there was anywhere he'd go. I talked to Ezra about it and neither one of us know where he'd run off to. I'd tell you if we did, that's for sure. Jon's a good guy. He's gotta be torn up about his mama."

Will watched the kid hug the grocery bag to his chest. He was more worried about losing the food than talking to a cop.

"Keep it," Will said. "I'm not going to tell anybody."

Relief flooded the kid's face. He walked around the standing freezer and got down on his knees as he hid the bag in what was clearly his usual spot. Will saw a dark oil stain had spread across the wood decking. There didn't seem to be a recycling tank, which meant the oil was going down the drain into the septic system, which could get into the groundwater, which was something the EPA frowned on. Will put the information in his back pocket in case he needed to pressure Bitty and Cecil with it later on.

"Thanks, mister." Gregg cleaned his hands on his apron as he stood back up. "I need to get back to work."

"Take a minute."

Gregg looked scared again. His eyes went to the hidden food.

"You're not in trouble. I'm just trying to get some idea of what Mercy's life was like before she died. Can you tell me about her?"

"Like what?"

"Like, whatever comes to mind. Anything."

"She was fair?" he asked, testing the waters. "I mean, she could tear you a new one sometimes, but not out of nowhere. You knew where you stood with her. Not like the rest of 'em."

"What are the rest of them like?"

"Cecil's mean as a snake. He'll cut you just as soon as look at ya. Not that he can move like that anymore, but before the accident, he was scary." Gregg leaned against the freezer. "Fish, he don't talk much. I guess he's okay, but he's weird. Bitty, she burned me real bad. Pretended she was my friend, then I didn't do something she asked fast enough and she turned on me something fierce."

"How'd she turn on you?"

"Cut me off," he said. "She helps me and Ezra out sometimes. Like, if you're nice to her, she'll slip you a ten- or a twenty-dollar bill. But now, I walk by and she won't even look me in the eye. Being honest, with Mercy gone, I'm gonna look for work in town. They already told all of us they're cutting back our wages on account of they don't know what's gonna happen next."

That tracked with what Will had learned about the McAlpines and money. "Have you ever seen Mercy talking to any of the male guests?"

He snorted. "That's a funny way of asking."

"What am I asking?"

His face turned red.

"It's okay," Will said. "It's just you and me. Did you see Mercy with any of the guests?"

"If she was talking to a guest, they were either asking her for something or complaining." He shrugged. "We're up here at six every morning, then back down the mountain by nine. There's a lot of work to do in between meals. Washing dishes, food prep, cleaning. Not a lot of time to watch what people are up to."

Will didn't ask him when he found time to go to school. The

kid was probably helping to support his family. "When's the last time you saw Mercy?"

"I guess around eight-thirty last night. She let us go early. Said she'd finish up."

"Was anyone in the kitchen when you left?"

"No, sir. She was alone."

"What about the chef?"

"Alejandro left when we did."

Will hadn't seen another car on the parking pad. "What does he drive?"

"We all take horses up and down. There's a paddock yonder down from the parking pad. Me and Ezra double up since it's his horse. Alejandro went the other way cause he lives on the other side of the range."

Will would follow up on the paddock. "What do you think of Alejandro?"

"He's all right. Takes his work real serious. Not a lot of joking around." He shrugged again. "Beats the guy who was here before. He was always looking at us funny."

"Did Alejandro spend time with Mercy?"

"Sure, she had to go over stuff with him a couple times a day on account of the guests are real particular about their food."

"Did Mercy and Alejandro have these conversations in front of you?"

Gregg's eyebrows went up, like he'd just put it together. "They'd go back to Mercy's office and shut the door. I never thought about the two of them together. I mean Mercy was kind of old."

Will guessed thirty-two was ancient to a fourteen-year-old.

"Mister," he said. "Sorry, but is that it? I gotta get the Hobart going or I'm gonna get my hide tanned."

"That's it. Thanks."

Will waited until the door was closed before going to the standing freezer. The lock was open. He looked inside. Nothing but meat. He walked around the back and spotted Gregg's stash shoved up against the wall of the lean-to. The trash cans were empty. The area was clean.

No bloody clothes. No broken knife handle.

Will got on his knees and used the flashlight from his phone to look under the freezer.

He heard voices from the forest. Will stayed down behind the freezer. He was obscured by the slats on the side of the lean-to. Christopher and Chuck were on the lower part of the trail below the dining hall. They were carrying fishing poles and tackle boxes. Chuck had the same gallon water jug he'd sported at dinner last night. He drank so loudly from the clear, plastic container that Will could hear his gulps from twenty yards away.

"Crap," Christopher said. "I forgot my stupid gaff."

Chuck wiped his mouth with the sleeve of his shirt. "You leaned it against the tree."

"Crap." Christopher looked at his watch. "We're supposed to have a family meeting. Can you—"

"Family meeting about what?"

"Hell if I know. Probably the sale."

"Do you think the investors are still interested?"

"Give me your stuff." Christopher wrangled Chuck's tackle box and pole alongside his own. "Even if they're not interested, it's over. I'm out of this business. I never wanted to do it in the first place. And without Mercy, it just won't work. We needed her."

"Fish, don't talk like that. We can figure it out. We can't give this up." Chuck held out his arms to indicate their surroundings. "Come on, buddy. This is a good thing we've got going. A lot of people are depending on us."

"They can depend on somebody else." Christopher turned and headed back up the trail. "I've made up my mind."

"Fish!"

Will ducked down so that Christopher didn't see him as he walked past.

"Fishtopher McAlpine. Come back here. You can't bail on me." Chuck was silent for way too long before he figured out Christopher wasn't coming back. "Dammit."

Will stuck up his head from behind the freezer. He could see Christopher heading toward the main house. Chuck was making his way down to the creek.

A decision had to be made.

Alejandro would probably be in the kitchen for the rest of the day. Unlike the rest of the men on the property, Chuck was a complete mystery. They didn't know his last name. They hadn't been able to do a background check. More importantly, Mercy had embarrassed the man in front of a group of people. Roughly eighty percent of the murders Will investigated were perpetrated by men who were furious about their inability to control women.

Will headed down the trail. If it could be called a trail. The narrow strip toward the creek wasn't lined with crushed stone like the others. Will could see why it wasn't meant for guests. The perilously steep trail could've resulted in some lawsuits. Will had to concentrate on his footing to get through the worst of it. Chuck was having an easier time of it. He was swinging the water jug as he traipsed through the forest. The man had a strange way of walking, like his pronated feet were kicking imaginary soccer balls. He resembled a lesser Mr. Bean. His back was swayed. He was wearing a bucket hat and fishing vest. His brown cargo shorts hit below his knees. Black socks slouched around his yellow hiking boots.

The trail turned even steeper. Will held on to a branch so he didn't slide on his ass. Then he grabbed a rope that was tethered to a tree like a handrail. He heard the shush of white water before he saw the creek. The sound was soft, more like white noise. This must've been the area Delilah had called the waterfall that wasn't really the waterfall. The terrain dropped about ten feet in the space of a dozen yards. Some flat stones had been placed in the water to create a footbridge at the head of the mini falls.

Will remembered seeing a photograph taken in this area on the lodge website. It showed Christopher McAlpine standing in the middle of the creek throwing out a fishing line. The water was up to his waist. Will guessed the rain had made it twice as deep. The bank on the opposite side was mostly submerged. The tree canopy was thicker overhead. He could see clearly, but not as clearly as he would've liked.

Chuck was taking in the same view, but from a lower vantage. He was kneading his back with his fist as he looked across the creek. Will catalogued the ways Chuck could hurt him if there was some kind of struggle. The hooks and lures on the man's vest would hurt like hell, but fortunately, Will only had one hand that would be shredded. He wasn't sure what a gaff was, though he had noticed that most of the instruments for fishing could easily be turned into weapons. The plastic jug was half full of water, but would feel like a hammer if Chuck swung it with enough force.

Will kept his distance, calling, "Chuck?"

Chuck whipped around, startled. His glasses had fogged at the edges, but his eyes easily found the revolver on Will's hip. He asked, "You're Will, right?"

"That's right." Will picked his way down the last part of the trail.

"The humidity is a bitch today." Chuck cleaned his glasses with the tail of his shirt. "We barely missed another storm coming through."

Will kept around ten feet between them. "Sorry we didn't get a chance to talk at dinner last night."

Chuck pushed his glasses up his nose. "Believe me, if I had a wife who was that hot, I wouldn't talk to anybody, either."

"Thanks," Will forced himself to smile. "I didn't catch your name."

"Bryce Weller." He reached out to shake Will's hand, then saw the bandage and waved instead. "People call me Chuck."

Will kept his response neutral. "That's quite a nickname."

"Yeah, you'll have to ask Dave how he came up with it. No one remembers anymore." Chuck was smiling, but he didn't look happy. "Thirteen years ago, I went up the mountain a Bryce and came down a Chuck."

Will wondered why the guy was suddenly speaking in an accent, but he didn't press it. "I should tell you I'm here in a work capacity. I was wondering if you wouldn't mind talking to me about Dave."

"He didn't confess?"

Will shook his head, glad that the word hadn't spread from town yet.

"I'm not surprised, inspector," Chuck said in another weird voice. "He's a weasely vermin. Don't let him get out of this. He should get the electric chair."

Will didn't tell him it was done by lethal injection. "What can you tell me about Dave?"

Chuck didn't answer immediately. He uncapped the water jug and gulped down half of what was left. He smacked his lips as he flipped the cap back in place. Then he let out a burp that was so putrid Will could almost taste it from ten feet away.

"Dave is a typical Chad." Chuck's jokey voice was gone. "Don't ask me why, but females can't resist him. The more terrible he is, the more they want him. He doesn't have a real job. He scrapes by on whatever scraps Bitty throws him. He smokes like a chimney. He's an addict. He lies, cheats and steals. He lives in a trailer. Doesn't own a car. What's not to love, right? Meanwhile, all the nice guys are relegated to the friend zone."

Will wasn't surprised that Chuck was an incel, but he was surprised the man was so open about it. "Did Mercy put you in the friend zone?"

"I put myself there, friend." Chuck seemed to really believe this. "I let her cry on my shoulder a few times, but then I realized nothing was ever going to change. No matter how much Dave hurt her, she always went back to him."

"You were aware of the abuse?"

"Everyone was." Chuck took off his hat and wiped the sweat off his forehead. "Dave didn't try to hide it. He would hit Mercy right in front of us sometimes. An open-handed smack, never a punch, but we all saw it."

Will held back his judgment. "That must've been hard to watch."

"I spoke up in the beginning, but Bitty pulled me aside. M'lady made it clear to me that a gentleman does not interfere in another gentleman's marriage." The stupid voice was back. Chuck leaned toward Will, pretending a confidence. "Even the harshest ruffian cannot say 'nay' to such a petite and delicate creature's request."

Will finally got what Sara meant when she said that Chuck was weird. "Mercy divorced him over a decade ago. Why was Dave even up here?"

"Bitty."

Rather than explain himself, Chuck decided to take another swig from the jug. Will was beginning to wonder if it was just water in there. Chuck drained the entire thing, his throat making gulping sounds like a slow toilet.

Chuck burped again before he continued, "For all intents and purposes, Bitty is Dave's mother. He has a right to see her. And of course Bitty has a right to invite him to every holiday. Christmas, Thanksgiving, Fourth of July, Mother's Day, Kwanzaa. Whatever the occasion, Dave's always here. She snaps and he jumps."

Will took that to mean that Chuck was always there, too. "How did Mercy feel about Dave being included in every family event?"

Chuck swung the empty jug in his hand. "Sometimes, she was glad. Sometimes, she wasn't. I think she tried to make it easy for Jon."

"She was a good mother?"

"Yeah." Chuck gave a curt nod. "She was a good mother."

The admission seemed to take something out of him. He took off his hat again. He tossed it onto the ground beside a black fiberglass rod that was leaning against a tree.

Which is how Will learned that a gaff is basically a four-foot-long pole with a big, nasty hook on the end.

"The property is huge," Chuck said. "Mercy could've avoided Dave. Hid in her room. Stayed out of his way. But she never did that. Every meal, she was at the table. Every family gathering, she was there. And invariably, she and Dave ended up screaming at each other or hitting each other and, honestly, it got boring after a while."

Will said, "I bet."

Chuck placed the empty jug beside his hat. Will had a sense of déjà vu taking him back to Dave and the boning knife. Was Chuck freeing up his hands or was he just tired of carrying things?

"The worst part was watching how all of this affected Fishtopher." Chuck started kneading his back again. "He hated how Dave treated Mercy. He was always saying that he was going to do something about it. Cut Dave's brake lines or throw him in the Shallows. Dave's a terrible swimmer. It's a wonder he's never drowned before. But Fish wouldn't do anything, and now Mercy's dead. You can see how it's weighing on him."

Will couldn't see anything. "Christopher is a hard man to read."

"He's devastated," Chuck said. "He loved Mercy. He really did."

Will thought he had a funny way of showing it. "Did you go back to your cottage after dinner last night?"

"Fish and I had a nightcap, then I retired to my cottage for some reading."

"Did you hear anything between ten and midnight?"

"I fell asleep with my book. That explains the kink in my back. I feel like I've been punched in the kidneys."

"You didn't hear a scream or a howl or anything like that?"

Chuck shook his head.

"When's the last time you saw Mercy alive?"

"Dinner." Irritation sparked his voice. "You witnessed what happened between us at cocktails. That's a prime example of how Mercy treated me. I was only trying to make sure she was okay, and she screamed at me like I had raped her."

Will watched his face change, like he regretted choosing the word *rape*. Before Will could follow up, Chuck reached for his hat on the ground. He hissed air between his teeth.

"Jesus, my back." He left the hat on the ground and slowly straightened up. "The body tells you when you need to take a break, right?"

"Right." Will was thinking about the fact that Mercy didn't have any defensive wounds. Maybe she had gotten in some punches before the knife had subdued her. "You want me to take a look at that?"

"My back?" Chuck sounded alarmed. "What would you see?"

Bruises. Bite marks. Scratches.

Will lied, "I worked as a physical therapist in college. I could—"

"I'm fine," Chuck said. "I'm sorry I can't be more helpful. That's all I can tell you."

Will could tell Chuck wanted him gone, which made Will not want to leave. "If you think of anything—"

"You'll be the first to know." Chuck pointed up the hill. "The trail will take you back to the main house. Just go past the dining hall on your left."

"Thanks." Will didn't leave. He wasn't finished making Chuck uncomfortable. "My partner will follow up with you later."

"Why?"

"You're a witness. We need to get your written statement." Will paused. "Any reason we shouldn't?"

"No," he said. "No reason at all. I'm happy to help. Even though I didn't see or hear anything."

"Thanks." Will nodded up the trail. "You heading to the house?"

"I think I'll stay out here for a while." Chuck started to rub his back again, then thought better of it. "I need some time for reflection. Despite the persiflage, I've suddenly realized how affected I am by her death, too."

Will wondered if Chuck's brain had told his face that news, because he didn't look like he wanted time for reflection. He was sweating profusely. His skin was pale.

Will asked, "Are you sure you don't want company? I'm a good listener."

Chuck's throat visibly worked. Sweat dripped into his eyes, but he didn't wipe it away. "No, thank you."

"Okay. I appreciate your talking to me."

Chuck's jaw was clenched.

Will lingered. "I'll be at the main house if you need me."

Chuck said nothing, but every part of his body said that he was desperate for Will to leave.

There was nothing to do but oblige him. Will started back up the trail. The first few steps were tricky, not because Will couldn't find his footing, but because he was calculating how far the gaff could reach. Then he was listening closely for the sound of Chuck running. Then he was wondering if he was being paranoid, which was statistically probable, but not all statistics corrected for reckless behavior.

Will kept his uninjured hand loose at his side, close to the gun on his hip. He saw a fallen log twenty yards ahead. The other part of the rope handrail was tied off to a large eye-bolt. He told himself he would turn back around to check on Chuck when he reached the log. His ears burned as he tried to pick out any sound other than the shush of the water flowing over the rocks. Going up the trail wasn't as easy as going down. His foot slipped. He cursed when he caught himself with his injured hand. He pushed himself up. By the time he'd made it to the log, he figured Chuck would be gone.

He was wrong.

Chuck was lying face-down in the middle of the creek.

"Chuck!" Will started running. "Chuck!"

Chuck's hand was trapped between two rocks. Water rushed around his body. He wasn't trying to lift his head. He wasn't even moving. Will kept running, unclipping his gun, the satellite phone, emptying his pockets because he knew he was going to have to go in. His boots slid in the mud. He made it down the slope on his ass, but he was a second too late.

The current pried Chuck's hand from the rocks. His body went spinning down the creek. Will had no choice but to go after him. He made a shallow dive into the water, then surfaced with an overhand stroke. The temperature was so cold he felt like he was moving through ice. Will pushed himself to keep moving. He was just barely keeping up with the flow. He pushed harder. Chuck was fifteen feet away, then ten, then Will reached for his arm.

He missed.

The current had grown stronger. The water frothed and churned as it hooked around a bend in the creek. He slammed into Chuck's body, his head jerking back on his neck. Will reached for him again, but suddenly, they were both tossed around by rapids. Will searched for the shore but he was spinning too fast. He tried in vain to find purchase with his feet. He heard a loud roar. Will thrashed, trying to get a lock on the horizon. His head kept going under. He pushed himself up and was momentarily paralyzed by what he saw. Fifty yards ahead. The turbulence flattened out as the surface of the water kissed the sky.

Shit.

This was the real waterfall Delilah had been talking about.

Forty yards.

Thirty.

Will made one last, desperate lunge toward Chuck, his fingers catching on the vest. He kicked his feet, trying to find something to brace against. The current wrapped around his legs like a giant squid, pulling him downstream. His head was dragged below the surface. He was going to have to let go of Chuck. Will tried to shake his hand loose, but he was caught on the vest. His lungs ached for air. He struggled to kick himself backward.

His foot landed against something solid.

Will pushed off with every ounce of strength he had left in his body. He flailed across the current, blindly reaching out his hand. His fingers touched something solid. The surface was rough and unyielding. He'd managed to grab onto the side of a boulder. It took three tries before he was able to pull himself up. He hooked his hips on the ledge to give himself time to breathe. His eyes were burning. His lungs were shaking. He coughed out a torrent of bile and water.

Chuck was still tethered to his hand by the fishing vest, but he was no longer dragging Will toward the waterfall. The man was floating on his back in a shallow gorge. His arms and legs were straight out, almost perpendicular to his body. Will looked at Chuck's face. Eyes wide. Water flowing through his open mouth. Well and truly dead.

Will crawled up the rest of the way onto the rock. He put his head between his knees. Waited for his vision to clear. His stomach to stop turning. Several minutes passed before he was able to survey the damage. The fishing vest was hanging off Chuck's shoulder. The other end was tightly twisted around Will's wrist and hand. The same hand that had been injured twelve hours ago. The same hand that was now pulsing like a bomb was ticking down inside.

There was nothing to do but get it over with. Will slowly peeled away the heavy, wet canvas, unwinding it like a puzzle. It took time. Hooks had doubled back on the material. They were in all shapes and sizes with multi-colored ends tied to look like insects. It felt like forever until Will got to his actual skin.

He stared in disbelief.

The bandage had saved him. Six hooks had clawed into the thick gauze. One hook was wrapped around the bottom of his index finger like a ring. The skin bled a little when he pulled the hook away, but it was more like a paper cut than an amputation. The last hook had clawed into the cuff of his shirt sleeve. Will wasn't going to mess with the barb. He ripped it out. He held up his hand to the light to make sure he was really unscathed. No blood. No sight of bone.

He'd gotten lucky, but the feeling of relief was short-lived.

Will had started out the day with one victim. Now he had two.

January 16, 2016

Dear Jon—

I sat down to write your gotcha letter and I just stared at the blank page so long because I didn't think there was much to tell you. Things have been real calm lately, which I'm grateful for. We've got a nice routine going. I get you up and ready for school and Fish drives you down the mountain and then we all get to work helping guests.

I know your uncle Fish would prefer to start his day in the creek but that's the kind of man he is, giving up his mornings for a little boy. Even Bitty is helping out, going to pick you up from school in the afternoons. I think she just needed you to get a little older. She's never liked babies. You two are getting real close. She'll let you in the kitchen when she's making cookies for the guests. Sometimes she'll even let you sit with her while she knits on the couch. And I'm okay with that for now. Just remember what I told you about how she can turn. Once you're on her bad side you will never see that sweet side again, and you can trust me on that cause it's been so long I don't even know what that side looks like anymore.

Anyway, I was thinking back on last year and wondering what I could tell you, but mostly that was the important part, that things have been easy for a stretch. It ain't much of a life up here on this mountain, but it's a life. I walk around this place and I think about you running it some day and that makes me happy enough.

But one thing I remembered was something that happened in spring of last year. Maybe you remember part of what happened, because I lit into you like my hair was on fire. I'd never done that to you before and I never will again. I know I can be short, and your daddy would be the first to tell you I've got some of Bitty's iciness, but you've never been on the bad end of one of my tempers. So I felt like I should tell you why I was so mad.

What I want to say right up front is that your uncle Fish is a good person. He can't help it that Papa beat the fight out of him. I know that him being the oldest and also being a man means he's supposed to protect me, but life just made it the other way around. Which I'm fine with to be honest. I love my brother and that's a fact.

Now this next thing I'm going to tell you should always be kept a secret, because it belongs to me and not to you. What happened was, you were reading in bed instead of going to sleep. I told you to turn off your light, then I went back to my room and lay down in bed. I was thinking I'd give it another minute before I checked on you again. Then I must've fallen asleep, because the next thing I know, I woke up and Chuck was on top of me.

I know you and me laugh about Chuck, but he's still a man and he is strong. I guess he's always had a thing for me. I went out of my way to never encourage it, but maybe I did something by mistake. I was always grateful that Fish had a friend. Your poor uncle gets so lonely up here. Truth be told, I think Fish would probably throw himself off the big falls if he didn't have Chuck up here keeping him company.

All of those thoughts were going through my head, believe it or not. The brain part of me was making the calculations about how much it would hurt Fish if I screamed and woke up the house. The body part of me had disappeared. I learned how to do that a long time ago and I hope you never find out why. But just know that I wasn't going to break my brother's heart.

But none of that ended up mattering because Fish walked in. Now I will say that in all my years, Fish has never just walked into my bedroom. He's always knocked first, then usually stood out in the hall. He's respectful like that. But maybe he heard me struggling since he's right next door. I don't know what brought him there. I'm sure as hell not going to ask him because we haven't talked about it since and never will as far as I'm concerned. But what happened was, this is the only time I think

I've ever heard him yell. He never raises his voice. But what he said was STOP!

Chuck stopped. He got off me so fast it was like it never happened. He ran out of the room. Then Fish just looked at me. I thought he was gonna call me a whore, but what he said was, "Do you want me to tell him to leave?"

There was a lot in that question, because it told me Fish knew I didn't ask for it. Being honest, that was what mattered the most. People always assume the worst of me, but Fish knew that I was never interested in Chuck that way. And he was willing to give up his only friend in the world to prove it.

So what I told him was, as long as it never happens again, Chuck can stay. Fish just nodded and left. And I'll say that Chuck has acted like it never happened, which is a relief. We're all just ignoring it. But it wasn't without a consequence, and that's why I'm telling you this story. I was real shaken when Fish closed my door. Some of my clothes were torn. And it's not like I can go into town and buy new things with all my money. Ain't nothing I've got up here that didn't come from a donation box.

But when I stood up, my knees gave out. I hit the floor. I was so angry at myself. What did I have to be upset about? Nothing actually happened. It just almost happened. And that was when I saw that your light was still on.

Now, I've lived my life watching shit roll downhill and come right for me. Papa gets mad and he takes it out on Bitty. Bitty takes it out on me. Or the other way around, but I'm always at the bottom of the hill. That night, I took it out on you, and I am sorry. This isn't an excuse, it's just an explanation. And maybe I just want to write this down so that somebody knows what happened. Because what I've learned with men like Chuck is that they get away with something once, they're gonna try to get away with it again. I've seen it happen so much with your daddy that I can set my watch by it.

Anyway, I'm gonna leave it at that.

I love you with all my heart and I'm sorry I yelled,

Mama

15

Penny had not lied about Rascal being gassed up. The horse had practically floated up the mountain on a cloud of flatulence. Unfortunately, Faith was at the closest end of the source. She'd brokebacked with Penny, clutching her arms around the woman's waist for dear life. Faith had been so terrified of falling and being trampled that she'd gone into some kind of hysterical fugue state. She'd found herself asking existential questions like *what kind of planet would her children inherit?* and *how come Scooby Doo, who is a dog, can't smell the difference between a ghost and a human?*

Penny clicked her tongue against her teeth. Faith had buried her face in the woman's shoulder. She looked up and nearly cried from relief. There was a sign on the road. McAlpine Family Lodge. She saw a parking pad with a rusted-out truck and a GBI UTV.

"Hold on," Penny said. She'd probably felt Faith's grip loosen around her surprisingly muscular abs. "Just another second."

The second was more like half a minute, which was too long. Penny *whoa'd* Rascal beside the truck. Faith put her foot on the hump over the back tire. She half-fell, half-stumbled into the truck bed, landing sideways on her Glock. The metal banged into her hip bone.

Faith let out a loud "Fuck."

Penny gave her a disappointed look. She clicked her tongue. Rascal pulled away.

Faith looked up at the trees. She was sweaty and bug-bitten and she was very tired of nature. She shifted off of her Glock.

She climbed down from the truck. She lifted her purse over her shoulder. She went to the UTV. Rested her hand on the plastic over the engine. It was cold, which meant the vehicle had been parked there for a while. The storage trunk was locked. Hopefully that meant they'd secured some evidence. She looked in the back seat. There was a blue Yeti cooler, an emergency first aid kit, and a backpack with a GBI logo on it. Faith tugged open the zipper. She found a satellite phone.

She clicked the button on the side, engaging the short-range walkie-talkie. "Will?"

Faith released the button. She waited. Nothing but static.

She tried again. "This is Special Agent Faith Mitchell with the GBI. Respond."

Faith released the button.

Static.

She tried a few more times with the same result. She tucked the phone into her purse, then headed to the center of the compound. Faith did a full turn. Not a soul was in sight. Even Penny and Rascal had disappeared. She tried to get a basic lay of the land. Eight cottages spoked out in a semi-circle from a large, higgledy-piggledy house. Trees were everywhere. You couldn't throw a rock without hitting one. Puddles dotted the ground. The sun was like a hammer pounding against the top of her skull. She could see entrances to a few trails. There was no telling where they led because she didn't have a map.

She needed to locate Will.

Faith reversed her three-sixty, checking each of the cottages. The hair on the back of her neck stood up. She felt like she was being watched. Why was no one coming out? It wasn't like she'd sneaked into the compound. The horse was snorty and loud. She'd banged into the truck like a mallet hitting a gong. Faith was dressed in her regs: tan cargo pants and a navy shirt with giant yellow GBI letters on the back.

She raised her voice, calling, "Hello?"

One of the cottage doors opened clear across the compound. Faith watched as a balding, unshaven man in a wrinkled T-shirt and baggy sweatpants trotted toward her. He was out of breath by the time he finally got close enough to speak. "Hi, are you with Will? Did you bring Sara? Is she on the horse? That didn't look like her. Will told me she's a doctor."

Faith guessed, "Frank?"

"Yes, sorry. Frank Johnson. I'm married to Monica. We're friends with Will and Sara."

Faith doubted that. "Have you seen Will?"

"Not for a while, but could you tell him that Monica finally turned a corner?"

Faith's cop brain woke up. "What was wrong with her?"

"She had a little too much to drink last night. She's better now, but it was rough there for a while." His laugh was sharp. He was clearly relieved. "She finally managed to keep down some ginger ale. I think she was dehydrated. But it would still be good if Sara had time to look at her, right? Better safe than sorry. Do you think she'd mind?"

"I know she wouldn't. She'll be here soon." Faith had to get away from this chatterbox. "Did Will go into the family's house?"

"I'm sorry, I don't know. I didn't see where he went. I can help you look if—"

"It's probably best for you to stay with your wife."

"Yes, right. Maybe I could—"

"Thank you."

Faith turned toward the main house to make it clear the conversation was over. She could hear Frank's plodding footsteps as he headed back the way he'd come. The eerie feeling returned as Faith walked across the open space. The area was quaint with the flowers and benches and pavers, but also someone had violently died here, so Faith was a little nervous that no one was around.

Where was Will? For that matter, where was Kevin Rayman? The agent was in charge of the North Georgia field office while his boss attended a conference. Faith told herself that Kevin wasn't some rookie off the street. He knew how to handle himself. So did Will. Even with one hand. So why had Faith broken out into a cold sweat?

This place was getting to her. It felt like that Shirley Jackson story right before the lottery numbers were called. She made herself take a deep breath and slowly let it go. Will and Kevin were probably at the dining hall. It was always better to isolate people when you interrogated them. Knowing Will, he had already found Mercy's killer.

A brown tabby blocked her way up the porch stairs. He was twisted on his back, front and rear paws going in opposite directions, as a ray of sunshine hit his belly. Faith leaned down to give him some pets. She instantly felt her stress level drop a few notches. She silently made a list of things she needed to do. At the top was locating a map. Faith had to figure out where Mercy's screams had come from and develop a more solid timeline. Then, she needed to figure out the best possible route that Mercy had taken down to the bachelor cottages. Maybe Faith would get lucky and find the broken knife handle on her way.

The front door opened. An older woman with long, stringy gray hair came out onto the porch. She was petite, almost doll-like. Faith guessed this was Mercy's mother.

Bitty stared down at her from the top of the stairs. "Are you a police officer?"

"Special Agent Faith Mitchell." Faith tried to establish a rapport. "I was just consulting with Hercult Purrot here."

"We don't name the cats. They're here for rodent control."

Faith tried not to wince. The woman's voice was high-pitched like a little girl's. "Is my partner inside? Will Trent?"

"I don't know where he is. I can tell you I don't appreciate him and his wife checking in under false pretenses."

Faith wasn't going to get into that. "I'm very sorry about your daughter, Mrs. McAlpine. Do you have any questions for me?"

"Yes, I do," the woman snapped. "When can I talk to Dave?"

Faith would consider Bitty's priorities later. For now, she needed to tread carefully. She didn't know if communications had been re-established to the lodge. Penny had promised to keep Dave's release a secret, but then again, she'd freely rattled a lot of skeletons in the McAlpine closet.

Faith told Bitty, "Dave's still in the hospital. You can call his room if you like."

"The phones are out. Internet, too." Bitty's hands went to her tiny hips. "I will never believe Dave had anything to do with this. That boy has his demons, but he wouldn't hurt Mercy. Not like that."

Faith asked, "Who else would have a motive?"

"Motive?" She sounded appalled. "I don't even know what that means. We're a family business. Our guests are educated, wealthy people. No one has a motive. Someone could've easily come up from town. Have you thought about that?"

Faith had thought about that, but it seemed very unlikely. Mercy seldom went into town. She had told Sara that her enemies were all up here. Plus, she had died on the property.

Still, Faith asked, "Who in town would want to murder her?"

"She's pissed off so many people, there's no telling who. We've had a lot of strangers coming into town lately, I can tell you that. Most of 'em have criminal records back in Mexico or Guatemala. Any one of them's probably a crazy ax murderer."

Faith steered her away from the racism. "Can I ask you about last night?"

Bitty's head started to shake like it didn't matter. "We had a little argument. Nothing unusual about that. We have them all the time. Mercy is a desperately unhappy person. She can't love anybody because she doesn't love herself."

Faith guessed they streamed Dr. Phil up here, too. "Did you hear anything or see anything suspicious?"

"Of course not. What a question. I helped my husband to bed. I went to sleep. There was nothing out of the ordinary."

"You didn't hear an animal howl?"

"Animals howl up here all the time. It's the mountains."

"What about the area you call the bachelor cottages. Does sound travel from there?"

"How would I know?"

Faith knew a dead end when she hit one. She looked up at the house. It was big, probably at least five or six bedrooms. She wanted to know where everyone slept. "Is that Mercy's room?"

Bitty looked up. "That's Christopher's. Mercy is in the middle, then Jon on the opposite side at the back end."

That still sounded close. "Did you hear when Christopher got in last night?"

"I took a sleeping tablet. Believe it or not, I don't like to argue with people. I was very upset about Mercy's behavior lately. She only ever thought of herself. She never considered what would be good for the rest of the family."

Will had prepared Faith for their apathy, but it was still equal parts sad and alarming. Faith would be on the ground if one of her children had been murdered.

Bitty seemed to pick up on the disapproval. "Do you have children?"

Faith was always careful with her personal information. "I have a daughter."

"Well, I'm sorry for you. Sons are much easier." Bitty finally walked down the stairs. She was even smaller up close. "Christopher never complained. He never threw a tantrum or pouted when he didn't get his way. Dave was an absolute angel. They let him run wild down there in Atlanta, but from the moment he stepped foot in my house, he was sweet as honey. That boy is my heart. I never wanted for anything when he was around. Took care of me when I was sick. Even washed my hair. Still to this day, he won't let me lift a finger."

Faith guessed Dave knew how to ingratiate himself. "Mercy wasn't like that?"

"She was terrible," Bitty said. "When she hit middle school, I was down at the principal's office every other week because Mercy had stirred up trouble with the other girls. Gossiping and fighting and acting like a fool. Spreading her legs for anybody who looked her way. How old is your girl?"

Faith lied to keep her talking. "Thirteen."

"So you already know that's when it starts. Puberty hits and everything is about boys. Then there's all the drama about their *feelings*. I tell you who had a right to complain, and that was Dave. What he went through down in Atlanta was unspeakable. They were not delicate with him, to put it politely. But he never used it as a crutch. Boys don't whine about their feelings."

Faith's boy had, but only because his mother had worked very hard to make him feel safe. "How did Mercy seem to you lately?"

"Seem?" she asked. "She seemed like her usual. Full of piss and vinegar and angry at the world."

Faith didn't know how to broach the pregnancy. Something told her to hold back. She doubted Mercy had ever confided in her mother. "Dave was thirteen when you and your husband adopted him?"

"No, he was only eleven years old."

Faith had been watching the woman's face closely when she'd answered. It had to be said that Bitty was a world-class liar. "How did Mercy and Christopher respond to having an eleven-year-old brother?"

"They were overjoyed. Who wouldn't be? Christopher had a new friend. Dave treated Mercy like a little doll. Would've carried her around in his arms all the time if he could'a. As it was, her feet never touched the ground."

"It must've been surprising when they ended up together."

Bitty lifted her chin in defiance. "It brought Jon into my life, and that's all I'll say about that."

"Has Jon come home?"

"No, and we're not looking. We're gonna give him the time he asked for." She patted her fingers to her chest. "Jon is a thoughtful boy. Kind and considerate, exactly like his daddy. He's going to break hearts just like his daddy, too. You should see how handsome he is. All the guests go crazy at the sight of him. I watch them out the window when Jon comes down the stairs. He likes to make an entrance. Your Sara looked like she wanted to eat him up."

Faith assumed Sara had asked him what subjects he enjoyed in school.

"My poor baby boys." Bitty patted her fingers to her chest again. "I did my best to keep Dave away from Mercy. I knew she would drag him down with her, and look at where he is now."

Faith struggled to keep her tone even. "I'm so sorry for your loss."

"Well, don't think I won't get him back. I've already reached out to a lawyer from Atlanta, so good luck keeping him in jail." She sounded very sure that the legal system would work. "Is that all?"

"Do you have a map of the property I can have?"

"Those maps are for guests." Her head turned toward the parking pad. "For the love of God, who's here now?"

Faith heard an engine rumbling. Another UTV had pulled up. Sara was behind the wheel.

"Another liar come up here to lie." Bitty ended the conversation with that. She walked up the stairs, went into the house, and shut the door behind her.

"Jesus." Faith hooked her purse over her shoulder and made her way to the parking pad. This place wasn't *The Lottery*. It was *Children of the Corn*.

"Hi." Sara was lifting a heavy duffel bag out of the UTV. She smiled at Faith. "Did you fall?"

Faith had forgotten she was covered in mud and horse farts. "A bird attacked my car and I ended up in a ditch."

"I'm sorry." Sara didn't look sorry. "I saw you were talking to Bitty. What do you think?"

"I think she's more worried about Dave than her murdered daughter." Faith still couldn't wrap her head around it. "What is it with these Boy Moms? She sounded like Dave's psycho ex-girlfriend. And don't even get me started on the Jon part. I hate when grown women speak in that breathless girlie voice. It's like Holly Hobby fucked the Devil."

Sara laughed. "Any progress?"

"Not on my end. I was about to go down to the dining hall to find Will." Faith glanced around, making sure they were alone. "Do you think Mercy knew she was pregnant?"

Sara shrugged. "It's hard to say. She was nauseated last night, but I assumed that was sequela to the strangulation. Mercy didn't tell me otherwise, but she wouldn't necessarily share that information with a stranger."

"My period is so irregular I can barely keep up with it." Faith wondered if Mercy had used an app on her phone or marked a calendar. "Who did you tell?"

"Only Amanda and Will. I think that Nadine, the coroner, figured it out when I did the manual exam to assess the uterus, but she didn't say a word. She knows that Biscuits is close to the family. She probably didn't want it getting out."

"Biscuits didn't see the X-ray?"

"You have to know what you're looking for," Sara said. "Normally, you would never X-ray a woman at any time during pregnancy. The risk of radiation exposure outweighs the diagnostic value. And at twelve weeks, there's not a lot to see. The fetus is roughly two inches long, so around the length of a double-A battery. The bones haven't calcified enough to show up on film. I only knew what I was looking at because I've seen it before."

Faith didn't want to think about how she'd seen it before. "I can't remember what it felt like to be twelve weeks along."

"Bloating, nausea, mood swings, headache. Some women mistake it for PMD. Some miscarry and assume it's just a bad period. Eight out of ten miscarriages happen before twelve weeks." Sara rested the duffel on the UTV. "When you look at who was around Mercy during conception, keep in mind that it's twelve weeks from the last reported period, not twelve weeks from the sexual encounter. Ovulation happens two weeks after your period, which puts the timeline around ten weeks, so you're talking two to two and a half months ago, if we're being picky."

"We definitely need to be picky." Faith got to the hard part. "What about rape?"

"I found trace amounts of seminal fluid, but that only indicates she had sexual contact with a man forty-eight hours prior to death. I can't rule out sexual assault, but I can't rule it in, either."

Faith could only imagine how annoyed Amanda had been with the equivocation. "But, between us?"

"Between us, I honestly don't know," Sara said. "She didn't have defensive wounds. Maybe she made the decision that it's safer to not fight back. There's a clear finding that Mercy suffered a high level of abuse. Broken bones, cigarette burns. I'm assuming a lot of it was at the hands of Dave, but some of the damage dates back to her childhood. If there was any fight in her, she used it judiciously."

Faith was struck by a profound sadness at the thought of Mercy's tortured life. Penny was right. She had never stood a chance. "Anything on the murder weapon?"

"That part I can help you with," Sara said. "So, in the design of a knife, you know that in a full tang, the metal extends all the way through from the tip of the blade to the butt of the handle."

Faith did not know this, but she nodded.

"The blade inside Mercy was a five-inch-long half-tang, which is a cheaper, less durable construction used in steak knives. With a half tang, you get a skeleton inside the handle, basically a horseshoe-shaped piece of thin metal that helps keep the handle attached to the blade. You following?"

"Half-tang skeleton inside the handle. Got it."

"The killer sank the blade in to the hilt. I could tell from the marks that were left on her skin that there wasn't a bolster. That's the metal collar at the transition between the blade and the handle. I found slivers of plastic around some of the deeper wounds. Under the microscope, the color skewed red."

Faith nodded again, but this time because she understood. "We're looking for the red handle of a cheap steak knife with a thin metal strip sticking out of it."

"Correct," Sara said. "All the cottages have kitchens, but ours didn't have any knives in it. And I don't remember seeing anything that would match a red-handled knife in the family kitchen. It would be worth searching again with this new information. I'd say it's about four inches long, maybe one quarter inch thick."

"Okay, I should talk to Will to see how we're going to proceed. You can run down the knife details for him." Faith started to go, but she caught herself. "I ran into Frank. He's worried about his wife. Apparently, she's more hung over than usual."

"I'll check on her now." Sara patted the duffel. "I brought up some medical supplies from the hospital in case we need them. Cecil's in a wheelchair, but I didn't see a van."

Faith hadn't realized that until now. "How do they get him into the truck?"

"I'm sure there are plenty of people around to help," Sara said. "Should I meet you guys at the dining hall when I'm finished?"

"That works."

Faith followed the wooden sign with the plate and silverware. She kept her eyes on the ground. The path was clear, but there was a lot of overgrowth on either side that could hide snakes and rabid squirrels. Or birds. Faith looked up. Branches hung down like fingers. A stiff wind rustled the leaves. She was certain an owl was going to attack her hair. She was relieved when the trail took a turn, but there was only more trail.

"Fucking nature."

She continued down, her eyes pivoting from the ground to the sky for possible danger. The path did another bend. The trees were less on top of her. She smelled the kitchen before she saw it. Emma's father was a second-generation Mexican-American whose spiteful mother loved cooking as much as she hated Faith, which was to say a lot. Coriander. Cumin. Basil. Cilantro. Faith's stomach was growling by the time she made it to the octagonal-shaped building. She bypassed the platform that was hanging dangerously over a gorge and walked through the door.

Empty.

The lights were off. There were two long tables, one already laid for lunch. Giant windows on the far wall showed more trees. She was going to be sick of the color green by the time she left this place.

"Will?" she called. "Are you in here?"

She waited, but there was no response. All she could hear was cooking noises behind the swinging door to the kitchen.

"Will?"

Still nothing.

Faith pulled out the satellite phone again. She pressed the walkie button. "This is Special Agent Faith Mitchell with the Georgia Bureau of Investigation. Anybody out there?"

She silently counted to ten. Then twenty. Then she felt herself starting to worry.

Faith dropped the phone back into her purse and walked into the kitchen. The sudden light was almost blinding. Two boys were at the long stainless-steel table that went down the middle of the room. One was cutting vegetables. The other was hand-mixing batter in a large bowl. The chef had his back to Faith as he cooked on the stove. The radio was tuned to Bad Bunny, which was probably why they hadn't heard her.

"Can I help you, ma'am?" one of the boys asked.

Faith felt her heart clench at the sight of him. He was just a kid.

"What do you need, officer?" the chef had turned around. This had to be Alejandro. He was incredibly handsome, but he also seemed incredibly irritated to see Faith, which was also reminiscent of Emma's father. "I'm sorry to be abrupt, but we're preparing lunch service."

Faith needed to find her partner. "Do you know where Agent Trent is?"

The boy said, "He went down Fishtopher Trail."

She let out a sigh of relief. "How long ago?"

His shoulders went up in an exaggerated shrug because he was a kid and he didn't understand time.

Alejandro provided, "I saw him outside the window about an hour ago, I think. Then there was a second man dressed like you about half an hour later. The trail is behind the building. I'll show you."

Faith felt some of her tension lessen over the Will and Kevin sighting. She followed Alejandro toward the back, checking out the rest of the kitchen on her way. The knives looked expensive and professional. No red plastic handles. She saw a bathroom that connected to an office. She wanted to go through those papers, see if she could get into the laptop.

"Lunch starts in half an hour." Alejandro opened the door and let Faith go first. "They usually shovel it down in twenty minutes. I could talk afterward."

Faith felt her attention snap to the chef like a rubber band. "Why do you think I want to talk to you?"

"Because I was sleeping with Mercy." He seemed to realize this conversation was happening now. He closed the door behind him. "We tried to be discreet, but obviously someone told you."

"Obviously," Faith said. "And?"

"It was casual. Mercy wasn't in love with me. I wasn't in love with her. But she was very attractive. It's lonely up here. The body wants what it wants."

"How long were you sleeping together?"

"From the moment I got here." He shrugged. "It was infrequent, particularly lately. I don't know why, but that was the nature of things with us, an ebb and flow. She was under a lot of pressure with her father. He's a very hard man."

"Did Dave know about you two?"

"I have no idea. I rarely spoke to him. Even when he was extending the viewing platform, I kept my distance. I suspected he was hurting Mercy."

"Why is that?"

"You don't get bruised like that from falling." He wiped his hands on his apron. "Let's just say if Dave had ended up murdered, you would be talking to me for very different reasons."

A lot of people kept saying that, but no one had done anything when Mercy was alive. "You said you weren't in love with her, but you also would've murdered for her?"

His smile showed all his teeth. "You're very good at this, detective, but no. It's my sense of duty."

"What did Mercy say when you noticed the bruises?"

The smile disappeared. "I asked her once, and she told me that we could either talk about it and never have sex again, or we could just keep having sex."

"Forgive me, but you don't seem conflicted by your choice."

He shrugged again. "It's different up here. The way they treat people—they just wear them out and throw them away. Maybe I did the same thing with Mercy. I'm not proud of myself."

"Was she seeing anyone else?"

"Maybe?" he asked. "Do you think Dave got jealous? Is that why he killed her?"

"Maybe," Faith lied. "What made you think Mercy could've been seeing someone else?"

"A lot of things, really. Like I said, the ebb and flow. Plus—" He shrugged. "Who am I to judge her? Mercy was a single mother with a demanding job, a difficult employer, and very few outlets for enjoyment."

Faith had never felt so seen. "Did she mention anyone in particular?"

"She wouldn't volunteer, and I wouldn't ask. Like I said, we fucked. We didn't talk about our lives."

Faith had enjoyed a few of those relationships herself. "But if you had to guess?"

He let out a short breath of air. "Well, it would have to be one of the guests, right? The butcher is older than my grandfather. Mercy hates the vegetable guy. He's from town. He knows about her past."

"What's there to know about her past?"

"She was very honest with me in the beginning," he said. "She did some sex work when she was in her early twenties."

"Did she do some sex work with you?"

He laughed. "No, I didn't pay her. I might have if she'd asked. She was very good at keeping things separate. Work was work and sex was sex."

Faith could see where that would be worth the money. "How was she yesterday?"

"Stressed," he said. "We cater to very demanding guests up here. Most of our conversations yesterday were like, 'don't forget Keisha doesn't like raw onions and Sydney doesn't do dairy and Chuck has a peanut allergy.'"

Faith watched him roll his eyes. "What do you think of Chuck?"

"He's here at least once a month, sometimes more. I thought he was a relative at first."

"Did Mercy like him?"

"She tolerated him," Alejandro said. "He's a lot to deal with, but then so is Christopher."

"Are Christopher and Chuck together?"

"As in lovers?" He shook his head. "No, not with the way they look at women."

"How do they look at women?"

"Desperately?" He seemed to struggle for a better description, then shook his head. "It's hard, because the problem is, they're both very awkward in general. I'll occasionally have a beer with Christopher, and he's an all right guy, but his brain is wired differently. Then you throw a woman into the mix, and he freezes up. Chuck has the exact opposite problem. You put him within ten feet of a woman and he's going to recite every line from Monty Python until she runs from the room."

Unfortunately, Faith knew the type well. "I heard about the fight Mercy had with Jon."

Alejandro winced. "He's a sweet kid, but very immature. Not a lot of friends in town. They know who his mother is. And his father. It's not right, but the stigma is there."

"Have you seen him drunk like that before?"

"Never," Alejandro said. "Honestly, I was like—no. Don't let this kid go down the addiction trail. He's got it in his blood. Both sides. It's just sad."

Faith silently agreed. Addiction was a lonely road to travel. "What time did you leave here last night?"

"Around eight, eight-thirty. The last conversation I had with Mercy was about clean-up. She let Jon have the night off, so she was doing it by herself. I didn't offer to help. I was tired. It was a long day. So I saddled up Pepe and I rode to my house, which is about forty minutes over the ridge. I was there all night. I opened a bottle of wine and watched a crime show on Hulu."

"Which show?"

"The one about the detective with the dog. You can probably check those things, right?"

"I can." Faith was more interested in the fact that he had anticipated all of her questions. It was almost like he'd crammed for the test. "Is there anything else you want to tell me about Mercy and her family?"

"No, but I'll let you know if I think of something." He pointed down a steep incline. "That's Fishtopher Trail. It's very muddy, so be careful."

He'd already opened the door, but Faith stopped him with a question. "Can you get to the bachelor cottages from Fishtopher Trail?"

He looked surprised, like he'd put together why she was asking. "You can if you follow the creek past the waterfalls, then walk along the lake, but the quicker route is down the Rope Trail. It goes around the side of the gorge. They call it the Rope Trail because there's a series of ropes you have to grab so you don't slip and break your neck. Only the staff uses it. It's not on the map. I only went down once because it scared the shit out of me. I'm not big into heights."

"How long did it take?"

"Five minutes?" he guessed. "Sorry, I really need to get back to work."

"Thank you," Faith said. "I'll need to get a written statement later."

"You know where to find me."

Alejandro disappeared into the kitchen before Faith could say anything else. She stared at the closed door. She tried to get a read on how the conversation had gone. In her experience, there were four ways a suspect could approach an interview. He could be defensive. He could be combative. He could be disinterested. He could be helpful.

The chef fell roughly between the last two. She would have to get Will to weigh in. Sometimes suspects were disinterested because they really weren't interested. Sometimes they were helpful because they wanted you to think they were innocent.

Faith started down Fishtopher Trail. Alejandro had not been lying about the mud. The going reminded her of a slip-n-slide. The angle was severe. She saw large footprints with heavy treads. Men going up the trail. Men going down.

She took a chance, shouting, "Will?"

The only response was a bunch of birds chirping, probably discussing a plan of attack.

Faith sighed as she continued her downward trajectory. Only a few seconds had passed before she was wrenching a boot out of the muck. This was why concrete had been invented. People weren't meant to be outdoors like this. She batted away dangling limbs as she navigated the steep slope. Part of her just accepted that she was going to end up on her ass at some point, but she was still annoyed when it happened. The trail was no less steep when she stood up. Faith had to go into the woods to avoid a slippery-looking section.

"Fuck!" she jumped away from a snake.

Then she cursed again because it wasn't a snake. A rope was lying on the ground. One end was attached to a boulder by a hook. The other end disappeared down the trail. Faith probably would've left it there if Alejandro hadn't told her about the other ropes on the Rope Trail. She let out a few more *fucks* as she grabbed on and continued down. She was sweating like a mother-fucker by the time she heard the rush of water over rocks. Thankfully, the temperature had dropped as the elevation lowered. She swatted away a mosquito that was circling her head. She wanted air conditioning and phone service and most of all, she wanted to find her partner.

"Will?" she tried again. Her voice didn't echo so much as compete with the forest racket. Insects and birds and venomous snakes. "Will?"

Faith grabbed a tree limb to keep her foot from slipping as she made her way down to the bank. Then her other foot slipped and her ass was on the ground again.

"Jesus," she hissed. She couldn't catch a break. She grabbed her satellite phone off the ground. She pressed the walkie button. "This is Agen—"

Faith let go of the button when an awful squealing sound nearly broke her eardrums. She shook the phone, then pressed the button again. The squeal returned. It was coming from her purse. She opened her bag. She saw her satellite phone.

She looked at the phone in her hand, then the phone in her bag.

How did she get two phones?

Faith stood up. She walked down a few feet. She could see the creek now. The water was swirling around large rocks. Faith took another step. The toe of her boot hit something heavy. She saw a paddle holster with a Smith and Wesson snub-nosed five-shot. Weirdly, it looked like Amanda's side piece. She searched the ground. Earbuds still in the case. Farther along, there was an iPhone. Faith tapped it awake. The lock screen glowed: a photo of Sara holding Will's dog.

"No-no-no-no . . ."

Faith's Glock was in her hands before her brain could fully process what she had seen. She did a three-sixty, wildly scanning the forest, panicked that she would find Will's body. There was nothing out of place but an empty half-gallon jug and a rod with a lethal-looking hook at the end. Faith rushed to the edge of the creek and looked right, then left. Her heart stopped until she was sure his body wasn't in the water.

"Will!"

Faith jogged along the creek. The terrain dropped. The water was flowing faster. In another fifty yards, it took a sharp turn to the left, bowing around some trees. Faith could see more rocks, more churning water. Something could've gotten swept up in the roiling current. Something like her partner. Faith started running toward the bend.

"Will!" she screamed. "Will!"

"Faith?"

319

His voice was faint. She couldn't see him. Faith holstered her Glock. She jumped into the water to cross to the other side. It was deeper than she'd calculated. Her knees bent. Her head dropped below the surface. Water swirled around her face. She pushed herself up, gasping for air. The only thing that kept her from going downstream was luck and a giant tree root sticking out from the side of the bank.

"Are you okay?"

Will was standing above her. His bandaged hand was pressed to his chest. His clothes were soaked. Kevin Rayman was behind him with a man's body slung over his shoulder in a fireman's carry. Faith saw a pair of hairy legs, black socks and yellow hiking boots.

She didn't trust herself to speak. She used the tree root to pull herself out of the water. Will held out his hand and practically lifted her up the bank. Faith didn't want to let go of him. She was breathless. She felt sick with relief. She'd been sure that he was lying dead somewhere. "What happened? Who is that?"

"Bryce Weller." Will helped Kevin lower the body to the ground. The man flopped onto his back. His skin was pale. His lips were blue. His mouth was open. "Also known as Chuck."

Kevin said, "Also known as heavy."

Faith turned on Will. "What the fuck are you doing coming down here without telling me where you were going?"

"I wasn't—"

"Shut your mouth when you're talking to me!"

"I don't think that's—"

"Why did I find Amanda's gun and your phones on the ground? Do you know how terrifying that was? I thought you'd been murdered. Jesus, Kevin."

Kevin held up his hands. "Whoa."

"Faith," Will said. "I'm okay."

"Well, I'm not." Her heart was clanging like a cow bell. "Jesus Christ."

"I was talking to Chuck," Will said. "He was sweaty and pale, but I didn't think anything about it other than maybe he was feeling guilty. I walked back up the trail. I got about twenty feet above him. I turned around and he was in the water. I got rid of the gun and my electronics because I knew I would have to go in."

Faith hated his calm and reasonable tone.

He continued, "The current took both of us downstream. I went after him. We almost went over a waterfall, but somehow, I managed to pull us both back. I couldn't leave his body down there, so I started carrying him toward the lodge."

"That's when I showed up," Kevin said. "I came looking for Will. Obviously, I carried the body farther than he did."

"I don't think that's true."

"Agree to disagree."

"I was actually in the water."

Faith was not up for bro jokes. She tried to focus her mind back on the case instead of the fact that she was standing dripping wet in the forest losing her shit because she'd thought that her partner was dead.

She looked down at the body. Bryce Weller's lips were dark blue. His eyes were like glass marbles. The current had pulled at his clothes. His shirt was open. His belt had come loose. More importantly, another person was dead. They could be searching for a killer with two motives instead of just one. Or Chuck could've murdered Mercy, then killed himself.

She asked Will, "What did Chuck say when you talked to him?"

Will said, "He used incel terminology. He was guarded. He acted like he wasn't into Mercy when he clearly was. I was liking him for the murder by the time we finished talking. He was hyper-focused on Dave. Openly jealous that Mercy wouldn't get rid of him. He kept rubbing his back. I wondered if she'd gotten some punches in."

Kevin said, "We can roll him over to check in a minute. I need to catch my breath."

Will told Faith, "Chuck described his altercation with Mercy before dinner in a weird way. He said, 'She screamed at me like I had raped her'. And I could tell he really regretted putting the word *rape* out there."

"Was that why he was sweating?" Faith asked. "He was nervous?"

"I don't think so. That would be some kind of flop sweat. It was dripping down his skull. His hair was plastered to his head. Looking back, I think he wasn't feeling well. He burped like his stomach was coming out of his mouth."

"Suicide?" she asked.

"If he drowned himself, he did it fast. No struggling. No splashing. It took me about a minute to get up that hill. By the time I turned around, his body had already floated out to the middle of the creek."

Faith looked at Chuck's face. She had attended more autopsies than she'd ever wanted to. She had never seen a corpse with lips that blue. "Was he eating something before he went in?"

"He was drinking water from a jug," Will said. "It was half-full when we started. He drank the rest while we were talking. What are you thinking?"

"Alejandro said that Chuck has a peanut allergy. Maybe someone slipped some peanut powder into his water."

"No," Sara said.

They all turned around. Sara was on the opposite side of the creek.

She said, "It wasn't peanuts. He was poisoned."

16

Sara wasn't happy with Will's guilty expression when he stared at her across the creek. The look was the same one he gave Amanda when she was about to rip him a new one.

Sara was not his boss.

"I'll bite," Faith said. "How can you tell he was poisoned?"

Sara would deal with Will later. Chuck hadn't been her favorite person, but he was still dead and he deserved some respect. "Anaphylaxis is a sudden, severe allergic reaction that causes the immune system to release chemicals that put your body into shock. It's not a quick death. We're talking fifteen to twenty minutes. Chuck would've exhibited chest discomfort and tightness, coughing, dizziness, flushing or redness in his face, skin rash, nausea or vomiting and most importantly, breathing issues. Will, did you notice that Chuck was having any of these symptoms?"

Will shook his head. "His breathing was fine. All that I noticed was that he was sweaty and pale."

"Look at how blue his fingernails and lips are." Sara pointed to the body. "That's caused by cyanosis, which is a lack of oxygen in the blood, which in this case indicates chemical poisoning. Chuck was drinking water before he died, so we can assume that's the source. The substance would have to be colorless, odorless, and tasteless. People with severe allergies know very quickly if the allergy has been triggered. Chuck didn't call for help. He didn't thrash around. He wasn't gasping for air or clawing at his neck for breath. I need to study the scene where he went into the water, but my theory is that he lost consciousness and rolled into the creek."

Faith asked, "What about a heart attack?"

"The lips and fingernails wouldn't be blue like that," Sara said. "Not all heart attacks lead to cardiac arrest. Sudden cardiac death is an electrical malfunction. The heart beats irregularly, or just stops, blood doesn't get to the brain, the person passes out. In a quiet setting like this, even over the sound of water, Will would've heard something before Chuck lost consciousness. Crying out, grabbing his arm in pain, the classic symptoms. At the very least, he would've made a heavy splash from falling into the water."

"I was listening to make sure he didn't come up on me," Will said. "When I turned around, he was just floating."

Faith asked, "What kind of poison would make his fingernails and lips blue like that?"

Sara had some ideas, but she wasn't going to volunteer them from thirty feet away. "Only toxicology can confirm, but I can give you some options once I have a closer look."

"We'll come to you," Will said. "We need to get him across the water. There's a stone footbridge upstream at the mini-falls. You guys okay without me?"

Will didn't wait for Kevin or Faith to answer. He jumped back into the creek to cross now. The current didn't seem to faze him. He climbed up the bank and stood in front of Sara with a resigned look on his face.

She handed him his iPhone and earbuds, asking, "How was the water?"

"Cold."

She wondered if a double-meaning was implied. "My love, I'm not going to lecture you for trying to save a man's life."

He gave her a curious look. "You're not mad?"

"I was worried," she told him. What she didn't add was that the panicked sound of Faith screaming his name had stopped Sara's heart. She had barely breathed until she'd seen that Will was all right. "I should change out the dressing on your hand. It's soaking wet."

He looked down at his hand. "Believe it or not, it saved my life."

Sara didn't know if she could hear specifics right now. "How much water did you swallow?"

"Somewhere between a little and a lot, but it all came back out."

"There's a slight risk of pulmonary embolism." She stroked back his wet hair. "I want you to tell me immediately if you have any trouble breathing."

"That's hard to judge," Will said. "Sometimes I look at my wife and she kind of takes my breath away."

Sara felt her lips turning up into a smile, but she was mindful that there were more important things that needed her attention. Faith and Kevin were already carrying Chuck back toward the crossing.

She walked along the bank, asking Will, "Did Faith tell you about the knife?"

He shook his head.

"Red plastic handle. I'm assuming a steak knife. The red is not typical. Usually, even if the handle is plastic, it's made to look like wood grain."

"Amanda should have the search warrant soon," he said. "I want to turn this place upside-down. I'm hoping the handle's not at the bottom of the lake."

"Any idea if Mercy knew she was pregnant?"

He shook his head again. "And there's no one to ask. She didn't trust anybody up here."

"I don't blame her." Sara started thinking ahead to next steps. "With the road washed out, we need to find a place to store the body until Nadine can safely remove it."

"There's a free-standing freezer behind the kitchen. There's not much in there. They've got another fridge inside they can probably move stuff to." Will had put his hand over his heart. The cold water and adrenaline were clearly no longer numbing the pain. "That reminds me, I told Frank I'd have you check on Monica."

"Already did," Sara said. "I gave her some fluids, but I'd feel better if she was closer to a medical facility. She's going to have to drink again or she'll go into withdrawal. From her symptoms, she was on the precipice of alcohol poisoning last night."

"Frank told me he was surprised she got that sick off what she drank."

325

"I'm not sure Frank is that reliable. He told me that he lied to you."

Will stopped walking.

"Last night, Monica filled out a request for another bottle of liquor. Frank went out onto the porch to leave it for Mercy, but he stuck the note in his pocket instead."

"And then he told me that Mercy had taken the note, which gave me the timeline we've been going by." Will looked understandably annoyed. "Why the hell did he lie about that?"

"He probably lies a lot to cover for his wife's drinking." Sara reminded him, "Paul said that he saw Mercy around 10:30-ish."

"I trust Paul even less than Frank." Will looked at his watch. "Lunch service is over. Maybe you can approach Drew and Keisha. Amanda ran a background on all the guests. Drew has a twelve-year-old assault charge."

Sara felt her lips part in surprise.

"I had the same reaction, but maybe that ties into what Drew was talking about when he told Bitty to forget that other business."

Faith asked, "What business?"

They had reached the mini waterfall. She was walking across the stone footpath with her arms out for balance. Will waited for her at the edge of the water. Sara tuned out their conversation. Neither one of them seemed interested in helping Kevin. Sara thought to help, but he was already crossing the creek with Chuck's full weight on his shoulder. Will was watching, too, but more out of envy than concern. He wanted to be the one balancing two-hundred pounds on his shoulder while he navigated what was basically an obstacle course.

Faith asked, "Could Monica be a poisoning victim, too?"

Sara realized the question was meant for her. "If so, the poison would've been a different agent by a different route. I can ask Monica's permission to draw blood, but we'll have to—"

"Wait for toxicology," Faith finished. "What about suicide?"

"With Chuck?" Sara shrugged. "Unless he left a note, I can't tell you."

"Except for the sweating, he wasn't acting guilty," Will said. "He seemed pretty confident Dave was the murderer."

Faith said, "I would be, too, without all the evidence that says he's not."

Sara remembered, "Wasn't Chuck wearing glasses?"

Will provided, "The current is fast. They're probably downstream."

"Thanks, guys." Kevin had made it across the creek. He went down on one knee, then he rolled Chuck onto the ground, then he sat back to catch his breath.

"Let's stay away from the bank over here." Sara indicated the point where she thought Chuck had gone into the water. "We'll need to bag the gaff and water jug, then start an inventory of anything that's found in his pockets."

"I'll get the supplies." Kevin pushed himself back up. "I need some water anyway."

"Make sure it's from a sealed bottle." Faith had found her purse on the ground. She took out her diabetic kit. "Can you guys start without me? I need to do my insulin thing."

Sara caught Will's eye as Faith walked a few feet up the trail and sat down on a fallen log. Faith was very good at her job, but she'd never been comfortable around the dead.

Sara asked Will, "Ready?"

He slipped his phone out of his pocket. "The creek was over the bank when I got here. We should video the area where Chuck went in before it's gone."

"Let's do it." Sara waited for him to start recording, then gave the date, time and location. "I'm Dr. Sara Linton. In attendance are special agents Faith Mitchell and Will Trent. This video is to document the scene where we believe the victim, Bryce Weller, also known as Chuck, went into Lost Widow Creek and subsequently expired."

She waited for Will to slowly pan across the area, starting with the base of the trail and making a broad sweep of the creek bank. Sara took the time to develop a theory about what had happened. There were three distinctive sets of shoe prints, one of which was made by a pair of sneakers. She looked at the bottom of Chuck's hiking boots. The soles were worn to the outsides where he pronated his feet. She already knew what Will's distinctive HAIX treads looked like. The elements had worked against them in preserving Mercy's crime scene, but the mud here had done them a favor. Chuck's last moments might as well have been set in stone.

"Okay," Will said. "Ready when you are."

Sara said, "The soles of the victim's boots match this W-shaped pattern in the mud. You can see where the victim's weight shifted to his toes here, facing the water. The heel imprint is more shallow than the toe. These two spots here indicate where the victim went down to his knees. They're not deep or irregularly shaped, which indicates it was a controlled action, not a sudden fall. There are two handprints on either side, here and here, so he was eventually on all fours."

Will said, "It must've hit him fast. I only took my eyes off of him for a minute. I didn't hear him call for help or cough or anything."

"Chuck's resources would've been directed toward staying conscious, not asking for help," Sara said. "My theory is that his blood pressure dropped, literally bringing him to his knees, then forcing him to put his hands down for balance. The right-side imprint is deeper than the left. You can see this long oval shape is probably where his right elbow buckled and he fell onto his right shoulder, then collapsed onto his right side. From there, my guess is that he rolled onto his back, but he was too close to the edge of the bank. Gravity took over from there, pulling him into the water. The current took him out to the boulders."

"His hand was caught when I saw him," Will said. "By the time I jumped in, he was already moving downstream."

"Did you see him twitch or make a gesture under his own volition?"

"No. He was floating. His arms and legs were straight out. There was no resistance."

"He must have been unconscious or already dead. I could be wrong, but my guess is that his lungs will show that he died by drowning." Sara looked into the water. She saw a pair of familiar-looking glasses stuck in the creek bed. "These are identical to the ones Chuck was wearing."

Will avoided the footprints as he leaned over the water with his phone to record the placement of the glasses.

Sara turned toward the body. Chuck was on his back, face up. She had barely looked at him the night before. Now, she took in his features. He was plain, though not unattractive, with black wavy hair he wore to his shoulders, olive skin, and dark brown eyes.

She asked Will, "When you were talking to Chuck, did you notice if his pupils were dilated?"

Will shook his head. "There's not a lot of sunlight down here with the trees. I was more focused on making sure he didn't grab that gaff and come after me."

"Can't you tell?" Faith was keeping her distance up the trail, but she was clearly listening. "Wouldn't his pupils still be dilated?"

"The iris is a muscle," Sara told her. "Muscles relax in death."

Faith looked queasy. "There's some gloves in my purse."

Sara located the gloves and put them on while Will did a full-body capture from the top of Chuck's head to the bottom of his hiking boots. The flash was on. Under the bright light, she could see the blue tint wasn't confined to Chuck's lips and fingernails. His face had a blue cast to it, particularly in the periorbital areas.

She told Will, "Make sure you focus in on his upper and lower eyelids and the eyebrows."

Sara waited until Will was done before she knelt beside the body. Chuck was wearing a short-sleeved shirt. She saw no scratch marks or self-defense wounds on his arms or neck. She unbuttoned his shirt. His chest and belly were hairy, but absent even a stray mark. She took a closer look at his fingernails. She studied his face. She tried to remember what Chuck had looked like the night before. For obvious reasons, Sara's attention had been firmly on Will.

She asked him, "Did you notice anything strange about how Chuck looked last night?"

He shook his head. "I wasn't really paying attention at cocktails until he grabbed Mercy's arm and she yelled at him. Then we went inside for dinner and the lights were low. I honestly don't remember looking at him again."

"Neither do I." Sara hadn't had much time for Chuck. "We need to talk to everyone who was at dinner. I want to know if anybody noticed this blue tint to Chuck's skin last night. Or even before that."

"You think Chuck was being poisoned before we got to the lodge?"

"It's hard to tell without the proper resources. When he was talking to you earlier, how much did he drink from the jug?"

"It was half-full when we started. He finished all of it while we were talking, which was approximately half a gallon in roughly eight minutes."

"Can't that kill you?" Faith asked. "Drinking a lot of water?"

"It can if you drink enough to dilute the sodium in your blood, but a half gallon won't do that. A two-hundred-pound man needs at least one hundred ounces as a baseline per day. One gallon is one-hundred-twenty-eight ounces. At worst, drinking half a gallon that rapidly might make you vomit it back up."

Will said, "It looks like there's still some water at the bottom of the jug."

Sara wanted to see the analysis of the jug's content, but that would take weeks. She asked Will, "Was his belt undone when you were talking to him?"

"No. I assumed it came loose in the water."

For the benefit of the camera, Sara pulled back the belt to show that the top button and part of the zipper of Chuck's cargo shorts was undone. She leaned down to smell his clothing. "What was his affect toward the end of your conversation?"

"He was really sweaty," Will said. "And really anxious for me to go."

"He might have been worried about diarrhea. Maybe he was trying to take down his pants when the other symptoms hit."

Faith said, "That explains why he didn't yell for help. You don't want another dude witnessing a blow-out."

Will asked, "Do you see any defensive wounds?"

"None, but I want to look at his back. I'll check his front pockets before I roll him." Sara gently patted the material, trying to see if there was anything sharp before she put her fingers into the upper and lower pockets of Chuck's cargo shorts. She called out her findings. "A tube of Carmex lip balm. A half-ounce bottle of Eads Clear eye drops. A folding line management tool. A folding fisherman's multi-tool. A retractable tether. A pocketknife."

Faith asked, "Is all that stuff normal for fishing?"

"Most of it." Sara had spent a lot of time with her father on the lake. He wore the equipment on his belt, but everyone was different. "Are you ready for me to turn him?"

Will moved back a few feet, then nodded.

Sara stabilized her hands on Chuck's shoulder and hip, then turned him onto his side.

Will made a noise. The back of his injured hand went to his nose. Sara took that as a confirmation on the state of Chuck's bowels. She was glad Faith was upwind.

Sara could only breathe through her mouth as she removed Chuck's wallet from his right back pocket and opened it flat on the ground. The black leather was polished. She laid out a Visa card, an American Express, a driver's license and an insurance card, all in the name of Bryce Bradley Weller. There was no cash in the inner compartment, just a single condom in a faded gold packet. Magnum XL lubricated and ribbed. Sara turned over the wallet. By the circular wear mark, she guessed that the condom had been there for quite a while. Something told her Chuck wasn't using one every night and replacing it.

Will said, "The seminal fluid you found in Mercy, could that have been lube?"

"No. The slide showed traces of spermatozoa under the microscope. And keep in mind that's not evidence of assault, just proof of intercourse." She lifted the back of Chuck's shirt. There were no scratch marks or signs of recent trauma. The only surprising discovery was a tattoo. "There's a large tattoo on the left shoulder blade, approximately four inches by three, of what appears to be a square whiskey glass with amber-colored liquid sloshing over the rim. Instead of ice, there's a human skull."

"Wow," Faith said. "Was he big into scotch?"

"I have no idea." Sara had deliberately avoided any small talk. "Will?"

He shrugged. "I didn't see him drinking anything but water all night."

"If I was going to poison him," Faith said, "I'd definitely spike the jug."

Sara gently rolled Chuck onto his back. "That's all the

preliminary findings. We'll have to wait for the autopsy and tox screens to give us the full picture."

Will stopped the recording. He asked Sara, "What's your theory?"

Sara nodded for him to follow her away from the body. She didn't like talking over victims as if they were problems to solve rather than human beings.

She waited for Faith to join them, then said, "Given our surroundings, my first thought was something natural, like atropine or solanine, which are found in nightshade. I've seen it before. The solanine is incredibly poisonous, even in small amounts. There's also horse nettle, pokeweed, black cherry and cherry laurel."

"Jesus, nature is so bad for you," Faith chimed in. "What was your second thought?"

"I'm wondering about the eye drops. There's an ingredient called tetrahydrozoline, or THZ, that's an alpha-1 receptor used to decrease redness by constricting blood vessels. By oral ingestion, it rapidly passes through the intestinal tract and absorbs into the bloodstream and central nervous systems. In higher concentrations, it can cause nausea, diarrhea, low blood pressure, decreased heart rate, and loss of consciousness."

Faith asked, "You're talking about the stuff you can buy over the counter?"

"The dose makes the poison," Sara said. "If THZ is the culprit, then you're looking for a few bottles."

Will said, "All of the garbage gets taken up the hill. We can search the bags for empty bottles, but we'll have to send anything we find to the lab to process for fingerprinting."

"Wait," Faith said. "There was a case in Carolina with this, right? The wife slipped the husband eye drops in his water? But it took some time for him to die."

Sara had read about the case, too. "The THZ could be a contributing factor in Chuck's death. The actual cause could be drowning."

"Suicide is probably out," Will said. "That doesn't sound like something you'd use to kill yourself."

"Unless you wanted to shit yourself to death," Faith added.

"Wasn't there a movie where the guy gave it to the other guy so he could get the girl?"

"*Wedding Crashers*," Will said. "Are we looking for one person or two? Who would have a motive to kill both Mercy and Chuck?"

"What do we know about Chuck?" Faith asked. "He was weird. He liked scotch enough to get a tattoo. He fished. He carried around a jug of water."

Will said, "He was Christopher's best friend. He had an unrequited obsession with Mercy. He was an incel or incel-adjacent."

"He had a condom in his wallet, so he hadn't completely given up all hope." Faith let out a heavy sigh. "Who had access to the jug?"

Sara looked at Will. "Everybody?"

Will nodded. "Chuck wasn't careful with it on the viewing deck during cocktails. He set it down on the railing a few times and walked away."

"It would be heavy to carry all the time," Sara said. "At capacity, a gallon of liquid is just under eight-and-a-half pounds."

"Emma was almost eight pounds when she was born," Faith said. "It was like carrying around an X-Box."

"Or a gallon of milk," Will said.

"So we're back to the suspect being everybody up here," Faith summarized. "And anybody who had access to Eads Clear eye drops, which is in every store."

Sara added, "And is fairly well-known as a poisoning agent."

"Let's take Mercy out of the equation," Faith said. "Who would have a motive to kill Chuck? He didn't have anything to do with the sale of the lodge. If someone was going to kill him because he was creepy and annoying, that would've happened a long time ago."

Will said, "Before I followed him down here, I heard Chuck talking about the investors with Christopher. They were on the part of the trail behind the kitchen. Christopher said he was going to be late for a family meeting that was probably about the sale. Chuck asked if the investors were still interested. Christopher said he didn't know, but he was out of the business. He never wanted to do it in the first place, and without Mercy, it didn't work. He said they needed her."

"That's odd," Sara said. "Did he mean out of the lodge business or another business?"

Faith supplied, "Mercy was running the place after Cecil's bike accident. According to Penny, she was doing a great job, turning a big profit, investing back in the property."

Will didn't seem persuaded. "One of the last things Chuck said to Christopher was something like, 'This is a good thing we've got going here. A lot of people are depending on us.'"

"Maybe Chuck was involved in the lodge?" Faith asked. "A silent partner?"

Will said, "It didn't sound like they were talking about the lodge."

The sound of footsteps drew their attention up the trail. Kevin was back with evidence bags and collection kits.

Faith said, "Agent Dogsbody has returned."

Kevin didn't seem to like the joke, probably because it cut too close. He told them, "I swung by the dining hall. I asked the chef to clear out the free-standing freezer, but I didn't tell him why."

Faith asked, "He couldn't figure that out when you told him to make a man-sized space?"

"I told him we needed to store evidence but didn't want to contaminate the food."

"Okay," Faith relented. "That was smart."

Kevin asked, "What's the plan on Chuck? Do we tell people? Do we keep it a secret?"

Sara said, "I have to notify Nadine of the death, but she won't be able to transport the body down until the road is accessible. I trust her to keep it quiet."

"The chef and waiters will see us taking the body into the freezer," Will said. "But if they stay in the dining hall and nobody from the house comes down, then the information won't make it to the compound."

Sara said, "If the lodge is still on the same schedule, guests won't come down for cocktails until six."

Kevin asked, "What about the Dave-didn't-do-it part? Still keeping that under wraps, too?"

"I think we have to," Faith said. "It's not like the family is crying out for the name of the murderer."

Sara asked, "What about Jon? He'll turn up eventually. Right now he thinks his father murdered his mother. Are we going to let him continue to believe that?"

"That's a complicated conversation," Will said. "You can't ask him to keep it a secret, and he might tip off the real murderer. We still need to find that missing knife handle. The killer might get sloppy because he thinks he got away with it."

Kevin said, "My vote is we keep it all under wraps—both Chuck and Dave."

"Agreed," Will and Faith said in unison, which made Sara's vote moot.

"Let's make a plan," Faith said. "We can use one of the empty cottages to conduct interviews so nobody is on their home turf. Start with Monica and Frank, figure out what else they're lying about. We need to get solid on the timeline. Then go for the app guys. I want to know why they lied about Paul Peterson's name."

"It's Ponticello," Will said. "Amanda found a marriage certificate. Paul Ponticello is married to Gordon Wylie."

Faith asked, "Why lie if you're married?"

"That's at the top of the list of questions," Will said. "I'm not sure how to handle Christopher."

"Because he was the last person to see Chuck and he had access to the water jug?" Faith snorted. "I mean, come on. He's suspect *numero uno*."

"What's his motive?"

"Fuck if I know." Faith let out a long, labored sigh. "We're just going around in circles. Let's stop talking and start doing things."

"You're right," Will said. "Kevin, I'll help you get Chuck to the freezer. I'm going to check the garbage pile while you process the scene down here. Faith, go ask for permission to use an empty cottage. If you can, rattle Christopher's cage. See if he asks where Chuck is. Sara, there's another satellite phone back at the UTV so you can call Nadine. Keep it on you in case I need you. Amanda told me she would call when the warrant is being sent, but check the fax machine anyway. Do you mind seeing if Drew and Keisha will talk?"

"I can try." Sara was more worried about the sutures in Will's hand. She'd brought antibiotics just in case. "I left the duffel with some medical supplies back at our cottage. I want to change out your dressing."

"Might as well wait until I'm finished going through the trash."

"Sounds good." Sara wasn't going to fight the infection battle, particularly in front of an audience. There was nothing for her to do but start back up the trail. The call to Nadine would be easy, but she wasn't sure how to approach Drew and Keisha. They seemed like genuinely nice people. They had every right to refuse to answer questions. But Sara would be lying if she told herself that Drew's assault charge didn't raise a giant red flag. He had been to the lodge twice before, maybe even as recently as ten weeks ago.

"Sara?" Will had clearly been making these same calculations. "Faith is going to come with you. She needs the map of the property."

Sara put on a smile just for him. "I can bring it back after I talk to Drew and Keisha."

Will put on a smile, too. "Or you could take Faith with you while you talk to them."

"For fucksakes." Faith wrapped her purse around her shoulder like a feedbag and started up the trail.

Sara went ahead of her up the trail. Faith didn't say much other than to complain about the mud, the trees, the undergrowth and nature in general. The path was narrow and the going was not easy because of the mud. Instead of worrying about Will's hand, Sara focused her attention in areas where she could be more effective. Nadine might have some information about Chuck. Small towns were notoriously wary of strangers. Barring that, a man like Chuck would stick out. There had to be stories about him around town.

"Jesus." Faith sounded more like she was praying as they finally reached the Loop Trail. "I have no idea why Will was so excited about this place. I'm covered in sweat, mud, and horse. Something bit me on my neck. My entire body feels sticky. Birds are everywhere."

Sara knew that Faith hated birds. "I've got some clothes you can change into."

"I don't know if you've noticed, but my body type is more husky teenage boy than tall and willowy supermodel."

Sara laughed. She was tall, but the other two adjectives were a stretch. "We'll find something."

Faith mumbled under her breath as they walked along the Loop. "Have you talked to Amanda?"

"Not about what she wants to talk about."

"I dunno, she kind of has a point about Will sticking his nose into things. He's on his honeymoon and he ends up running into a burning house, getting stabbed in the hand, and now he almost went over a waterfall."

Sara had to swallow before she could speak. The waterfall detail was new to her. "I didn't marry him to change him."

"Your level of healthy interaction can be really annoying sometimes."

Sara laughed again. "How's Jeremy?"

"Oh, you know, ready to become an FBI agent and throw himself on a dirty bomb."

Sara glanced down at her. Faith was generally easy to read, mostly because she volunteered whatever came into her head, but she was fiercely guarded about her children. "And?"

"And," Faith said, "I don't know what to do. Before this, the most shocking thing he ever said to me was that the United States keeps 1.4 billion pounds of cheese stored in a cave in Missouri."

Sara smiled. She loved Jeremy's random facts. "Have you tried talking to him?"

"I'm going to keep yelling a little longer to see if that works, then maybe I'll try the silent treatment, then I'll sulk for a while and use it as an excuse to eat too much ice cream." Faith crossed her arms as she looked up at the sky. "It's weird here, right?"

"You mean all the birds?"

"Yes, but I keep coming back to Mercy's mom," Faith said. "The way Bitty talked about her own daughter . . ."

Sara shared her disgust. "I can't imagine what kind of person you'd have to be to hate your own child. What a miserable human being."

"Kids can teach you who you are," Faith said. "With Jeremy, I tried so hard to be perfect. I wanted to prove to my parents that I was adult enough to take care of him on my own. I made schedules and spreadsheets and kept all the laundry done, and then one morning, I realized it's okay to eat food off the floor if it's closer to your mouth than the garbage can."

Sara smiled. She'd watched her own sister make these same calculations.

"Emma is teaching me how good a mother my own mother is. I wish I'd listened to her more. Not that I'm going to start listening to her now, but the thought is what counts." Faith's smile didn't last for long. "Talking to Bitty, all I could think is that she didn't learn anything. She had this beautiful little girl, and she could've made the world a wonderful place for her, but she didn't. Worse, she chose Dave over Mercy and Christopher. And now, Mercy is dead, and Bitty hasn't learned anything from that, either. She can't stop shitting on her own daughter. I know I joked about her acting like Dave's jealous, psycho-ex, but it feels pathological."

"I wouldn't say she's done any better by Christopher," Sara pointed out. "She basically ignored him at cocktails. I saw her slap his hand when he tried to get more bread."

"What about Cecil?"

"Mercy said something to me last night that's really been in my head a lot today," Sara said. "She asked me if I had married my father."

Faith looked at Sara. "What did you say?"

"That I did. Will is a lot like my dad. They have the same moral compass."

"My dad was a saint. No man will ever measure up, so why even try?" Faith shrugged, but she hadn't really given up. "What made her ask the question?"

"She was telling me that Dave is like her father. Which makes sense after seeing her X-rays. She suffered a tremendous amount of childhood abuse." Sara wondered how much Will had told Faith about Dave. She didn't want to overstep. "From what I've heard, Dave has two sides. Like Cecil, he can be the life of the party. Then there's the other side that can hurt the mother of his child."

"Most abusers are like that. They groom their victims, they

don't come in showing their entire asshole. But don't let Bitty off the hook," Faith said. "She could've physically abused her kids, too."

"I wouldn't be surprised," Sara said. "In my experience, women like that take more pleasure in psychological torture."

"I know finding Mercy was hard for Will, but I'm glad she wasn't alone when she died."

"She was worried about Jon," Sara said. "She told Will to make sure that Jon knew she forgave him for what happened at dinner. Her last words, her last thoughts were only about her son."

Faith rubbed her arms like she was cold. "It would kill me all over again if I thought Jeremy had to carry that kind of guilt around for the rest of his life."

"Jeremy has a lot of people who would look after him. You made sure of that."

Faith clearly didn't want to get emotional. She looked up the trail. "Fuck me, is that your cottage?"

Sara felt a pang of sadness when she saw the beautiful flower boxes and the hammock. They had lost their perfect week. "It's really sweet, isn't it?"

"Are you kidding me?" Faith sounded ecstatic. "It's like something Bilbo Baggins would live in."

Sara hung back as she watched Faith bolt toward the stairs. There was a familiar, sickly sweet odor in the air that she couldn't quite place. "Do you smell that?"

"It's probably me. You don't want to know what came out of that horse." Faith slapped at the side of her neck. "Another mosquito. Look, do you mind if I take a quick rinse off? I can't tell you how gross I feel."

"Let yourself in. Check the chest of drawers for some clothes. I'll wait for you outside. It's too pretty to be indoors."

Faith didn't ask questions. She dashed up the stairs.

"Faith!" Sara's heart had shot into her throat. "Stay out of my suitcase, okay?"

Faith gave her a look, but said, "Okay."

Sara watched her disappear. She prayed this would be the one time Faith wasn't nosey. Will would quit his job and move to a deserted island if she found the giant pink dildo Tessa had packed in Sara's suitcase.

She waited until the door had closed to turn back to the view. Her body felt shaky from exhaustion. Neither she nor Will had slept the night before. And not for the reason you shouldn't sleep on your honeymoon. Sara took a deep breath. The sickly sweet odor was still there.

On a hunch, she continued around the Loop Trail. Most of the guests had been assigned cottages close to the main house, but she remembered from the map that cottage nine was tucked away between her own cottage and the rest of the compound.

Sara had only walked along the top side of the Loop Trail twice, once with Will and Jon and the second time in darkness. On neither occasion did she see the ninth cottage. Sara was wondering if she was on a fool's errand when she finally spotted a footpath winding up another hill. The sweet smell got decidedly stronger as she walked the path. Sara knew from Jon that the odor was from a cartridge of Red Zeppelin. She also knew that he had lied about only having one vape pen. The one he held to his mouth now was silver.

Jon was sitting on the porch swing staring into the woods. His face was swollen, his eyes bloodshot, from mourning the loss of his mother. He was so deep in thought that he didn't notice Sara until she stood on the porch. He didn't startle. He just looked at her. Judging by his heavy eyelids and the glassy look in his eyes, he'd smoked more than Red Zeppelin today.

She said, "This is a nice place to hide out."

Jon used the excuse of putting the pen back to his mouth to quickly brush away his tears.

Sara asked, "Do you have enough food?"

He nodded as he blew smoke into the air.

"I'm not going to tell you to go home, but I need to make sure you're safe."

"Yes, ma'am, I'm—" He cleared his throat. "I'm safe."

She could see what the admission had taken out of him. Jon's mother was dead. For all he knew, his father was the murderer. He was probably feeling completely alone.

Sara asked, "Were you on the path by my cottage just now?"

He cleared his throat again. "The lookout bench was the last time . . . I mean, not the last time, but the last place . . ."

Sara watched a tear slip down his face. She wasn't going to inundate him with questions, but she sensed that he needed someone to listen. "You sat with your mother on the bench?"

His face looked pained by the memory. "She wanted to talk. We used to do that a lot when I was little. I thought I was in trouble, but she wasn't mad. She was real sad, though."

Sara leaned against the railing. "What was she sad about?"

"She told me Aunt Delilah was here." Jon rested the vape pen on the swing beside him. "She told me to ask Papa what was going on. It was about the sale. She wanted me to hear it from Papa instead of her. But not because she was a coward."

Sara's heart ached at the protective tone in his voice.

"I was mad at her, though. After I talked to Papa, I mean. Cause why did she want to stay up here? What was the point? We could all get a house in town and she could do her thing and I could . . . I don't know. Make some friends. Go out with . . ."

Sara listened to his voice trail off again. "It's a beautiful place. It's been in your family for generations."

"It's boring as shit." He tucked his chin into his chest. "Sorry, ma'am."

Sara said, "I don't imagine there's a lot for you to do up here."

"Work is all there is." Jon used the tail of his shirt to wipe his nose. "At least Bitty started paying me some a few years back. Papa never gave us a dime. I didn't even have a phone till Bitty sneaked me one. Papa said everybody I need to talk to is on this mountain."

Sara watched him start playing with the vape pen, turning it end-over-end. "When you were on the bench with your mother, did she say anything else to you?"

"Yeah, she gave me the night off. Then told me to get some liquor for the lady in seven. Only, I forgot."

Sara wondered if he'd really forgotten. "Did you drink it yourself?"

Jon's expression told her the truth.

Sara said, "I'm very sorry she's gone. Mercy seemed like a nice person."

341

His eyes cut toward her. She could tell he wasn't sure whether she was joking. Jon obviously wasn't used to hearing Mercy painted in a positive light.

Sara continued, "I didn't have much time with your mother, but we talked a bit. The one thing that was clear to me is that she loved you very much. She wasn't upset about the argument. I think like all mothers, she just wanted you to be happy."

Jon cleared his throat. "I said some awful things to her."

"It's what kids do." Sara shrugged when he looked up at her. "All of those emotions you were feeling last night are perfectly normal. Mercy understood that. I promise you she didn't blame you for being mad at her. She loved you."

Jon's tears started back in earnest. He started to put the pen to his mouth, then changed his mind. "She didn't want me vaping."

Sara wasn't going to lecture him about quitting right now. "When you're ready, I want you to talk to Will. He has some things he wants to tell you."

Jon wiped his eyes. "He's not mad at me for calling him Trashcan?"

Sara had almost forgotten about the exchange. "Not even the littlest bit. He would be very glad to talk to you."

"Where's my—" his voice caught. "Where's Dave?"

"He's in the hospital." Sara chose her words carefully. She knew that she couldn't tell him the truth right now, but she wasn't going to lie. "Your father is fine, but he was injured when he was taken into custody."

"Good. I hope he's hurting the same way he always hurt her."

Sara heard the bitterness in his tone. His fist had clenched around the vape pen.

Jon said, "A while back, he told me that he'd probably end up dying in prison. He was looking for pity, but I guess he was right, huh? It was gonna happen eventually."

"Let's talk about something else," Sara said, as much for her own sake as for Jon's. "Did you have any questions about what's going to happen with your mother?"

"Papa said we're gonna cremate her but—" His lip started to tremble. He turned his head away, looking into the forest. "What's that like?"

"Cremation?" Sara gave the answer some thought. She never talked down to children, but Jon was in a delicate place. "Your mother is being transported to GBI headquarters now. Once the autopsy is complete, she'll be taken to a crematorium. There's a specially designed chamber that uses heat and evaporation to render the body to ash."

"Like an oven?"

"More like a funeral pyre. Do you know what that is?"

"Yes, ma'am. Bitty let me watch *Vikings* on her iPad." Jon leaned forward, resting his elbows on his knees. "You don't need to do the autopsy if they already know who did it, right?"

"We still have to. It's part of the procedure. We need to collect evidence to legally establish a manner of death."

He looked startled. "It wasn't because she was stabbed?"

"Ultimately, yes." Sara skipped the explanation on cause vs. manner vs. mechanism of death. "Remember what I said. This is part of a legal procedure. Everything will have to be documented. Evidence will have to be collected and identified. It's a lengthy process. I can walk you through the steps if you like. You're still at the beginning."

"But if my dad would go ahead and confess to murdering her, then you wouldn't have to do any of that?"

Sara felt the guilt start to well back up for hiding Dave's innocence. She still kept strictly to the truth. "Jon, I'm sorry. That's not how it works. An autopsy has to be performed."

"Don't say you're sorry." He was crying in earnest now. "What if I don't want it? I'm her son. Tell them I don't want it."

"Legally, it's still required."

"Are you kidding me?" he yelled. "She's already been stabbed to death and now you're gonna cut her up some more?"

"Jon—"

"How is that fair?" He stood up from the swing. "You said you liked her, but you're just as bad as the rest of them. Hasn't she been hurt enough already?"

Jon didn't wait for an answer. He walked into the cottage and slammed the door.

Sara longed to follow him inside. He had a right to know about Dave. But he was also a sixteen-year-old kid who was angry and hurting. Ultimately, finding the person responsible for killing his mother would give him some sense of peace. For now, Sara could only ensure the bare minimum was being met. He was sheltered. He had food. He had water. He was safe. Everything else was out of her control.

Instead of going back to her cottage, she decided to find the satellite phone in the UTV. Sara had a duty to report Chuck's death to Nadine. That, at least, was one task she could complete. She put Jon's pain to the back of her mind. She called up the details from Chuck's crime scene so her report to Nadine would be succinct. Analyzing the contents of the water jug would be key. Motivation would also play a factor in the prosecution. If Sara's theory was correct, the eye drops would be listed as the cause of death, but the mechanism would be drowning, and the manner would be homicide. Any mitigating factors were for the jury to decide.

She took a deep breath to clear her lungs. Cottage six came into view. A little farther on, she found herself in the compound, passing the other cottages. When Will and Sara had first arrived, Sara had thought of the clearing as idyllic, almost like a painting from a storybook. Now, she felt a heavy weight on her shoulders as she got closer to the main house. Cecil was sitting on the porch. Bitty was beside him. Both of them had angry expressions on their faces. No wonder Jon hadn't wanted to go home.

"Sara?" Keisha was standing in the open doorway of her cottage. Her arms were crossed. "What the hell is going on? You need to get us off this mountain."

Sara walked toward her, trying to swallow back her dread. Drew was a legitimate suspect. Sara had to keep up the lie a little while longer. "I'm sorry I can't help you. I would if I could."

"There's two off-road vehicles over there with four seats each. You could let us borrow one. We could take Monica and Frank. They're ready to go, too."

"That's not my decision to make."

"Well whose decision is it?" Keisha asked. "We're scared of hiking down because of mudslides. God knows what the road is like. We can't call an Uber. There's no internet or phones. You've got us trapped up here."

"You're not technically trapped. You can leave at any time. You're just choosing not to because of valid reasons."

"Goddam, did you always talk like you're married to a cop or am I just noticing?"

Sara took a deep breath. "I'm a medical examiner with the Georgia Bureau of Investigation."

Keisha looked surprised, then impressed. "Seriously?"

"Seriously," Sara said. "Can you tell me anything about Mercy's family?"

Keisha's eyes narrowed. "What do you mean?"

"This is your third time up here. You and Drew know the McAlpines better than we do. Their response to Mercy's death seems very guarded."

Keisha crossed her arms as she leaned against the doorjamb. "Why should I trust you?"

Sara shrugged. "You don't have to, but I think you cared about Mercy. We need the case against her killer to be airtight. She deserves justice."

"She sure as hell didn't deserve Dave."

Sara swallowed down her guilt. She had been outvoted. What's more, she wasn't an agent. This wasn't her case to solve. "Do you know Dave well?"

"Only well enough to despise him. Reminds me of my lazy piece of shit ex-husband." Keisha's gaze had settled on the main house. Bitty and Cecil were looking at them, but the couple was too far away to hear anything. "The family has always been reserved, but you're right. They're all acting strange. The McAlpines have a lot of secrets up here. I guess they don't want them getting out."

"Secrets about what?"

Keisha narrowed her eyes again. "Being a medical examiner—does that mean you're a cop, too? Because I don't know how it works."

Sara returned to an honest approach. "I can still be a witness to anything you say."

Keisha groaned. "Drew doesn't want me getting involved in this."

"Where is he now?"

"Looking for Fishtopher down at the equipment shed so he can fix our damn toilet. It's been acting up since we got here, and Drew doesn't know the difference between a faucet and his asshole."

"What's it doing?"

"Making a dripping sound."

Sara spotted a way to earn back some of her trust. "My father is a plumber. I used to help him out every summer. Do you want me to take a look?"

Keisha's eyes went to the main house again, then back to Sara. "Drew told me the cops don't have a right to search anything without a warrant."

"He's not completely correct on that," Sara said. "The McAlpines own the property. Ultimately, they're the ones who are responsible for granting permission. And if I see anything laying around your place like a murder weapon, then I'm obviously going to tell Will."

"Obviously." Keisha took a second to think about it, then she let out a loud groan as she threw open the door. "I can't be trapped up here with that dripping noise. Don't mind the mess."

Sara guessed the two drinking glasses and half-eaten pack of crackers on the coffee table were the mess that Keisha was referring to. Cottage three was smaller than ten, but the furnishings were similar. A set of French doors off the living room offered spectacular long-range views. Sara glanced through the open door to the bedroom. The bed was made, unlike what Faith would find at Sara and Will's. There were two suitcases waiting by the front door. The backpacks were overstuffed where they'd been hastily packed. To her great relief, there were no empty bottles of Eads Clear eye drops in the trash can.

"Come on back." Keisha walked through to the bathroom. Two sets of toiletries were lined up by the basin, but still no eye drops. "Have you tried the liquor up here?"

"No." Sara had really wanted to after the last twelve hours, but she said, "Will and I don't drink."

"I'd keep it that way. Monica had a rough night." Keisha lowered her voice, though they were alone. "I saw Mercy talking to the bartender. I'm sure they were trying to cut her off. That shit is dangerous. You get somebody really sick up here, that's a helicopter trip to Atlanta, and insurance doesn't pay if you're the one serving."

Sara guessed that Keisha knew about liability from her catering business. "Did you hear anything last night? A noise or a scream?"

"Not even the damn toilet leaking." Keisha sounded exasperated. "This was supposed to be a romantic escape, but we're at that sexy stage in our marriage where I sleep with a fan on so I don't have to hear Drew's CPAP machine."

Sara laughed, trying to keep things light. "When were you up here last?"

"When the leaves started to come out. I guess that was two and a half months ago, give or take. It's beautiful that time of year. Everything's in bloom. I'm really sad we're not coming back."

"Me, too." Sara couldn't help but do the math. Drew was squarely in the frame for Mercy's pregnancy. "Did you guys ever spend any time with Mercy?"

"Not much this last trip because the place was packed," she said. "Now, during our first stay, we had drinks with Merce after dinner maybe three or four times. She drank seltzer water, but she could be fun once the tension drained away. I know how that feels. When you're in the service industry, people are always pulling at you. All day, you're getting nibbled to death by ducks. Mercy understood how that feels. She let her hair down with us. I was glad we could give that to her."

"I bet she appreciated it," Sara said. "I can't imagine how lonely it must be up here."

"Right?" Keisha said. "All she's got is her brother and that weirdo. Drew calls him Chuckles."

"Did you notice anything between Mercy and Chuck?"

"Same thing that you saw last night," Keisha said. "Chuck was here the first time we came. I guess the second time all the cottages were full, so he slept in the house. Papa was not happy with that, let me tell you. Neither was Mercy, come to think on it. She said something about keeping a chair against her door."

"That's strange."

"It is now, but you know how you joke about those kinds of things."

Sara did know. A lot of women used dark humor as a talisman to downplay fear of sexual assault. "Why doesn't Papa like Chuck?"

"You'd have to ask him, but I doubt there's any one reason," Keisha said. "Being honest, Papa doesn't have a neutral. He either loves you or hates you. No in between. I'd hate to be on the wrong side. He's a hard man."

"Did you ever get a chance to talk to Chuck?"

"What would I talk to him about?"

Sara had felt the same way. "And Christopher?"

"He's sweet, believe it or not," Keisha said. "Once you get past his shyness, he's easy to be around. Not to have a drink with, but as a guide, he knows his shit. That boy loves fishing. He can tell you everything about the water, the fish, the equipment, the science, the ecosystem. He bored me to tears, but Drew loves that stuff. It's good for him to get outside of himself every now and then. That's why I'm so sad this place is ruined for us. I doubt they'll be able to hold on to it without Mercy."

"Can't Christopher run the business?"

"You get a chance to see that equipment shed of his?" She waited for Sara to nod. "Drew calls it the Fish Palace. Everything nice and neat in its proper place, and that's fine, because it makes Fish happy, but you can't run a business like that unless you're the only employee. People are unpredictable. They want to do their own thing. Shit goes crazy on a minute-by-minute basis. You're juggling all these balls, freaking out about making payroll, dealing with customers who pull at you all day long, and then in the middle of it all the van breaks down or the toilet starts leaking. You've gotta roll with that shit or roll on out the door."

Sara was familiar with the pressure. She had owned a pediatric practice in her former life.

"Let me tell you this, one time, Drew went into the shed to put his fishing pole back on the rack, trying to be nice and help out, right? And Fishtopher comes running in there all bent out of shape because he wants to make sure it's put back *correctly*." She shook her head at the memory. "The only business he can run is fishing in the morning and drinking scotch at night."

Sara remembered Chuck's tattoo. "Is he into scotch?"

"I don't know what they're into, and I don't care. Once we get off this mountain, I'm never looking back."

Sara found it interesting that the question had been about Christopher, but Keisha had thrown Chuck in there, too.

"What about my toilet?" Keisha asked. "You figure out the dripping noise?"

Sara had figured out Keisha knew more than she was letting on. "It's probably the rubber flapper around the flush valve. It can wear out over time and let water seep through. If they don't have a spare, you could move to one of the empty cottages."

"I already told Drew that we should move, but he wouldn't listen to me. Said we were staying right here in the same cottage we're always in. You know how men can be."

"I do." Sara lifted the lid off the tank. Then she felt like she'd been kicked in the throat. She was right about the source of the leak, but wrong about the flapper being worn out.

A jagged piece of metal was keeping the rubber from making a seal. It was attached to a piece of red plastic that was about four inches long and approximately one-quarter of an inch thick.

She had found the broken knife handle.

17

Will watched thermal paper inch out of the portable fax machine like a snail squeezing through a pasta maker. The search warrant for the compound had finally come through.

"Okay." He pressed the satellite phone to his ear, telling Amanda, "It's printing."

"Good," she said. "I want you to wrap this up within the hour."

Will would've laughed if not for the fact that she could make his working life a miserable hell. "Faith is still with Sara, but they should be back soon. I asked Penny, the cleaner, to set up cottage four so we can do the interviews. Kevin is securing the body in the freezer. The kitchen staff probably saw what we were doing, but they're knee-deep in meal prep. I think we'll be able to keep Chuck's death a secret until dinner at least."

"I'm still trying to track down the file on Drew Conklin's assault charge," she said. "What about the family?"

"Their time is coming." Will started walking toward the woodpile. He wanted to see it in daylight. "I was steering clear of the parents while I waited for the warrant. I don't know where Christopher is. I'll send Kevin to find him once he gets back. Jon's still missing. I think Sara will peel off to look for him again. The aunt's Subaru is on the parking pad, so she must be back at the house."

"There's more to get from the aunt."

"Agreed." Will stood in front of the massive stacks of wood. There was enough split oak to last the winter. "I took a look around Chuck's cottage. It's a mess, but there was nothing interesting. No bloody clothes. No broken knife. No eye drops, even. Which isn't surprising. I went into all the cottages after the murder looking for Dave. If I didn't see anything then, I doubt I'll find anything now."

"Would you find it surprising to know that Mr. Weller has two hundred thousand dollars in a money market account?"

"Christ." Will had dipped into his emergency reserve to pay for the honeymoon. "I can halfway see why Christopher would be sitting on some cash. He doesn't have any bills. But what's Chuck's story?"

"Very similar to Christopher's. He paid off his student loans one year ago, almost in the same week. He's got a fishing license, driver's license, and two credit cards that are consistently paid off. There's no next of kin that I can locate. And as with Christopher, this seems to be a recent windfall. I did a deep dive going back ten years. They were both covered up in debt until one year ago."

"We need to see their taxes."

"Give me a reason and I'll give you a subpoena."

"Stock market? Lottery scratch-off?"

"I looked, and no."

"The money's got to be legit. They wouldn't put it in the bank if they hadn't paid taxes on it." Will walked down the stacks of wood. One looked different from the others. "What did Chuck do for a living?"

"I couldn't find any reference. From his social media, it seems that he primarily spent his time paying for lap dances in strip clubs."

Will moved the phone to his shoulder to free his hand. "There's no employment listed anywhere?"

"Nothing," she said. "He rents a condominium in Buckhead. We're in the process of executing a search warrant. Perhaps we'll find any next of kin or paperwork related to his employment there."

"Look for Eads Clear eye drops."

"The killer could've used a different brand. I left it open-ended in your search warrant."

"Good." Will picked up a piece of chestnut. The grain was

tight. It was an expensive choice for firewood. "I already searched all the trash bags. I didn't find anything."

"How did you manage that with one hand?"

Will had felt like a toddler when he'd asked Kevin to help him put on the glove. "I managed."

"How many bottles are you looking for?"

"I don't know." Will ran his fingers along a piece of figured maple. Another expensive choice. "I want to talk to Sara, but I think I remember a case where a guy was using eye drops as a date rape drug."

"If Mr. Weller was using them on women, why would he use them on himself?"

"I can't answer that right now," Will tapped a piece of acacia. It was soft and dried out from exposure, not the kind of thing you wanted in your fireplace. "What do you know about wood?"

"More than I'd like. Back in the day, I worked a sexual assault case against a carpenter."

Will didn't ask for details. "I get the feeling Christopher and Chuck had a side-hustle. Mercy was important to the operation. The aunt told me that Christopher and Chuck were hanging around the woodpile when she drove in."

"Find out why," Amanda said. "The clock is ticking."

The line went dead. Will had to hand it to her. She knew how to end a conversation.

He clipped the phone to the back of his pants. He knelt down in front of the stacked logs. Everything but this one section was oak. Why were they storing expensive wood outside in the elements? What kind of business would put two hundred grand each in Christopher's and Chuck's pockets? And why wasn't Mercy being paid?

"Will?" Sara's voice sounded tense.

He stood up. Faith was nowhere in sight. "What's wrong?"

"I found the broken knife handle in Keisha and Drew's toilet tank."

Will stared at her. "What?"

"Keisha told me her toilet was dripping, so I looked and—"

"Does she know you saw it?"

"No. I put the lid back on and told her she would need to talk to Christopher."

"Where's Drew?"

"He went to the equipment shed to find Christopher."

"Did you see him? Where the fuck was Faith?" All he could think to do was physically put himself between Sara and Drew's cottage. "What were you doing going in there by yourself?"

"Will," she said. "Look at me. I'm okay. We can talk about this later."

"Fuck." Will unclipped the phone. He hit the walkie button. "Faith, come in?"

There was static, then Faith said, "I'm heading toward the main house. Where's Sara?"

"With me. Hurry up." He clicked the button again. "Kevin, come in?"

"Right here." Kevin was walking toward them. He was covered in mud and debris from wrangling Chuck's body up the trail. "What's going on?"

"I need you to locate Drew. He's supposed to be at the equipment shed with Christopher. Keep an eye on him. Don't approach. He could be armed."

"Got it." Kevin set off at a brisk pace.

"Will," Sara said. "Keisha told me that the last time they were up here was two and a half months ago."

He didn't need a reminder. "Around the time Mercy got pregnant."

"What's up?" Faith had passed Kevin as she walked across the compound. She was wearing her Glock and a pair of baggy black pants. "Sara, where did you go? I wanted to look over the map."

Will told her, "We need to secure cottage three. The broken knife handle is in Keisha and Drew's toilet tank."

Faith didn't ask questions. She started jogging toward the cottage, her Glock down by her side.

Will kept pace with her. "There's a set of French doors off the back."

"On it." Faith peeled off.

Will scanned the area, checking windows and doors to make sure no one was going to surprise them. He knew that the front door wouldn't be locked. He walked in without knocking.

"Shit!" Keisha jumped up from the couch. "What the fuck, Will?"

It was the same reaction she'd had before, but this time, Will knew exactly what he was looking for. "Stay here."

"What do you mean, stay here?" Keisha tried to follow him to the back, but Faith stopped her. "Who the hell are you?"

"I'm Special Agent Faith Mitchell—"

Will pulled a glove out of his pocket as he approached the toilet. He used the nitrile as a barrier between his fingers and the porcelain as he removed the lid.

The broken knife handle was exactly where Sara had described. A thin piece of metal was preventing the flapper from making a seal. Which didn't make sense. If Drew had put the handle in the toilet tank, why was he looking for Christopher to stop the leak?

Or, was Drew worried about the cottages being searched, so he'd cleverly rigged the toilet to make it seem like he wasn't the one who'd hidden the knife handle?

Will wasn't sure about anything except that the killer liked water. Mercy had been left in the lake. Chuck had died in the creek.

"Will!" Keisha shouted. "Tell me what the hell is going on."

He carefully laid the tank lid on the bathmat by the tub. Faith was physically blocking Keisha when he went back into the living room. He told her, "Secure the evidence."

"What evidence?" Keisha asked. "Why are you doing this?"

"I need you to go to the cottage next door with me."

"I'm not going anywhere with you," Keisha said. "Where is my husband?"

"Keisha," Will said. "Either go with me on your own or I will physically take you there."

Her face turned ashen. "I'm not talking to you."

"I understand," he said. "But I need you to go to the other cottage so we can search your things."

Keisha's teeth were clenched. She looked angry and terrified, but thankfully, she walked out onto the porch.

Sara was standing in the middle of the compound. Will knew why she was there. She wanted to face Keisha, to give her a chance to yell at the person who had caused this. Will didn't care about Keisha's feelings of betrayal. He wanted Sara off this mountain as soon as possible.

"This way." Will directed Keisha toward cottage four. She glanced back at Sara before she walked up the stairs. She opened the door. Four was exactly like three. Same layout. Same furniture. Same windows and doors.

Will said, "Sit down on the couch, please."

Keisha sat with her hands between her knees. The anger had left her. She was visibly shaken. "Where's Drew?"

"My associate is looking for him."

"He didn't do anything, okay? He's cooperating. We're both cooperating and following orders. We're complying. All right? Sara did you hear that? We're complying."

Will felt his stomach twist into a knot at the sight of Sara.

"I heard," Sara told Keisha. "I'll stay with you while we work this out."

"Yeah, well, I made the mistake of trusting you before, and look where I'm at now." Keisha put her fist to her mouth. Tears streamed from her eyes. "What the hell happened? We came up here to get away from this shit."

Will watched Sara sit down in one of the club chairs. She was looking at him like she wanted guidance when his guidance had been for her to stay outside.

There was a burst of static, then, "Will, copy?"

Will reached back for his phone. He had no choice but to step out onto the porch. He left the door open so he could keep his eye on Keisha. "What is it?"

Kevin said, "Subjects are fishing from a canoe on the lake. They haven't seen me."

Will tapped the phone to his chin. He thought about all the tools that Drew would have access to on the boat, including knives. "Stay back, keep an eye on them, let me know if anything changes."

"Will?" Faith came up onto the porch. She was holding an evidence bag with the broken knife handle inside. "Nothing in their suitcases or backpacks. The cottage was clean. Want me to lock this in the UTV?"

"Bring it inside."

Keisha was sitting ramrod straight on the couch when Will walked back into the room. Her eyes went to his gun, then Faith's. Her hands were shaking. She was clearly terrified that they had brought her inside the cottage away from witnesses so that they could hurt her.

Will took the evidence bag and motioned Faith outside. She left the door ajar so she could stand on the porch and listen. He sat down in the other chair, which wouldn't have been his choice, but Sara was seated closest to Keisha. He placed the plastic evidence bag on the table.

Keisha stared at the handle. "What is that?"

"It was in your toilet tank."

"Is it a kid's game or—" She leaned forward. "I don't know what that is."

Will looked at the red plastic handle with a thin piece of curved metal jutting out at the broken end. If you didn't know what you were looking at, you might mistake it for a kitchen implement or an old-fashioned toy.

He asked her, "What do you think it is?"

"I don't know!" Her voice raked up in desperation. "Why are you even asking me about this? You've got the killer. We all know you arrested Dave."

Will guessed now was as good a time as any to let out the truth. "Dave didn't kill Mercy. He has an alibi."

Keisha's hand slapped to her mouth. She looked like she was going to be sick.

Will said, "Keisha—"

"Jesus Christ," she breathed. "Drew told me not to talk to you guys."

"You can choose not to talk," Will said. "That's your right."

"You're gonna jam us up anyway. Goddammit. I can't believe this is happening. Sara, what the fuck?"

"Keisha," Will didn't want her talking to Sara. "Let's try to clear this up."

"The fuck you say," she yelled. "Do you know how many idiots are rotting in prison because the cops told them they needed to clear some shit up?"

Will said nothing. Thankfully, neither did Sara.

"Jesus." Her hand went back to her mouth. She looked at the bag on the table. She'd finally put it together. She knew that it was part of the murder weapon. "I've never seen that before, okay? Not me, not Drew. Neither one of us. Tell me how to get out of this, okay? We didn't do it. Neither one of us had anything to do with this."

Will asked, "When did you first hear the toilet leaking?"

"Yesterday. We were unpacking and we heard it dripping, so Drew went to find Mercy. She was upset because Dave was supposed to fix the toilet before we checked in."

Will heard her audibly gulp for air. She was terrified.

"Mercy told us to go for a walk while she took care of it, so we went up the Judge Cecil Trail to look down at the valley. When we came back, the toilet was fixed."

"Was Mercy still here?"

"No. We didn't see her again until cocktails."

"When did you notice the noise from the toilet again?"

"This morning," she said. "We went to breakfast and—that's when it happened, isn't it? Somebody put that thing in our toilet. They're trying to frame us."

"Who else was at breakfast?"

"Uh—" She gripped her hands to her head, trying to think. "Frank and Monica were there. He tried to get her to eat something, but she couldn't handle it. They left before we did. And the guys—the app guys. Did you know his name is Paul?"

"I did."

"They didn't show up until we were leaving. They're always late. They were late to cocktails last night, too. Remember?"

"What about the family?"

"They never come to breakfast. At least not that I've seen." She turned to Sara. "Please, listen to me. The doors are always unlocked. You know we had nothing to do with this. What could possibly be our motivation?"

Will said, "Mercy was twelve weeks pregnant."

Keisha's jaw dropped. "Who was—"

Will heard her teeth click together when she closed her mouth. She glared at Sara with a look of red-hot betrayal. "You tricked me."

"I did," Sara said.

"Keisha." Will pulled the focus back his way. "Drew was convicted of assault."

"That was twelve years ago," Keisha said. "My ex, Vick, kept fucking with me, showing up at work, sending me texts. I told him to stop, then he shows up drunk at our house. He tried to grab my arm. Drew shoved him back and Vick fell down the stairs. Bumped his head. He was fine, but he insisted on going to the hospital, making it a thing. That was all. You can look it up."

Will rubbed his jaw. The story sounded believable, but then Keisha was desperate to be believed. "Did Drew ever spend time alone with Mercy?"

"You want me to say yes, don't you?" Desperation made her voice raw. "What if I saw Dave last night? He was walking on the trail, okay? I'll swear to that on a stack of Bibles."

Will didn't believe her, but he said, "Okay."

"Dave used to beat Mercy. You both know that. Whatever alibi he has, that can be broken, right? So if I saw him on the trail before she was murdered . . ."

Keisha stood up, so Will did, too.

She said, "Jesus Christ, I just need to move. Where would I go?"

He watched her pace the small room until Sara caught his eye. He could tell she was conflicted. He could also tell her presence was distracting him. Keisha was angry and upset. Will didn't need to be worrying about Sara. He needed all of his attention to be placed on the possible accomplice to murder.

"Tell me what to say," Keisha begged. "Just tell me what to say and I'll say it."

"Keisha." Will waited for her to look at him. "When I brought everybody out to the compound to tell them that Mercy was dead. Do you remember what happened?"

"What?" she looked perplexed. "Of course I remember what happened. What are you talking about?"

"Drew said something to Bitty."

Her gaze locked onto his, but she didn't say anything.

Will said, "Drew told Bitty, 'Forget about that other business. Do whatever you want up here. We don't care.'"

Keisha crossed her arms. She was a textbook example of someone with something to hide.

"What did Drew mean?" Will asked. "What was that other business?"

She didn't answer the question. She was looking for a way out. "We can make a trade, right? That's how it works?"

"How what works?"

"You need somebody to pin this on. Why not Chuck?" She was genuinely asking him the question. "Or one of the app guys? Or Frank? Leave Drew alone."

"Keisha, that's not how I work."

"Said every dirty cop ever."

"All I want to know is who killed Mercy."

"Chuck has the motive," Keisha said. "You saw how he freaked Mercy out. We all saw it. You wanna know who was here two and a half months ago? Chuck. He's always here. He's creepy as fuck. Sara, you know what I'm talking about. Dude gives off rapey vibes. Women know it. Ask your partner right now. Better yet, put her in a room alone with Chuck for five minutes and she'll see for herself."

Will gently nudged her away from Chuck. "What are you trying to trade?"

"Information," she said. "Something that gives a motive—that gives Chuck a motive."

Will wasn't going to tell her what had happened to Chuck, but he had learned a long time ago that people were drawn to solving puzzles. Even if the solution didn't necessarily benefit them. "Both Chuck and Christopher had a couple hundred grand in their bank accounts."

"Are you shitting me?" Keisha looked astounded. "Jesus, they were on to something."

"What were they on to?"

"No." She started shaking her head. "I'm not saying another word until Drew is standing beside me. Unharmed. Do you understand?"

"Keisha—"

"No, sir. Not another word."

She sat down on the couch, hugging her arms to her waist,

staring at the door like she was praying for her husband to walk through.

Will tried again, "Keisha."

"If I ask for a lawyer, if I make that request, you've got to stop asking me questions, right?"

"Right."

"Then don't make me ask for a lawyer."

Will relented. "My partner's going to come in to sit with you."

"No," Keisha said. "Where am I gonna go, man? I'd already be off this mountain if I could. I don't need a fucking babysitter."

He said, "If you want to make a deal, then you need to keep what I said about Mercy's pregnancy to yourself."

"And you need to keep out of my goddam way."

Will opened the door. Faith was still on the porch. They both watched Keisha go into her cottage. Faith asked Will, "What do you think?"

He shook his head. He didn't know what to think. "Christopher and Chuck were in a business with Mercy. Drew knew about it. Now Chuck and Mercy are dead."

She said, "So go talk to Christopher and Drew?"

He nodded. "Kevin's already down at the lake. You want to come?"

"I want to get this map straightened out. Something's not right on the timing."

Will had seen what Faith could do with a timeline. "I'll let you know if I need you."

He held the door open for Sara. She walked onto the porch. He felt his teeth clench as he followed her toward the Loop Trail. The walk to the cottage would take about ten minutes. He would use the time to explain to her why she needed to stay the hell in her own lane. She had been a distraction while he was interrogating Keisha. Will couldn't let that happen again.

Sara was oblivious to what was coming. She strolled onto the Loop, nodding toward cottage five. Paul and Gordon were on opposite ends of the hammock on their front porch. Gordon tossed them a wave. Paul drank straight from a bottle of alcohol.

The door to cottage seven creaked open. Monica came out, squinting in the sunlight. She was wearing a black nightgown and holding a glass of what was probably alcohol, because apparently Sara was right about drinking being the only thing to do up here.

Sara changed her trajectory. She headed toward Monica, asking, "How are you feeling?"

"Better, thank you." Monica looked down at the glass in her hand. "You were right. This took the edge off."

"Do you mind if I have a taste?"

Monica looked as surprised as Will felt, but she handed Sara the glass anyway.

He watched her take a sip. She grimaced. "That burns."

"You get used to it." Monica gave a sad laugh. "Don't take drinking advice from me. I need to apologize to both of you for my behavior last night. And this morning. The entire time, really."

"You have nothing to feel guilty about." Sara handed back the glass. "At least not as far as we're concerned."

Will wasn't sure about that. He told Monica, "I need to ask you about last night, just before midnight."

"Did I hear anything?" Monica asked. "I was passed out in the bathtub when the bell started clanging. I thought it was the fire alarm. I couldn't find Frank."

Will felt his teeth grit. "Where was he?"

"I guess he was sitting on the back porch, taking a break from my antics. He came through the French doors in a panic." Monica shook her head with sorrow. "I honestly don't know why he stays with me."

Will was more concerned with Frank's alibi. This was the second time he'd lied. "Where's Frank now?"

"He went down to the dining hall to find some ginger ale. My stomach's still not great."

Will guessed that Frank would bring back word of Chuck's death, which would bring its own set of problems. "Tell him I need to talk to him."

Monica nodded, telling Sara, "Thank you for your help. I really appreciate it."

Sara squeezed her hand. "Let me know if you need anything else."

Will followed Sara back toward the Loop Trail. He was glad that her pace was quicker this time. She wasn't going on a stroll.

Will worked to get a plan straight in his head. He would leave Sara at their cottage, then continue down to the lake. He would check in with Kevin and figure out an approach to Drew and Christopher, because no matter what Keisha said, Drew wasn't entirely in the clear. He had obviously known about the *business*. The knife handle had been found in his toilet. He had immediately invoked his rights, which was technically his right, but it was also Will's right to be suspicious.

The best thing to do was work Christopher and Drew off each other. Kevin could take Drew to the boathouse. The man was probably going to lawyer up again. Will could keep Christopher at the shed. Mercy's brother wasn't as sophisticated as Drew. He would be terrified that Drew was talking. Will would put it into his ear that the first rat gets the cheese. Hopefully, Christopher would panic and not realize until it was too late that he should've kept his mouth shut.

Will stuck his hand in his pocket. He watched Sara walk ahead of him. He needed to make sure she stayed in the cottage, which meant he was going to have to have a very uncomfortable conversation before they got there.

He said, "You shouldn't have been in the room with me and Keisha. I was conducting an interview and you threw me off my game."

Sara glanced up at him. "I'm sorry. I didn't think about that. You're right. Let's talk about it back at the cottage."

Will hadn't expected this to be easy, but he took the win. "You need to pack. I want you off this mountain before nightfall."

"And I want your hand to not get infected, but here we are."

This was more what he'd been expecting. "Sara—"

"I've got some antibiotics at the cottage. We can talk about—"

"My hand is fine." His hand was killing him. "It's not just about you being in the room. I told you to stay with Faith and you ran off on your own. What were you doing talking to Keisha by yourself? What if Drew had shown up? Forget about Mercy and Chuck. He has a record of assault."

She stopped in the middle of the trail. She looked up at him. "Anything else?"

"Yeah, what about you drinking in the middle of the day? Is that something you're going to start doing?"

"Jesus," she whispered.

"Jesus yourself." Will caught a whiff of alcohol on her breath. "You smell like lighter fluid."

Sara pressed her lips together. She waited. When he didn't speak, she asked, "Are you finished?"

Will shrugged. "What else is there to say?"

"When I *ran off on my own*, I found Jon. He's staying in cottage nine, which is over there. I don't want him hearing what I have to say."

Will looked over the top of her head. He could see the sloped shingled roof nestled in the trees. "I searched it this morning when I was looking for Dave. Jon must've gone there after I left."

Sara didn't comment. She started back down the trail. Will followed behind her again. He wondered if Jon was still in the cabin, and if so, how much he'd heard. Will had only raised his voice about the alcohol. He knew that he was too uptight about drinking. But it had been strange that Sara had taken a sip from Monica's glass. Which made him start wondering what Sara had meant when she'd told Will that she didn't want Jon hearing what she had to say.

He didn't have to wait much longer. Sara stopped a few yards from their own cottage. She looked up at him. "The side-business that Mercy, Christopher and Chuck are involved in. What are your theories?"

He hadn't gone into the theories yet. "The property is buffered by a state and national forest. Maybe illegal timber harvesting?"

"Timber?"

"The woodpile has some expensive species—chestnut, maple, acacia."

"Okay, that makes sense." Sara was nodding her head. "The app guys told me the bourbon tasted like turpentine. Monica is drinking top-shelf whiskey, but it tastes and smells like lighter fluid. She was on the edge of alcohol poisoning last night, but both she and Frank were surprised because usually she can handle it better. And twenty minutes ago, Keisha asked me if we'd tried the liquor. She warned me off it, and then launched into a speech about liability if a guest has to be airlifted off the mountain."

Will felt blind for not putting it together sooner. "You think the business Chuck and Christopher were talking about is selling bootleg liquor."

"Keisha and Drew run a catering business. They would notice if the alcohol was off. Maybe they brought it up with Cecil and Bitty. Some of the higher-end brands have a smokey flavor. Oak, mesquite—"

"Chestnut, maple, acacia?"

"Yes."

Will kept going back to the conversation he'd heard on the trail behind the dining hall. "Chuck told Christopher, 'A lot of people are depending on us'. Amanda said Chuck's social media puts him in a lot of strip clubs."

"Where there's usually a two-drink minimum."

Will asked, "Do you think Drew went to Bitty because they wanted a piece?"

"I don't think so," Sara said. "Maybe I'm giving them too much of the benefit of the doubt, but Keisha and Drew loved it up here. It seems more likely they were trying to stop it. Keisha flagged the liability. She warned me off drinking anything. I don't see her going in to something where she knows that people could die. Plus, think about what she said about trading information. She wouldn't give up Drew. She was giving up the bootlegging."

"Their credit check came back clean. They're not sitting on piles of cash." Will rubbed his jaw. He was still missing something. "The thing that's not adding up is, why kill Mercy and Chuck when you can kill Drew?"

"You're the one who likes a money motive," Sara said. "With Mercy and Chuck gone, Christopher gets whatever money is in the pot, plus he gets the business to himself. Then he ties up Drew with a murder charge."

Will pulled out his phone, he pressed the walkie. "Kevin, update?"

"Just a couple of dudes sitting by the lake drinking some beers."

Will caught Sara's worried expression. Chuck's water had been spiked with some kind of poison and now the guy who had the most access to Chuck had served Drew a beer. "Kevin, try to keep them from drinking anything, but don't let them know what you're doing."

"On it."

Will started to go, but then he remembered Sara.

"Go," she said. "I'll stay here."

Will clipped the phone on his belt as he ran toward the lake. He passed the fork, the lookout bench. He didn't know much about liquor, but he knew everything about the state and federal laws restricting the unlicensed manufacture, transportation, distribution, and sale of alcohol. The question he needed to answer most was how they were doing it. Testing the bottles of alcohol on the property would take weeks. Were they substituting cheaper stuff for top-shelf, which would cost them their liquor license and a heavy fine? Or were they making it themselves, which broke all kinds of state and federal laws?

Will took the dogleg down toward the shed. He could see ahead to the lake. There were two empty lawn chairs, each with a can of beer in the plastic cupholder. Kevin was lying on the ground holding his leg. Christopher and Drew were standing over him. Will's heart felt like it had been sucked into a vacuum hose, but then he realized that Kevin had found a way to keep the men from drinking.

Kevin accepted Will's hand to help him up. "Sorry guys, I get these bad leg cramps."

Drew looked skeptical. "Fish, I'm heading back. Thanks for the beer."

Christopher tipped his hat as Drew walked toward the trail. Will nodded for Kevin to follow. Drew was not going to be happy when Keisha told him that she'd talked to Will.

"So?" Christopher said. "What is it? Did Dave confess?"

Will figured the news was already out. "Dave didn't kill your sister."

"Well." Christopher's expression was unchanged. "I knew he'd manage to squirm out of it eventually. Did Bitty give him an alibi?"

"No, Mercy did." Will had been expecting at least some surprise, but Christopher gave him nothing. "Your sister called Dave before she died. Her voicemail rules him out."

Christopher looked out at the lake. "That's surprising. What did Mercy say?"

"That she needed Dave's help."

"Also surprising. Dave never once helped Mercy when she was alive."

"Did you help her?"

Christopher didn't respond. He crossed his arms as he stared at the water.

Will said nothing. In his experience, people couldn't tolerate silence.

Evidently, Christopher was immune. He kept his arms crossed, his eyes on the lake, and his mouth closed.

Will had to find another way to rattle the man.

He looked back at the equipment shed. The doors were propped wide open. The knives were in the same place as before, but they looked sharper in the light of day. The blades weren't Will's only concern. A paddle to the head or a punch to the gut with one of the wooden handles on a net could do a lot of damage. Not to mention that Christopher probably had the same fishing gear in his pockets as Chuck. A folding line management tool. A folding fisherman's multi-tool. A retractable tether. A pocketknife.

Will only had one hand. The other one was hot and throbbing because Sara was right about the infection. Then again, the hand that wasn't infected was in easy reach of a Smith and Wesson snub-nosed revolver.

He went inside the shed. He started loudly opening cabinets and drawers.

Christopher rushed inside, clearly distressed. "What are you doing? Stay out of there."

"I've got a search warrant for the property." Will raked open another drawer. "If you want to read the warrant, you can go back to the compound and ask my partner to show it to you."

"Wait!" Christopher was rattled now. He started closing the drawers. "Hold on, what are you looking for? I can tell you where it is."

"What would I be looking for?"

"I don't know," he said. "But this is my shed. Everything in here is there because I put it there."

He seemed to realize a second too late that he'd just taken ownership of whatever Will found.

Will asked, "What do you think I'm looking for?"

Christopher shook his head.

Will walked around the shed like he'd never seen it before. He kept his eye out for any sudden movements from Christopher. The man came across as passive, but that could easily change. What struck Will about the shed was that everything was back in its place. Early this morning, Will hadn't been gentle when he'd rifled around looking for a way to tie up Dave. The tools had been returned to their outlined spots. The nets hung at the same intervals along the back wall. The daylight streaming in gave Will a clear view of the hasp lock to the room in the back. And the well-worn padlock.

"Look," Christopher said. "Guests aren't allowed in here. Let's go back outside."

Will turned to face him. "There's some interesting species of wood you've got stored up by the house."

Christopher's throat made a gulping sound. He'd started to sweat. Will hoped like hell this wasn't another eye drop situation. He wanted to move this along quickly. He decided to take a risk.

He said, "Last night when we all went in to dinner, you stayed outside with Mercy."

Christopher's face remained impassive, but he said, "So?"

Will guessed the risk had paid off. "What did you talk to her about?"

Christopher didn't answer. His eyes went to the floor.

Will repeated his question. "What did you talk to Mercy about?"

He shook his head, but said, "The sale, of course. I'm sure you've heard about it from Papa and Bitty."

Will nodded, though he hadn't talked to the parents yet. "Do you know what else they told me?"

"It's no secret. Mercy was blocking the sale. She was hoping that I would join her, but I'm tired. I don't want to do this anymore."

"That's what you told Chuck, isn't it?" Will's brain was imprinted with the conversation the two men had had on the trail. "You said that you never wanted to do it in the first place. That it didn't work without Mercy. That you needed her."

Christopher finally looked surprised. "He told you that?"

Will studied the man's face. The surprise seemed genuine, but Will had learned the hard way not to trust a potential psychopath. "You don't really need the money from the sale, do you?"

Christopher licked his lips. "What do you mean?"

"You're pretty set, right?"

"I don't know what you're trying to say."

"You've got a couple hundred grand in a money market. Paid off your student loans. Chuck is in the same boat. How did that happen?"

Christopher's eyes went to the floor again. "We've both made some savvy investments."

"But you don't have any investment or brokerage accounts in your names. You're not officers in any corporations. Your only job is being a fishing guide with your family's business. So where did the money come from?"

"Bitcoin."

"Is that what your taxes will say?"

Christopher cleared his throat loudly. "You'll find paystubs from the family trust. It's part of my profit-sharing."

Will guessed he would find evidence of money laundering. That was probably where Mercy came in. "Dave's part of the family trust, right? Where's his money?"

"I'm not in charge of who gets what."

"Who is?"

Christopher cleared his throat again.

"Mercy wasn't getting her portion of the profit-sharing. She doesn't have a bank account. She doesn't have any credit cards or a driver's license. She had nothing. Why is that?"

He shook his head. "I have no idea."

"What's back here?" Will knocked on the wall. The nets banged against the wood. "What am I going to find when I break open this door?"

"Don't break it. Please." Christopher's eyes stayed on the floor. "The key is in my pocket."

Will didn't know if the man was truly complying or if this was some kind of trick. He made a show of resting his hand on the butt of the revolver. "Empty all of your pockets onto the bench."

Christopher started with his fishing vest, then worked his way down to his cargo shorts. He laid an array of tools on the counter that were the exact same brand and color as the ones Chuck had kept in his pockets. He even carried a tube of Carmex lip balm. The only thing missing was a bottle of Eads Clear eye drops.

The last item Christopher placed on the counter was a ring of keys. There were four in all, which was strange considering none of the doors at the lodge locked. Will recognized a Ford ignition key. A barrel key that probably opened a safe. The remaining two keys were of the smaller padlock variety with black plastic grips. One had a yellow dot. The other had a green one.

Will kept his hand on the revolver as he stepped back from the wall. "Open it."

Christopher's head stayed down. Will made sure to watch his hands because the man was clearly not going to convey his intentions through facial expressions. Christopher selected the key with the yellow dot, slid it into the lock, pulled back the hasp, opened the door.

The first thing Will noticed was the smell of stale smoke. Then he saw the pieces of foil where they'd been test-burning combinations of wood. There were oak barrels. Copper tanks. Spiraling pipes and tubes. They weren't putting cheap liquor in expensive bottles. They were making their own.

"There's two keys," Will said. "Where's the other still?"

Christopher would not look up from the floor.

Will was going to have to rattle him again. Nothing freaked out a man more than feeling the cold metal of a pair of handcuffs ratcheting around his wrists. Will didn't have cuffs, but he knew where Christopher kept the zip ties. He reached down to open the drawer.

Early this morning, Will had felt guilty for leaving the zip ties loose. Sometime between then and now, someone had banded them back together. He assumed that someone was the same man who'd left six empty bottles of Eads Clear eye drops in the drawer.

18

Faith longed to take another shower. And not just because she was sweating her ass off. Keisha had looked at her with such disgust that Faith had felt like a stand-in for all the shitty cops all over the world.

This was why she didn't want her son to join the FBI, the GBI, or any other law enforcement agency. Nobody trusted the police anymore. Some of them had damn good reasons. Others were inundated with constant examples of bad cops. It wasn't just a matter of bad apples anymore. Entire departments were bad barrels. If Faith had to do it over again, she would've become a fireman. Nobody was mad at the people who rescued cats from trees.

Faith shook her head as she traveled along the bottom half of the Loop Trail. That was enough wallowing about things she couldn't change. For now, she had two murders and one suspect. Will wanted her to take the lead on interrogating Christopher. He figured the man shared Chuck's incel-adjacent beliefs, which meant that being interviewed by a woman would irritate the hell out of him. Faith agreed with the strategy. Christopher sounded too calm for his own good. She needed to find a way to scare the shit out of him. Fortunately, he'd given her a lot of ammunition.

In the state of Georgia, simply owning a still that produced anything but water, essential oils, vinegar and the like was a felony. Add to that the distribution, transportation and selling, and Christopher was looking at hard time in state prison. But that was only part of his problem. The federal government was supposed to get a piece of every drop of alcohol sold in the country.

If the two murders didn't keep Christopher in prison for the rest of his life, the tax evasion would.

"Hi." Sara was waiting at the bottom of the stairs. "Will and Kevin are still down at the lake. Christopher is taking them to the boat dock to show them the second still."

Faith grinned. Will was dragging Christopher around like a dog on a leash so that by the time Faith got to him, he would feel completely helpless. "His timing is great. Dave showed up at the house right before I left, so now they all know he didn't kill Mercy."

Sara frowned. "How did he get up here?"

"Dirt bike," Faith said. "He's gotta be hurting butt to nuts."

"He probably scored some fentanyl as soon as he left the hospital," Sara said. "I called Nadine to tell her about Chuck. The problem is, the death notice moved the lodge up the list to get the road fixed, so we won't be isolated up here much longer."

"Well I've got even worse news. The phones and internet are back up, so this place is no longer our little slice of Cabot Cove."

Sara looked worried. "Jon's been hiding out in the cottage next door. I should tell him that Dave is here. He's probably looking for a reason to go home."

"I don't know, look at what he has to go home to." Faith thought of a better idea. She tapped the side of her purse. "Jon can't get online from cottage nine anyway. Can I show you the map? Maybe you can help me fill in some blanks while I wait for Will to give me the heads-up on Christopher."

"Sure." Sara motioned for Faith to follow her up the stairs.

Faith had to readjust herself first. She'd borrowed a pair of Sara's yoga pants. They were about a foot too long and an inch too snug. She'd had to roll the waistband three times to keep the crotch from dangling down to her knees, then roll up the legs like puckered mouths around her calves. Her milkshake was bringing exactly zero boys to the yard.

The cottage had been cleaned since Faith had showered. Sara had obviously straightened up. Or maybe Penny had, because

Faith picked up the scent of oranges and, while Sara was tidy, she wasn't that tidy.

Sara asked, "What've you got?"

"Colored markers and a taste for vengeance." Faith sat down on the couch and dug around in her purse for the map. She laid it on the table. "I walked around the property with my phone to test the Wi-Fi signal. The yellow lines approximate the reception area. Mercy had to be inside these areas to make the phone calls to Dave."

Sara nodded. "So, that includes cottages one through five, plus seven and eight, plus the main house, plus the dining hall."

"The relay in the dining hall covers the viewing platform and halfway down Fishtopher Trail, which is where Chuck died. On the other side, the signal extends a bit into the area below the viewing platform. I didn't want to get too far away from civilization without someone knowing I was down there. Also, there was a shit-ton of birds."

Sara said, "It's interesting that both bodies were found in water."

"Christopher loves the water. Did you know there's a FishTok?"

"My father is on it."

"So is Christopher. He's really into rainbow trout. Let's start here." Faith pointed to the area where Mercy's body had been found. "Lost Widow Trail links the bachelor cottages and the dining hall. That's the way you guys went with Nadine to get to Mercy's crime scene. Will ended up taking the same trail when he was running toward the first and second scream. You following?"

Sara nodded.

"You can see the trail kind of meanders around the ravine, which is why it takes about ten or fifteen minutes to get down. But there's a faster way from the dining hall to the bachelor cottages that's not on the map. Alejandro told me about it. They call it the Rope Trail. I found the ropes, and basically it's a controlled fall down the side of the ravine. If Mercy was running for her life, that's the route she would've taken. Alejandro estimates it would take about five minutes to get down. I'll need Will to help me time it out. We can use it to backstop whatever story Christopher comes up with."

"So, you're saying the first scream, the howl, came from the dining hall, and the last two screams came from the bachelor cottages." Sara looked at the map. "That makes sense, but last night, in the moment, I could only tell that the two screams came from this general direction. The way sound travels here is strange because of the elevations. The lake is in a caldera."

Faith looked through her notes. "You were at the compound with Jon when you heard the second scream for help?"

"Yes. We had a brief conversation, then I heard the scream for help. There was a pause, then another scream—*please*. Jon ran back into the house. I went to look for Will."

"Back into the house," Faith repeated. "So, when you first saw Jon, he was coming out of the house?"

"I didn't recognize him at first because it was so dark. He was walking down the stairs with a backpack. He fell to his knees and vomited."

"What was the conversation?"

"I asked him to sit on the porch and talk. He told me to fuck off."

"Sounds like a drunk teenager," Faith said. "You were looking at him when you heard the two screams, though, so that's Jon off the list."

Sara looked startled. "Was he ever on it?"

Faith shrugged, but as far as she was concerned, every male up here but Rascal was on it.

"Amanda told me that she wants to get a statement from Jon," Sara said. "He could help with the timeline. After the scene at dinner, Mercy would've checked on him, at least."

"Maybe not," Faith said. "She could've been giving him space."

"Either way, I don't imagine he'll be much help. He was probably too drunk to remember anything." Sara pointed at the map. "I can help you identify where everyone else should've been. Sydney and Max, the investors, were in cottage one. Chuck was in cottage two. Keisha and Drew are in cottage three. Gordon and Paul are in five. Monica and Frank are in seven. The Wi-Fi area covers all of them, so Mercy could've made the calls to Dave from any of these cottages. According to Paul, she was on the trail at 10:30."

"Paul Ponticello sounds like Pippa Pig's pal." Faith turned back the pages to find the timeline. "Whatever happened must have kicked off at 11:10, right? Mercy called Dave five times in the space of twelve minutes. You don't do that unless you're frantic, scared, angry, or all three. Mercy left the voicemail at 11:28, so we know she was talking to the killer by then. She said, '*Dave will be here soon. I told him what happened.*'"

"What happened?"

"That's what I need to find out," Faith said. "But let's assume that Christopher is the murderer. He kills Mercy, takes out Chuck, frames Drew, which shuts down Keisha, easy peasy lemon squeezy."

Will said, "It's complicated."

Faith turned around. He was standing in the doorway with his bandaged hand over his heart. She knew Will wasn't speaking ironically. Most crimes were very straightforward. Only comic book villains relied on dominos falling in the right order to take out the right people.

Faith told Will, "Dave's at the main house. Came up on a dirt bike."

Will didn't respond. Sara had returned with a glass of water. She held up two pills. Will opened his mouth. She dropped them in, then gave him the glass. He drank the water. He gave her back the glass. Sara went into the kitchen. Faith folded the map and pretended like none of this was weird.

Faith asked, "Any word on whether forensics was able to save Mercy's notebook?"

She had asked Sara the question, but Sara was looking at Will. Which was odd, because forensics was Sara's department.

Will gave a tight shake of his head. "No word on the notebook yet."

"Okay." Faith tried to ignore the weirdness. "What about the pregnancy? I know the preliminary autopsy didn't rule sexual assault in or out, but are we thinking Christopher could be the father?"

Sara looked horrified, but she still didn't speak.

Faith tried again, "I know we'll eventually get DNA from the fetus, but Mercy was hooking up with other men. It'd be easy for Christopher's defense attorney to argue that one of her hook-ups found out about the pregnancy, got jealous, and stabbed Mercy to death."

Will did the tight headshake again, but not as an answer. "Sara, could you talk to Jon again? You've got a good rapport with him. He's probably seen a lot of things up here. People tend to forget when kids are around."

Sara asked, "Are you sure?"

"Yes," he said. "You're part of this team, too."

She nodded. "Okay."

He nodded. "Okay."

Faith watched them stare at each other in that secret way that excluded everyone else. She was yet again the hilarious sidekick in their romcom. Though she would like an award for not looking in Sara's suitcase when she'd had the chance.

She asked Will, "Ready?"

"Ready."

He stepped back so Faith could go down the stairs first. Which was gentlemanly, but also dangerous because Faith had nobody to land on if she fell. She slapped a mosquito off her arm. The sun was like a laser beam drilling into her retinas. She was so ready to get out of this place.

Will was more relaxed than usual as they walked down the trail. He stuck his left hand in his pocket. His right was still pressed to his chest.

Faith couldn't think of a way to be subtle, so she asked, "Tell me about you and Dave when you were kids."

He looked down at her, clearly needing an explanation.

"Dave ran away from the children's home," she said. "Whatever he was doing down in Atlanta, he probably did to Christopher up here."

Will grunted, but he answered, "He made up stupid nicknames. Stole your stuff. Blamed you for shit he did. Spit in your food. Found ways to get you in trouble."

"Sounds like a winner." Faith still couldn't figure out a way to be delicate. "Was Dave sexually abusing anyone?"

"He was definitely having sex, but that's not unusual. Kids who are sexually abused tend to focus on sex for connection. And sex feels good, so they want to keep doing it."

"Was it boys, girls, both?"

"Girls."

Faith took the way his jaw tightened to mean that Dave had been with Will's ex-wife. Which hardly made him an outlier.

Will said, "Being sexually abused as a kid doesn't mean you grow up to sexually abuse kids. Otherwise, half the world would be pedophiles."

"You're right," she said. "But let's isolate Dave from that statistic. He was thirteen when he got to the lodge, but they aged him down to eleven. Being thirteen with everyone treating you like you're eleven is infantilizing. Dave must have felt angry, frustrated, emasculated, confused. But he was also grooming Mercy. He was having sex with her at least by the time she was fifteen, and he was twenty. Where was Christopher when Dave was raping his baby sister?"

"Not protecting her, you mean?"

"I mean, Christopher was afraid of Dave, too."

"That'd be a really great motive if Christopher had murdered Dave."

"Maybe we'll get back to the compound and he'll have a bomb strapped to his chest and you'll have to defuse it before it detonates."

Will glanced down at her.

"Come on, Danger Dog. You've already run through a burning building and nearly tumbled over a waterfall."

"I would really appreciate it if you didn't describe it that way in your report."

He directed her down yet another steep path. Faith saw the lake first. The sun bounced off the surface like a disco ball from hell. She shielded the blinding light with her hand. Kevin was standing by the equipment shed. They'd put a canoe on the ground. Christopher sat in the middle. His wrists were zip tied to the bar that went across the center of the boat.

Will said, "Sara told me the bar's called the crosspiece. The upper edge is called the gunwale."

Faith was reminded of when Will had first met Sara. He'd found the stupidest reasons just to say her name.

"Hey." Kevin jogged up to meet them. "Hasn't made a peep."

Faith said, "Did he ask for a lawyer?"

"Nope. I got it on video when I read him his Miranda Rights. Dude looked into the camera and said he doesn't need a lawyer."

Faith said, "Well done, Kev."

"Agent Dogsbody continues to deliver." He pulled a ring of keys out of his pocket. "I'll hit you up if I find the safe."

Will watched him go. He asked Faith, "Is Kevin mad at you for the dogsbody joke?"

"No idea." Kevin was mad at her for ghosting him after they'd hooked up two years ago. "I need you to do the scary lurking thing while I talk to Christopher, okay?"

Will nodded.

Faith studied Christopher as she walked toward the canoe. They'd faced him away from the water, giving him a wide-open view to the illegal still in the back of the shed. He was average-looking. Not muscular but not pudgy. His blue T-shirt showed a small paunch. His dark hair was a little mullet-y in the back, just like Chuck's.

She walked past him, taking a deep breath as she looked out at the water. Gnats were swirling near the floating dock. Birds were circling. She let out a fake sigh of contentment. "God, it's gorgeous out here. I can't imagine having nature as my office."

Christopher said nothing.

"You should ask your lawyer to look into Coastal State Prison," Faith said. "It's in Savannah. If the wind shifts the right way, you can occasionally get a whiff of salt air over the scent of raw sewage."

Christopher still didn't respond.

Faith walked back around the boat. Will was leaning against the open door of the shed looking intimidating. She gave him a nod before turning to face Christopher. The suspect was sitting on one of two benches. He was hunched over because his hands were zip tied to the bar. The second bench was smaller, tucked into the back end.

She pointed to it, asking, "Is this the bow or the starboard?"

He looked at her like she was an idiot. "Starboard is the right side. The bow is at the front. You're standing at the stern."

"Talk about stern," Faith joked. She stepped into the canoe.

The fiberglass made a grinding noise as it dug into the rocky shore.

"Stop," Christopher said. "You're ruining the hull."

"*Hull*." Faith made it extra crunchy as she sat down. "Believe me, you do not want me on the water. I don't know a crossbar from a gun-whale."

"It's cross*piece* and gun-*wall*."

"Oh, my mistake, sorry." Faith pretended like she had never been corrected by a man. She picked up a piece of rope that was tied to a metal loop. "What's this thing called?"

"A rope."

"Rope," she repeated. "I feel like a sailor."

Christopher gave a put-upon sigh. His head turned. He stared down at the ground.

"Did they feed you? Are you hungry?" Faith opened her purse and found one of Will's Snickers bars. "Do you like chocolate?"

That got his attention.

Faith peeled apart the wrapper. She gave Christopher an apologetic look as she placed the bar in his upturned hand. He didn't seem to mind. He let the wrapper drop to the bottom of the boat. He held the Snickers longways between his hands instead of straight up. Then he leaned over and nibbled it like corn on the cob.

She let him enjoy himself as she tried to figure out a better approach. There couldn't be that many more parts of a canoe that she could get wrong. Normally, Will used his broody silence to pull the truth out of suspects, but you could get away with that when you were six-three and naturally terrifying. Faith's particular talent was making men incredibly uncomfortable every time she opened her mouth. She waited until Christopher had taken a large bite of Snickers to ask her first question.

"Christopher, were you fucking your sister?"

He choked so hard that the boat shook. "Are you insane?"

"Mercy was pregnant. Are you the father?"

"Are you f-fucking kidding?" he stuttered. "How could you even ask me something like that?"

"It's an obvious question. Mercy was pregnant. You're the only man up here except for your father and Jon."

"Dave." He wiped his mouth on his shoulder. "Dave is up here all the time."

"You're telling me that Mercy was fucking her abusive ex-husband?"

"Yes, that's exactly what I'm telling you. She was with him yesterday before the family meeting. They were rolling around on the floor like animals."

"Which floor?"

"Cottage four."

"What time was the family meeting?"

"Noon." He shook his head, still hung up on the incest. "Jesus. I can't believe you even asked that."

"Did Dave ever try to fuck you?"

The shock wasn't as extreme this time, but he still looked disgusted. "No, of course not. He was my brother."

"He fucked his sister but he wouldn't fuck his brother?"

"What?"

"You just told me Dave was fucking his sister."

"Can you stop saying that word?" he said. "It's very unlady-like."

Faith laughed. If Amanda couldn't shame her, this guy didn't stand a chance. "Okay, buddy. Your sister was brutally raped and murdered, but you're hung up on me saying *fuck*."

"What does any of this have to do with bootlegging?" he demanded. "You've caught me red-handed."

"We sure as fuck did."

Christopher huffed out his breath like he was trying to control his temper. He looked at Will. "Sir, could we please get this over with? I'll take the blame. It was my idea. I built both stills. I was in charge of everything."

"Hey, ding-a-ling." Faith snapped her fingers. "Don't talk to him. Talk to me."

Christopher's cheeks turned red with anger.

Faith didn't let up. "We already know that Chuck was balls deep in your little liquor operation. He's even got the tattoo on his back to prove it."

Christopher's nostrils flared, but he gave in quickly. "Okay, I'll flip on Chuck. Is that what you want?"

Faith opened her arms wide. "You tell me."

"Chuck and I are connoisseurs, okay? We love whiskey, scotch, bourbon. We started making small-batch for ourselves. Just a little bit at a time. Experimenting with flavors and various species of exotic woods to bring out the richness."

"And then?"

"Papa had his bike accident. Mercy started making changes at the lodge. She fixed up the bathrooms. Started offering cocktails. More money started coming in. Big money. Primarily from the alcohol. Chuck said we should cut out the middleman, use our hooch instead. At first, Mercy didn't know that we were refilling the bottles with our own stuff, but then she figured it out. She didn't care. All she wanted to do was prove to Papa that she could turn a profit."

"It wasn't just the lodge," Faith said. "Chuck was selling to strip clubs in Atlanta, too."

Christopher looked caught out. He had finally realized that Faith knew a hell of a lot more than she was letting on.

She asked, "Did your parents know?"

"Absolutely not."

"Drew and Keisha did, though."

"I—" He shook his head. "I didn't know that. What did they say?"

"You're not asking the questions," Faith told him. "Let's go back to Mercy. How did she feel about being left off the money train?"

"I didn't leave her off. She's my sister. I created a trust for Jon. I put the money in an account. He'll be able to draw from it when he's twenty-one."

"Why not give the money to Mercy?"

"Because Dave would get his greedy hands on it. Mercy can't— she couldn't—say no to Dave. He needled everything out of her. There was nothing he wouldn't take from her. And you're telling me she was pregnant? She would've been stuck with him for the rest of her life." Christopher suddenly looked sad. "I guess she was, right? Mercy died before she could get away from him."

Faith gave him a few seconds to catch his breath. "Did Mercy know about the trust fund you created for Jon?"

"No, I didn't even tell Chuck." He leaned forward, straining against the zip ties. "You're not listening to me, lady. I'm telling you how this works. Mercy would've eventually told Dave, and Dave would've hounded Jon into the ground until the trust was empty. There's only two things he cares about: money, and Mercy. In that order. He'll do anything to control both of them."

Faith regrouped. "Tell me how it worked. How did you launder the money?"

He sat back. Looked down at his hands. "Through the lodge. Mercy's really good at bookkeeping. She opened an online account, set up payroll. She made sure that we paid taxes on everything. All of the records are in the office safe."

"You said that Mercy was good with money, but she didn't have a dime to her name."

"That was her choice," Christopher said. "I gave her whatever she wanted, but she knew if she had money in the bank, or a credit card, or debit card, Dave would find out about it. She depended on me for everything in her life."

Faith felt a crushing sense of claustrophobia thinking about how helpless Mercy had truly been.

"That's what we were really talking about before dinner." Christopher was looking at Will again. "Mercy was pushing me to turn down the investors. She told me that she had nothing to lose. I told her that I could take away the rest of her life. Maybe I did. Maybe I should've just cleaned out my accounts and handed everything to her. She might've left Dave before it was too late, right?"

He had asked Faith the question. She couldn't answer him. She only knew the statistics, and they were soul crushing. It took an abused woman an average of seven tries to leave her abuser, and that was if he didn't kill her first.

She asked Christopher, "What about Chuck?"

"I told you, he doesn't know about Jon's trust. He's more afraid of Dave than I am."

"No, what about Chuck meaning, why did you murder Chuck?"

There was no reaction this time, just a blank stare. "What?"

"Chuck is dead, Christopher. But you knew that. You're the one who spiked his water jug with the eye drops."

Christopher looked at Faith, then at Will, then back at Faith again. "You're lying."

"I'll take you to him right now," Faith offered. "We had to store his body in the freezer outside the kitchen. He's hanging there like a side of beef."

Christopher stared at Faith like he was waiting for her to laugh, to say it was all a joke. When Faith didn't, he gulped air into his mouth. His head dropped to his chest as he started to sob. He was more torn up about Chuck than he'd ever been about Mercy.

She gave him a moment to cry. Faith had played the bully. Now, she played the mother. She leaned forward, rubbing Christopher's back to soothe him. "Why did you kill Chuck?"

"No." Christopher shook his head. "I didn't."

"You wanted out of the liquor business. He was trying to force you to stay in."

"No." Christopher kept shaking his head. "No. No. No."

"You told Chuck that the business didn't work without Mercy."

He was shaking so hard that she could feel it through the hull.

"Christopher, you're so close to telling me the truth." Faith kept rubbing his back. "Come on, buddy. You'll feel better once you get it all out."

"She hated him," he whispered.

"Mercy hated Chuck?" Faith patted his shoulder, but she kept her mothering tone. "Come on, Christopher. Sit up. Tell me what happened."

He sat up slowly. Faith watched his stoicism crumble. It was like every emotion he'd ever suppressed had been unleashed. "Chuck embarrassed Mercy in front of everybody. I was—I was taking up for her. I wanted to teach him a lesson."

"What kind of lesson?"

"To stop messing with her," Christopher said. "I don't understand. How did he die? I used the same amount as before."

Faith was seldom caught out by anything suspects said, but this one gave her pause. "You've spiked Chuck's water jug before?"

"Yes, that's what I'm telling you. I'm a distiller. I'm very exact with my measurements. I put the same amount in his water as the previous times."

"Times?" Faith repeated. "How many times have you poisoned him?"

"He wasn't poisoned. His stomach was upset. He had the shits. That's all it ever did. Chuck would say something rude to Mercy and I would slip some drops into his water to teach him a lesson." Christopher looked genuinely confused. "How did he die? It has to be something else. Why are you lying to me? Are you allowed to do that?"

Faith had heard Sara's theory at the crime scene. Chuck hadn't died from the eye drops. He had died because he'd rolled into the water and drowned.

She had to ask, "Christopher, did Chuck kill Mercy?"

"No."

Faith heard the certainty in his voice. She expected he would say something delusional, like *Chuck was in love with Mercy, how could he kill her?* But he didn't.

"I knocked him out."

"You what?"

"We always end the evening with a nightcap. I put some Xanax in his drink to make sure he didn't do anything stupid. Chuck was reading on his iPad, then he fell asleep." Christopher shrugged. "The bedroom window in cottage two lines up to the window in the back staircase off the kitchen. I checked on him before I went to sleep. He never left."

Faith was momentarily at a loss for words.

"I loved my sister," Christopher said. "But Chuck was my best friend. He couldn't help it that he loved Mercy, too. I kept him in check. I stood up for Mercy the only way I knew how."

Faith was almost at a loss again. "Did Chuck know that you were drugging him?"

"It doesn't matter." Christopher shrugged away the multiple felonies. "Mercy was kind to me. Do you even know how that feels when no one else in the world is kind to you? I know I'm weird, but Mercy didn't care. She looked after me. She put herself between me and Papa over and over again. Do you know how many times I watched him beat her down? I'm not talking with his fists. He whipped her with a rope. He kicked her in the stomach. Broke her bones. Wouldn't let her go to the hospital.

383

And then her face—the scar on her face—that's all Papa's fault. He let Mercy carry that guilt around for—"

Faith saw the look of fear in Christopher's eyes before his head bobbed down again. He had said too much. But maybe not by accident. Christopher wanted Faith to try to pull the truth out of him. What he didn't understand about Faith was that neither of them was going to leave this canoe until she did.

She said, "Penny Danvers told me your sister got the scar on her face from a car accident at Devil's Bend. Mercy was seventeen years old. Her best friend was killed."

Christopher didn't respond.

Faith asked, "How is Mercy's scar your father's fault?"

Christopher shook his head.

"How is your father responsible for the scar?"

Faith waited, but he still didn't answer.

"What guilt did your father let Mercy carry?"

Again, he didn't answer.

"Christopher." Faith leaned forward, edging into his personal space. "You told me that you tried to protect Mercy the best way you knew how, and I believe that. I really do. But I don't understand why on earth you would protect your father right now. Mercy was violently murdered. She was left to bleed out on your family's land. Can't you give her soul some peace?"

Christopher was silent a few seconds longer, then he took a quick breath and pushed out the words, "It was him."

"It was who?"

"Papa." Christopher glanced up before looking back down again. "He's the one who killed Gabbie."

Faith could feel Will's tension behind her. She had to take her own quick breath before she could speak. "How did—"

"Gabbie was so beautiful. And kind. And sweet. I was in love with her." Christopher was looking at Faith in the eye now, his voice strident. "People laughed at me, because I didn't stand a chance, but I loved her so much. A pure kind of love. Nothing that could be tainted. That's why I understood how Chuck felt about Mercy. He couldn't help himself."

Faith worked to keep her tone even. "What happened to Gabbie?"

"Papa happened." The strident tone was gone. His voice had the familiar deadness to it. "He couldn't stand the way Gabbie flitted around the world like a beautiful butterfly. She was always so happy. She had this lightness inside of her. She flirted with the guests. She laughed at their stupid jokes. She loved Mercy. She really did. And Mercy loved her. Everyone loved Gabbie. Everyone wanted her. So Papa raped her."

Faith felt like her mouth had filled with sand. It was the matter-of-fact tone he'd used to describe something that was almost indescribable. "When did this happen?"

"The night of the so-called accident."

Faith kept silent. She didn't need to push him anymore. Christopher was finally ready to tell the story.

"I was out collecting nightcrawlers," he said. "Papa raped Gabbie in my bed. He left her there for me to find. Papa told me he wasn't going to let anybody have something that he didn't have first."

Faith tried to swallow the sand in her mouth.

"He didn't just rape her. He beat her face. All of her beauty, her perfection, it was just gone." Christopher took another sharp breath. "I went to get Mercy, but she was passed out on her bedroom floor with a needle in her arm. She had so much pain in her body. She was so desperate to get away. She and Gabbie were going to leave together at the end of summer, but . . ."

Faith didn't need him to finish the sentence. She had heard about their plan from Penny Danvers. Gabbie and Mercy were going to move to Atlanta and get an apartment together and wait tables and make lots of money and live it up the way that only teenagers can.

And then Gabbie had died, and Mercy's life was changed forever.

Christopher said, "Papa made—he made me carry Mercy to the car. He just threw her in the back seat like a sack of garbage. Then we put Gabbie in the front. She wasn't even moving by then. I guess the shock or maybe being punched in the head so many times—I don't know. Maybe Gabbie was already dead. I was glad she didn't know what was going on."

He'd started crying. Faith listened to his nose wheeze as he tried to control his breathing. She recalled another detail from Penny—that Christopher had been so inconsolable after Gabbie's death that he had taken to his bed for weeks after.

"Papa told me to go back inside the house, so I did. I watched them drive away from my bedroom window. I fell asleep with my head on my arm." Christopher gulped another quick breath. "Three hours later, I heard a car door slam. Sheriff Hartshorne was there. My mother came into my room. She was crying so hard she could barely talk. We all went down to the kitchen. Papa was there, too. The sheriff told us that Gabbie was dead and Mercy was in the hospital."

"What did your father say?"

He gave a bitter laugh. "He said, 'Goddammit, I knew Mercy would end up killing somebody.'"

His tone had a finality to it, but Faith wasn't going to let him stop there. "Bitty didn't hear anything the night before?"

"No, Papa had slipped her some Xanax. Nothing would wake her up." He leaned down to wipe his nose on his arm. "All Mother knew was that Mercy had gotten high and ended up crashing her car and killing Gabbie. We never asked for the details. We didn't want to know."

Faith knew the official version from Penny. Mercy was the driver who'd been going down the rollercoaster hill that led to Devil's Bend. The EMTs had told the town that Mercy had laughed like a hyena in the back of the ambulance. Mercy had insisted that they were parked in front of the lodge. Which made sense, because Mercy was in her bedroom when she'd nodded off with a needle in her arm. She had no memory of being carried to the car.

Now, Faith could only assume that Cecil McAlpine had put the gear in neutral and hoped that gravity would rid him of his daughter and the young woman he'd beaten and raped.

She told Christopher, "The car dropped twenty feet into a gorge. Mercy got thrown through the front window. That's how her face was ripped off. Gabbie's head was crushed, but that happened before the accident. Your father's good friend Sheriff Hartshorne said that her feet were on the dashboard at impact. The coroner said that her skull was pulverized. They had to use dental records to identify her at the autopsy. It was like someone had taken a sledgehammer to her head."

Christopher's lips were trembling. He couldn't look Faith in the eye, but she knew that Christopher couldn't look a lot of people in the eye.

She asked, "What was Gabbie's full name?"

"Gabriella," he whispered. "Gabriella Maria Ponticello."

19

Will's brain was vibrating with self-recriminations. Paul had been right in front of him the entire time. Will should've pushed the man about checking in under an alias. He should've done a deeper dive into Paul's past. Delilah had told Will about Gabbie less than an hour after Mercy's death. Will had a sick feeling that he knew exactly what the tattoo on Paul's chest said. You didn't have a word permanently imprinted over your heart unless that word was important to you.

Will had looked right at it and hadn't been able to read it.

Faith had needed less than a minute on her phone to confirm Paul's connection to Gabbie. She'd found an obituary in the *Atlanta Journal-Constitution* archives. Gabriella Maria Ponticello had been survived by her parents Carlos and Sylvia, and her younger brother Paul.

"Kevin," Faith said. "Circle around to the other side. I want you to take Gordon to cottage four. Listen to whatever story he spins, then we'll compare notes with whatever we get out of Paul."

Kevin looked surprised, but he gave her a salute. "Yes, ma'am."

Will felt his teeth start to ache from clenching his jaw. Faith was giving the interview to Kevin because she felt the need to babysit Will.

He couldn't blame her. He had fucked up so much of this already.

The door to the main house opened. Delilah came out first. She bounded down the stairs. Bitty pushed Cecil out onto the porch. Dave was behind them. He lit a cigarette, then blew out a stream of smoke as he followed them to the wheelchair ramp off the back of the house.

Faith tugged at Will's sleeve, pulling him into the forest. They were waiting for the compound to clear out. Christopher was zip tied to a paddle wheel inside the boathouse. Sara was with Jon. Cocktails had started five minutes ago. Monica and Frank had been the first to leave. Then Drew and Keisha. With the rest of the family heading down, that left Gordon and Paul. The lights were on in cottage five, but the men hadn't come out. And why would they? Thanks to Will, Paul was confident that he'd gotten away with murder.

Will couldn't hold it in any longer. He told Faith, "I fucked up. I'm sorry."

Faith said, "Tell me how you fucked up."

"Paul has a tattoo on his chest. I know it says Gabbie. I saw it, but I couldn't read it fast enough. He covered it with a towel."

Faith was silent a beat too long. "You don't know that."

"I know it. You know it. Amanda will know it. Sara will—" He felt like his stomach had filled with diesel fuel. "Keisha told me that Paul and Gordon were late to breakfast. That's when Paul hid the broken knife handle in their toilet tank. I scared the shit out of her and Drew for nothing. They were terrified of being shot. And Chuck would probably still be alive. Christopher was supposed to be guiding guests this morning. Chuck would've been asleep in his bed."

"Wrong," Faith said. "The activities were cancelled because of Mercy."

Will shook his head. None of it mattered.

"Penny told me about the car accident," Faith said. "I could've followed up on it hours ago. I had Gabbie's first name. I could've cross-referenced it with all the other names, including Paul's. That's how I found the obituary."

Will knew she was clutching at straws. "We've got to get a confession out of Paul. I can't let him get away with this because of my mistake."

"He won't get away with it," Faith said. "Look at me."

Will couldn't look at her.

"Christopher's going to do serious time. We'll use his testimony to get Cecil for murdering Gabbie. We'll arrest Paul for killing Mercy. God knows how many strip clubs in Atlanta were buying moonshine off Chuck. They almost killed Monica with that shit. None of this would've happened if you weren't up here. Do you think Biscuits would've investigated Mercy's murder? You're the only reason Paul is going to get caught. And Christopher. And Cecil."

"Faith, I know you're trying to make me feel better, but every word out of your mouth sounds like pity."

The door to cottage five opened. Gordon came out first, then Paul. They were laughing about something because they had no idea that hell was about to rain down on them both.

Will said, "Let's go."

He jogged across the compound. Kevin came from the other side. He grabbed Gordon by the arm.

"Excuse me?" Gordon said, but Kevin was already pulling him away.

"Hey!" Paul tried to go after him. Will put a firm hand on the man's chest.

Paul looked down. There was no flirty banter this time. His mouth went into a straight line. "All right. I guess we're doing this now."

Faith said, "Let's go back inside."

Will kept close to Paul's heels in case he tried to run. Kevin took Gordon into cottage four. The lights came on. The door closed, but not before Gordon gave Paul a steady look. Will made sure that Faith had caught it, too.

Both men were in on it.

The living room smelled like a dive bar. There were half-empty bottles of liquor and overturned glasses. The trash can was overflowing with potato chip bags and candy wrappers. Will caught a whiff of pot. He spotted an ashtray by the chair. It was filled with the butt ends of too many joints to count.

Faith said, "Looks like you guys had quite the party. Anything in particular you were celebrating?"

Paul raised an eyebrow. "Are you sorry we didn't invite you?"

"Gutted." Faith pointed to the couch. "Sit."

Paul sat down with a huff. He leaned back, his arms crossed. "What's this about?"

Faith asked, "You're the one who said I guess we're doing this. What are we doing?"

Paul looked at Will. "You saw the tattoo."

Will felt like a metal spike had gone into his chest.

Paul said, "I kept watching you guys circling around all day. Was it Mercy? Did she tell someone before she died?"

Faith asked, "What did she have to tell?"

Will watched Paul unbutton his shirt, then pull back the material to show his chest. The tattoo was ornate, decorated with red hearts and multicolored flowers. From this distance, all that Will could make out was the G, but that was probably because he already knew the name.

Faith leaned forward. "That's clever. You can't really see the name unless you know what you're looking for. Do you mind?"

Paul shrugged as Faith took out her iPhone.

She snapped several photos, then sat back in the chair with a sigh.

Paul asked, "Am I a suspect or a witness?"

"I can see why it's confusing," Faith said. "Because you're acting like you're not either one of those things."

"White male privilege am'aright?" Paul reached for a bottle of liquor. "I need a drink."

"I wouldn't do that," Faith said. "It's not Old Rip."

"It's still alcohol." Paul took a large gulp straight from the bottle. "What are you guys looking for?"

Faith looked at Will like she expected him to take over. He assumed that his silence would outlast her, but this time, it didn't.

Paul said, "Hello? Witness-slash-suspect calling. Anybody home?"

Will felt his face flush. He couldn't keep being the reason this got fucked up. He asked Paul, "Did Mercy see your tattoo?"

"I let her see it, if that's what you mean."

"When?"

"I don't know, an hour or so after we checked in. I took a shower. I was in the bedroom about to get dressed. I looked out the window. I saw Mercy coming toward our cottage. I thought, 'Why not?'" Paul rolled the bottle between his hands. "I wrapped the towel back around my waist and I waited."

Will asked, "Why did you want her to see the tattoo?"

"I wanted her to know who I am."

"Did Mercy know that Gabbie had a brother?"

"I imagine so. They only knew each other for a few months over the summer, but they formed an intense bond very quickly. All of Gabbie's letters back home were about Mercy and how much fun they were having together. It sounded like—" Paul stopped, searching for the right words. "You know how it is when you're young and you meet somebody and you just click, and it's like two magnets getting stuck together? You can't see how you lived before you met them, and you don't want to live the rest of your life without them."

Will asked, "Were they lovers?"

"No, they were just two perfect, beautiful friends. And then it was ruined."

"You checked into the lodge under a fake name. That would've been the time to let Mercy know you're Gabbie's brother."

"I didn't want her family to find out."

"Why?"

"Because—" Paul took another drink. "Jesus, that's terrible. What the hell is it?"

"Illegal." Faith reached over and snatched the bottle out of his hands. She put it on the floor. She waited for Will to continue.

All he could do was let his mouth work on autopilot. "Why?"

"Why didn't I want the McAlpines to find out?" Paul sighed as he thought it through some more. "I wanted to keep it between me and Mercy, okay? I wasn't even sure I wanted to do it, but I saw her and I . . ."

Paul shrugged instead of finishing the sentence.

Will listened to the silence in the room. He looked down at his hands. Even the injured one was trying to make a fist. There was a bone-deep ache in his jaw from clenching his teeth. His body was familiar with this anger. He'd felt it in school when the teacher berated him for not finishing the sentence on the board. He'd felt it at the children's home when Dave made fun of him for not being able to read well. Will had developed a trick where he took his mind out of the situation, unplugging it from his body like the cord on a lamp.

But he wasn't sitting in the back of a classroom anymore. He wasn't in the children's home anymore. He was talking to a murder suspect. His partner was counting on him. More importantly, Jon was counting on him. Will had felt the last beat of Mercy's heart. He had made a silent promise to the woman that her killer would see justice. That her son would know the peace of seeing the man who had stolen her away from him punished for the crime.

Will moved the coffee table back from the couch. He sat directly in front of Paul. "You were arguing with Gordon on the trail yesterday afternoon."

Paul looked surprised. He had no way of knowing that Sara had overheard them.

Will said, "You told Gordon, 'I don't care what you think. It's the right thing to do.'"

"That doesn't sound like me."

"Then Gordon said, 'Since when do you care about the right thing?'"

"Are there cameras?" Paul asked. "Is this place bugged?"

"Do you know what you told Gordon?"

Paul shrugged. "Surprise me."

"Gordon asked, 'Since when do you care about the right thing,' and you said, 'Since I saw how she fucking lives.'"

Paul nodded. "Okay, that sounds like me."

"Gordon said that you have to let it go. But you didn't let it go, did you?"

Paul worked the hem of his shirt, folding it into tight pleats. "What else did I say?"

"You tell me."

"Probably something like, 'Let's discuss this over a barrel of Jim Beam.'"

"You told me that you saw Mercy on the trail around 10:30 last night."

"I did."

"You said she was making the rounds."

"She was."

"Did you talk to her?"

Paul started unfolding the pleats. "Yes."

"What did you say?"

393

"You won't believe me," Paul said. "Gordon told me to stay away from you. He said that you were just a big dumb cop looking to arrest anybody with half a reason."

"You've got more than half a reason," Will said. "What did you say to Mercy on the trail last night, Paul? She was doing her job, making her rounds, and you came out of your cottage around 10:30 and you talked to her."

"That's accurate."

"What did you say?"

"That—" He let out another long sigh. "That I forgive her."

Will watched Paul start back in on the pleats.

"I *forgave* her," Paul said. "I blamed Mercy for so many years. It ate me up inside, you know? Gabbie was my big sister. I was only fifteen when it happened. There was so much of her life—our lives together—that was stolen from me. I never got to know her as a real person."

"Is that why you killed Mercy?"

"I didn't kill her," Paul said. "You have to hate someone in order to kill them."

"You didn't hate the woman who was responsible for your sister's death?"

"I did for many years. And then I found out the truth." Paul looked up at Will. "Mercy wasn't driving the car."

Will studied the man, but he gave nothing away. "How do you know she wasn't driving?"

"The same way that I know Cecil McAlpine raped her."

Will felt like all of the oxygen had been burned out of the room. He checked in with Faith. She looked just as thrown as Will.

Paul continued, "I also know that Cecil and Christopher put Gabbie in the car with Mercy. I'm hoping that Gabbie was dead by then. I don't want to think about her waking up like that, watching the car barrel toward that sharp curve in the road and knowing that there was nothing she could do to stop it."

Will glanced at Faith again. She had moved to the edge of her chair.

"Her pelvis was crushed, too," Paul said. "My mother told me that little detail last year. The poor woman was on her deathbed.

Pancreatic cancer, plus dementia, plus a raging urinary tract infection. She was on high doses of morphine. Her brain—her beautiful brain—kept her trapped inside the summer Gabbie died. Helping her pack for the mountains, making sure she had the right clothes, waving goodbye as my father drove her away. Then picking up the phone. Hearing about the car crash. Learning that Gabbie was dead."

Paul leaned down and picked up the bottle from the floor. He took a long drink before continuing.

"It was just me at my mother's bedside. My father died of a heart attack two years ago." Paul hugged the bottle to his chest. "Dementia knows no patterns. The strangest little detail would come and go from her mind—that Gabbie had forgotten to pack her stuffed bear. Maybe we could mail it to her. Or that she hoped the McAlpines were feeding Gabbie well. Weren't they such nice people? She'd talked to the father on the phone when Gabbie applied for the internship. His name was Cecil, but everyone called him Papa. He was the one who called to tell us that Gabbie was dead."

Paul started to drink, but changed his mind. He handed the bottle to Will. "That phone call from Cecil—that's what really stuck with her. Papa gave her all the details from the accident. My mother assumed that he was trying to be helpful with his brutal honesty, but that's not what it was about. He was reliving the violence. Can you imagine what kind of psychopath you'd have to be to rape and murder a woman's child, then call her up and tell her all about it?"

Will had met that kind of psychopath, but he hadn't realized that Cecil McAlpine was one until now.

"That phone call hounded my mother to the grave. She only had a few hours left, and it was all she could talk about. Not the happy times, like one of Gabbie's violin recitals or track meets or when I surprised everybody and got into medical school, but that phone call from Cecil McAlpine telling her all the gory details about Gabbie's death. And I had to listen to every single word, because those were the final moments that I would ever have with my mother on earth."

He looked out the window, his eyes glistening in the light.

Faith asked, "How did you find out that Cecil killed your sister?"

"I had to go through my mother's papers after she died. My father's too. She had never really bothered to sort them out. There was a folder in the back of his filing cabinet. It had everything to do with the accident. Not that there was a lot to see. A four-page police report. A twelve-page autopsy report. I'm a plastic surgeon. I've worked on people after car accidents. I've testified at criminal and civil trials about the damage. I have never seen a case that didn't have boxes of paperwork. And that's not even with a death. Gabbie died. Mercy almost died. You're telling me that only took sixteen pages?"

Will had read his share of autopsy reports, too. The man was right. "Did they run a toxicology?"

"You're not just a pretty face after all." Paul's smile had a sad quality. "That was what really stood out. Gabbie had marijuana and a high concentration of alprazolam in her system."

"Xanax," Will said. The McAlpines had a predilection for the drug.

"Gabbie smoked, but she liked being up," Paul said. "She took stimulants—Adderall, molly, sometimes coke if anybody had it. She wasn't addicted. She just liked to party. It's one of the reasons my father forced her to do the internship at the lodge. He's the one who found the listing. He thought the fresh air, hard work and exercise would put her on the right track."

Will said, "Mercy was never charged with anything related to the accident. Your parents didn't find that odd?"

"My father was a big believer in truth, justice, and the American way. If a cop said there was nothing to see here, then there was nothing to see here."

Faith cleared her throat. "Which cop?"

"Jeremiah Hartshorne the first. Number two has the job now, which is an appropriate designation."

"Did you talk to him?"

"No, I hired a private detective," Paul said. "He made phone calls, knocked on doors. Half the people in town refused to talk to him. The other half seethed every time he mentioned Mercy's name. She was a whore, a junkie, a murderer, a bad mother, a waste, a witch, possessed by Satan. Every single one of them blamed her for killing Gabbie, but it wasn't really about Gabbie. They just fucking hated Mercy."

Will asked, "How did you find out what really happened?"

"We were approached by an informant. Very cloak and dagger." Paul's smile turned bitter. "It cost me ten grand, but it was worth it to finally hear the truth. Obviously, I wasn't able to do anything about it. The asshole shut up as soon as he had the cash. Wouldn't testify. Refused to go on the record. We looked into him. He's an oily little turd. I doubt his testimony could've sent Jeffrey Dahmer to jail for jaywalking."

Will knew the answer already, but he had to ask, "Who was the informant?"

"Dave McAlpine," Paul said. "You arrested him for Mercy's murder, but for some reason let him go. You know he's not just her ex-husband, right? He's also her adopted brother."

Will rubbed his jaw. There wasn't anything Dave touched that didn't turn to shit. "What did you say to Mercy on the trail last night?"

Paul slowly let out a long breath. "First, you should know a bit more about Gabbie's letters. She wrote at least once a week. She loved Mercy so much. They were going to rent an apartment in Atlanta and—you know how stupid you are when you're seventeen. You do the math and you can live off mac and cheese for ten cents a week. Gabbie was so happy to have found a friend. It wasn't easy for her in school. I told you about the violin. She was in band. She'd been teased for years. It wasn't until she blossomed into her looks that she finally had some kind of life. And Mercy was her first friendship as part of that life. It was special. It was perfect."

Will asked, "What's the second thing?"

"Gabbie also wrote about Cecil. She felt like he was hurting Mercy. Abusing her physically, maybe something else. I don't know the specifics because she didn't say. I doubt she had the words, really. Gabbie didn't grow up with fear. This was before the internet took away our innocence. We didn't have twenty zillion podcasts about beautiful, young women being raped and murdered."

Will could hear the sadness in his voice. The one thing that was clear was that Paul had loved his sister. Still, he hadn't answered the original question. "What did you say to Mercy on the trail last night?"

"I asked her if she knew who I was. She said yes. I told her that I forgave her."

Will waited, but he had stopped.

Faith prompted, "And?"

"And, I had this long speech prepared about how I knew that she had loved Gabbie, that they were best friends, that Mercy hadn't been at fault, that it was her father all along, that she had nothing to feel guilty about—all of those things. But Mercy never gave me the chance to say any of them." Paul forced a smile onto his face. "She spit on me. Literally. Just horked up something ungodly and let loose."

"That's all?" Faith asked. "She didn't say a word?"

"Yeah, she told me to go fuck myself. Then she walked toward the house. I watched her until she went inside and slammed the door."

Faith asked, "And then what?"

"And then—nothing. I was stunned, obviously. And I wasn't going to chase her down after that. She made it clear how she felt. So, I walked back inside and sat down exactly where I'm sitting now. Gordon had heard everything. We were both kind of speechless, to be honest. I hadn't been expecting a Hallmark moment, but I thought I would at least start a dialogue, maybe help both of us get some closure."

The sadness had left his voice. Now, he sounded perplexed.

"Okay, I need to rewind a bit." Faith obviously shared Will's skepticism. "Mercy spit on you, and you didn't do anything?"

"What could I do? I wasn't mad at her. I pitied her. Look at how she's living up here. Everyone in town despises her. She's trapped on this mountain with the father who framed her for killing her best friend. The whole family buys into her guilt. She lost her face because of that man. Think about that part. Mercy's own father took away her face, and she's living with him, working with him, eating meals with him, taking care of him. And on top of that, her own ex-husband, or brother, or whatever you want to call him, took ten grand off me for the truth, but he's never told her what really happened? It's just so fucking sad."

Will asked, "How did Dave know the truth?"

"That part I cannot tell you." He shrugged. "Offer him another ten grand. I'm sure he'll capitulate."

Will would get to Dave later. "You didn't seem fazed this morning when I announced that Mercy had been stabbed to death."

"I was very drunk and very high," Paul said. "Gordon stuck me in the shower to sober up. That's why I wasn't at my best when you saw me. The water had turned brutally cold."

Faith asked, "How are you sure that Mercy didn't know her father was responsible for Gabbie's death?"

"The husband/brother told me she had no idea. Worse, he came across as a bit of a prick about it. Arrogant, like *ha-ha I know this thing that she doesn't know, look at how clever I am.*"

That sounded like Dave all right.

"I knew it was true the very first time I talked to Mercy," Paul said. "I was trying to pull it out of her, right? To see if she really knew what her father had done. I talked about the money this place brings in, how nice it is up here. I thought maybe she was in on it, or was covering for her father."

"But?" Faith asked.

"I asked her about the scar on her face, and she tried to cover it with both hands." Paul shook his head. The memory clearly stirred up some emotion. "Mercy looked so damn ashamed, you know? Not just regular ashamed, but the kind of shame where you feel like your soul has been punched out of your body."

Will knew about that kind of shame. The fact that Dave had forced it onto Mercy, that he had used it to punish the mother of his child, was unconscionably cruel.

"That's why Gordon and I were fighting on the trail. I knew I had to tell her the truth. And I tried, but she made it clear she wasn't interested. Gordon was right. I've already lost my sister and both my parents. It's not my job to fix this fucked up family. It's all beyond repair."

Faith put her hands on her knees. "Do you remember anything else about Mercy last night? Or the family? Did you see anything?"

"Maybe I listen to too many podcasts, too, but it's always the thing you don't think that matters that actually ends up mattering. So—" Paul shrugged. "When Mercy went into the house and slammed the door, I was still absolutely stunned. I stood there for a moment staring in disbelief. And I swear to God I saw someone on the porch."

"Who?" Faith asked.

"I'm probably wrong. I mean, it was dark, right? But I swear it looked like Cecil."

"Why would you be wrong about that?"

"Because after the door slammed, he stood up and walked back inside."

20

Sara matched her pace to Jon's shuffling stride as they followed the Loop Trail to the dining hall. She had delayed their departure because she wasn't going to take a sixteen-year-old to cocktails. This seemed like a silly line to draw considering Jon was stoned when she'd knocked on the door to cottage nine. She'd bribed her way in with bags of potato chips and two Snickers bars that Will was certain to miss.

Jon had absorbed the news of his father's innocence in shocked silence. He was clearly overwhelmed by the events of the last twenty-four hours. He'd stopped trying to hide his tears. He'd only stared at Sara in disbelief, his hands trembling, his lower lip quivering, as she'd relayed the facts: Dave was innocent. They had another suspect, but Sara wasn't at liberty to tell him any more than that.

She had offered to take him to his grandparents, but Faith had been right. The boy was in no hurry to go home. Sara had kept him company as best she could. They had talked about trees and hiking trails and anything but the fact of his mother's murder. Sara could tell by the way he spoke—the lack of *uhms* and *ers* and *likes* that peppered most teenagers' sentences—that he had been predominantly raised in the company of adults. That those adults all shared the last name McAlpine was a very bad luck of the draw.

Jon kicked a pebble off the path, his foot raking through the dirt. He was visibly anxious. He knew better than Sara that they were close to the dining hall. He was probably thinking that his presence after being gone for so many hours would create a stir.

The last time he'd been inside the building, he'd been blind drunk and screamed at his mother that he hated her.

Sara asked, "Are you sure you want to do this? It's not exactly private. A lot of the guests will be there, too."

He nodded, his hair flopping into his eyes. "Will he be there?"

Sara knew he meant Dave. "Probably, but I could be the one to tell your family that you're back. You could wait for them at the house."

He kicked another pebble, shook his head.

She assumed they would continue on in silence, but Jon cleared his throat. He glanced at her before his eyes went back to the ground.

He asked, "What's your family like?"

Sara considered her answer. "I have a younger sister who's got a daughter. She's studying to be a midwife. My sister, not my niece."

Jon's mouth turned up in the hint of a smile.

"My father is a plumber. My mother does the bookkeeping and scheduling for the business. She's very involved in civic causes, and activities at her church, which she often reminds me of."

"What's your dad like?"

"Well—" Sara was aware that Jon had a complicated relationship with his own father. She didn't want to shame Dave by proxy. "He loves dad jokes."

Jon's eyes slid her way again. "What kind of dad jokes?"

Sara thought about the card her father had put in her suitcase. "He knew I was going to be in the mountains this week, so he gave me a dollar in case there were any deer parties."

"Deer parties?"

"Yeah, it costs a buck to get in."

Jon snorted.

"He wanted to make sure I had the doe."

Jon laughed out loud. "That's pretty corny."

Sara thought it was pretty wonderful. If Jon had been unlucky, Sara had hit the jackpot. "Remember what I told you about Will. He wants to talk to you about your mom. He has some things to tell you."

Jon nodded. His eyes were back on the ground. She thought

about the young man she had met the day before. He had been so confident when he'd walked down the front steps of his family home. At least he'd been that way until Will had cut him down to size. Now, Jon seemed nervous and cowed.

As a pediatrician, Sara had witnessed the dualities in children. Boys in particular were desperate to figure out how to be men. Unfortunately, they often looked to the wrong men for their role models. Jon had Cecil, Christopher, Dave, and Chuck. Clearly, he could do worse than a creepy incel who was being routinely poisoned by his best friend, but you could also do a hell of a lot better.

"Sara?"

Faith was waiting for her on the viewing platform. She was alone. The lights were on inside the dining hall. Sara heard silverware clattering, the low hum of conversation. Everyone had been isolated up here for hours, watching guests being selected for scrutiny one by one. The kitchen staff had probably told them about the body in the freezer. Christopher was nowhere to be found. And then Dave had shown up like an atom bomb going off, and Gordon and Paul had not come down for drinks. Sara assumed they were all abuzz with theories.

She asked Jon, "Do you want to wait for me to go inside?"

"No, ma'am. I've got this." Jon straightened his shoulders as he walked through the door. He was putting on his armor. Her heart ached at the sight of his fragile courage.

"Sara," Faith repeated. "This way."

Sara followed her up the Chow Trail. Earlier, Faith had caught Sara up on Christopher's revelations while Kevin and Will secured the man in the boathouse. Now, Sara tried to catch Faith up on her end of the investigation. "Nadine called. The creek receded. They put two metric tons of gravel on the road. She'll be here within the hour. It won't be long before the news spreads that people can leave. They're already talking to each other. Whatever you say to one person, you might as well say to all."

Faith said, "Tell me about the autopsy."

Sara couldn't think in bullet points right now. "You mean about the pregnancy or—"

"What samples did you collect for the lab?"

"The sperm in her vagina. Urine and blood. I swabbed her thighs, mouth, throat, and nose, for saliva, sweat, or touch DNA. I collected some fibers—red, mostly, but some black, which isn't consistent with Mercy's clothing. There was some hair with the follicles intact. I took fingernail scrapings. I performed a—"

"Okay, that's good. Thank you."

Faith went uncharacteristically silent. She was clearly rolling ideas around in her head. Sara figured she would learn what was happening soon enough, which is exactly what happened when they made the last turn in the trail and saw Will.

He was studying the map Faith had marked up. Sara could tell from the weary expression on his face that something had gone terribly wrong during the interview with Paul.

She asked, "It wasn't him?"

"No," Will said. "Paul already knew that Cecil killed his sister. Gordon's story matched his almost exactly. It wasn't him."

Before Sara could recover from the surprise, Faith asked, "As a doctor, what did you notice about Cecil?"

Sara shook her head. The question had come from nowhere. "Be more specific."

Faith said, "Can he get out of the wheelchair?"

Sara shook her head again, but more to try to clear the confusion. "I don't know the extent of his injuries, but two-thirds of mobility device users fall under some degree of ambulatory."

Faith prompted, "Which means?"

"They're not paralyzed. They can walk short distances, but they use the chair because of chronic pain or injury or exhaustion or because it's physically easier." Sara mentally flashed through her brief interaction with Cecil at the cocktail party. "He can use his right arm. He shook our hands last night, remember?"

Will said, "His grip was strong."

"You're right, but there's no way to extrapolate from that data point absent a full exam." Sara tried to think it through, but she couldn't see a way to be helpful. "I can't tell you whether he can walk unless I see his medical chart and talk to his doctors. Even then, willpower is amazing. Look at how long Mercy stayed alive after being stabbed so many times. Science will never explain everything. Sometimes, bodies can do things that don't make sense."

Faith asked, "Can they get an erection?"

Sara felt the shock of the implication. They had honed in on Cecil. "Give me more information."

Will said, "You were in the house. Did you see where Cecil was sleeping?"

"They converted one of the sitting rooms on the ground floor," Sara recalled. "He's using a regular bed, not a hospital bed. But— this might not mean anything, but I would expect a bedside commode. The downstairs toilet is too narrow for a chair. The bathtub didn't have a transfer seat. Cecil was in boxers when I saw him on the front porch this morning. He wasn't wearing a urine collection bag. There weren't any catheters in the bathroom. I also saw a set of men's toiletries laid out on a shelf above the toilet. Even if the bathroom was accessible, he wouldn't be able to reach them from a chair."

Faith said, "You told me it was weird that there's not a wheel-chair van in the parking pad."

"I didn't say it was weird. I said that he probably had people to help lift him in and out of the truck. Bitty's too small to do it on her own. She could've asked Jon or Christopher. Or Dave, for that matter."

"Wait," Will said. "When I rang the bell, Cecil was the first to come out. Then I saw Bitty, but I didn't see her pushing the chair. Cecil was just there, and then Bitty was there. Christopher didn't show up until later. Neither did Jon. Delilah was still upstairs when I came back from Gordon and Paul's cottage. You said it yourself. There's no way Bitty could lift Cecil on her own. She's not even five feet tall, maybe a hundred pounds in her socks. So how did Cecil get in his chair?"

"He got up and walked," Faith said.

Sara couldn't debate the walking anymore. "What did Paul tell you that set all of this off?"

Will provided, "He saw Mercy at 10:30, but she didn't go up the trail. She went inside the house. Paul watched Cecil get up from the porch and follow her inside."

Sara didn't know what to say.

"The first call from Mercy to Dave was at 10:47," Faith said. "Dave didn't answer. Mercy stewed. Then she went to talk to her father. Maybe Cecil panicked because he thought Mercy would talk to Paul again and find out how Gabbie really died. What did Cecil do to Mercy in those ten minutes?"

Sara put her hand to her throat. She had heard the kinds of things that Cecil McAlpine was capable of.

"Whatever happened with Cecil put Mercy into a tailspin. She called Dave at 10:47, 11:10, 11:12, 11:14, 11:19, 11:22. We know she was somewhere in the Wi-Fi area when she made these calls."

Will held up the map so that Sara could see. "Mercy was probably still inside the house when she started making the calls. She packed her backpack, stuck in her clothes and the notebook. She ran down to the dining hall. She kept trying to get in touch with Dave."

"There's an office safe in the back of the kitchen," Faith said. "Kevin opened it with Christopher's key. It was empty."

Will said, "Remember what Mercy said on the voicemail: 'Dave will be here soon.'"

Faith said, "She was talking to Cecil."

Sara looked at the map, taking in the distance between the house and the dining hall, the dining hall, and the bachelor cottages. "Cecil could possibly make it to the dining hall, but not down to the bachelor cottages. He wouldn't be able to manage the Rope Trail, and Old Widow would take him too long. Not to mention having the physical strength to stab Mercy that many times."

Will said, "Which is why he sent someone else to take care of her."

Sara needed a moment to process exactly what they were saying. She looked at Will. Now she understood the haggard expression on his face. "You think Cecil had an accomplice?"

Will said, "Dave."

Sara felt it all clicking together. "Mercy was trying to block the sale. With her out of the way, Dave would control Jon's vote. He's got a money motive."

"He's got more than that," Will said. "He's helped Cecil clean up his messes before."

Faith took over. "Dave knew that Cecil staged the car accident. He told Paul last year in exchange for some cash. Look—"

Sara watched Faith swipe her finger across her phone to pull up a county map.

"Devil's Bend is near the quarry on the outside of town, about a forty-five-minute drive from the lodge. Christopher said three hours elapsed between the time Cecil drove away with Gabbie and Mercy in the car and the time the sheriff came to notify them about the accident. There's no way Cecil could've hiked home in three hours. There's an entire mountain between the two locations. Someone had to drive him."

Sara said, "Dave."

"Fourteen years ago, Dave helped Cecil cover up Gabbie's murder," Faith said. "And last night, Dave helped Cecil kill Mercy to cover up for him again."

Sara was convinced. "What are you doing? What's the plan?"

Will said, "I want you to find a way to get Jon out of there. I'm going to stir up Dave."

"Stir up Dave?" Sara didn't like how that sounded. "How are you going to stir him up?"

Will told Faith, "Give us a minute."

Sara felt every hair on the back of her neck stand on end when Faith walked down the trail. She told Will, "You need Dave to turn on Cecil."

"Yes."

"So you're going to goad Dave into saying something stupid."

"Yes."

"And he's probably going to try to hurt you."

"Yes."

"And he probably has another knife."

"Yes."

"And Kevin and Faith are going to let it happen."

"Yes."

Sara looked at his right hand, which he was still holding against his chest. The bandage was frayed and almost black from dirt and sweat and God only knew what else. She let her eyes travel down. He wasn't wearing the revolver Amanda had given him. His left hand was at his side. She could see the wedding ring on his finger.

Will's first marriage proposal to Sara had not actually been a proposal. She hadn't answered the question because he had not actually asked her the question. The fact of this should not have been surprising. He was a remarkably awkward man. He was given to grunting and long silences. He preferred the company of dogs to most people. He liked to fix things. He preferred not to discuss how they'd been broken.

But he also listened to Sara. He respected her opinion. He valued her input. He made her feel safe. He was a lot like her father. Which got to the heart of why Sara was so profoundly, irrevocably in love with him. Will was always going to stand up when everyone else stayed seated.

She said, "Beat the hell out of him."

"All right."

Sara felt shaky as she walked toward the dining hall. She twisted her wedding ring around her finger. She thought about Jon, because that was the one person she wanted to protect. The last twenty-four hours had been crushingly traumatic for the young man. He'd gotten blind drunk. He'd argued with his mother. He'd thrown up in his own front yard in front of a stranger. He'd been surrounded by more strangers when he'd learned that his mother had been murdered. Then his father had been arrested, then his father was put in the clear, and now Will was about to goad Dave into bragging about the fact that he had murdered the mother of his child.

Sara had to get Jon out of there before it happened.

Faith was waiting on the viewing deck again. Kevin had joined her.

He said, "I got the kitchen staff out of the way. They're up in cottage four until this blows over. What about the guests?"

Will said, "We'll play it by ear. We want Dave to put on a show. He might want an audience."

Sara looked up at Will. "What if I can't get Jon to leave?"

"Then he'll hear what he hears."

Sara took a deep breath. That was a hard reality to swallow. She nodded. "Okay."

Faith warned, "Keep an eye on Bitty. Remember what I said about her acting like Dave's psycho ex. She might be unpredictable."

That part Sara was ready for. Nothing that happened in this place could surprise her anymore. "Let's get this over with."

Kevin opened the door.

Sara walked into the dining room first. The scene was familiar. Two tables, only one of them set for dinner. Supper had already been served. Dessert plates were scraped clean. Wine glasses were half-empty. Instead of being grouped together, the couples had spread out, each of them in different camps. Frank and Monica were with Drew and Keisha. Gordon and Paul were seated with Delilah. Cecil's chair was at the head of the table. Bitty was on his left with Dave beside her. Jon was on Cecil's right, directly across from his grandmother.

Sara felt all eyes on her as she sat down beside Jon. Being so close to his father had sapped the young man's courage. His hands were gripped together in his lap. There were sweat marks on his shirt. His head was bowed, but even Sara could feel the white-hot hate that he was directing across the table at Dave.

"Jon." Sara touched his arm. "Can I talk to you outside?"

"Hell no," Dave said. "You people've already deprived me of enough time with my boy."

Bitty said, "That's the damn truth. I want all of y'all out of here as soon as the road is open."

"Quiet," Cecil said. He was gripping his fork in his right hand. He stabbed a piece of cake. He chewed noisily in the silence.

Jon kept his head down. His anguish was as palpable as his anger. Sara wanted to wrap her arms around him and whisk him away, but she couldn't interfere with the investigation. Will and Faith had already taken up their positions. Kevin was blocking the entrance. Faith stood at the opposite end of the table. Will had put himself close to Dave, which also gave him proximity to the kitchen door. They had formed a perfect triangle.

"So?" Cecil barked. "What's this about?"

Bitty asked, "Where is my son?"

Faith said, "Christopher's been arrested for producing, distributing and selling illegal alcohol."

There was a short period of silence that was broken by Dave's laughter.

"Damn," he said. "Way to go, Fishtopher."

"Hear, hear." Paul raised a glass. "To Fishtopher."

Monica tried to join the toast, but Frank held down her hand. Sara looked at Bitty. The woman's attention was squarely on Dave.

His demeanor had changed. He knew this was not a friendly conversation. He rapped his fingers on the table as he looked first at Kevin, then Faith, then finally, he turned his head to look up at Will. "Hey, Trashcan. How's your hand?"

Will said, "Better than your balls."

Jon snickered.

"Jon." Sara kept her voice low when she suggested, "Why don't we leave?"

Dave said, "Keep your ass in that chair, boy."

Jon had frozen at the sharp order. Bitty made a tutting sound. Sara looked at the silverware settings. Two types of forks, a knife, a spoon. Any one of them could be turned into a weapon. She knew that Will had made the same calculations. His gaze had stayed not on Dave's face, but on his hands. Sara looked at Bitty's hands, too. They were folded on the table.

"So?" Dave said. "Whattaya got, Trashcan?"

Faith answered, "The coroner called. She found some evidence during Mercy's autopsy."

Bitty huffed, "Is this an appropriate venue to discuss such matters?"

Paul said, "I think tonight would be a great night for all of us to hear the truth."

Sara caught Faith shutting him down with a look.

"Or not." Paul returned his glass to the table.

Faith said, "The coroner scraped under Mercy's fingernails. She found pieces of skin, which means that Mercy scratched whoever attacked her. We're going to need DNA from every person in here."

Dave laughed. "Good fucking luck, lady. You need a warrant for that."

"Judge Framingham is signing off on it right now." Faith spoke with such authority that Sara almost believed her. "You know the judge, don't you, Dave? He presided over a couple of your DUIs, right? He's the one who pulled your driver's license."

Dave traced his finger along the fork beside his plate. "You're just gonna take everybody's DNA here?"

"That's right," Faith said. "Every single person."

Drew said, "You can't do that. There's no reason to suspect—"

"You don't need my fucking DNA," Cecil said. "I'm her goddam father."

Sara flinched at the explosion of rage. Her mind immediately went to Gabbie, then Mercy.

"Mr. McAlpine." Faith kept her voice calm. "There's something called touch-DNA, which means that anybody who came into physical contact with Mercy, whether it was Bitty or Delilah or you or Jon or even one of the guests, left some of their genetic material on her body. We have to establish profiles on everyone so we can isolate the killer's. The kitchen staff and Penny have already given samples. It's really not that big a deal."

"Okay." Delilah surprised everyone by speaking first. "I held Mercy's hand. It was before dinner, but sign me up. How do we do this? Spit? Swab?"

"Fuck. No." Keisha slapped the table. "I'm not keeping your secret anymore. This is bullshit."

"What secret?" Delilah asked.

Faith provided, "Mercy was twelve weeks pregnant."

Bitty gasped. Her eyes went straight to Dave.

Sara looked at Dave, too. The news had clearly unsettled him.

Faith said, "We know that Mercy had sex with some of the guests."

There was cross-talk at the end of the table, but Sara could only watch Bitty place a calming hand on Dave's arm. His jaw was tight. He kept clenching and unclenching his fist.

He said, "What are you saying about my wife?"

Will chose now to jump in. "Mercy wasn't your wife."

Dave's fist clenched tight. He ignored Will, training all his rage on Faith. "What bullshit just came out of your fucking mouth?"

Will said, "It wasn't just the guests. Mercy was fucking Alejandro on the regular."

Dave stood up so fast that his chair fell over. He was looking at Will now. "Shut your fucking mouth."

Sara tensed along with everyone else at the table. The two men were facing off, both ready to kill each other.

"Dave." Bitty tugged at the back of his shirt. "Sit down, baby. If they had a warrant, they'd be showing it to you."

Dave's mouth twisted into a vulgar grin. "She's right. Show me the paper, Trashcan."

"You think I can't get your DNA?" Will asked. "You're gonna toss out a cigarette or throw away a bottle of Coke or smear your ass on a toilet seat and I'm gonna be right there collecting it. You can't help yourself. You leave your stink on everything you touch."

"I don't smoke," Frank weighed in, always trying to make peace. "But there's no need to follow me around. I'm happy to give a spit or a swab, too."

Gordon said, "Sure, why not? Count me in."

Paul asked, "Can we choose what type of donation we give?"

Sara watched Jon drop his face into his hands. He let out a sharp cry as he pushed away from the table. He ran across the room, almost barreling into Kevin. The door banged shut behind him. The sound echoed in the silence. Sara didn't know what to do, whether to go after him or stay.

"My precious boy," Bitty whispered in the silence.

Dave looked down at his mother. Bitty was still stretched across the table, reaching for Jon's empty chair. She slowly sat back. Clasped together her hands. Dave's gaze lifted to the door Jon had just escaped through. There was something unguarded in his expression. His lower lip started to tremble. Tears welled into his eyes.

Then just as suddenly, they were gone.

Dave's demeanor changed so quickly that Sara thought she'd witnessed a magic trick. One moment, he looked utterly broken, the next he was enraged.

Dave kicked his overturned chair. The wood splintered against the wall.

He screamed, "You want my DNA, Trashcan?"

"Yeah," Will said. "I do."

"Take it from that baby I put in Mercy's belly. Ain't nobody else ever touched her. That fucking kid is mine."

"There he is," Will said. "Father of the year."

"You're goddam right I am."

"You're so full of shit," Will said. "Mercy was the only real parent Jon ever had. She kept him safe. She provided for him. She put a roof over his head and food in his mouth and love in his heart and you took that from him."

"*We* gave Jon those things!" Dave yelled. "Me and Mercy. It was always me and her."

"Ever since you were eleven, right?"

"Fuck you." He took a menacing step toward Will. "You got no idea what we had. Mercy loved me since she was a baby."

"Like a good little sister?"

"You motherfucker," Dave muttered. "You know exactly what we had. I was the one she loved. I was the one she cared about. I was the only man who ever fucked her."

"You fucked her all right."

"Say it again," Dave said. "Say that one more time to my face, you stupid bitch. You want me to write it down for you? You want me to spell it out, Trashcan? Mercy loved *me*. All she ever cared about was *me*."

"Then why didn't she say anything about you?" Will asked. "Mercy was still alive when I got to her, Dave. She talked to me. She didn't even mention your name."

"Bullshit."

"I asked her to tell me who stabbed her. I begged her. You know what she said?"

"She didn't say it was me."

"No, she didn't," Will said. "She knew she was going to die, and all she cared about was Jon."

"*Our* Jon." He slammed his fist to his chest. "*Our* son. *Our* boy."

"She wanted Jon to get away from you," Will said. "That's the first thing she told me. 'Jon can't stay. Get him away from here.' Get him away from *you*, Dave."

"That ain't true."

"They argued at dinner," Will said. "Jon was angry at Mercy for blocking the sale. He said he wanted to live with his grandmother in a house with you. Who put that in his head, Dave? Was it the same asshole who told him to call me Trashcan?"

Dave started shaking his head. "You're full of shit."

"Mercy wanted me to tell Jon that she forgave him," Will said. "She didn't want him carrying around any guilt from the fight. Those were literally the last words out of her mouth. Not about you, Dave. Never about you. Mercy could barely speak. She was bleeding out. The knife was still inside of her chest. I could hear the breath wheezing through the holes in her lungs. And with her last ounce of strength, her literal last breaths, she looked me right in the eye and said it three times in a row. *Three times.* Forgive him. Forgive him. Forgive—"

Will's voice caught. He stared at Dave with a look of horror on his face.

"What?" Dave said. "What did she say?"

Sara didn't understand what was happening. She watched Will's chest rise and fall as he took in a deep breath and slowly let it go. His gaze was still locked with Dave's. Something passed between them. Maybe their shared history. They were two fatherless boys. Jon had been raised a fatherless son. And now his mother was gone. They both knew better than most what it meant to be truly alone.

Will told Dave, "Mercy's last words were *Tell Jon that I forgive him.*"

Dave said nothing. He stared up at Will, his head back, his mouth closed. He gave a slight nod, no more than a dip of his chin. Then the magic trick happened again, but this time in reverse. Dave deflated like a balloon. His shoulders rolled in. His fists relaxed. His hands dropped to his sides. The only thing that didn't change was the mournful expression on his face.

He asked, "Mercy said that?"

"Yes."

"That's exactly what she said?"

"Yes."

"Okay." Dave nodded once, like his mind had been made up. "Okay, it was me. I killed her."

Bitty gasped. "Davey, no."

Dave picked up a paper napkin from the table. He dried his eyes. "It was me."

"Davey," Bitty said. "Stop talking. We'll get a lawyer."

"It's all right, Mama. I stabbed Mercy. I'm the one who killed her." Dave waved toward the door. "Go on now. You don't need to hear the details."

Sara couldn't take her eyes off Will. The pain in his eyes was killing her. She had seen him at the lake with Mercy. She knew what her death had taken out of him. He looked down at his injured hand. He'd placed it back over his chest. Sara longed to go to him, but she knew that she couldn't. She could only sit helplessly as the room started to clear. First the guests, then Bitty finally stood up to push Cecil's chair, then they were gone.

Will finally looked at Sara. He shook his head. He told Faith, "Take over."

Sara felt his hand on her shoulder as he walked past. He'd pressed down, telling her to stay. He needed time alone. Sara had to give it to him.

Faith acted quickly. She had her Glock in her hands. Kevin had moved closer. She told Dave, "Show me that knife. Slowly."

Dave started with the butterfly knife in his boot. He laid it on the table. He said, "I knew Mercy was fucking around. I knew she was pregnant. I didn't know about the bootlegging, but I knew that she was making money and she wasn't giving any to me. We got into an argument."

"Where did you argue?"

"In the kitchen." Dave took out his wallet, his phone. "I cleaned out the safe. That's why you didn't find anything."

Faith asked, "What was in there?"

"Money. The books she was cooking so everybody got paid."

Faith said, "What about the knife?"

"What about it?" Dave gave an exaggerated shrug. "Red handle. Piece of metal sticking out of the broken-off part."

"Where did you get it?"

"Mercy kept it in her desk drawer. She used it to open envelopes."

"How did she end up at the bachelor cottages?"

"I chased her down the Rope Trail. I stabbed her and left her for dead. I started the fire to cover my tracks."

"She wasn't found in the cottage."

"I changed my mind. I wanted Jon to have a body to bury. I

dragged her out to the water. Figured that would wash away any evidence. I didn't know she was still alive or I would've drowned her." He shrugged. "Then I hid out at the old camp. Caught some fish, made myself some dinner."

"Did you rape her?"

Dave hesitated, but only slightly. "Yeah."

"What did you do with the knife handle?"

"I sneaked into cottage three after Trashcan rang the bell. Same toilet I fixed before the guests hiked in." Dave shrugged again. "I figured Drew would go down for it. I guess you caught me though."

Sara watched Dave raise his hands, offering his wrists so that Faith could handcuff him.

"Not yet," Faith said. "Tell me about Cecil."

Dave shrugged yet again. "What do you want to know?"

21

Will ran through the woods. He was off the trail again, cutting straight across the Loop. Low-hanging limbs and branches sliced at his face. He held up his arm to block his eyes. He remembered last night, the blind confusion as he'd searched for the source of the screams. The locations hadn't been set in his mind yet. He'd gotten turned around, sent in two different directions. He'd smelled the smoke from the burning cottage. He'd run inside to search for Mercy. He'd rushed to the shore to rescue her. He'd stabbed his own hand trying to save her. And then he'd heard exactly what he'd wanted to hear.

Forgive him . . . forgive him . . .

Will kept his tread light as he climbed the stairs to the front porch. The door was ajar. He inched his way inside. Darkness had come, the moon obscured by clouds that held the promise of another storm. Will could see a figure in the bedroom. Drawers had been rifled. Suitcases were open on the floor.

Dave had figured it out a few minutes before Will. A spark of understanding had thrown the Jackal off his game. He had known Mercy since she was a child. He was her brother. He was her husband. He was her abuser.

He was also cunning and clever and manipulative.

The confession Dave gave Faith would be pristine. It would also be a lie. He had probably picked up enough details over the last twelve hours to answer every single one of Faith's questions. Everyone in the compound had been awakened by Will ringing the bell. Biscuits knew that Mercy had been found at the lake. Delilah had sat with her body near the burned-out cottage. Keisha

417

had seen the broken knife handle. Dave probably knew where it had been kept before it was used as a weapon. The kitchen staff had watched Kevin open the empty safe. It wasn't hard to guess what Mercy would store inside. Dave knew where the Wi-Fi worked, where a call could be made or not.

Forgive him. Forgive him.

At the lake, Will had been on his knees begging Mercy to hold on for Jon. She had coughed blood into Will's face. She had grabbed his shirt, pulled him close, looked him in the eye, and spoken her last words. But her dying wish hadn't been to Jon. It had been to Will.

Forgive him.

You, a police officer, *forgive my son* for murdering me.

Will heard a zipper rake back. Then another. Jon was frantically searching Sara's backpack. He was looking for the vape pen Sara had bribed him into surrendering. Back in the dining hall, Will had just as good as told the kid that the metal could be swabbed for DNA, and that the DNA would link him to Mercy's murderer.

He waited until Jon had found the Ziploc bag in the front pocket.

Will turned on the lights.

Jon's mouth gaped open.

"I-I-I-" Jon stuttered. "I n-needed, uh, I needed to calm my nerves."

"What about your other vape pen?" Will asked. "The one that's in your back pocket?"

Jon reached for it, then stopped. "It's broken."

"Let me see it. Maybe I can fix it for you."

Jon's eyes darted furtively around the room—the windows, the door. He started to turn toward the bathroom because he was sixteen years old and still thought like a kid.

"Don't," Will told him. "Sit down on the bed."

Jon sat on the corner of the mattress, his shoes flat to the carpet in case he got a chance to run. He was gripping the plastic bag like his life depended on it. Which was true, because it did.

Dave wasn't Cecil's accomplice.

Jon was.

Sara had almost caught him right after the murder. Jon was

carrying a backpack, ready to make his way down the mountain. He was also hidden in darkness. Sara had only been guessing when she'd called Jon's name. She'd assumed he was throwing up because he'd been drinking. She had no way of knowing that he'd just murdered his mother.

That the Jackal had made the realization before Will wasn't surprising. That he had tried to lay down his own life for his son was the only good thing the man had ever done.

Will peeled the Ziploc bag from Jon's grip. He placed it on the table and sat down in the chair. He said, "Tell me what happened."

Jon's Adam's apple bobbed.

"Sara told me she was looking right at you when your mother screamed for help," Will said. "Mercy didn't die immediately. She passed out. She woke up. She must've been in agony, disoriented, afraid. That's why she cried for help. That's why she screamed *please.*"

Jon kept his silence, but he started picking at the cuticle on his thumb. Will watched the kid's eyes tracking back and forth as he desperately tried to think his way out of this.

Will asked, "What did you do to your mother?"

Blood welled around Jon's cuticle.

"Sara told me that you were carrying a dark-colored backpack," Will said. "What was in there? Your bloodstained clothes? The knife handle? The money from the safe?"

Jon pressed into the nail, squeezing out more blood.

"After you heard Mercy scream for help, you ran inside the house." Will paused. "What made you go inside, Jon? Was someone waiting for you?"

Jon shook his head, but Will knew Cecil's bedroom was on the ground floor.

"Your hair was wet when I saw you. Who told you to take a shower? Who told you to change your clothes?"

Jon smeared the blood down his thumb, across the back of his hand. He finally broke his silence. "She kept going back to him."

Will let him speak.

"Dave was all she ever cared about," Jon said. "I begged her to leave him. For it just to be us. But she always went back to him. I didn't—I didn't have anybody."

Will listened to his tone as much as his words. Jon sounded helpless. Will knew the particular anguish of being a child at the mercy of an unreliable adult's whims.

"No matter what Dave did," Jon continued. "Beat her, choke her, kick her—she would always take him back. Every time, she always chose him over me."

Will leaned up in the chair. "I know it's hard for you to understand now, but Mercy's relationship with Dave had nothing to do with you. Abuse is complicated. No matter what happened, she loved you with every piece of her heart."

Jon shook his head. "I was an albatross around her neck."

Will knew that Jon hadn't come up with that description on his own. "Who told you that?"

"Everybody, all my life." Jon looked up at him, defiant. "You guys said it yourself. Mercy was screwing guests, screwing Alejandro, getting pregnant again. Go on and talk to people in town. They'll tell you the exact same thing. Mercy was a bad person. She murdered a girl. She was a prostitute. Drinking and drugging. Letting somebody else raise her kid. Letting her ex-husband knock the shit out of her. She was nothing but a stupid whore."

Will said, "It makes it easier to call her those names, doesn't it?"

"Makes what easier?"

"The fact that you stabbed her so many times."

Jon didn't deny it, but he didn't look away, either.

"Your mother loved you," Will said. "I saw the two of you together when we checked in. Mercy practically glowed when you were around. She fought your aunt Delilah for custody. She got sober. She turned her life around. All for you."

"She wanted to win," Jon said. "That's what she really cared about. She wanted to beat Delilah. I was the trophy. Once she had me, she put me on a shelf and didn't think about me again."

"That's not true."

"It is true," he insisted. "Dave broke my arm once. Put me in the hospital. Did you know that?"

Will wished he felt less surprised. "What happened?"

"Mama told me I had to forgive him. She said he felt bad, that he promised he would never touch me again, but it was Bitty who finally protected me," Jon said. "She told Dave if he ever hurt me again, he wouldn't be able to come back up here. And she meant it. So he left me alone. That's what Bitty did for me. She protected me. She still protects me."

Will didn't ask him why his grandmother had never used this same threat to protect her own daughter.

"She saved me," Jon said. "If I didn't have Bitty, I don't know what would've happened to me. Dave probably would've killed me by now."

"Jon—"

"Can't you see what Mama drove me to?" Jon's voice strained on the last words. "I would've just disappeared up here. I would'a been nothing. Bitty's the only woman who ever loved me. Mama didn't care about shit until she saw that she'd lost me."

Will had to weigh his desire for a confession against Jon's mental health. He couldn't crush this kid into pieces. Jon would probably spend the rest of his life in prison, but at some point, he would have to look back at what he had done. He deserved to know his mother's last words.

"Jon," Will said. "Mercy was still alive when I found her. She was able to talk to me."

His reaction was not what Will had been expecting. Jon's mouth gaped open. His face went ashen. His body went still. He'd even stopped breathing.

He looked absolutely terrified.

"What—" Panic robbed Jon of words. "What did—did she—"

Will silently played back the last few seconds of the conversation. Jon had been passive when Will had accused him of murder. What had set him off? What was he afraid of?

"What she saw—" Jon had started panting again, almost hyperventilating. "It wasn't—we didn't—"

Will slowly sat back in the chair.

Can't you see what she drove me to?

"I didn't mean—" Jon gulped. "She had to go away, okay? If she had just left us alone so we could—"

Mama didn't care about shit until she saw that she'd lost me.
"Please—I didn't—please—"
Will's body started to accept the truth before his brain did. His skin felt hot. His ears buzzed with a loud, piercing ring. His mind spun back to the dining hall like a carousel of nightmares. He saw Dave's rattled expression when Jon ran out the door. The slow change in his demeanor. The nod of understanding. The sudden capitulation. It wasn't Jon's departure that had triggered his confession. It was hearing Bitty's soft whisper—
My precious boy.
Faith had joked that Bitty acted like Dave's psycho ex-girlfriend. But it wasn't a joke. Dave had been thirteen when he'd run away from the children's home. Bitty had aged him down to eleven. She had infantilized him, made him feel angry, frustrated, emasculated and confused. Not all sexually abused kids grow up to be abusers, but sexual abusers are constantly on the prowl for new victims.
"Jon." Will could barely get the name out of his mouth. "Mercy called Dave because she saw something, didn't she?"
Jon's hands covered his face. He wasn't crying. He was trying to hide. The shame was punching his soul out of his body.
"Jon," Will said. "What did your mother see?"
Jon wouldn't answer.
"Tell me," Will said.
He started shaking his head.
"Jon," Will repeated. "What did Mercy see?"
"You know what she saw!" Jon screamed. "Don't make me say it!"
Will felt like a thousand razor blades were slicing into his chest. He had been so fucking stupid, still only hearing what he'd wanted to hear.
Mercy hadn't told Will that Jon had to get away from *here*.
She'd told him that Jon had to get away from *her*.

THIRTY-SEVEN MINUTES BEFORE THE MURDER

Mercy stared out the slitted foyer window. The moon was so bright it was like a spotlight shining on the compound. Paul Ponticello was probably bitching with his boyfriend inside cottage five. He had a right to. The famous Mercy Temper had roared out like a lion and now she was overcome with regret. The truth was, she had been stunned by Paul's offer of forgiveness.

Mercy deserved a lot of things for killing Gabbie, but forgiveness was not one of them.

She pressed her fingers into her eyes. Her head was killing her. She was glad Dave hadn't picked up the phone when she'd called to tell him what had happened. God knew he loved a good *go fuck yourself* story, but he would've riled her up even more.

Her body already felt on edge. She was bloated and gross. She was probably about to start her period. Mercy had stopped using the app on her phone to track it. She'd read horror stories online about cops getting your data and cross-referencing credit cards to see the last time you'd bought tampons. All Mercy needed was Fish getting his financial records combed over. She had to talk to Dave about wearing a condom again. This time she would mean it. No amount of his sulking was worth the risk to her brother.

Dave's brother, too, if you wanted to get technical about it.

She closed her eyes again. Every bad thing that had happened

423

today suddenly caught up with her. Plus her thumb was aching like a motherfucker. Another stupid mistake she'd made, dropping that glass when Jon had yelled at her. The stitches had gotten soaked when she was cleaning the kitchen. Her throat felt raw and bruised from Dave choking her. She couldn't take anything stronger than Tylenol.

Worse, what the fuck had she been thinking, talking to that doctor? Sara had been so nice that she'd lulled Mercy into forgetting that the woman's husband was a cop. Will Trent already had a hard-on for Dave. The last thing Mercy needed was a GBI agent sniffing around the property. Thank God a storm was coming up over the ridge. Mercy doubted the honeymooners needed much of an excuse to stay inside their cottage for the rest of the week.

She thought about stupid Chuck waving around that smoking foil outside the equipment shed this morning. He was getting sloppy, distilling too much moonshine too fast to keep up with the quality control. It was time to shut that shit down. Fish had been making noises for months about how he wanted out. And it wasn't just about the bootlegging. He wanted free from this claustrophobic prison that generations of McAlpines had built not out of pride but out of spite.

The shocking truth was, Mercy wanted out, too.

Her threats at the family meeting had been hollow after all. She would never show anyone her childhood diaries that detailed Papa's rage. No one would find out that Papa had taken control of the lodge by attacking his own sister with an ax. Bitty's crimes would roll away with the statute of limitations. Mercy's letters to Jon that called out Dave's abuse would never see the light of day. Fish could rid himself of the bootlegging and live out his solitary life on the water.

Mercy was going to break the cycle. Jon deserved more than being tied to this cursed land. She would vote to sell to the investors. She would take a hundred grand for herself and put away the rest in a trust to benefit Jon. Delilah could be the trustee. Let Dave try to get blood from that stone. Mercy would rent a small apartment in town so Jon could finish school and then she would send him off to a good college. She didn't know how much money it took to live on your own, but she had found work the last time. She would find work again. She had a strong back. A solid work ethic. Life experience. She could do this.

And if she failed, she could always move back in with Dave.

"Who's there?" Papa barked.

Mercy held her breath. Her father had been on the porch when she'd told Paul to go fuck himself. Papa had demanded details, but Mercy had refused. Now, she could hear her father stirring in his bed. He would stagger into the hall soon, dragging his legs like Jacob Marley's chains. Mercy slipped up the front stairs before he could reach her.

The lights were out, but the moon poured through the windows at either end of the hall. She kept to the right side. Mercy had sneaked in and out of the house enough times to know which floorboards would squeak. She looked toward the bathroom at the end of the hall. Jon had left his towel on the floor. She could hear Fish snoring like a freight train behind his closed door. Bitty's door was ajar but Mercy would just as soon stick her face inside a hornet's ass.

Jon's door was closed. Soft light fanned out from underneath.

Mercy felt some of her earlier anxiety return. On the scale of all the fights she'd had with her son, the one at dinner hadn't been the worst, but it had been the most public. She had lost count of the number of times that Jon had screamed at the top of his lungs that he hated her. He usually needed a day or two to cool off. He wasn't like Dave, who could punch you in the face one minute then pout because you were mad at him the next.

Lord knew that Mercy had never deluded herself into thinking she was a good mother. She was a hell of a lot better than Bitty, but that was a pathetically low bar. Mercy was an okay mother. She loved her son. She would lay down her life for him. The Pearly Gates wouldn't be swinging open for her in the afterlife— not after all the people she had hurt, the precious life she had taken—but maybe the pureness of Mercy's love for Jon would land her a nice spot in purgatory.

She should tell Jon about the sale. He couldn't be mad at her for giving him exactly what he wanted. Maybe they could go somewhere together. They could vacation in Alaska or Hawaii or one of the dozens of places he used to talk about visiting back when he was a chatterbox little kid with big dreams.

Money could help some of those dreams come true now.

Mercy stood outside Jon's door. She heard the tinkling sound of a music box. Her eyebrows furrowed. Her son listened to Bruno Mars and Miley Cyrus, not *Twinkle, Twinkle, Little Star*. She gave a light rap on the door. God knew she didn't want to catch Jon with a bottle of lotion again. She waited, listening for his familiar lope across the floor. All she heard was the tinny sound of metal bars pricking against a rotating spool.

Something told her not to knock again. She turned the doorknob. She opened the door.

The car accident that had killed Gabbie had always been a blank in Mercy's mind. She had nodded off in her bedroom. She had woken up in an ambulance. Those were the only two details that Mercy could recall. But sometimes, her body had a memory. A flash of terror burning through her nerves. A cold fear freezing the blood in her veins. A hammer shattering her heart into pieces.

That was how she felt now when she found her mother in bed with her son.

It was a chaste scene. They were both clothed. Jon was lying in Bitty's arms. Her lips were pressed to the top of his head. The music box was playing. His baby blanket was wrapped around his shoulders. Bitty's fingers were curled into his hair, her legs intertwined with his, her hand up the front of his shirt as she stroked his belly with her fingers. It could have passed for normal except for the fact that Jon was nearly almost a grown man and she was his grandmother.

Bitty's expression removed any shred of doubt. The guilt on her face told the entire story. She scrambled to get out of the bed, clutching her robe tight, saying, "Mercy, I can explain."

Mercy's knees buckled as she stumbled to the bathroom. She retched into the toilet. Water and vomit splashed back into her face. She grabbed the bowl with her hands. She retched again.

"Mercy," Bitty whispered. She was blocking the door. She clutched Jon's baby blanket to her chest. "Let's talk about this. It's not what you're thinking."

Mercy didn't need to talk. It was all coming back to her now.

The way her mother had treated Jon, the way she had treated Dave. The cloy looks. The constant touching. The relentless babying and coddling.

"Mama . . ." Jon stood in the hall. His entire body was shaking. He was in his pajamas, the ones Bitty made him wear that had cartoons on the bottoms. "Mama, please . . ."

Mercy swallowed down the vomit in her mouth. "Pack your things."

"Mama, I—"

"Go back into your room. Change your clothes." She physically turned him around and steered him into his room. "Pack your stuff. Take whatever you need because we're never coming back here."

"Mama—"

"No!" She pointed her finger in his face. "Do you hear me, Jonathan? Pack your fucking clothes and meet me at the dining hall in five minutes or I will tear this fucking house down!"

Mercy ran into her room. She grabbed her phone off the charger. She called Dave. That motherfucker. He had known all along what Bitty was.

"Mercy!" Cecil yelled. "What the hell is going on up there?"

Mercy listened through to the fourth ring. She ended the call before Dave's voicemail picked up. She looked around her room. She needed her hiking boots. They were going down the mountain tonight. They were never coming back to this godforsaken place.

"Mercy!" Papa yelled. "I know you can hear me!"

Mercy found her purple backpack on the floor. She started shoving in clothes. She didn't pay attention to what went in, didn't care. She called Dave again.

"Pick up, pick up," she demanded. One ring. Two rings. Three, four. "Fuck!"

Mercy started to go, but then she remembered her notebook. Her letters to Jon. She dropped to her knees in front of her bed. She reached under the mattress. Suddenly, there was no air in her lungs. Jon's childhood flashed through every molecule of her body. Her boy. Her gentle, sensitive young man. She held the notebook to her heart, hugged it like she was hugging her baby. She wanted to go back, to read every word in every letter, to see what she had missed.

Mercy held in a sob. Dave wasn't the only monster here. Mercy had missed the signs. Everything had happened inside this very house, down that very hall, while she was sleeping.

She shoved the notebook into her backpack. The nylon was so tight she could barely get the zipper closed. She stood up.

Bitty was blocking the doorway.

"Mercy!" Papa yelled again.

She grabbed her mother by the arms and gave her a violent shake. "You wicked cunt. If I ever see you near my son again, I will fucking kill you. Do you understand me?"

Mercy shoved her back against the wall. She dialed Dave's number as she walked into Jon's room. He was sitting on the bed. "Get up. Now. Pack your shit. I mean it, Jon. I am your mother, and you will do what I fucking say."

Jon stood up. He looked around the room, dazed.

Mercy ended the call to Dave. She went to Jon's closet. She started throwing out clothes. Shirts. Underwear. Shorts. Hiking boots. She didn't leave until Jon had started to pack. Her mother was still in the hall. Mercy heard a creaking sound from the floorboards. Fish was standing on the other side of his closed door.

"Stay in there!" Mercy warned her brother. She couldn't let him see this. "Go back to bed, Fish. We'll talk about this in the morning."

Mercy waited for him to comply before she headed toward the back stairs. She felt snot and tears running down her face. Papa was waiting for her below. Both of his arms were hugging the banister for support.

She jabbed a finger at him. "I hope the Devil fucks you in hell."

"You little bitch!" He grabbed at her arm, but he only managed to catch the laces on her hiking boots. She threw them in his face as she ran out the door. Mercy jogged down the wheelchair ramp. She dialed Dave's number again. Counted through the rings.

Fuck!

Mercy's knees gave out as she hit the Chow Trail. She fell to the ground, pressed her forehead to the crushed stone. She kept seeing images of Bitty. Not with Jon—the very thought was too agonizing—but with Dave. The way their mother demanded a kiss on her cheek every time she saw him. The way Dave washed Bitty's hair in the sink and let her pick out his clothes. It wasn't the cancer that had started those rituals. Dave would fetch Bitty's morning coffee and rub her feet and listen to her gossip and paint her fingernails and put his head in her lap while she played with his hair. Bitty had started training him the second Papa had brought him through the door. He had been so grateful. So desperate for love.

Mercy sat back on her heels. She stared blankly into the darkness.

What if Dave didn't know about Jon? What if he was just as clueless as Mercy had been? Dave had been molested by his PE teacher. He had never known his mother. He had spent his life surrounded by damaged people. He didn't know what normal looked like. He only knew how to survive.

Mercy called his number again. Waited through the four rings before hanging up. Dave was probably at a bar. Or with a woman. Or sticking a needle in his arm. Or drowning a handful of Xanax with a bottle of rum. Anything to numb himself to the memories. Anything to escape.

Mercy would not let their son end up the same way.

She stood up. She went down the Chow Trail, walked across the viewing platform. She needed to get into the safe. There was only five grand in petty cash, but she was going to take it and hike down with Jon and then she would figure out what to do about all of this when she had a moment to catch her breath.

Mercy felt a minuscule bit of relief when she saw that the lights were already on in the kitchen. Jon had come down the back trail. Mercy tried to get hold of herself as she walked around the building, worked to take the torment off her face when she opened the door.

"Shit." Drew was standing at the rolling bar cart. He held a bottle of liquor in his hand. Uncle Nearest. Mercy longed for the smooth taste burning down her throat.

She dropped her backpack by the door. She didn't have time

for this. "You caught me. It's fake. The big still is in the equipment shed, the little one is in the boathouse. Tell Papa. Tell the cops. I don't care."

Drew put the bottle back on the cart. "We're not going to tell anybody."

"Really?" she asked. "I saw you pull Bitty aside after dinner. You told her you had some business you wanted to talk about. I thought you were gonna complain about the fucking water spots on the glasses. What is it, you and Keisha want a piece?"

"Mercy." Drew sounded disappointed. "We love it up here. We just want you to stop. It's dangerous. You could end up killing somebody."

"If it was that easy, I would pour every bottle we have down my mother's fucking throat."

Drew clearly didn't know what to do. He was the dog that caught the car.

"Just go." Mercy propped open the door for him.

Drew shook his head as he walked past. She followed him around to the viewing platform to see if Jon was there. She heard rustling behind the kitchen. Her heart nearly leapt. Jon was coming down Fishtopher Trail.

Except it wasn't Jon she found standing beside the outside freezer.

"Chuck." Mercy spit out his name. "What the hell do you want?"

"I was worried." Chuck put on that stupid bashful look that made her stomach turn. "I was asleep, and I heard Cecil yelling, and then I saw you running across the yard."

"Was he yelling for you?" Mercy asked. "No? He wasn't? Then go on back up the trail and mind your own goddam business."

"Jesus, I was trying to be a gentleman. Why are you always such a bitch?"

"You fucking know why, you pervert."

"Whoa." Chuck patted the air like she was a rabid animal. "Calm down, mi-lady. There's no need to get nasty."

"Why don't I take mi'nasty ass to cottage ten? That guy with the redhead is a cop. You want me to get him for you, Chuck? You want me to tell him about your little side-business down in Atlanta?"

His hands dropped. "You're a fucking cunt."

"Well congratulations. You finally got close to one." Mercy went into the kitchen and slammed the door. She looked at the clock. She had no idea what time she'd left the house. She'd told Jon to be down here in five minutes, but it felt more like an hour.

She jogged into the dining hall to look for him, but it was empty. Then her heart jumped into her throat. The viewing platform. The ravine was a deathtrap. What if Jon couldn't face her? What if he'd decided to take his life?

Mercy ran outside. She grabbed the railing. Looked over the side, the sheer, fifty-foot drop that cut straight down the mountain like the blade of an ax.

Clouds were rolling in over the moonlight. Shadows danced across the ravine. She listened for anything—whimpers, cries, the sound of labored breathing. She knew what it felt like when you had reached your end, when the pain was too much, when your body was too tired, when all you wanted was the welcome embrace of darkness.

She heard laughter.

Mercy pulled back from the railing. Two women were on Old Bachelor Trail. She recognized Delilah's long white hair. Mercy hadn't even noticed that the old bitch wasn't inside the house. She craned her neck to see who Delilah was holding hands with.

It was Sydney, the investor who wouldn't shut up about horses.

"Jesus Christ," Mercy whispered. Every fucking ghost was coming up on her tonight.

Mercy ran back into the building. Through the empty dining hall, into the kitchen. She looked back to the bathroom, clear to her office. Fish had cut a safe into the wall when they'd started bootlegging. There was a calendar hanging over the door. Mercy jogged to the back, rummaged through the desk drawers for the key. She found one of Fish's old backpacks gathering dust in the corner. Every item she pulled from the safe brought her and Jon closer to freedom.

Five thousand dollars, all in twenties. The bootlegging ledger. Payroll stubs. Two sets of books from the lodge. The diary Mercy had kept when she was twelve years old. She dropped them all into Fish's brown backpack. She tugged the zipper closed. She tried to think through a plan—*where could she hide Jon, how could she help him, how long before the money ran out, where could she find a job, what did a child psychiatrist cost, who could she turn to, was it the cops or a social worker, would she be able to find someone Jon trusted enough to talk with, how in God's name could she even find the words for what she had seen . . .*

The questions were too much for her brain to handle. Mercy had to think about one hour at a time. The hike was dangerous at night. She zipped a book of matches inside the front pocket of the backpack. Grabbed the red-handled knife out of the desk drawer. She used it to open envelopes, but the blade was still sharp. She would need it in case they ran into any animals on the trail. Mercy shoved the knife into her back pocket. The blade sliced through the seam, creating a kind of sheath. She knew how to pack for a hike. Safety, water, and food. She returned to the kitchen. Tossed the backpack beside her own against the closed door. She filled up two water bottles. There was trail mix in the fridge. She would need extra for Jon.

Mercy looked up.

What was she doing?

The kitchen was still empty. She walked back into the dining hall. Still empty. Her heart sank as she yet again returned to the kitchen. The panic had died down. Now the reality hit her like a freight train.

Jon wasn't coming.

Bitty had talked him out of leaving. Mercy should've never left him alone, but she had been shocked and disgusted and scared, and as usual, she had let her emotions take over instead of looking at the cold hard facts. She had failed her son just like she had failed him a thousand times before. Mercy would have to go back to the house and drag Jon away from Bitty's clutches. There was no way she could do this next part alone.

Mercy had to place her phone on the counter because her hands were too sweaty to hold it. She called Dave one last time. Her desperation amped up with every ring. He wasn't answering again. She had to leave him a message, to get out this sickness that was rotting her soul. Mercy thought about what she would say, how she would tell him what she had seen, but when the fourth ring passed and his greeting played, the words flowed out of her mouth in a panic—

"Dave!" she screamed. "Dave! Oh my God, where are you? Please, please call me back. I can't believe—oh, God, I can't— Please call me. Please. I need you. I know you've never been there for me before, but I really need you now. I need your help, baby. Please c-call—"

She looked up. Her mother was standing in the kitchen. Bitty was holding Jon's hand. Mercy felt like a fist was punching up her throat. Jon's eyes were on the floor. He couldn't look at his own mother. Bitty had broken him just like she'd broken everyone else.

Mercy struggled to find her voice. "What are you doing here?"

Bitty reached toward the phone.

"Don't!" Mercy warned. "Dave will be here soon on. I told him what happened. He's on his way."

Bitty had already tapped the screen to end the call before she'd finished. "No, he's not."

"He told me that—"

"He didn't tell you anything," Bitty said. "Dave has been sleeping at the bunkhouses. His phone doesn't work over there."

Mercy put her hand to her mouth. She looked at Jon, but he wouldn't look back at her. Her fingers started to tremble. She couldn't catch her breath. She was scared. Why was she so scared?

"J-Jon . . ." She stuttered out his name. "Baby, look at me. It's okay. I'm going to get you out of here."

Bitty stood in front of Jon, but Mercy could still see his down-turned face. Tears were pooling into the collar of his T-shirt.

"Baby," Mercy tried. "Come over here, okay? Just come over here to me."

"He doesn't want to talk to you," Bitty said. "I don't know what you think you saw, but you're acting hysterical."

"I know what I fucking saw!"

"Watch your language," Bitty snapped. "We need to talk about this like adults. Come back to the house."

"I'll never step foot inside that fucking house again," Mercy hissed. "You fucking monster. You're the Devil standing right in front of me."

"Stop this at once," Bitty commanded. "Why do you make everything so difficult?"

"I saw—"

"What did you see?"

Mercy's brain flashed up the image: legs intertwined, a hand up Jon's shirt, lips pressed to the top of his head. "I know exactly what I saw, *Mother*."

Jon flinched at her sharp tone. He still couldn't look up at her. Mercy's heart splintered. She knew what it felt like to bow your head in shame. She had done it for so long that she barely knew how to look up anymore.

"Jon," she said. "It's not your fault, baby. You didn't do anything wrong. We're gonna get you some help, okay? It's all gonna work out."

"Get help from who?" Bitty asked. "Who's going to believe you?"

Mercy heard the question echo straight through every year of her life. When Papa flayed the skin off her back with a rope. When Bitty stabbed her so hard with a wooden spoon that blood had run down her arms. When Dave had pressed the glowing end of a cigarette into her breast until the smell of her own burning flesh had made her vomit.

There was a reason Mercy had never told anyone.

Who's going to believe you?

"That's what I thought." Bitty's face had a look of complete triumph. She reached down, lacing her fingers through Jon's.

He finally looked up. His eyes were red. His lips were trembling.

Mercy watched in horror as he lifted Bitty's hand to his mouth and gave it a gentle kiss.

She screamed like an animal.

All the pain of her life came out in a wordless howl. How had she let this happen? How had she lost her son? She couldn't let him stay. She couldn't let Bitty devour him.

The knife was in Mercy's hand before she knew what she was doing. She jerked Bitty away from Jon, shoved her against the counter, held the point of the blade to her eye. "You stupid bitch. Did you forget what I told you this morning? I'm gonna put your bony ass in federal prison. Not for fucking my boy, but for cooking the books."

There was nothing sweeter in Mercy's entire life than watching the arrogance drain from Bitty's face.

"I found the ledgers in the back of the cabinet. Does Papa know about your slush fund?" Mercy could tell from her shocked expression that her father had no idea. "It's not just him you should be worried about. You've been cheating on your taxes for years. You think you can get away with that? The government goes after fucking presidents. They're not gonna stop at some dried-up old pedophile. Especially when I put the proof in their hands."

"You—" Bitty's throat gulped. "You wouldn't—"

"I fucking would."

Mercy was finished talking. She jammed the knife back into her pocket, turned to grab the two backpacks, swung both over her shoulder. She turned back to tell Jon to move, but he was leaning down so that Bitty could whisper in his ear.

Bile flooded back into Mercy's mouth. The time for threats was over. She shoved her mother hard enough to send her sprawling across the floor. Then she clamped her hand around Jon's wrist and jerked him out the door.

Jon didn't try to pull away. He didn't work to slow her down. He let her use his wrist like a rudder to steer him away. Mercy listened to his quick breaths, the heavy fall of his feet. She didn't have a plan except to go somewhere Bitty couldn't follow.

She easily found the boulder that marked the Rope Trail. She made Jon go ahead so she could keep her eyes on him. They both made quick work of the ropes, grappling from one to the next, sliding most of the way around the ravine. Finally, they were back on solid ground. Mercy grabbed his wrist again to lead the way. She picked up the pace, started jogging. Jon jogged behind her. She was going to do this. She was actually going to do this.

"Mom . . ." Jon whispered.

"Not now."

They trampled through the forest. Limbs slapped at her body. She didn't care. She wasn't going to stop. She kept running, using the bright light of the moon to keep her bearings. They would shelter at the bachelor cottages tonight. Dave would show up in the morning for work. Or maybe she would take Jon to Dave right now. They could follow the shore, pick up a canoe, and paddle over. If Dave was sleeping at the bunkhouses, he would have fishing rods, fuel, blankets, food, shelter. Dave knew how to survive. He could talk to Jon, keep him safe. Mercy could hike into town and find a lawyer. She wasn't going to give up the lodge. She sure as hell wasn't going to be the one leaving on Sunday. Mercy would give her parents until noon tomorrow to pack up their shit and go. Fish could stay or he could leave, but either way, Mercy and Jon were going to be the last McAlpines standing.

"Mom," Jon tried again. "What are you going to do?"

Mercy didn't answer. She could see the moonlight hitting the lake at the bottom of the trail. The last section was terraced with railroad ties. They were only a few yards away from the bachelor cottages.

"Mom," Jon said. It was like he had woken up from a trance. He was finally resisting, trying to break away from her grasp. "Mom, please."

Mercy tightened her grip, pulling him so hard that she felt the muscles in her back straining. By the time they reached the clearing, she was panting from the effort of dragging him behind her.

She dropped both backpacks on the ground. There were cigarette butts everywhere. Dave hadn't prepared for the storm. Everything was laid out exactly where he had left it. Sawhorses and tools, a can of gasoline with the cap off, a generator turned onto its side. The shitty state of the worksite was a sharp reminder of who Dave really was. He didn't take care of things, let alone other people. He couldn't even bother to pick up after himself. Mercy couldn't trust him with this.

Yet again, she was on her own.

"Mom," Jon said. "Please, just drop this, okay? Let me go back."

Mercy looked at him. He had stopped crying, but she could hear the whistle of air through his stuffy nose.

"I n-need to go back. She told me I could go back."

"No, baby." Mercy pressed her hand to his chest. His heart was pounding so hard that she could feel it through his ribs. She couldn't stop the sob that came out of her mouth. The enormity of what had just happened caught up with her all at once. The terrible things that her mother had done to her son. The rot that had taken hold of her family.

She said, "Baby, look at me. You're never going back. That's settled."

"I don't—"

She grabbed his face in her hands. "Jon, listen to me. We're going to get help, okay?"

"No." He peeled her hands away from his face. He took a step back, then another. "Bitty doesn't have anybody but me. She needs me."

"I need you!" Mercy's voice was hoarse. "You're my son. I need you to be my son."

Jon's head started to shake. "How many times did I ask you to leave him? How many times did we pack our bags, and the next day, you were fucking him again?"

Mercy couldn't argue with the truth. "You're right. I've failed you, but I'm making up for it now."

"I don't need you to do anything," Jon said. "Bitty's the one who protected me. She's the one who kept me safe."

"Safe from what? She's the one who's hurting you."

"You know what Dave did to me," he said. "I was only five years old. He broke my arm, and you told me I had to forgive him."

"What?" Her whole body was shaking. That wasn't what happened. "You fell out of a tree. I was standing right there. Dave tried to catch you."

"She warned me you would say that," Jon said. "Bitty protected me from him. You told me I had to forgive him, to let him do whatever he wanted so he didn't get mad again."

Mercy felt her hands go to her mouth. Bitty had filled him with disgusting lies.

"Jon—" She said the first thing that came to mind. "We're going to cottage ten."

"What?"

"The couple in cottage ten." She could finally see a way out of this. The solution was there all along. "Will Trent is with the Georgia Bureau of Investigation. He won't let Biscuits sweep this under the rug. His wife is a doctor. She can look out for you while I tell him what happened."

"You mean Trashcan?" His voice raked up in alarm. "You can't—"

"I can and I will." Mercy had never felt more certain of anything in her life. Sara had told her that she trusted Will, that he was a good man. He would fix this. He would save them both. "That's what we're doing. Come on."

Mercy reached for the backpacks.

"Go fuck yourself."

The coldness in his voice stopped Mercy in her tracks. She looked up at him. Jon's face was so hard it could've been cut from a single piece of marble.

"All you care about is winning," he said. "You only want me now because you know you can't have me."

Mercy realized that she needed to be very careful. She'd seen Jon angry before, but never like this. His eyes were almost black with rage. "Is that what Bitty told you?"

"It's what I've fucking seen!" Spit flew out of his mouth. "Look at how pathetic you are. You're not trying to protect me. You're running to that cop because you can't accept that I found some-body who makes *me* happy. Who cares about *me*. Who loves only *me*."

He sounded so much like Dave that it nearly took her breath away. That bottomless pit, that never-ending quicksand. Her own child had been running alongside her all this time and Mercy hadn't bothered to notice.

"I'm sorry," she said. "I should've seen. I should've known."

"Fuck your sorry. I don't need it. Fuck!" He threw his hands in the air. "This is exactly what she warned me about. What the fuck do I have to do to stop you?"

"Baby—" She reached for him again, but he slapped her hands away.

"Don't fucking touch me," he warned. "She's the only woman who gets to touch me."

Mercy held up her hands in surrender. She had never been scared of Jon, but she was scared of him now. "Take a breath, okay? Just calm down."

"It's you or her," he said. "That's what she told me. I have to decide. You or her."

"Baby, she doesn't love you. She's manipulating you."

"No." He started shaking his head. "Shut up. I need to think."

"She's a predator," Mercy said. "This is what she does to boys. She gets in their heads and she fucks them up so bad—"

"Shut up."

"She's a monster," Mercy said. "Why do you think your daddy's so fucked up? It wasn't just what happened to him in Atlanta."

"Shut up."

"Listen to me," Mercy begged. "You're not special to her. What she's doing to you is the exact same thing that she did to Dave."

He was on her before she knew what was happening. His hands snaked out, wrapping around her neck. "Shut your fucking mouth."

Mercy gasped for air. She grabbed his wrists, tried to pull away his hands. He was too strong. She dug her fingernails into Jon's chest, tried to kick out with her feet. She felt her eyelids start to flutter. He was so much stronger than Dave. He was squeezing too hard.

"You pathetic bitch." Jon's voice was deadly quiet. He had learned from his daddy that you didn't make too much noise. "I'm not the one who's leaving here tonight. You are."

Mercy felt light-headed. Her vision blurred. He was going to kill her. She reached back to her pocket, wrapped her fingers around the red plastic handle of the knife.

Time slowed down to a crawl. Mercy silently took herself through the motions. Pull out the knife. Slice him on the forearm. Were there arteries there? Muscle? She couldn't damage him—he was already hurt almost beyond repair. She should show him the knife. The threat would be enough. That would stop him.

It didn't.

Jon snatched the knife away from her. He swung the blade over his head, ready to drive it down into her chest. Mercy ducked down, crawling on her knees as she scrambled across the ground. She felt the air move as the blade slashed within inches of her head. Mercy knew a second blow was coming. She grabbed her backpack, held it up like a shield. The blade skipped across the thick, fireproof material. She didn't give Jon time to recover. She swung the backpack at his head, knocking him backward.

Instinct took over. She clutched the backpack to her chest and started running. Past the first cottage, the second one. Jon was fast on her heels, closing the gap. She sprinted up the stairs to the last cottage. Slammed the door in his face. Fumbled to send the bolt home on the lock. Heard the loud punch of his fist against the solid wood.

Mercy gasped for air, her chest heaving as she listened to him pacing across the porch. Her heart felt like it was inside of her throat. Mercy put her back to the door, closed her eyes, listened for her son's loping gait. There was nothing but silence. She could feel a breeze drying the sweat on her face. All the windows were boarded up but one. The moon put a blue glow on the grain in the rough-hewn walls, the floor, her shoes, her hands.

Mercy looked up.

Dave had not been lying about the dry rot in cottage three. The back wall of the bedroom had been completely stripped away. Jon had slipped in through the studs. He stood with the knife in his hand.

Mercy blindly reached behind her. Slid back the bolt. Twisted the handle. Threw open the door. She turned, and it felt like a sledgehammer hit between the shoulders as Jon drove the blade in to the hilt.

The blow knocked the wind out of her. She stared at the lake, mouth open in horror.

Then Jon pulled out the knife and slammed it in again. And again. And again.

Mercy careened off the porch, falling down the stairs, landing on her side.

The knife cut through her arm. Her breast. Her leg. Jon straddled her, driving the blade into her chest, her belly. Mercy tried to buck him off, to twist away, but nothing would stop him. Jon kept swinging back and forth, stabbing the knife into her back, taking it out, plunging it in again. She felt the crack of bones, the explosion of organs, her body filling with piss and shit and bile until Jon wasn't just stabbing her, he was beating her with his fists because the blade had broken off inside her chest.

Suddenly, Jon stopped.

Mercy could hear him panting like he'd finished a marathon. He was spent from the attack. He could barely stand. He stumbled away from her. Mercy tried to take in a breath. Her face was in the dirt. She inched onto her side. Every part of her body was alive with pain. She had fallen across the stairs. Her feet were still on the porch. Her head rested on the ground.

Jon was back.

She heard liquid sloshing, but it wasn't the waves hitting the shore. Jon walked up the stairs with the gasoline can. She heard him spreading the fuel around the inside of the cottage. He was going to burn the evidence. He was going to burn Mercy. He dropped the empty can beside her feet.

He walked back down the stairs. Mercy didn't look up. She watched blood drip from his fingers. Stared at the shoes that Bitty had bought him in town. She could feel Jon looking down at her. Not with sadness or with pity, but with a kind of detachment she had seen in her brother, her father, her husband, her mother, herself. Her son was a McAlpine through and through.

No more so than when he struck a match and tossed it into the cottage.

The *whoosh* brought a blast of hot air across her skin. Mercy watched Jon's blood-soaked shoes shuffle through the dirt as he walked away. He was going back to the house. Back to Bitty. Mercy wheezed in a slow breath. Her eyelids started to flutter. She felt blood gurgling inside her throat. She was overcome with the sensation of floating. Her soul was leaving her body. There was none of the expected calmness, the sense of letting go. There was only a cold darkness that worked its way from the edges, the way the lake froze in the winter.

Then there was Gabbie.

They were both hurtling through the air, but they weren't angels in heaven. They were being thrown from the car at Devil's Bend. Mercy turned to look at Gabbie's face, but only a bloody pulp remained. An eye dangling from a socket. An eruption through her skin of shattered teeth and bone. Then an intense, searing heat that threatened to engulf her.

"Help!" Mercy screamed. "Please!"

Her eyes opened. She coughed. Droplets of blood sprayed across the ground. Mercy was still on her side, still draped across the porch stairs. Smoke fouled the air. The heat from the fire was so intense that she could feel it drying the blood on her skin. Mercy forced her head to turn, to look back at what was coming. The flames were working themselves across the porch. Soon, they would chew their way to the stairs and find her body.

Mercy braced herself for more pain as she rolled onto her belly. She pulled herself off the stairs with her elbows. The broken knife inside her chest scraped into the dirt like a kickstand. She propelled herself forward, the threat of the fire spurring her to keep moving. Her feet dragged uselessly behind her. Her pants had come undone. Dirt caked into the material, pulling her jeans down around her ankles. The exertion quickly caught up with her. Mercy's vision started to swim again. She willed herself not to pass out. Delilah had said that McAlpines were hard to kill. Mercy wasn't going to live to see the sun rise over the mountains, but she could make it to the goddam lake.

As usual, even these last moments were a struggle. She kept passing out, waking up, pushing herself forward, passing out again. Her arms were shaking by the time she felt water on her face. She used the last of her strength to roll onto her back. She wanted to die looking up at the full moon. It was such a perfect circle, like a hole in the blackness. She listened to her heartbeat as it slowly pumped blood from her body. She heard the soft cupping of water around her ears.

Mercy knew that she was close to death, that there was nothing that was going to stop it. She didn't see her life flash before her eyes.

She saw Jon's life.

Playing in Delilah's yard with his little wooden toys. Cowering in the back of the room when Mercy showed up for her first court-appointed visitation. Being dragged from Delilah's arms by Mercy in front of the courthouse. Sitting in Mercy's lap as Fish drove them up the mountain. Hiding with Mercy when Dave was on one of his tears. Bringing Mercy books on Alaska and Montana and Hawaii so that they could get away. Watching her pack their bags again and again. Watching her unpack them because Dave had written her a poem or sent her flowers. Being handed off to Bitty while Mercy sneaked away to one of the cottages with Dave. Being abandoned with Bitty because Mercy had to go to the hospital for another broken bone, a cut that wouldn't heal, a suture that wouldn't hold.

Being constantly pushed into the arms of Mercy's mother, his grandmother, his rapist.

"Mercy . . ."

She heard her name like a whisper inside of her skull. She felt her head being turned, saw the world as if she was looking through the wrong end of a telescope. A face came into view. The man from cottage ten. The cop who was married to the redhead.

"Mercy McAlpine," he said, his voice faded like a siren passing down the street. He kept shaking her, forcing her not to give in. "I need you to look at me right now."

"J-Jon . . ." Mercy coughed out the name. She had to do this. It wasn't too late. "Tell him . . . tell him he h-has to . . . he has to g-get away from h-her . . ."

Will's face swam in and out of her vision. She saw him there one moment, then gone the next.

Then he screamed, "Sara! Get Jon! Hurry!"

"N-no . . ." Mercy felt a trembling in her bones. The pain was unbearable, but she couldn't give up now. She had one last time to get it right. "J-Jon can't . . . he c-can't . . . stay . . . Get away from . . . from . . ."

Will spoke, but she couldn't make sense of his words. What she knew was that she couldn't leave things with Jon like this. She had to hold on.

"L-love . . . love him . . . s-so much . . ."

Mercy could feel her heart slowing. Her breaths were shallow. She fought against the ease of slipping away. She needed Jon to know that he was loved. That this wasn't his fault. That he didn't have to carry this burden. That he could get out of the quicksand.

"I'm s-sorry . . ." She should've said this to Jon. Should've told him to his face. Now all she could do was ask this man to tell him her last words. "F-forgive . . . him . . . Forgive him . . ."

Will shook Mercy so hard that she felt her soul snap back into her body. He was leaning over her, his face close to hers. This cop. This detective. This one good man. She grabbed his shirt, pulling him even closer, staring so deep into his eyes that she could practically see his soul.

She had to suck in a breath before she could push out the words, telling Will, "F-forgive him."

He nodded his head. "Okay—"

That was all that Mercy needed to hear. She let go of his shirt. Her head cradled back in the water. She looked at the beautiful, perfect moon. She felt the waves pulling at her body. Washing away her sins. Washing away her life. The calmness finally came, and with it, a powerful sense of peace.

For the first time in her life, Mercy felt safe.

ONE MONTH AFTER THE MURDER

Will sat beside Amanda on the couch inside her office. Her laptop was open on the coffee table. They were watching the taped interview of Jon's confession. He was wearing a tan jumpsuit. His wrists were not handcuffed because he'd been committed to a juvenile psychiatric facility, not an adult prison. Delilah had hired a top criminal defense attorney out of Atlanta. Jon was going to remain institutionalized, but maybe not for the rest of his life.

On the video, Jon said, "I blacked out. I don't remember what happened next. I just knew she would go back to him. She always went back to him. She always left me."

"Left you with who?" Faith's voice was faint. She was off-screen. "Who did she leave you with?"

Jon shook his head. He still would not implicate his grandmother, even though she was dead. Bitty had swallowed a bottle of morphine before they could arrest her. The autopsy had revealed that she had terminal cancer. The woman hadn't just cheated justice. She had cheated a prolonged and painful death.

Faith said, "Let's go back to that night. After you left the note that you were running away, where did you go?"

"I stayed at the horse paddock, then the next morning, I went to cottage nine cause I knew nobody was staying there."

"What about the knife handle?"

"I knew Dave . . ." Jon let his voice trail off. "I knew Dave fixed the toilet, so I thought that would be evidence against him. Cause you'd already arrested him for killing her. He should go to prison no matter what. I know Mercy said it wasn't true, but he broke my arm. That's child abuse."

"Okay." Faith didn't get sidetracked, though they'd both seen the hospital report on the broken arm. Jon had fallen from a tree. "When Dave was arrested, you'd already run away from home. Who told you what happened?"

Jon started shaking his head. "I had to make a choice."

"Jon—"

"I had to protect myself," he said. "Nobody else looked out for me. Nobody else cared."

"Let's go back to—"

"Who's gonna protect me now?" he asked. "I've got nobody. Nobody."

Will looked away from the screen as Jon started to cry. He thought about the last conversation he'd had with the kid. They were sitting in the bedroom in cottage ten. Will had told Jon that abuse was complicated, but it seemed really fucking straightforward right now.

Don't hurt children.

Amanda said, "All right, you get the gist."

She closed the laptop. She held on to Will's hand for a few seconds. Then she got up from the couch and walked toward her desk.

She said, "Catch me up on the bootleg case."

Will stood up, glad emotion-time was over. "We've got Mercy's ledger that details the pay-outs. The spreadsheets on Chuck's computer list all the clubs he was selling to. We're coordinating with ATF and IRS-CI."

"Good." Amanda sat down behind her desk. She picked up her phone. "And?"

"Christopher's set to plea negligent homicide on poisoning Chuck. He'll get fifteen years as long as he testifies against his father on the murder of Gabriella Ponticello. Plus we've got the second set of books on the lodge to hit Cecil with tax evasion. He says he didn't know anything about it, but the money's sitting in his accounts."

She typed on her phone. "And?"

"Both Paul Ponticello and his private detective provided sworn statements about what Dave told them. It's hearsay, though. We need to find Dave to make it a slam dunk."

"We?" Amanda looked up. "You're not working that part of the case."

"I know, but—"

Amanda cut him off with a sharp look. "Dave disappeared the day after his mother committed suicide. He hasn't tried to contact Jon. His phone has gone dark. He hasn't been back to his trailer. He was not at the campground. The North Georgia Field office put a notice on the wire. I'm sure he'll show up eventually."

Will rubbed his jaw. "He's been through a lot, Amanda. The only family he's ever known just disintegrated."

"His son is still here," she reminded him. "And don't forget about what he did to his wife. I'm not only speaking to the physical and verbal abuse. Dave knew years ago that Mercy wasn't responsible for Gabbie's death. He hid it from her as a means of control."

Will couldn't argue with that part, but there were plenty others. "Amanda—"

"Wilbur," Amanda said. "Dave McAlpine is not going to suddenly become a better man. He will never be the father that Jon needs. There is not a piece of logic, or a sage bit of advice, or a life lesson, or any amount of love, that will turn him around. He lives the way he does because he chooses to. He knows exactly who he is. He embraces it. He won't change because he doesn't want to change."

Will rubbed his jaw again. "A lot of people would've said that about me when I was a kid."

"But you're not a kid anymore. You're an adult." She rested her phone on her desk. "I know better than most what you had to overcome to get here. You have earned your happiness. You have a right to enjoy it. I will not allow you to throw all of it away in some misguided attempt to save everyone. Especially the ones who do not want to be saved. You cannot serve two masters. There's a reason Superman never married Lois."

"They were married in 1996, in *Superman: The Wedding Album.*"

She picked up her phone. She started typing again.

Will waited for her to respond. Then he remembered how good she was at ending conversations.

He stuck his hands in his pockets as he walked down the stairs. There was a lot to unpack about Jon, but Will was more of a mover than an unpacker. He reached for the exit door with his injured hand. The knife wound had Frankensteined. Sara had not been kidding about that infection. One month out, he was still taking pills that were approximately the size of a hollow-point bullet.

The lights were off on his floor. Technically, Will was off the clock, though he noticed Amanda hadn't chastised him for staying late. What she'd told him was wrong, and not just because Will was clearly more Batman than Superman.

Change was possible. Will had spent his eighteenth birthday in a shelter, his nineteenth in jail, and by his twentieth, he was enrolled in college. The grade-school kid who was routinely sent to detention for not reading all of the assignment had graduated with a college degree in criminal justice. The only difference between Will and Dave was that someone had given Will a break.

"Hey," Faith called from her office.

Will stuck his head in. She was using a lint roller to get the cat hair off her pants. Faith had brought the McAlpine cats down to Atlanta to put them in a shelter. Then Emma had seen them and one had gotten out of his carrier and killed a bird and that was the story of why Faith had two cats now, one named Hercule and the other named Agatha.

She said, "Some jackass kid at daycare showed Emma TikTok. She keeps trying to steal my phone."

"It was bound to happen sooner or later."

"I thought I had more time." Faith tossed the lint roller into her purse. "Meanwhile, I've got the FBI knocking down my door because they want to expedite Jeremy's application. Why is everything happening so fast? Even frozen dinners get to sit a minute after you pull them out of the microwave."

Will felt his stomach growl. "I watched the interview with Jon. You did a good job."

"Well." Faith lifted her purse onto her shoulder. "I finished reading Mercy's letters to Jon. They broke my fucking heart. I could've written them to Jeremy. Or Emma. It's just Mercy trying to be a good mom. I hope Jon gets to a place one day where he can read them."

"He'll get there," Will said, mostly because he wanted it to be true. "What about Mercy's diary?"

"Exactly what you'd expect from a twelve-year-old girl who was in love with her adoptive brother and terrified of her abusive father."

"Anything from Christopher?"

"He's still saying he had no idea what was going on. Bitty never touched him that way. I guess he wasn't her type." Faith shrugged, but not to dismiss it. Because it was too much. "Mercy saw it happening with Dave, you know? Some of it's in her diary. A lot of it's in the letters. Bitty would stroke Dave's hair or Mercy would walk into a room and Dave would have his head in Bitty's lap. Or he'd be rubbing her feet or massaging her shoulders. It felt weird—I mean, Mercy calls that out herself, that it's weird—but she never really put it together."

"Abusers don't just groom their victims. They gaslight everybody around the victim so that if you say anything, you're the one who's sick."

"You wanna know sick, you should read some of the texts between Bitty and Jon."

"I did," Will said. He'd felt so nauseated that he'd skipped lunch.

"She hated babies," Faith said. "Do you remember Delilah telling you that Bitty wouldn't even pick up her own kids? She let them stew in their dirty diapers. And then Dave comes along and he's exactly her type. Or she ages him down to make him her type. Do you think Dave knew that she was abusing Jon all along?"

"I think he put it together in the dining hall, and he did what he could to save his son."

"I'm going to let myself believe that, because the alternative is that he confessed to save Bitty."

Will didn't want to entertain that scenario. He had other things to keep him up at night. "I'm sorry I missed Paul's tattoo."

"Shut up," Faith said. "I'm the dummy who kept saying Bitty was Dave's psycho ex like she wasn't actually Dave's psycho ex."

Will knew he had to let this go. "Try not to fuck up like that again."

"I'll try." Faith started grinning. "How did I get an Agatha Christie locked-room mystery with a VC Andrews twist?"

He winced.

"Too soon?"

Will stole a play from Amanda and walked back down the hall toward his office. He turned into the doorway and got a familiar lightness in his chest when he found Sara sitting on the couch. Her shoe was off. She was rubbing her pinky toe.

He loved the way her face glowed when she looked up at him.

She said, "Hey."

"Hey."

"I stubbed my toe on the chair." She slipped her shoe back on. "Did you watch the interview?"

"Yep." Will sat down beside her. "How did lunch go with Delilah?"

"I think it's good for her to have someone to talk to," Sara said. "She's doing everything she can for Jon. It's hard right now because he doesn't want to accept help. Every time she visits, he stares at the floor for an hour, then she leaves and comes back the next day and he stares at the floor again."

"He knows she's there," Will said. "Do you think it would help if Dave visited Jon?"

"I would leave that to the experts. Jon has a lot of damage to process. Dave has his own damage. He needs to help himself before he can help his son."

"Amanda told me Dave doesn't want to be fixed because being broken is all he has."

"She's probably right, but I wouldn't give up on Jon. Delilah is in it for the long haul. She really loves him. I think that makes a big difference in these situations. Hope is contagious."

"Is that your medical opinion?"

"My medical opinion is that my husband and I should leave

work so we can eat lots of pizza, binge some *Buffy*, and make sure my toe isn't the only thing that gets banged tonight."

Will laughed. "I need to send this report, then I'll see you at home."

Sara gave him a very nice kiss before leaving.

Will sat down at his desk. He tapped his keyboard to wake the screen. He was about to slip in his earbuds when the phone on his desk rang.

He punched the speakerphone button. "Will Trent."

"Trent," a man said. "This is Sheriff Sonny Richter from Charlton County."

Will had never gotten a call from Georgia's southernmost county before. "Yes, sir. How can I help you?"

"We stopped a fella on a broken tail light. Found a brick of heroin taped under his seat. There's a notice on him from the North Georgia Field office, but he said to call you. Claims he has some information to trade for a lighter sentence."

Will knew what was coming before the man even finished.

"His name is Dave McAlpine," the sheriff said. "You want to come down here or should I call the field office?"

Will twisted the wedding ring around his finger. The slim piece of metal encompassed so many things. He still didn't know what to do with the feeling of lightness he got inside his chest every time he was around Sara. He had never experienced this type of prolonged happiness before. They were one month out from the wedding, and the euphoria he had felt during the ceremony still hadn't subsided. If anything, the intensity was heightened with every passing day. Sara would smile at him, or laugh at one of his stupid jokes, and it was like his heart turned into a butterfly.

Amanda was wrong again.

There actually was a certain amount of love that could turn a man around.

"Call the field office," Will told the sheriff. "I can't help him."

ACKNOWLEDGMENTS

First thanks always goes to Kate Elton and Victoria Sanders, who've been there pretty much from the get-go. I would also like to thank my confrere, Bernadette Baker-Baughman, as well as Diane Dickensheid and the team at VSA. Thanks to Hilary Zaitz Michael and the folks at WME. And speaking of all that, thanks very much to Liz Heldens for following up on that dinner in Atlanta and making the magic happen, and also for bringing Dan Thomsen into my life. Y'all are the best.

At William Morrow, special thanks to Emily Krump, Liate Stehlik, Heidi Richter-Ginger, Jessica Cozzi, Kelly Dasta, Jen Hart, Kaitlin Harri, Chantal Restivo-Alessi, and Julianna Wojcik. At HarperCollins worldwide, thank you so much Jan-Joris Keijzer, Miranda Mettes, Kathryn Cheshire and last but not least, the amazing and indefatigable Liz Dawson.

David Harper has been giving me (and Sara) free medical advice for far too long, and I remain eternally grateful for his patience and kindness, especially when I go off into a Google hole and have to be pulled out by my funny bone. The incomparable Ramón Rodríguez was very kind to suggest some menu items that a Puerto Rican chef would serve. Tony Cliff made the map a reality. Dona Robertson answered a few GBI questions. Obviously, any mistakes are my own.

Last but not least, thanks to my father for hanging in there, and to DA—my heart. You can always be sure of me. I will always be sure of you.